VERA WONG'S UN

MW00852155

"Vera Wong is my new favorite sleuth! This book is comfort food for the soul. Every chapter is bursting with wisdom and heart."
—Elle Cosimano, *USA Today* bestselling author of *Finlay Donovan Is Killing It*

"Jesse Sutanto has once again weaved her magic and gifted us with another winner. *Vera Wong's Unsolicited Advice for Murderers* is a signature Sutanto creation, a feel-good genre-defying comedic whodunnit with a superb cast of characters headed by the indomitable, chaotically funny Vera, indubitably one of the best senior protagonists I've seen in a long while."
—Lauren Ho, bestselling author of *Last Tang Standing* and *Lucie Yi Is Not a Romantic*

"Vera is a force, and so is author Jesse Q. Sutanto, spinning a compulsively readable story with intrigue, humor, and above all, heart. . . . Smart, wholly original, and brimming with emotion, *Vera Wong's Unsolicited Advice for Murderers* feels like the warmest hug that you'll never want to end."
—Laurie Elizabeth Flynn, author of *The Girls Are All So Nice Here*

"Following the success of *Dial A for Aunties*, Sutanto is back with another charmer, this time following the exploits of orthopedic-sneaker-wearing Vera Wong Zhuzhu. . . . Sutanto excels at skewering with affection, and an earnest hilarity shines through in this entertaining whodunit."
—*The Washington Post*

VERA WONG'S GUIDE to SNOOPING (on a DEAD MAN)

JESSE Q. SUTANTO

BERKLEY

NEW YORK

BERKLEY

An imprint of Penguin Random House LLC

1745 Broadway, New York, NY 10019

penguinrandomhouse.com

Copyright © 2025 by PT Karya Hippo Makmur

Book design by Daniel Brount

Library of Congress Cataloging-in-Publication Data

Names: Sutanto, Jesse Q, author.
Title: Vera Wong's guide to snooping (on a dead man) / Jesse Q. Sutanto.
Description: First edition. | New York: Berkley, 2025. | Series: A Vera Wong novel
Identifiers: LCCN 2024046865 (print) | LCCN 2024046866 (ebook) |
ISBN 9780593546253 (trade paperback) | ISBN 9780593546246 (hardcover) |
ISBN 9780593546260 (ebook)
Subjects: LCGFT: Detective and mystery fiction. | Novels.
Classification: LCC PR9500.9.S88 V46 2025 (print) | LCC PR9500.9.S88 (ebook) |
DDC 823/.92—dc23/eng/20241214
LC record available at https://lccn.loc.gov/2024046865
LC ebook record available at https://lccn.loc.gov/2024046866

First Edition: April 2025

Printed in the United States of America
1st Printing

The authorized representative in the EU for product safety and compliance is
Penguin Random House Ireland, Morrison Chambers, 32 Nassau Street,
Dublin D02 YH68, Ireland, https://eu-contact.penguin.ie.

*To those of us whose ambition is
to turn into a Vera when we grow up.*

VERA WONG'S GUIDE to SNOOPING (on a DEAD MAN)

ONE

VERA

Vera Wong Zhuzhu should be having the time of her life. She is, in fact, having the most wonderful, lovely, delightful time. Today, like every day, she wakes up at four thirty in the morning and jettisons out of bed like an army general with a new troop of terrified soldiers to scream at. And today, like every day, she puts on her gear, protecting every inch of her skin from the sun, and bustles out of the house to go on her extremely aggressive morning walk. But today, unlike most other days, Vera does not open up her tea shop after her morning routine. No, today is Sunday, Vera's favorite day. After a freezing, character-building shower and a simple breakfast, Vera marches to the kitchen, where she gets to work.

She's planned the menu with the meticulous care of Ralph Fiennes's character from that strange movie *The Menu*, and she's rather excited to get going, because tonight's meal will include mud-baked chicken. Vera rarely makes this dish because, to be honest, the idea of cooking with mud seems like something a hippie would do, but she is making it tonight because she knows how much it would delight little Emma, and she would do anything for Emma. She lugs the bag of clay she's bought from the garden center for this occasion alone outside of her teahouse and mixes in some water.

"Aiya, why are you making such a mess so early in the morning?" someone calls out in Mandarin. Someone extremely irritating.

Vera scowls before she even turns around. "Mind your business, Winifred," she says.

"What?"

"I said, 'Mind your business, Winifred'!"

"Eh, don't shout so loud so early in the day!" Winifred shouts back. "People are trying to sleep."

Vera sucks in a deep breath and goes back to mixing the clay. Aiya, thanks to Winifred, she's poured in too much water. She grits her teeth and shakes out more clay from the bag.

"Playing with clay, are we?" Winifred says, walking out of her bakery while stretching her arms over her head. "I'm glad you're finding a hobby, Vera. I was starting to get worried about you."

Vera straightens up so fast that her back clicks. "Why would you be worried about me? I have a roaring social life. It is you who people should be worried about."

Winifred raises her eyebrows. "Oh? I have twin grandbabies. I barely have time to run my extremely successful patisserie—"

"Chinese bakery," Vera mutters. The mention of twin grandbabies stings. To make matters worse, against all rules of nature, Winifred's grandkids are actually cute. Considering their genes, Vera thinks sulkily, those two babies should have been born with fangs and a forked tongue, but no, they are so adorable they belong in the pages of parenting magazines. How unfair life can be sometimes.

"My extremely successful French bakery," Winifred continues. "And every day I get to see my little baobei—oh, they love me so much, you know! The other day, little Frieda actually said, 'Ah Ma!'"

"They're two months old, they're hardly going to be saying anything," Vera says flatly. "Maybe you hallucinated it because you're going senile."

Instead of looking scandalized, Winifred merely smirks. "Oh, you know my little grandbabies, they have such good genes. They are geniuses, of course. I expect any day now, they will be invited to join MENSA."

Vera wants so badly to say something snippy about MENSA lowering its standards, but when she thinks of Winifred's chubby little grandkids, all she wants to do is snuggle them and squish their round cheeks and tell them what precious treasures they are. Damn it, if she can't bring herself to be mean about them, she'll lose this round. Oh, who is she kidding? She was always going to lose their sparring matches. Those annoyingly cute little bundles are Winifred's trump cards.

"Well," Vera huffs, "if you'll excuse me, I am very busy cooking a feast for my weekly family dinner." She stirs the bucket of clay mix so aggressively that it squelches, and droplets of sticky clay splat onto Winifred's trousers.

"Aiya!" Winifred cries. "Look what you did! These are pure cotton, you know. My daughter-in-law bought them for me from that fancy organic shop down at Union Square. They cost three hundred dollars."

"For those pajama pants? What is this European nonsense?"

"They are not pajama pants, they are called lounging pants."

"They look like pajama pants to me. In fact, I have a pair just like them from Costco. Are you sure your daughter-in-law didn't get them from Costco?"

Winifred huffs. "My Kelly is a good girl, very filial. She likes to spoil me. I hope that if you ever get a daughter-in-law, she will be half as good as my Kelly."

"*When* I get a daughter-in-law, you mean," Vera says cunningly.

"Oh?"

"Tonight's dinner is so special," Vera says with a small smile.

Winifred falls for her bait. "And why is that?"

"Because it will be at Tilly's new place. Tilly and Selena's new place."

Winifred's eyebrows rise to her hairline. "Oh? They are moving in together, your Tilly and that police officer?"

"Yes!" When Vera thinks of this fact, she feels a joy so fierce it bubbles up inside and bursts into a huge grin. "And once that happens, you know it won't be any time at all before they get engaged."

"Hmm," Winifred grunts. "Maybe. But you know young people these days, they think nothing of moving in or breaking up. So I wouldn't count your chickens just yet, Vera."

And with that, Winifred saunters back to her accursed bakery, muttering about her expensive pants. Vera hopes they are forever stained. She looks down at the bucket of clay and takes a deep breath. She's being silly, she knows it. There is no need for her to be nervous. Tilly and Selena will settle nicely into their new place, and before she knows it, there will be a proposal, then a wedding, and then . . . twin grandbabies. Nay, triplets! When Vera closes her eyes, she can just see it—Vera sitting on an overstuffed sofa with one arm around Emma and the other arm around three fat babies. She is manifesting like the TikTok told her to. She can practically smell their milky baby smell.

Tonight is going to go perfectly. She can tell, it will be the beginning of an amazing chapter in her life.

Tilly and Selena's new place is a sweet little duplex in the Mission District, just a short ten-minute drive from Vera's house. Oliver arrives at two with Julia and Emma in tow to pick Vera up. They come out of the car to help Vera with the ungodly amount of food she's prepared, even little Emma. She carries a thermos of cold winter melon drink that is nearly as tall as she is and totters down the driveway, and the sight of her makes Vera's heart ache with affection.

"Vera, don't you think that you've made too much food?" Oliver says, grunting as he heaves a cooler stuffed to the gills with food into the trunk.

Julia elbows him viciously. "No, she didn't." She turns to Vera and says firmly, "No, you didn't, Vera."

"There's enough food here for twenty people," Oliver says.

"And I will happily take any leftovers home," Julia says. "Stop telling her to cook less, Ollie. You know Emma and I basically live off Vera's Sunday leftovers."

Oliver rolls his eyes. "Well, yes, so do I. I'm just saying, you should take it easy, Vera."

"Tch," Vera tuts. "I'll take it easy when you young people learn to take care of yourselves. But you are like children, I have to make sure you get fed." Ever since Vera solved the mystery of Marshall's death last year, she's remained close to the people who'd been involved in the case. Oliver, Marshall's twin brother; Julia, Marshall's ex-wife; and Emma, Marshall's daughter. Now, she steps inside the car and helps strap Emma into her car seat.

"You haven't kissed me yet," Emma says in her usual solemn voice.

"You supposed to kiss me, I'm your elder."

Emma considers this for a second, then nods and plants a kiss on Vera's papery cheek. Vera smiles and returns the kiss. They hold hands the entire way to Tilly and Selena's.

When they arrive at Tilly's, there are lots of hugs to be given and received, and everyone oohs and aahs over the amount of food that is being carried inside.

"Hi, Vera," Selena says.

It had taken Vera a while to stop thinking of her as Officer Gray and to start thinking of her as Selena, and now Vera has started thinking of Selena as her future daughter-in-law, and what she really wants is for Selena to stop calling her Vera and start calling her Ma. But Tilly has made Vera swear on Jinlong's soul not to ask Selena to call her Ma, so here she is, being referred to as Vera by her future daughter-in-law as though Vera were a stranger.

"Hi, Xifu," Vera says, enveloping Selena in a tight hug. "Xifu" means "daughter-in-law," and when Vera started calling Selena that a month ago, Selena asked what it meant, to which Tilly had screamed, "It means 'dear' in Chinese!"

They all pile into the house, and Vera nods with satisfaction when she sees how much unpacking Tilly and Selena have done in the past few days. There are only a couple of boxes left in the living room, marked POLICE FILES. Everything else seems to have been unpacked and sorted out, and though they only moved in less than a week ago, the place looks like a home, with houseplants adorning it here and there. Tilly and Selena make a good couple. Vera watches Tilly get onto his knees to speak to Emma at eye level, and her heart swells at the sight.

"Hey, Emms, there was a sale at the corner bookstore, so guess what I got?" Tilly says.

Emma regards him with reservation.

"Ta-da!" Tilly pulls out two picture books, and Emma smiles shyly. "Do you wanna read them with me?"

Emma nods. The two of them settle on the couch and Tilly starts reading out loud. Vera sneaks a glance at Selena, hoping her future xifu had witnessed this heartwarming sight, but Selena is too busy chatting with Julia and Oliver. Aiya! If only Selena would look over at Tilly, she'd know what a good father he would make. Vera coughs.

Julia looks over. "You okay, Vera?"

Now they're all looking over at her with concern.

"Yes, don't make such fuss," Vera says, her cheeks reddening. She shifts her attention to the food, lifting the mud-packed chicken from its container and going to the backyard with it. The grill has already been prepped beforehand, so all Vera has to do is slide the heavy load inside and close it. Three hours of baking, and it will be fall-off-the-bone tender when dinnertime rolls around.

The rest of the afternoon is spent chatting and playing various games. At four, Riki, his younger brother Adi, and Sana arrive, bearing homemade samosas and mint chutney, and the little house starts feeling too packed, so they spill out into the backyard. Riki and Sana had been Vera's other suspects in Marshall's death, and Vera is glad that none of them turned out to be the killer. Everyone is talking and laughing and snacking, and by the time dinner is ready, they're almost too full to eat. Vera, Adi, and Emma hammer away at the mud-packed chicken, and everyone cheers when the baked clay finally cracks apart. Vera unwraps the layers of aluminum foil and lotus leaves to reveal the perfectly baked chicken, and despite the ridiculous amount of snacks they've had throughout the afternoon, nobody can resist the food. Aside from the chicken, there's also braised pork belly, grilled carp with Szechuan chili sauce, and half a dozen side dishes.

"Oh my god, this chicken is so juicy," Sana says, her mouth full.

"Mmm. Worth the mess," Selena says.

"Oh yeah, totally," Oliver agrees.

Vera beams at them. Her little ragtag family. Sometimes, she can't believe how lucky she is, to have found this wonderful group of people. Sometimes, she wonders if she's dreamed them up, if she will one day wake up to find herself alone once more. The thought is so painful that she always shakes her head when she thinks of it, as though to shake it off.

Life couldn't be better. She is surrounded by a loving family, and her tea shop has a steady stream of customers. Vera should be content. And she is, really. But she's also kind of—dare she say it—bored.

Sometimes, all an old lady wants is a murder to solve. Is that too much to ask for?

TWO

VERA

Vera should have known better than to wish for a murder to solve. Because of course the universe wasn't ever going to do what she asked it to. When has it ever? And anyway, she isn't the kind of awful person who would wish death upon a stranger just so she could solve it. Well, maybe she is, but only if said stranger was a horrible person like Marshall Chen, may he rest in peace.

But no, the universe did not grant her wish. What it did do was give her a knockoff, kind of like ordering something from Wish. Here's what actually did end up happening:

On Friday morning, Vera is just returning from her morning walk when she hears her phone ringing. To have someone call her so early in the morning must mean there's urgent news. Vera hurries back into the house, locates her cell phone, and answers the call with "Who is it? Who died?"

There is a slight pause, then the person on the other end of the line says, "Um, is this Miss Vera Wong?"

"Yes, who are you?"

"Miss Wong, I'm from the Bank of San Francisco. Can you please confirm your credit card number with us is 4257-6329-6990-3467?"

Vera falters. She's too ashamed to admit that she does not actually know her credit card account number by heart. "Wait," she says shortly to the caller before scuttling to her bedside table, where she takes out her notebook, where she's jotted down every important number, including her bank account and credit card details. Tilly has repeatedly told her that this is incredibly unsafe, but what else is Vera going to rely on if not her trusty notebook? She flips through it, squints at the numbers, and recites them into the phone.

"Thank you. I'm calling to confirm the charge of four thousand dollars made to your credit card this morning."

"WHAT?" Vera squawks. When she was young, Vera had tried for a bit to be the kind of girl that squeals instead of squawks. But now that she is in her sixties, she's given up trying to remove the squawk. The squawk is here to stay, she might as well embrace it. And she does. The one she emits now is particularly impressive, conveying shock, rage, and fear all at once.

To give the bank teller some credit, he doesn't react to Vera's squawk. Merely says, "Yes, ma'am, at five thirty-seven a.m. there was a charge made on Target.com for the amount of four thousand, two hundred, and fifty-eight dollars on your credit card. As part of our security, we like to double-check that you are aware of this transaction."

"No!" Vera squawks again. She clears her throat. "No, it was not me. Not me! Block it. Cancel the card!"

Another short pause, then the teller says, "Ma'am, are you saying that your card was stolen?"

"No." Well, was it? Vera rushes out into the living room, where she finds her handbag and rummages through it for her wallet. Sweat trickles down the small of her back. Her scalp itches, and she wishes she could scratch it, but she must find her credit card quickly. She feels sure there is something lodged in her throat, preventing her from breathing. Oh, right, it's her heart. After what seems like ages, Vera finally locates her wallet. Her hands are trembling so badly that it takes a couple of tries before she gets it open. She slides out her credit card and breathes a huge sigh of relief, then feels silly for being relieved, because what does it matter if her credit card is physically here, given that someone's managed to use it virtually anyway? "I have it with me," she says.

"I see. Then I think what's most likely happened is that someone managed to clone your card—"

"Clone?" Images of her poor little credit card floating in a tube in some nefarious lab alongside several other tubes filled with identical credit cards cross Vera's mind. Is that how they clone things, including credit cards?

"It's just a way of saying someone got hold of your credit card details. Ma'am, I will try to block this transaction, and in the meantime, I will connect you to the police to report this incident. Is that okay?"

Relief surges through Vera. She sags onto the couch. "So, you going to block it? I won't lose four thousand dollars?" She blinks away the tears that have been threatening to fall without her realizing it.

"I should be able to block it. Don't worry, ma'am. This happens a lot."

"Does it?" Vera's chest puffs out. Now that the immediate fear of losing so much money is past, indignation floods her. "Well, if it happen a lot, then you people should fix it. Is a problem, you know! Oh, I just feel so unsafe, I better change bank."

If the teller is taken aback by this sudden switch from helpless old lady to annoyed warrior, he doesn't show it. "I apologize for the inconvenience, ma'am. I'll transfer you right now. Please hold."

Vera fumes quietly for the next few moments. By the time the line is picked up by a gruff voice saying, "Inspector Kevin Pan speaking," she is ready with her tirade.

"I just get scam!" Vera crows into the phone. "You need to solve this, you catch the no-good bad guy who did it, and you tell him, 'How dare you scam elderly folk?' We are the most vulnerable people in society, we should be—"

"Uh . . . ma'am, can you—let's start from the beginning. Please state your name and date of birth." Vera tells him, and he says, "Sixty-one years old. That's hardly elderly, ma'am."

Vera sniffs. "Oh, is very old. Any day now I will die, which is why I always say to my family to treat me well."

"You sound very healthy to me. Um, right, I will need to know a few more details, in addition to a photo of your ID, and you'll be all set. The report will be filed and—"

"And you catch this bad guy?"

"We will catch whoever was behind this."

Vera nods happily and rattles off the answers to Inspector Pan's questions, including, strangely enough, her social security number. After they end the call, she takes a picture of her ID and sends it to the email address the inspector gave her, and he replies less than a minute later, confirming receipt and telling her he is on the case. Only after that does Vera let out a huge sigh. She glances at the clock. Oh my, not even seven in the morning, and already she's had quite the adventure. Still, she supposes, she was the one who had asked the universe for some excitement.

"Not the kind of excitement I ask for," she says out loud, in case the universe is still listening. "I ask for murder, not credit card scam. Murder is exciting, credit card scam is scary and very stressful. You trying to drive me early to my grave?"

After a while, Vera, who is not one to dwell, gets up and sets about making herself some breakfast. While slurping up her congee, she shoots off another email to Inspector Pan, asking if he's made any leads yet, since it has been at least twenty minutes since she made her report, but to her surprise, she immediately gets a response: "This email address does not exist."

Vera stares at her phone, then she tries sending another email. Again, she is told that Inspector Pan's email address does not exist. Frustration bubbles inside her. Why is it that technology seems to always be fighting her? She tries so hard to keep abreast of all of modern tech; she's even got the Threads app, for goodness' sake. Huffing, Vera calls Selena instead.

"Morning, Vera," Selena says in a tone of voice that can only be described as long-suffering but good-natured. Exactly how a xifu should sound. "How's it going?"

"Hi, Selena, you have good sleep? Sometime Tilly snore, I know. All you need to do is poke him on the left side of his lower back, just a small poke, not to wake him, you know, but it work wonders."

"Vera," Selena sighs. Then she pauses and says, "Actually, I will try that, thank you."

"You are welcome," Vera says, pleased at her contribution.

"You didn't call just to tell me that, did you?"

"No, of course not. I have important business. I need to know the email—or, better yet, I need to know phone number of your colleague, Inspector Pan."

"Who?"

"Kevin Pan. Aiya, Selena, you really should socialize more, not just hole up in your office solving murder."

"Solving murder's my job. Hang on, let me look him up." There is a series of clacking keys as Selena types, then she says, "Nope, he's not on our roster. Are you sure he's from this precinct?" Then she suddenly adds, "Wait, why do you need to speak to an officer? Whatever it is—god, I'm gonna regret this, aren't I?—whatever it is, Vera, you can talk to me. I'm also an officer."

"Yes, you a good girl, a good officer," Vera says placatingly, "but you are not my case officer."

"Uh-oh. What case would this be?"

And so Vera fills Selena in on the credit card fraud incident. But instead of applauding Vera for acting quickly and getting her report in with such efficiency, Selena draws in a breath in an unhappy hiss. "Vera," she says, and now her voice has lost all traces of good humor and turned very serious. "Tell me you didn't send this guy photos of your ID and your social security."

"Well, I—" Vera falters. She'd been so calm, so confident, just moments ago, but now that fear is back, clutching at her chest, tightening her rib cage around her lungs and making it hard to breathe. "I did. He say I need to do that to make police report . . ."

"Oh, Vera," Selena sighs. "The police would never ask you to make a report over the phone, never mind send your personal, private details over email."

"Is it bad?" Vera says, and her voice comes out small and unsure, like Emma's does sometimes.

"Yes, it's—" Selena stops abruptly. When she speaks again, her voice is more level. "How about you just drop by the precinct now, and I'll help you file a proper report, okay? And Vera? Don't be scared; it's going to be okay. We'll get this fixed."

"I'm not scared," Vera snaps, but the snap has very little snap to it. In fact, it comes out more like a whine than a snap.

"Okay, good. Nothing to be scared of. I'll see you in a bit, Vera." With that, Selena hangs up.

Vera looks at the phone and mutters, "Aiya." She looks up at the universe—or rather, the ceiling. "Are you happy now?"

No matter how frantic and stressed out and scared Vera might feel, she still can't bring herself to drop by the precinct without bringing some food. What would people think? She's visited Selena plenty of times to make sure her future xifu has a nutritious lunch to eat, and the other officers have taken to calling Vera "Auntie V," which sounds rather badass, if Vera says so herself. And she always took care to bring extra food for everyone. Unfortunately, she has no time to rustle up a slow-cooked pork rib soup, so she whips up a quick fried noodle dish with an assortment of seafood, followed by three-cup chicken, and packs it up in large containers. It's hardly a feast, so on her way to the station, Vera swallows her pride and steps inside Winifred's bakery.

"Five egg tarts, five pork floss buns, and two youtiao," she says curtly to Winifred.

"You mean Bâtonnets de pâte frits? Right away."

Lucky for that Winifred, Vera has no time to correct her faux French names. She practically snatches the bag of pastries from Winifred and marches out of the bakery with her chin up high. As usual, she places a quick curse on the Café as she walks past it. At this time of day, San Francisco has woken up, and the streets are filled with honking cars and the sidewalks with students and office workers rushing, coffee cup in one hand and phone in the other. Not a single one thinks to stop and ask if Vera needs any help. Young people nowadays. But maybe it's not all their fault. Vera has excellent skin, after all, so maybe they are mistaking her for a spry forty-year-old. *Or maybe*, a small voice pipes up in the back of her mind, *sixty just isn't that old*. Vera mentally swats that voice away. She enjoys being old. Many people across many Asian cultures do, because being seen as old is considered very respectful. Ever since Vera turned fifty, she has been telling Tilly that she is "ancient" and will "die any day now," and it worked wonders getting him to do chores around the house. So, if she wants to be regarded as a venerable old lady, then she will be regarded as a venerable old lady, damn it.

Outside of the police station, a girl catches Vera's attention, because unlike everyone else in the city, this girl doesn't seem to be in a hurry. In fact, she seems to be rather at a loss, standing outside of the double doors and gazing up with wide, scared eyes at the sign that says, SAN FRANCISCO POLICE DEPARTMENT. She chews on her thumbnail and hugs herself with her other arm. Vera's maternal instinct picks her out right away as a vulnerable person (almost as vulnerable as Vera the old lady).

"Why you just standing there?" Vera says kindly to the girl. "You coming in or not?"

The girl's head whips around and her fearful gaze locks on Vera. Her mouth drops open. "Uh, I—"

"I am about to see my daughter-in-law in there. She is police officer, you know," Vera says with pride. "Come, you talk to her too, she will listen."

"Oh, that's not—it's okay, thanks," the girl cries, and hurries off.

She is very obviously not okay, but Vera is carrying way too many bags of food to hurry after her. Plus, she has resolved not to meddle so much this year. With one last look at the girl's retreating back, Vera turns and walks into the police station.

Making the police report turns out to be a lot more painless than Vera had expected, though the expediency of the process might have to do with Selena's help.

"Honestly, Selena," Vera says, "you doing things so fast, people might think is because you don't want me hanging around here."

Selena laughs weakly as she types into her computer. "Now, why would anyone ever think that?"

"I don't know, I am a treat."

"Yes, you are," Selena says dryly.

"Well, your food definitely is, Auntie V," a burly police officer calls out, his mouth full of noodles.

Vera simpers, then turns to Selena and says, "You better take some food first before all these people eat them up."

Selena sighs. "I just want to make sure that we take care of this ASAP."

The seriousness in Selena's voice makes Vera's stomach curdle. "Is it bad, what happen to me? Will I lose all my saving?"

Selena's mouth thins. "No, not if I can help it. We've checked with your bank to make sure there hasn't actually been a charge made to your credit card, and we've blocked the card, so as far as we know, your money is safe. And now I'm putting it into the system that your identity has been compromised, and this will help safeguard you for the future."

Vera scrambles to follow all of this. Ugh, if there is one thing she hates more than anything, it's feeling small and helpless. She only likes acting like a helpless little old lady; she doesn't actually like being one, for goodness' sake.

"In short, everything will be okay," Selena says, as though she's realized that Vera is struggling to understand everything she just said. She reaches out and places a gentle hand on Vera's arm. "You'll be fine."

Vera puts her hand over Selena's. "You are such good xifu. If only Jinlong were here to see you. He will be so happy. He will say, 'Wah, son, you get such a pretty girlfriend!'"

Selena laughs. "Everything Tilly's told me about his dad has been so sweet. I wish I could've met him. Speaking of Tilly, we're taking a weekend trip to Tahoe, and—"

"You need me to come and feed Chichi," Vera finishes. "Say no more. I will do it."

Selena smiles. "Thanks, Vera. Tilly wanted to ask Oliver, but . . ."

"Oliver!" Vera cries. "What he knows about feeding cats?" To be fair, a small voice in her head whispers, *It's not exactly rocket science, but still.* The thought of them asking someone else instead of her to do this is offensive. Vera needs to set a precedent to be the one they turn to when they need someone to take over, whether it be cat sitting or babysitting. "I will do this. I feed the heck out of Chichi."

"Okay. Thank you." Selena hits a key on her keyboard and leans back. "There you go. All done. And, Vera, take note, because of what happened, scammers will know you are vulnerable. Expect more scam calls to your number. They'll come in various forms. They'll pretend to be from your long-lost family or even from the police. They'll tell you that you broke some traffic law or something and you're overdue on your fines, and you must pay up or face prison time . . ."

"What?" Vera snaps. "This is . . ." She is about to wail about how awful all of this sounds when it hits her that, actually, it isn't. Because, what could be better than picking up the phone and telling off a few scammers? Oho, she'll give them a piece of her mind. First, she will tell them that their ancestors are very disappointed in them. Then she will launch into a tirade about young people nowadays. Finally, she will ask if they have eaten, and if not, she will impart some recipe and tell them to go cook themselves a nice meal and ponder their life choices. This is her chance to make a real difference in the world. "Okay," she says finally. "I understand."

Selena narrows her eyes. "Vera," she says in a warning tone, "when you get another scam call, the right thing to do would be to put down the phone. Not give them life advice or offer them food. Okay?"

Aiya, how did Selena guess what Vera had been thinking? Ah, her police instincts. *My word*, Vera thinks, *Selena is going to make an excellent mom*. She's almost as good as a Chinese mom at sniffing out the truth. "Of course I know that," Vera says, then busies herself with getting up and calling out, "Eh, you all stop eating my food! I cook for my daughter-in—ah, for my Selena, and you all finishing it up!"

Guilty faces look up, most of them chewing, and then look away. Vera walks over to the food containers where, sure enough, there is none left for Selena. "Aiya!"

"Sorry, Auntie V," someone says.

Vera harrumphs.

"It's okay, Vera," Selena says. "I've had breakfast anyway."

Still, Vera shoots the other officers dirty looks as she packs up her containers. "Next time, I make sure to leave some aside for you," she says to Selena.

"Okay. I'll see you later, Vera."

As Vera goes down the elevator, she realizes that her chest is no longer as tight as it was when she'd arrived. Thank goodness for Selena. Still, when Vera thinks of her credit card, she feels exposed, as though someone had found out her deep, dark secret. Not that she has any deep, dark secrets. She is a respectable Chinese mother, after all. No deep, dark secrets to be found here, no sir. She's making a mental note to drop by her bank to have them issue her a new credit card when, while exiting the building, she nearly bumps into the same girl she'd noticed while walking in. The girl's mouth drops open, but she doesn't say anything. Anxiety is plainly written across her face.

I mustn't meddle. I don't do that anymore, Vera thinks. *Whatever is bothering this girl, she's clearly got the right idea, coming to the police station. She knows what she's doing. I will mind my own business and walk away.* She turns away and starts walking.

To give Vera some credit, she actually manages to walk three whole steps before she swings around, her face set in a determined expression. The girl shrinks back as Vera marches toward her. Vera's expression softens when she gets to the girl. She pats the girl lightly on the shoulder and says, "Come. We will have tea."

THREE

MILLIE

Millie's mind is a mess. Granted, it's been this way for a while now. Ever since she came to this place. Everything feels a bit like a dream. No, a nightmare. There's such a sense of surreal-ness about life, as though she were standing behind herself, watch-ing herself going through the motions every day. Sometimes, Millie can barely remember her own name. *Millie,* she reminds herself every morning, as she gazes into her cracked mirror. *I am Millie. Just go through the motions, and you'll be okay.*

Except now she's not going through the motions. She's going through something else. Something entirely unexpected, and Mil-lie doesn't know what to do. Mother and Father don't like unex-pected. They've explained to her many times that unexpected is bad. She watched in the past week as they explained this to her little sister Mina. She'd nodded and agreed with them about the dangers of the unknown and how they should always, always play it safe.

But this strange old lady has taken Millie by the hand, and

Millie could probably yank her hand out of her grasp and run away, if Millie wanted to. And she should, really. But there's something about this old lady that reminds Millie of her grandmother, her nainai back home, and Millie can't imagine doing anything as horrible as pulling her hand away from her grandmother. And anyway, the old lady promised her tea, and Millie really wants tea. And maybe unexpected is bad, but how bad can it be when it includes a little old lady? Little old ladies are known for being harmless.

And so Millie lets the strange old lady lead her down the streets of San Francisco to Chinatown, past numerous grocery shops and cake shops, where everyone calls out to the old lady and she waves back at them. It's clear that whoever she is, the woman is a beloved part of the community, and again, Millie gets the sensation that she's outside of her own body, watching this scene play out before her. She can almost hear background music, something light and playful to serenade this scene. In a past life, Millie used to be a beloved part of a neighborhood. She thinks. She can't be sure. Everything is such a blur these days.

The woman stops suddenly, and Millie almost bumps into her. She looks up at the huge sign above the door as the woman takes out her keys. VERA WANG'S WORLD-FAMOUS TEAHOUSE. Millie's eyes widen and she stares at the woman. To think, she is with the famous dress designer herself. Her mouth goes dry. Should she curtsy? She should definitely curtsy.

Vera opens the door and glances over her shoulder at Millie, then frowns. "What you doing?"

"Miss Wang, it is such an honor to meet you."

Vera looks confused for a second, then she laughs. "Oh! No,

no, I'm not that fashion lady. I'm just Vera Wong, tea expert and crime solver."

Millie straightens up. Now she feels stupid. Of course it wouldn't have been Vera Wang the dress designer. Why would Vera Wang own a teahouse in the middle of San Francisco's Chinatown? Stupid, stupid. This is why they get angry with Millie so often. Why she gets punished so much. And why, after so many years of working for them, she still owes them so much.

"Come, come. Why you stand outside?" Vera calls out.

Millie blinks, gives herself a little shake, and steps inside the shop gingerly. Her breath catches in her throat as she takes in her surroundings. Has she stepped into a magical place? The walls are painted in colors so rich and vivid that she can practically smell them. She's transported into a starry night in Shanghai—she's only ever been to Shanghai once, but she was kept in the dark for most of that day, and then she'd left the country altogether, so she doesn't think it counts, not really, and anyway, this is a very different Shanghai. There is a boathouse and people spilling out of it, laughing, drinks in hand. Red lanterns adorn the boat and the waters around it, and the scene is so beautiful Millie can only stop and stare.

"Very good, isn't it?" Vera says from behind the counter. "My niece draw it, you know. Very talented artist. She is in such high demand now, I tell her, Sana, don't keep coming to visit me, you must be so busy. But she says, Auntie Vera, you are most important person in my life, of course I must come visit you always." She laughs to herself as she measures out some ingredients into a teapot. "Oh, that Sana."

Millie feels an inexplicable surge of envy toward this Sana, a complete stranger she's never met, and yet already, she knows Sana must be everything she's not. Sana is ultra-confident and has never known what it is like to hate herself with so much passion that she wants to peel her skin off. She also feels jealous because Sana has an aunt like Vera. Millie has the feeling that if she had an aunt like Vera, she wouldn't be in the mess she's currently in.

"Sit," Vera commands, and Millie's body listens without consulting her brain. Vera then bustles out from behind the counter with a tray of accoutrements. As Millie watches in wonderment, Vera brews her tea just like her nainai used to, pouring scalding hot water all over the teacups and then throwing out the water. She smiles at Millie as the tea steeps, then lifts the tiny teapot daintily and pours it into four teacups. "Two each," Vera says. "Come, you drink while is hot."

Millie does so and then has to stop because tears have filled her eyes. She sits there, blinking rapidly, begging her tear ducts to quit doing whatever they're doing. Vera pretends not to notice, sipping her tea with exaggerated enjoyment.

"Dried candied winter melon peel with goji berries and rose petals. I make the candied winter melon peel myself, you know," Vera says. "With my granddaughter Emma. Oh, she eat half of it before I manage to stop her."

Millie swallows the knot in her throat and takes another sip. "You have such a big family here," she says finally.

Instead of agreeing, Vera gives her a strange look before smiling. "Yes, I do, don't I? Now, you tell me what is your name and why you act so strangely."

She really shouldn't be here. She should run. Drop this teacup and just bolt out of here. But there's something about Vera that makes going against her not just hard but nearly impossible. "My name is Millie," Millie says.

"Millie," Vera says, nodding with approval. "Where are you from, Millie?"

"Yunnan," Millie says.

"Oh, Yunnan!" Vera switches to Mandarin. "My dear, I'm from China too. I had some relatives in Yunnan, we used to visit in the springtime. The fruits there are beautiful. The soil is so rich there. I can still smell the fragrance of the mushrooms we went picking this one morning . . ."

Millie is swept away by Vera's words. She knows exactly what Vera is talking about. Yunnan is indeed blessed with rich, fertile land that rewards its people with an abundance of glorious fruits and vegetables. Grapes so sweet they taste like candy, and green beans that are tight and bursting with flavor. Mushrooms that are fat and tender and smell like rich broth. Tears fill her eyes once more. God, how she misses home.

"What brings you here, child?"

"Work," Millie says, and she's so glad to be speaking Mandarin once again. It's been so long since she's been able to speak her mother tongue. "My family has a farm back home, but it's been given to my brothers. I have nothing to my name, and my parents wanted me to get married, but I was scared, so I chose to come here. They said there would be good work to be found here."

"Oh, good for you," Vera says. "You've got a good head on your shoulders, I can see that. You shouldn't have to get married just because your parents were too shortsighted to let you take care of part of the family farm."

I don't have a good head on my shoulders, Millie wants to say, but the lump in her throat is once again too large, and anyway, she isn't here to talk about her head or her shoulders.

"And why were you standing outside of the police station?" Vera says, her voice gentle. "Are you in some kind of trouble?"

"Me? No. Of course not." Has she said that too quickly? Does she look guilty now? And anyway, she has no idea what she should tell Vera. She'd been at the police station because—well, she's not sure why she was there in the first place. Maybe because she'd just felt so lost, so devoid of hope. But now that she's here in this teahouse with this strange woman, Millie is at a loss. She can't just come out and tell Vera the truth. Or can she? No, definitely not. Oh god, she's hesitated for too long now. Vera is looking shrewdly at her like she knows exactly what's going through Millie's head, and she's been silent for too long. She needs to say something, anything. Millie swallows, then says, "It's my friend. He's missing, and I think something bad has happened to him." As soon as the words are out of her mouth, Millie wishes she could kick herself. That was quite possibly the worst thing she could have told Vera.

Vera's entire body perks up like a meerkat. "Tell me everything."

Even though this is the first time Millie has met Vera, she somehow knows that there is very little point in trying to hide things from her. She can't possibly tell Vera the truth, so she's just going to have to make it up as she goes along.

Thomas was one of the first people Millie had met when she arrived in America. They'd been shuffled into one large group of extremely exhausted, bedraggled people, and Millie was so scared. She'd been convinced that she'd made a grave mistake, and she was shivering with fear and tiredness. Then something warm was draped across her shoulders, and when she looked up, there he was. He said something in a language she didn't recognize, and at her look of confusion, he switched to English.

"You look cold. You take jacket."

She tried to take it off—she knew the dangers of owing strangers a debt—but Thomas placed his hand over her arm, just for a second, and said, "You take jacket."

"Thank you," she said. Her English was terrible, but so was his, and she felt an immediate kinship between them. "I am Millie."

"I am Thomas."

What a nice name. It suited him though, this kind-looking stranger with a thick foreign accent. "I am from China," Millie said.

"China, I have always want to go. I am from Indonesia."

"Oh, I have always want to go there too."

They smiled at each other, smiles that were weighed down because they both knew they would never have a chance to visit each other's countries.

Their rooms ended up being on the same floor, and though their work didn't much overlap, they always found pockets of time to spend with each other. Millie would often come back to her room to find a small plastic bag hanging from her doorknob. The bag would contain little treasures, like a Hershey's chocolate bar (her favorite was cookies 'n' creme) or a keychain that spelled out her name or a mug with a teddy bear resting on top of its handle.

"So, he was your boyfriend?" Vera says.

"No!" Millie says, again too quickly. She was in love with him, but she knew they would never work for a million reasons.

"Tch," Vera tuts. "I don't know why you young people always overthink these things. If you find a boy sexy, just tell him!"

Anyway . . .

She was in love with him, but there were many reasons why they couldn't be together, and she knew that, which was why she never told him how she truly felt. All she did was return the kind gestures with little offerings of her own. And they were always finding ways of hanging out with each other, mostly on the roof of their building. They'd sit there and watch the glimmering lights of the city and come up with impossible dreams.

"I want to bring you to Fisherman's Wharf one day," Thomas had said at one point.

"I don't see what so special about wharf." Millie had had enough of wharfs and piers and all that. She'd seen plenty of them on her way here, and they had all been highly unpleasant experiences.

"Ah, but this is a tourist place. Tourists come from all over the world to see it." They'd been getting English lessons every day, and Thomas was improving a lot faster than she was. His Indonesian accent had gone from a thick one to a mere musical lilt. She missed it. She missed everything about the boy she'd met her first day here. Sometimes, Millie felt like she was watching Thomas slip right through her fingers. He was getting to be so good at what he did. Much better than her, anyway. Soon, he would be promoted, or maybe he'd have saved enough money to get his own place. The dream.

Millie shook off the lonely, awful thought and fixed her eyes to an awe-inspiring structure in the distance. "I rather see Golden Gate Bridge." Everything in San Francisco promised wealth. In

Mandarin, San Francisco is called Jin Shan, which translates to Gold Mountain, named during the Gold Rush, when so many Chinese immigrants had been drafted into mining for gold. No doubt a few of Millie's ancestors had come too. She wondered what their lives had been like, if they'd had it as rough as—no. Stupid girl. How could she even compare their hardships to hers? Hers was nothing compared to theirs, to the horrors that they had to go through. "Tell me about Indonesia," she'd ask Thomas.

"You know how you have siu mai?" Thomas would say.

Yes, of course she did.

"Well, we have it too. We call it siomay Bandung, but ours is flat and made of shrimp and fish paste. No pork, because most of the country is Muslim. And we serve it with spicy peanut sauce. Like satay sauce."

It sounded delicious. She'd lose herself in his words, wondering if there would come a day when he'd be able to take her to his hometown, where she'd eat Indonesian food and marvel at how similar and yet different it was to Chinese food. Everything about Thomas was like that—similar but different.

Wah, this sounds very delicious," Vera says. "Wait, what are they called again? Siomay Bandung? I must ask Riki why he's never mentioned them to me, that silly boy."

Millie doesn't have the heart to tell Vera she's kind of interrupting her story. She watches obediently as Vera taps a message into her phone. It's a painstaking process; Vera types with just her index finger, muttering the words as she does so.

"Riki—why you—don't—tell me—about—Siomay—Bandung?

Silly—boy. There." Vera puts down her phone and looks up at Millie. "Sorry, where were we? Oh my, look at the time. You better hurry and tell me the juicy details before the shop is crowded with customers. It's a very happening place these days, you know. Now, tell me, what happened to this Thomas?"

"Well I—that's just it. I don't know," Millie cries. Her entire face feels like it's burning. "The last few months or so, Thomas has been so different. Glued to his phone. Even when we spent time with each other, he'd be checking his phone most of the time and smiling to himself. I think maybe he met someone." Her voice almost breaks then. "But he wouldn't tell me who. He didn't tell me anything. He just said, 'Millie, it's all about building the life you want for yourself. Fake it till you make it.'"

"This is actually not bad advice," Vera says. "Okay, so you said he went missing? When was this?"

Millie kicks herself inwardly for the millionth time. Why had she said that to Vera? "Um. Well, I don't know, he might've just left . . ."

"Okay, when was the last time you saw him?"

"Three nights ago."

"And he didn't say anything to you?"

Millie shakes her head.

"How about his apartment? Have you checked where he lives?"

"Oh, um . . ." Millie thinks hard. "Sure. Yeah, um, there's someone else living there."

"You mean there's a squatter in his apartment?"

Millie shakes her head. "Someone else has moved in."

"Just one day after your friend went missing?" Vera says. "Even for the Bay Area, that's pretty fast. Did you ask your landlord about it?"

Millie's insides clam up. "Um, sort of. They said he told them he wouldn't be back."

Vera narrows her eyes in that way of hers that's starting to become familiar to Millie. Behind her glasses, her eyes are sharp and shrewd. "Why didn't you report it to the police? I was just there reporting this scam that I—well, I wouldn't say I fell for it, but I became involved in a phone scam—well, not involved as a guilty party. Okay, I fell for a phone scam, and that was why I was at the police station, and they were very helpful."

Oh god. She knew it. She knew she'd made a mistake coming here. "I—I can't. I tried, but I—there are things that I can't . . ."

"Hmm." Vera regards her for a moment, watching as she flails. Then she says, "You know, Millie, over the past year, I got to know a bunch of people. Young people, like you. And, oh my, the things they were hiding. Well, they thought they were very bad things, things worth keeping secret until their hearts festered with it. To be honest with you, their secrets were really quite tame. So, whatever it is you're hiding, I'm sure it's not that bad. Can't be as bad as murder, eh?"

Millie's mouth opens and closes like a fish on land. She certainly feels like a beached fish. "It's not murder," she manages to say.

"Of course not. What does this Thomas look like?"

Millie finds a photo of him on her phone and shows it to Vera. It is of her and Thomas, hanging out in his room. She's sitting on his bed and he's sitting on the floor, and they both look so young and so happy.

"What a handsome boy. You don't often see such K-pop good looks," Vera says. "All right, don't you worry, child. I'll take care of this. I solved a murder case last year, you know. I'm practically a detective by now. And I have access to information most people don't."

Millie doesn't dare ask how an old teahouse owner like Vera has access to any sort of sensitive information, unless said information has to do with tea. All she does is give a weak nod and hope that she hasn't just spilled the tea to the wrong person.

FOUR

VERA

So maybe it was a slight exaggeration when Vera told Millie that she has access to information that most people aren't privy to. But what is life without a little exaggeration now and again? Or, as Vera likes to call it, a little razzle-dazzle.

The truth is, Vera has no idea where to even begin looking for Thomas. She looks down at her trusty notebook, in which she has jotted down everything Millie told her about Thomas. Apparently, his full name is Thomas Smith. Unfortunate, that, because when Vera did a search of "Thomas Smith" on the Google, it came up with about twelve million Thomas Smiths. His birth date is September 7, 2001. He is Chinese-Indonesian, but apparently his family has been in Indonesia for so many generations that he doesn't speak Chinese. Not much to go on. Vera takes out her phone and enlarges the image of Thomas, zooming in on his face. He really is very good-looking. She tries googling "Thomas handsome San Francisco" and gets a whole lot of rubbish results. She scrolls through them, slowing down at the images of topless men, before her sensibilities get the better of her, then she slams down the phone and mutters, "What a waste of time." Though that last Thomas with the six-pack was maybe worth a second look . . .

As Vera pries one side of the phone up for another guilty look, it rings. "Aiya!" She jumps, flipping the phone up into the air. She makes a frantic grab for it before it can crash to the floor and catches it just in time. She taps Answer and presses the phone to her ear. "Yes, hello, this is Vera Wong speaking!"

"Ma? You okay? You sound kinda out of breath."

"Tilly. Yes, I'm okay, what silly question to ask." Vera flaps a hand at her face, trying to cool it down. Of course the universe would have her son call right now. "Why you call?"

"Selena told me about the phone scam, and I wanted to make sure you're okay."

"Oh, that." Somehow, even though it happened only earlier this morning, it feels like much more time has passed. *That's what getting involved in a proper case does for you*, Vera thinks smugly. Modulating her voice so it comes out flippant and casual, she says, "Silly boy, no need to worry, it was very small issue only."

"Okay . . ." Tilly doesn't sound convinced.

"Anything else? I am very busy, you know," Vera says quickly, to stop him from asking her more questions.

"Uh, well, if you're sure you're okay. Oh, I also wanted to ask if you're still up for feeding Chichi this weekend? I could just ask Oliver—"

"Aiya, of course I am still up for that. Mothers do everything for their children, especially Chinese mothers." If Vera were completely and ruthlessly honest with herself, she might have admitted to feeling a frisson of excitement at this point, because being alone in Tilly and Selena's house means snooping will be achieved.

Unfortunately for Vera, the rest of the day whizzes by with a steady stream of customers wanting this tea and that tea—both the drinking kind and the gossiping kind—and so she doesn't have much time to do another search for Thomas—both Millie's kind and the kind with washboard abs. At some point, Riki messages her with a sheepish apology for not telling her about siomay Bandung and she huffs, making a mental note to surprise him with the dish next Sunday.

The next evening, which is a Tuesday, Vera goes to Tilly and Selena's place after closing up the tea shop. She lets herself in, then calls out for Chichi. The cat slinks past her leg, and Vera pats it lightly on the back. "Are you lonely, dear?" she says, bustling to the kitchen and finding the stack of cat food and a few short instructions written in Tilly's handwriting. She pours out a can of food for Chichi, then straightens up and looks around the house.

They've done a satisfactory job with the house. Some might even say an "amazing" job, but Vera is not one for overt praise. She can tell which were Tilly's touches—the bookcase filled to the gills with thrillers and fantasy novels, the coffee table that is lovingly made out of repurposed crates, and the black-and-white photos adorning one wall of the living room. And the rest, well, the rest must be Selena's. Vera strolls around the house, admiring Selena's effect on the living space. The kitchen cabinets, which have glass doors, are filled with rows of mismatched cups and bowls. Though not a single one comes from the same set, the riot of colors somehow comes together to paint a beautiful picture. Vera smiles at that. Tilly used to live in a gray apartment with all-white plates and bowls. She likes this for him. The sofa is lined with colorful cushions, all of them mismatched and yet, like the cups, they somehow work together, transforming the space into something warm and inviting. Then there are the houseplants. Selena has a green thumb. Who would've thought? The plants are everywhere, their vines snaking across Tilly's books and around lampshades. Ah, Selena. What a catch. Vera thanks the ancestors for bringing such a wonderful lady into Tilly's life. Then she prays to the ancestors to watch over Tilly and make sure he doesn't do anything to mess this up.

A loud thump from the bedroom makes Vera jump. She whirls around, her arms up. "I know kung fu!" she shouts. She doesn't. Slowly, Vera creeps toward the bedroom, her hands still in the stance she reckons is martial arts–esque.

Vera slinks her arms through the crack in the doorway and flaps them a little just to show whomever's inside that she means business. When there is no reply, she peeps around the door. Chichi looks at her guiltily from the dresser. Well, as guiltily as a cat can look, which isn't very.

"Aiya, Chichi. You nearly give me heart attack. Bad cat. Bad." Vera hurries over to retrieve the fallen object. Her heart, which was racing just moments ago, stops. Because what's fallen from the dresser is a briefcase, and it isn't Tilly's. She picks it up and puts it upright on the dresser. Then she shoos Chichi out of the bedroom, closing the door tightly behind her. Outside of the bedroom, Vera smiles. She is proud of herself. A lesser person might get curious. A lesser person might give in to their curiosity. A lesser person might start snooping. But that's not Vera, is it? No, Vera is a pillar of her community, a respectable woman with a thriving, busy life of her own to live. She does not need to snoop. She is fulfilled, content, totally and utterly—

The door to the bedroom swings open. Vera stands in the doorway, casting a long shadow across the bedroom, breathing hard. "Aiya, to hell with it," she says, and strides in, then grabs the briefcase with a firm hand. It's locked. Yet another sign that she shouldn't pry. But there is no stopping Vera now. Like a shark that's scented blood in the water, all of her senses have left her, and she is operating through primal instinct alone. Without hesitation, she reaches into her hair and pulls out a hairpin. These silly built-in briefcase locks are so flimsy. If Selena did not want anyone breaking into it, then she should've invested in a padlock. The lock practically springs open at the barest touch of Vera's hairpin, so can Vera be blamed for opening it? Okay, yes, in truth it took Vera nearly fifteen minutes of fiddling with the hairpin before she managed to get the briefcase open.

And then it's wide open, like a yawning mouth, and Vera stares at the treasure trove in front of her. Swallowing, she takes out the folders and places them with reverence on the coffee table. There are three folders in total. Three murder cases. Vera bites her lower lip to keep from squealing with childlike excitement. She allows herself a mental squeak. *Eee! So exciting!* Taking a deep breath, she opens the first one. Oh dear.

It's a sadly not uncommon case: domestic violence that ended fatally. Vera winces at the photos and closes the folder with a heavy heart. She's relieved to know that the abusive husband was apprehended at the scene of the crime, but sadness weighs on her narrow shoulders at the thought of the poor woman. And poor Selena, having to go through crime scenes like this one and study all the details to give to the prosecutor. No wonder she is often so tense. Vera makes a mental note to brew Selena some chrysanthemum tea to help her relax.

She opens the next folder. An armed robbery. Ooh. She reads the reports with wide eyes, the scene unfolding in her mind's eye. Three armed robbers had burst into, of all places, a hedge fund. Vera doesn't know why a fund that deals with hedges is worth robbing, but she soldiers on. In the ensuing chaos, one of the employees was shot. The police arrived soon after, and a shoot-out occurred, during which one of the robbers was killed and the other two apprehended.

"Wah," Vera says, shaking her head. "Terrible stuff. Awful." She opens the third and last file eagerly.

A dead body had been fished out of the water at Mile Rock Beach a day ago. Age approximately between twenty to thirty-five, Asian American male, five foot ten, 175 pounds. A John Doe. Suspected suicide.

How young to have taken his own life. The sadness weighing on Vera's shoulders presses down harder. She thinks back to last year, when she came across Riki, Sana, Oliver, and Julia. Before meeting them, she'd assumed that young people nowadays were making up problems when there weren't any to be had. What could possibly plague them? They're so lucky, what with the Internet and smartphones basically opening up the world like a fat oyster, glistening with nothing but endless possibilities? But the more she learned from the four youngsters, the more she realized that though they are armed with new technology, their burdens are equally as deep as hers, if not worse. They live in a world full of unchecked capitalism that requires them to move at breakneck speed or threatens to leave them behind. So now, Vera is more attuned to the needs of the younger generation. She wishes she'd met this mysterious John Doe (what a name, she thinks, very spy-

esque, like James Bond) so she could've stuffed him full of homemade food and well-meaning unsolicited advice.

Sighing, Vera turns the page. And freezes. Because there, in
front of her, are photos of John. And he isn't John at all but Millie's
missing friend Thomas.

The next two days plod along with excruciating slowness. Having
taken photos of Thomas's file, Vera returns the folders to Selena's briefcase, locks it, and places it back on the dresser. Selena really should think of a new hiding spot if she really doesn't want
people to find this stuff. Then, Vera walks home with a troubled
mind, torn between wanting to update Millie on what she has found
and also not wanting to be the bearer of bad news. Still, she assures
herself, there is no one better to receive bad news from. Coming
from Vera, there is also added reassurance that it will be accompanied by a hot meal to stave off the sharp edges of sorrow.

But then Vera remembers that Millie hadn't actually given her
a contact number or any other way to get in touch with her. "Aiya!"
How could Vera have missed such an obvious detail? "I'll be
back," Millie had said, and like a complete fool, Vera had nodded
and waved goodbye. Some sort of detective she is.

And so there is no choice but to wait patiently for Millie to return, and that is exactly what Vera will do. The next morning, she
takes Emma to the park, where she tells off other children for various things, like not greeting their elders and for pronouncing
their Rs as Ws. "Sorrrrry," Vera says. "Not sowie."

The little boy looks at her with plain confusion on his face. "I
said that."

"No, you say, 'Sowie.' Just because you're—how old are you? Three? Yes, you are old enough to enunciate."

"What is enun-sit?"

Vera sighs. Clearly there is no hope for this one.

The next day she spends with Sana and two of her friends, both of whom are artists. They take her to San Francisco Museum of Modern Art, where she complains about the ridiculousness of modern art. "I can do that," Vera says, pointing to a concrete canvas that has been painted completely black. "I do for big discount, only fifty thousand dollars, a steal. Call the museum manager."

Sana merely laughs and squeezes Vera's arm. "Oh, Vera. You're so tetchy today."

"I'm not tetchy!" Vera says tetchily.

"It's true though," Sana's friend says. "I mean, anyone could do that black thing. The only problem is, we didn't think to do it before this dude did."

Her other friend adds, "And we're not white men, so we can't just hand in a completely black canvas and say it is symbolic of the hopelessness of life and be lauded as artistic geniuses."

Vera can't help but smile at that. She likes Sana's friends, even if one of them has purple hair and the other one has an eyebrow piercing. After that, she herds them back to her tea shop, where she feeds them to bursting and sends them home with containers filled to the brim with food.

The third day, Vera wakes up just about ready to scream with frustration. She's been grateful for the company the past couple of days, but Thomas's death has been quietly eating away at her. As she opens up the tea shop, she slips her phone out and opens up her Images folder for the umpteenth time, zooming in so she can read his case file again even though she's pretty much memorized it by now.

Thankfully, during the late afternoon lull, the door tinkles open and Vera looks up, and there she is.

"Millie!" she cries, hurrying out from behind the counter.

Millie freezes, as though not expecting such an excited greeting. She looks like she has half a mind to turn and run away, but then Vera says, "I find your friend!" and Millie gasps.

"Come in, sit down," Vera says, switching to Mandarin. "I'll make us some tea."

Millie perches gingerly on the chair as Vera bustles around and starts brewing tea. She chooses to make chrysanthemum tea, which she sweetens with rock sugar and dates, for its soothing effect. Now that Millie is actually here, Vera finds herself embarrassingly nervous, so she makes small talk as she fusses with the tea. To her credit, Millie answers all of Vera's inane questions with impressive patience, even though she must be bursting with curiosity about poor Thomas. Only after Vera pours the tea does she sit down with a sigh. She waits for Millie to take a sip of the soothing tea before she breaks the news.

"I'm so sorry, my dear girl, but I'm afraid I have bad news for you."

Millie utters a small gasp, the teacup halting halfway from her mouth. "Is he . . . ?"

"He is—well, there is no easy way to say this, but Thomas is dead." Vera catches Millie's hand before she can drop the teacup, guiding her hand gently until the cup is placed on the table.

"How?" Millie whispers.

In answer, Vera takes out her phone and shows Millie the pictures she took of Thomas's file. She is thoughtful enough not to show Millie Thomas's dead body, just a photo of his face. "This is him, yes?"

"I—yes. How did you get these?"

"Ah, I cannot reveal my sources." It's a line Vera has heard numerous times on *CSI*, and she finds great pleasure in finally being able to say it herself.

Millie stares at the image of her dead friend. "He's dead," she mutters hollowly.

"I'm sorry, dear. And here it says, 'Suspected suicide.' Was he having a difficult time?"

Millie laughs, a choked, humorless sound. "Yes, I suppose you could say that. We all are, to be quite honest."

Vera's instincts prick up. Here is another young person in need, and what she needs is Vera. "Maybe you can talk to me, tell me why you're having a hard time."

"I can't." There is such finality to Millie's tone that Vera knows better than to keep pressing.

Though she wants to, of course. It goes against her every instinct as a Chinese mother not to pry. But she has a feeling that if she does, she is bound to chase Millie away. So instead, she changes tack. "Is there a reason why the police think Thomas's name is John?"

Confusion clouds Millie's face. "I don't understand."

"Here, see? It says John Doe."

"Oh. I think that's just what they call people they can't identify. The female version is Jane Doe."

Vera frowns down at the image in her phone. "John and Jane Doe. Strange names for unidentified people. Well, anyway, why wouldn't they know who Thomas is?"

Millie's shoulders hunch up even smaller. "I don't know."

"Shall I go to the police and tell them his real name?"

If Millie were to shrink even more, she'd turn into a 2D line. "I don't think Thomas is his real name either."

Vera narrows her eyes. It doesn't take a super sleuth like herself to know that Millie is hiding something. But again, she senses that Millie is like a jittery bird. Step toward her too quickly and she will take flight, and Vera has a feeling if that were to happen, she would never see Millie again. A soft tread, that's what this needs. Aiya, she hates soft treads. She has always marched like an army general looking for a new recruit to bully, and now look at her, measuring her steps like a guilty child. Still, Vera prides herself as the odd old dog who can learn new tricks.

And now, she is about to reveal some important information to Millie, and Vera has prepared herself so she'll catch every minute detail on Millie's face when she does her dramatic reveal. Keeping her eyes on Millie, Vera scrolls to the next picture. "Did you know, though, that Thomas—or whoever he really was—was a social media star?"

Millie stares. The next image is a shot of an Instagram profile of someone named @XandaPanda. @XandaPanda has 1.1 million followers and what looks like a roaring social life filled with fancy parties and private jets. And @XandaPanda is undoubtedly Thomas. Vera herself had been extremely confused when she saw this in the police file, because isn't this proof of Thomas's identity? Vera had logged on to the Instagram herself and looked up @XandaPanda. According to his bio, he is "Xander Lin, dreamer and entrepreneur." Why the police report hasn't identified him as Xander Lin is beyond Vera's understanding.

"Do you think this could be his real name?" Vera says.

Millie doesn't answer. She's still gaping in complete shock at the photo. She zooms in and Xander/Thomas's laughing face expands across Vera's phone screen. "I—this can't be possible. Is that a private jet? But Thomas never—he wouldn't be able to—" she sputters. Then, with a frustrated sigh, she says, "I have no idea what this is, but it can't be Thomas. Even though it looks very much like him."

Vera looks hard at Millie, trying to sense if she's lying, but finds no traces of dishonesty. "Okay," Vera says finally. "Don't you worry about this. I will take care of it."

Millie looks at her with wide eyes. "What do you mean? What's there to take care of?"

"I'll find out everything about Thomas or Xander or whoever he was. Why he died, why this, why that. Trust me, dear, I can smell an unfinished story miles away. Now, why don't you give me your phone number so I can text you once I find something?"

Millie blanches, clearly not wanting to give Vera her number.

Soft tread, Vera reminds herself. "That's all right. Here, take my number. Call me every afternoon so I can give you updates, okay?" Then she stands and goes around to the back of the counter, where she takes out a container. "I made you some almond cookies to take home."

Is it just her, or does Millie look like she's about to burst into tears? Vera pats Millie's hands gently and pretends not to see the trembling of Millie's chin. Millie nods wordlessly at her, takes the cookies, and rushes out the door. Vera sighs. Oh, young people nowadays. Everything seems to be so complicated for them. It's a good thing they have her around to solve their problems for them.

VERA'S NOTEBOOK

Victim: Thomas/Xander/John

Age: ?? Definitely Gen Z, anyway.

Cause of death: Fall from bridge. Suspected suicide. But also maybe not?

Suspects: Maybe Millie? But she seem very sad when she talk about him. But maybe she is sad because she KILLED HIM?? Hmm. Okay, no jumping to conclusion.

Strategy: OK, this is very complicate case, so I must be ~~methodick~~ ~~menthos~~ mentaldical.

1. Must find out who he really is. But how??
2. What are clues so far? Police file. The Instagram!
3. Oh yes, I will look through the Instagram and see who tag in his profile! Yes, very good.
4. Need to buy more sesame oil and soy milk. And fortune cookie for Emma (but remind her they are not actually real Chinese).

FIVE

TJ

It's been a rough morning for TJ. Though, come to think of it, TJ can't remember the last time mornings weren't rough. But this one has been particularly unpleasant. He's pretty sure Robin genuinely hates him by now, not just the typical *I hate everything* that comes with puberty but actual, specific hatred directed toward him. And TJ can't blame her. He takes a few deep breaths in his car and immediately regrets it. When was the last time he cleaned this thing? Smells like something's died in here. With a sigh, he climbs out. He gives another sigh when he sees the office in front of him. When he first started up his firm over a year ago, he'd been so hopeful, practically skipping all the way from the parking lot to the front door and greeting his employees with a hearty "Good morning." Now he dreads seeing them.

Somehow, TJ manages to trudge to the front door. A sign on the window says, TJ VASQUEZ TALENT MANAGEMENT. TJ wants to lolsob every time he sees it now. He can't even manage his own life. He braces himself before pushing the door open.

Elsie looks up from her desk and says, "Hi, boss."

"Hi, Elsie. How're you feeling today?"

Elsie pats her pregnant belly and smiles. "This one was treating my bladder like a soccer ball all of last night, but other than that, I'm good."

TJ returns the smile. Elsie is having a girl. He's sure she'll be a way better parent than he is. Robin would probably agree. There are two other agents working at TJV Talent—Kit and Lomax—and they're both at their desks scrolling through their phones. TJ greets them as he walks by but doesn't stop to chat. He's the only one who has an office, and he can't wait to get inside so he can slump over his desk and close his mind off to the world. As soon as the door shuts behind him, TJ sags, the breath hissing out of him as though he were a sad, deflating balloon.

Who would've thought that just one single teen could ruin his entire career? But then, TJ thinks, there's a reason why they're called influencers. Because they influence. And anyway, it was his fault. He should've seen the whole mess coming. Then there was the horrible thing with Xander. TJ had barely been able to keep it together when the cops came to talk to him. He wonders, for the millionth time, how much longer he can keep the business up and running before he has to close up shop and leave Elsie, Kit, and Lomax unemployed.

A knock at TJ's door makes him jump. He hurries to his chair, sits down with a straight back, and places his hands on his desk. Then he takes his hands off his desk and places them on his lap. After a moment, he places his right hand on his desk. Then he says, "Come in."

The door opens. Kit and Lomax stand in the doorway, carrying a contraption that looks like a sex toy that a very adventurous couple might use on their wedding night. "Hey, TJ, we got something for you," Lomax says. Lomax dropped out of high school junior year and, since then, bounced from job to job until TJ hired him. TJ likes him. He likes all three of his employees. They're all good kids.

"Whatever it is you've got there, I think I would prefer you leave it outside," TJ says.

Kit narrows her eyes. "Why? What do you think it is?"

TJ clears his throat, not quite meeting Kit in the eye. Kit had spent a couple of years in a correctional facility, and it shows. She's tough and sharp as hell, and TJ is maybe a little terrified of her sometimes, but she's still a good kid at heart. He thinks.

"Oh my god," Kit says. "You think it's a sex toy, don't you?"

"No!" TJ says.

"That is some kinky shit, boss," Lomax says.

"I wasn't—"

"How would this even work as a sex toy?" Kit says.

"Well, there's that bulbous thing on the end," TJ mumbles.

"This is a neck and shoulder massager," Kit says flatly.

"Oh." TJ sets his mouth in a thin line. "A neck and shoulder massager. Yeah, of course, I can see that."

At that, both Kit and Lomax burst out laughing. "It's totally a sex toy," Lomax says. "I don't even know what it does. We got it off a site named WeirdSexToys.com."

TJ buries his face in his hands and groans. "This is so inappropriate. Get outta here and do your work."

They linger in the doorway, the laughter melting from their faces. "We're here if you need to talk about shit," Kit says, her face shining with earnestness.

TJ's heart cracks open. If the business were to fold, what would happen to Kit, Lomax, and Elsie? The world would only see an ex-con, a high school dropout, and a single mother-to-be. They're unhirable. Though maybe he should focus on his own shit, because it's not like people would be scrambling to hire him either. "Thanks. I really appreciate that," he says. "Now, please get that thing outta here."

"Aye, aye," Kit says, saluting with the terrible dildo. As they turn to leave, she adds, "By the way, there's some old lady here to see you."

TJ frowns. "What's her name?"

"Vera Wang."

The Vera Wang? TJ's eyebrows practically disappear into his hairline. His hairline, which he's noticed is slightly receding, just because life hasn't been hard enough for him lately. But maybe things are about to look up for TJ. Why else would Vera Wang be here, if not to look for a new talent manager? TJ rises from his seat, then lowers himself again. Shouldn't look overly eager. He clears his throat and says, "Send her in." His voice comes out squeaky with excitement.

But the woman who strides in is very much not Vera Wang. She looks the opposite of Vera Wang, in fact, with a cloud of gray hair hidden under a visor so large it might as well be an umbrella, and is pulling along a foldable shopping cart behind her.

TJ gapes at her. "Who are you?"

"Vera Wong. I told your assistant. She didn't tell you?"

TJ bites the inside of his cheek to keep from groaning out loud. Of course he would get the knockoff Vera Wang. He takes a deep breath and refocuses on the old lady. "Right, sorry. Are you . . . looking for representation?"

The old woman cocks her head to one side. "Representation? No, no, my son is lawyer. If I need representation, I go to him. Even though he will say conflict of interesting, but in the end he will represent me because he is a good boy."

It takes TJ a moment to digest what she's just said. Then the penny drops. "Oh, you think I'm a lawyer. I didn't mean that kind of representation. I'm a talent manager."

"What? What is that? Why would talent have to be manage?" Then she utters a small gasp of understanding. "Ohhh, you mean like that Kim Kardashian girl and her mom? Her mama is her momager. Like that?"

TJ is about to say no when he considers it. "Sort of, yes. I do most things for my clients, including booking them shows, coming up with collaborations for them, marketing and publicity, all that good stuff. But hang on, if you're not here looking for a manager, then why—"

"Oh yes, I come here to ask you about Xander Lin." The old woman rummages in her shopping cart and takes out a notebook.

And of course the knockoff Vera Wang is here to interrogate him about Xander. TJ's neck and shoulders, which had only just begun to relax a few minutes ago, immediately knot up. He swallows to make sure his voice comes out even. "What about him?"

"Well, he is your client, right?"

"He was. I heard the news of his passing. Are you—was he of relation to you?" Did that come out sounding as awkward as he thinks? God, he's bad at this.

"I think I ask the questions around here, young man."

How could TJ have seen this woman as a kindly old lady? She's obviously someone far more dangerous. An undercover cop. Yes, that's got to be it. And at her age, she's probably one of the more senior and most experienced cops they have. Which is why they've sent her to talk to him, because they know what he did—

Stop it! TJ mentally shouts at himself. *Stop. Spiraling. You're always doing that. Just stop.*

He pulls at the collar of his shirt. "Uh, okay? What—uh, what would you like to know?"

"Well, I want to know what really happen to him," she says, emphasizing "really" in a way that makes TJ's pores open and start sweating. "But maybe you can start by telling me how you come to know Xander."

"Okay." TJ thinks fast. "Well, like you said earlier, Xander Lin was my client. I represent social media influencers. When an influencer gets over three hundred thousand followers on TikTok or one hundred thousand followers on Instagram, I reach out to them and ask if they would like representation. Sometimes they say yes, sometimes they say no. That's usually how it works in this business."

"So, you reach out to Xander Lin and offer to representing him, and he say yes?"

TJ nods.

"How long ago?"

TJ has no idea if the answer he gives would incriminate him or not, so in the end, he fudges it a little. "Three months ago. Maybe. I can't remember. I have a lot of clients." A complete and utter lie.

Vera's shrewd eyes laser into him as though she can read the guilty thoughts scurrying through his head.

"And what was Xander like?"

"Polite," TJ says immediately. Was that a good answer to give?

It was true, to a point. Xander was polite until he was very much not. "A hard worker."

"Mm," Vera grunts as she scribbles in her notebook. "That not saying much about him. What else?"

"I mean . . . to tell you the truth, I didn't know him that well." That's sort of true. The best lies all have a grain of truth in them, don't they? "In fact, I never even met him in person."

Vera's head snaps up. "You never meet him? Aiya, how can? You are his manager, but you don't even care to spend time with him?"

"This is how things work in the industry," TJ says. *Too defensive*, he thinks. He must reek of guilt. But he's not lying about this. He hasn't met most of his clients. But maybe that's the whole problem. That's why he's in this mess now. Because when it comes down to it, who are all of these people he's representing? And what a word—"represent." Such a heavy one, and yet he's rarely stopped to think about it. What they do reflects on him, and vice versa. So much trust placed in each other, and yet they are in effect strangers.

"Oh, if I am in industry, it would not be how it works," Vera says smartly, and TJ believes her. "You never meet with Xander, so how you contact each other?"

"Mostly over email and text. Occasionally, if there is a significant offer being made, I would make a phone call, but you know young people nowadays, they're allergic to calls."

"Not the young people I know," Vera says, and again, TJ believes her. If there's anyone who could make a young person pick up their phone, it would be this surprisingly terrifying old lady in front of him. "So, what kind of deal you get for Xander?"

"Let me think." Again, that question running through his

head: What can I tell her? What can't I? "A couple of sponsorship deals. One was with a local IPA, and another was with a sneaker company. Then there were the collabs."

"What is collabs?"

TJ can't figure out if she really doesn't know what a collab is or if she's testing him. "They're collaboration deals between two or more promising influencers. I reach out to my other clients or other influencers who I think might work well together and ask if they want to do a few posts with each other. That way, you hit both audiences with one shot. It's a great way to get more exposure."

"I see. Like networking."

"Yeah, exactly." Then it hits TJ that he really, really shouldn't have told Vera about collaborations. Oh my god, he really is bad at this. But then again, she probably knew the entire time what they were since she's an undercover cop. Or maybe she's the FBI. He can see that. But then, wouldn't she have flashed her badge at him? The FBI does that a lot. They're like that proverbial Harvard grad—how can you find out if a guy went to Harvard? You don't, he'll tell you within five minutes of meeting you. The FBI's like that, right? In all the movies, they talk to someone—anyone—and first thing they do is show their badge. TJ doesn't blame them. If he were an FBI agent, he'd do the same. And it would probably annoy the hell out of Robin. He can practically see her rolling her eyes and saying, "Okay, Dad, no one's impressed." Why is he thinking about this right now when he should be thinking about what a massive mistake it was talking to this woman?

"Anyway, I have a lot of work to do, so . . ."

"Oh yes, young people are so busy nowadays." But she doesn't make a move to leave. Instead, she rummages once more in her shopping cart and lifts a couple of containers out. "Claypot rice with Chinese sausage and mushrooms, and this one is crispy roasted pork belly. I cook for my family, but you looking like you need it more."

"I can't possibly—"

But already she's opened one of the containers, and the smell that wafts out is so delicious that TJ's brain zaps his mouth shut. And fills it with saliva. *Shut up and eat,* his brain tells his entire body, and TJ finds himself reaching out and picking up a piece of roasted pork belly. The skin is crunchy and salty, and the meat is juicy, and it is quite possibly the best thing TJ has ever put in his mouth. His eyes close, and a sound that's almost scandalous comes out of him.

"Don't forget to share with your colleagues," Vera says.

"Oh, I don't think so," TJ mumbles through a mouth full of delicious pork. "Thank you."

"You're welcome. I will be back. I bring more food next time."

Yay, goes TJ's stomach. *Nooo,* goes his survival instincts. He can only watch helplessly as Vera marches out of his office, her foldable shopping cart trundling along behind her.

SIX

AIMES

Aimes is trying to get a photo of herself with her beautiful cup of dirty matcha, but neither the drink nor her face is cooperating. It's one of those days where even the most flattering angles don't seem to be doing her any favors, and the sheen of condensation sticking to her plastic cup is making it hard to see the beautiful swirls of brown and green. The swirls are the whole reason why she'd ordered a dirty matcha. She really prefers straight coffee, but straight coffee doesn't get as many likes as a swirly, multicolored drink, so here she is. She tries pouting, but her chin trembles, and before she knows it, a tear slips down her cheek, then another. "Fuck," she mutters, swiping at her face savagely.

"Amy?" someone says.

"It's Aimes, actually," Aimes says automatically. Story of her life, correcting people about her name. She dabs at her face again before looking up. Standing in front of her is a tiny old woman. "Um . . . I'm not interested."

The old woman sits down anyway.

Aimes looks around the café. Is this a prank? She wants to ask the old lady to leave, but that would be rude, and she looks like a helpless little grandma, and what kind of monster would be rude to a helpless little grandma? "Are you lost?" she says kindly.

"No, my dear. Come, I help you with that." She plucks the phone smartly out of Aimes's hand, aims the camera at her, and takes a picture before Aimes realizes it.

"Wait, you can't just—huh." The picture is actually a good one. Aimes's green eyes are somehow brighter, and her expression of slight surprise makes her look really pretty and innocent. For a split second, Aimes experiences a tiny shot of endorphins at the sight of the flattering photo, then reality overwhelms her once more. She takes the phone back from the old lady and mumbles, "Thanks."

"I come here to talk to you, Aim-zee."

"It's just Aimes."

"Aimes," the old woman says. "I like that name. Very good name."

"What did you come here to talk to me about?" Aimes says.

"Oh yes. I come here to see how you doing. You sleeping well? Eating healthy?"

"What?" Again, Aimes looks around the café, wondering if there's a hidden camera somewhere. This has got to be a prank. "Who are you?"

"I'm Vera, and I worried about you."

"Why would you be worried about me?"

Now it's Vera's turn to look confused. "Because your boyfriend die. I think that make most people sad, when boyfriend die. Unless he is bad boyfriend?"

"Oh." Of course she is here about Xander. Very few people

have actually heard the news of Xander's death, but Aimes had known it was only a matter of time before the Internet found out. And when that happens, what would they find out about her? Aimes gives herself a mental shake. If this old woman is here to ask about Xander, she must be related to him. She softens with pity. "Are you his mom? His grandma?"

"Nothing like that. In fact, I am very confuse about who he is, I am hoping you can tell me."

Panic churns in Aimes's stomach. "I don't know—" She stops herself. Her eyes brim with tears again. She is so bad at this. She is so bad at everything. "I'm sorry," she sputters.

"Oh dear. Don't get upset. Come, you eat this." Somehow, Vera has produced a steaming container of what looks like pork rib soup. Aimes looks down at it blankly. A spoon is placed in her hand. "Eat," Vera says, and Aimes does so without really comprehending just what the hell is going on.

The broth is somehow light and yet rich, a clean flavor that speaks of hours of gentle simmering that goes straight to Aimes's belly and warms her up from within. If it were possible to be brought back to life by food, then that is what Aimes is experiencing. Except she doesn't deserve to be brought back to life. Not after what she did to Xander.

"How long you been together with Xander?" Vera says, then adds, "Try the pork, fall off the bone."

The pork rib is so tender that all it needs is a soft poke of the spoon before the meat slides off completely. Aimes's brain is torn between squealing, *Don't eat food from strangers! Stranger danger!* and *OMG this is so good. I feel like a child again. I want a bedtime story now, please.* Her mouth opens and says, "About eight months."

"Quite long. You two look very good together."

Yes, they do—did—look very good together; that was the whole point.

"What he like, this Xander? He treat you well?"

"Yes. He's—he was—the perfect boyfriend." The answer comes out automatically. She's said it so many times. The perfect boyfriend. Whenever anyone asks, that's the word Aimes and Xander always used. "Perfect." Of course, all of their Instagram post captions talk about how impossible it is to reach perfection, how we shouldn't strive for it, how we should always strive for authenticity instead. But that's the thing about captions. You want to convey perfection while at the same time appearing like you haven't toiled away at achieving it. You want to be effortlessly perfect. And that was what she and Xander were. Naturally, casually, perfectly perfect.

What Aimes expected Vera to do is go, "Awww," like most people do. But what Vera actually says is, "Sound boring."

"You can't say that," Aimes blurts out.

"Why not?"

Before Aimes can answer, a tall thermos *thunks* down next to the container of broth. "Chinese tea. Pu-erh. Very invigorating, bring you back to life. You need it." Vera unscrews it, pours out a cup, and puts it in Aimes's hand. "Drink."

Again, Aimes obeys without really thinking and nearly burns her mouth with it. She takes a smaller sip, and this time, she tastes it. A taste that is completely different from the dirty matchas and the oat milk lattes she's been having every day for the last however many years. The word that comes to mind is . . . "authentic." She looks down at the cup of tea. It looks completely unremarkable, something utterly un-Instagrammable and therefore uninteresting to her. And yet. Aimes takes another sip.

"Xander was a kind boy?" Vera says.

Aimes nods wordlessly. The less she says about Xander, the better.

"How was he kind? Give me example."

Damn it. This old woman is something else. "Um, I don't know, like the normal way." She struggles to come up with an anecdote, but her brain seems to have been replaced by scrambled eggs.

"How you meet him?"

Ah, well now, this she does have an answer for. The perfect answer. "We were at Trader Joe's," she says, and the words flow out smoothly, she's recited this so many times. "We reached for the last carton of milk at the same time, and our hands brushed each other's. I looked up and there he was." Normally, people sigh dreamily at this point. Vera narrows her eyes, but Aimes keeps going. "I said, 'I'll make you a banging cup of latte with this if you let me have it.' And the rest is history." The perfect meet-cute. Unfortunately, it also happens to be a complete fabrication.

"Sound like a movie," Vera says.

"Yeah, it was kind of a movie-quality moment," Aimes says.

"No, I mean, I think I see in a movie before."

Aimes swallows. Despite the amazing food and tea, she really wants Vera to leave now. "Anyway, who are you? I don't—why are you here? How did you find me?"

"I told you already, I am Vera."

"Yes, but why are you here?"

"Oh. I forget that part. I am such an old lady, you know. So helpless and frail."

Vera clearly looks anything but helpless or frail. In fact, next to

Vera, Aimes feels helpless and frail. But she's too scared of Vera to challenge her, so she says nothing.

"I am investigating Xander's death. I am investigator." Vera slides a business card across the table.

It says:

VERA WONG.

Tea expert. Murder investigator. Entrepreneur.
Owner: Vera Wang's World-Famous Teahouse. Est. 1974

"Investigator?" Aimes's voice feels like it's coming from afar. She's pretty sure her soul has left her body. Her entire mind has imploded and is screaming, *What if she finds out?*

"Oh yes. I solve a murder case last year that the police couldn't. Actually, they think it was accident, but I know—aha—must be murder. I always know, because I am Chinese mother; there is nothing we don't know."

Aimes can feel her left eyelid twitch. She forces a smile. "But why are you investigating Xander's death? The police told me it looked like a suicide." Does she sound sad? She should. She is. But the fear is kind of overriding the sadness.

"Maybe it is suicide, maybe not. Someone ask me to look into it, so I do, and my instincts are going off. Something not right here."

Oh god. It was Aimes, wasn't it? The "something not right." Vera can probably sniff the guilt coming off Aimes in rank waves. "Who asked you to look into it? His family?"

"No. Actually, I want to get in touch with his family, but I can't find them. Can you give me their number?"

Noooo, a small, high-pitched voice in the back of Aimes's mind squeaks. Why does she keep making things worse for herself? "Um, I—he wasn't close to his family. Never really mentioned them." Oh no, that was bad. This is bad. This whole thing is catastrophic, and she needs to stop talking before Vera catches her in too many lies.

"Oh? You been together almost a year and you never meet his family?"

"Well, they're . . . yeah. I don't know. We don't—we didn't really talk about that stuff."

Vera narrows her eyes. Anytime now, she's going to leap across the table and slap handcuffs around Aimes's wrists and—

"Hmm. I don't understand young people relationship nowadays," Vera says. "In my day, first thing you do when you start dating is get to know each other family."

"Yeah, well, things are different now," Aimes mumbles. "So anyway, how did you know where to find me?"

Vera still wears a thoughtful expression when Aimes asks that. She snaps back to the present. "Oh yes, the Instagram, of course." She takes out her phone, squinting down at it, and taps on it with her index finger. "Here. Your profile. You always posting drinks from same place every morning. I just look at the label on the cup and I visit the café. You should stop drinking coffee, is not good for you, will give you wrinkles. Look at me, I am so old, sixty-one already, but my face look so young because I don't drink coffee."

Aimes's eyes are glued to the phone screen, where there are, indeed, a ton of photos of herself carrying a coffee cup clearly labeled SALTHOUSE COFFEE. From a very far distance, she hears herself mumbling: "My grandma is seventy and she runs marathons. I don't think sixty is that old . . ." But inside, her mind is squawking, *You stupid, dumb girl. Why would you post these photos every morning? Of course any random stranger online could find you. Where are your survival instincts, you moron?* But Aimes has been living her life according to fulfilling anything and everything Instagram desires, and posting her morning coffee has been something that garnered a ton of likes, so she never really thought about things as pesky as personal safety. And now here she is, confronted by an actual, real-life investigator. "I know I asked this before, but who hired you?" she blurts out after a while. Possibilities whiz through Aimes's head, so many of them. So many people hate her, want nothing more than to see her fall.

"Someone who is close to Xander. But you don't worry about that, is not your problem, okay? Now, you sit here and finish your soup and your tea, and when you are done, you return the containers to me, okay? These things cost money, you know."

"Wha . . . where should I take them to?"

Vera taps on the business card. "My teahouse, of course. You come by on Wednesday at seven p.m. I cook dinner for you. Crispy roast duck." And with that, Vera is gone, leaving behind a plastic container of delicious homemade soup, tea, and a giant crater in Aimes's aesthetically pleasing life.

SEVEN

VERA

Vera is having so much fun she half wonders if she shouldn't write a book about it. A self-help book titled *The Ancient Chinese Secret to Long Life: Solving Murders*. Is that too long for a title? She knows, as everyone does, that titles should be snappy and memorable. But she does like the word "ancient" in there because it's rather impressive and mysterious. Maybe *The Ancient Chinese Secret to Solving Murders*. Ooooh, yes, that is a good one. As she sits on the bus on the way back home, Vera composes the book in her head.

Chapter One: Call Your Mother.

Every mother holds the answer to all of your life's problems. If you do not have a mother, you may call me. My number is—

Hmm. Perhaps it wasn't the wisest of ideas to share her personal number with the millions of strangers who would no doubt be buying her book.

If you do not have a mother, you may slip and slide into my DMs.

Yes. Yes! Not only does that show how approachable Vera is, it reminds everyone that she is very much up to date with young people these days. She is basically an honorary Gen Z. This whole writing-a-book thing is so easy, no wonder Sana's mother writes four of the things every year. Vera is sure she can bang out at least six books a year if she wanted to.

By the time she alights from the bus back in Chinatown, she has composed two chapters in her mind (Chapter Two: Finding a Murder to Solve). She hums to herself as she unlocks the door to the teahouse and walks in. She checks the floor to make sure there are no dead bodies on it. One can never be sure. She spends some time updating her notebook, adding Millie, TJ, and Aimes as possible persons of interest. Vera likes the term "person of interest." It's more vague than "suspects," so if it turns out she was wrong to suspect them, she can just say, "I never suspected them, I was just interested in them."

The problem is, she likes these three youngsters. Just like the brood of lost chicks she gathered last year, she doesn't want any of them to be guilty of Xander's death. And they are so clearly guilty of something. Vera sniffs. Why don't young people learn to lie better? She rearranges her facial expression into one of innocent surprise. "Huh? Xander dead? I have nothing to do with it." See? That's how you lie.

"Talking to yourself is a sign of senility, Vera," someone calls out from the doorway.

Vera turns around, her face hot. Of course she recognizes that voice without even looking. "Winifred." The name comes out practically in a hiss. "What brings you here?" Vera says, switching to Chinese.

"Oh, it's a rare day I'm not so busy with customers, so I thought I'd drop by and keep you company. It can be so lonely for a lone, elderly woman with a forgotten tea shop," Winifred says, slinking inside the tea shop. She plops a bag on the table. "I brought some of my bestselling breads. Brew some tea, Vera."

The audacity of her! Winifred marching in like she owns the place and ordering Vera to brew tea? "I do not need company. I'm hardly alone. And, yes, even though I am your elder, which means you should speak to me with more respect, I am hardly elderly."

"Oh, save it, Vera. I've heard you refer to yourself as a helpless old woman countless times."

"That's to remind young people to respect me."

"Funny that," Winifred sniffs. "I never have to remind them to respect me. I guess I just command it naturally."

"The only thing you command naturally is body odor," Vera mutters, but for some reason, she does as Winifred says and gets the kettle going.

Winifred settles on a chair and begins taking out the pastries. "I am considering changing the bakery name," she says.

"Oh? People finally caught wind of your ruse, then? Realized it's not a French bakery?"

"No. It's just . . . Korean bakeries are the latest rage, haven't you heard? I see it all over the TikTok. It's K-pop this, K-drama that, everything K."

"You're not Korean, Winifred."

"I am on my grandmother's side." Winifred says something in Korean.

It takes an awful lot of willpower for Vera to refrain from asking Winifred what she just said, but that's exactly what Winifred wants, isn't it? So Vera looks on blandly, until Winifred finally says, "It means 'good afternoon' in Korean."

"Impressive," Vera says in a monotone voice, measuring out

ingredients for the tea. It had taken her a moment to decide what to brew. Part of her was very tempted to brew something disgusting for Winifred, but she decided against it since she would likely have to drink it herself, and anyway, there isn't anything disgusting in Vera's tea shop, of course not. So ginseng it is. As Vera brews the tea, Winifred points to each pastry.

"Here we have kkwabaegi."

"Looks like a mahua to me."

Winifred narrows her eyes. "Well, yes, to the untrained eye, it is very similar to a Chinese twisted doughnut, but the Korean version is coated in sugar."

"So is mahua. Sometimes."

With a sniff, Winifred points to the next pastry. "This one is gyeran-ppang. Egg bread."

Vera looks at the oblong-shaped dough with a whole egg in the center of it and tries very, very hard to think of a Chinese equivalent, but her traitorous brain refuses to come up with anything. Gah! She pours out the tea slowly, still thinking hard.

"Oh dear, is it the dementia?" Winifred says. "That often gets worse when one has no friends or family."

"I have plenty of friends and family," Vera snaps. "And my mind is perfectly fine, thank you very much. I drink gingko tea every day." She serves Winifred her tea and sits down across from her.

"Have the gyeran-ppang," Winifred says, sliding it across the table to Vera.

With a small huff, Vera unwraps it and takes a bite. The sweet, fragrant dough coupled with savory egg makes for a comforting combination. It really is very good. Vera chews slowly, annoyed at how delicious it is. She follows the bite with a sip of her tea.

Winifred watches her with hawk eyes. "Well?"

Vera shrugs. "It's not bad."

Winifred grins. "I knew you'd be a fan. Now try this one. Honey butter toast. I think it will bring the Gen Z into both our shops. It's the kind of thing you have over a nice cup of tea."

"I don't need your help to bring the Gen Z into my tea shop," Vera says.

Winifred says nothing, merely gives a pointed look around Vera's empty shop.

"Today is a bit slower because it's a weekday."

"Are you going to wait around until the fad from that dead guy fades before you actively do something to promote your tea shop?" Winifred says.

The nerve of her, coming into Vera's shop and spouting such rubbish. Vera's temper stirs. "I'll have you know I am very busy investigating another case," she snaps.

"Yes, I thought so. That's why I'm really here," Winifred says as she takes another sip of ginseng tea.

Vera can practically feel her blood pressure bubbling up. "I thought you're here because you wanted to increase the flow of customers to our shops."

Winifred waves a hand flippantly. "Oh, Vera. You should know better than anyone what a snooper looks like when they are snooping."

For a moment, Vera considers the wisdom of slapping the table and going, "How dare you insinuate that I am a snooper!" but, oh, who's she kidding? Winifred, being another Chinese mother, isn't going to fall for Vera's usual tactics. Instead, she tries a different tack. "Winifred, I know you are very bored and very lonely, but you should look for your own cases."

"Unfortunately, Vera, I do not have the good fortune of having young men dropping dead in my shop."

"Well, my dear Winifred, maybe that means the universe does not think you are capable of handling such a thing."

"Or maybe, dear Vera, it means that you are attracting bad luck. Nothing but death around you."

"Choi, choi!" Vera raps her knuckles on the wooden table to dispel Winifred's petty ill-wishing.

"I don't mean to wish you bad luck, Vera. I am merely here to help dispel some of the bad luck you've been having. Share your burden with me. What are friends for?"

"I have plenty of friends to share my burdens with."

Winifred raises her eyebrows. "Those little youngsters barely out of their diapers are not your friends; they are your adopted children. Do you even have friends your own age?"

"Yes," Vera snaps.

"Who?"

"There's Sister Zhao, who owns the vegetable shop down the street, and Brother Hua, who—"

"Owns the dried fruit shop, yes. These are neighbors, Vera. I know them too. But do you actually spend time with them?" Winifred adds, "Aside from when you're buying fruits and vegetables from them, I mean."

Vera grows quiet. "Well, there was Alex."

"Ah yes, Alex counts as a friend, I'll give you that. But he can't really spend time at your tea shop anymore, can he? Not since he was arrested for murdering his own son."

"I visit him once a month," Vera mutters. She didn't think it possible, since her life has so much love and laughter in it nowadays, but now that Winifred mentioned it, Vera realizes that she

indeed does not have any friends her own age. She has plenty of
family, of people she considers her children or nephews or nieces
or grandchildren, but peers? Goodness, what a sobering thought.

"It's quite all right, Vera. It's nothing to be ashamed of," Winifred says smugly. "You may be my friend."

Vera glowers at her, then sniffs. "I don't need your help. But
since you are obviously so bored, I'll tell you a little bit about the
young man I'm looking into." As she takes her phone out of her
pocket, it strikes Vera that, dare she say it, she's having a little bit
of fun. To her surprise, a large part of her wants to share bits and
pieces about Xander's case with Winifred and discuss possibilities
and gasp in horror at the twists and turns that will no doubt crop
up. It's what Julia and Sana would call "girl talk." So she opens up
the Instagram and shows Winifred Xander's profile. "This poor
boy drowned at the Mile Rock Beach. They found him a few
days ago."

"Oh dear, such a young man." Winifred takes out a pair of
glasses and squints at the phone screen. "Very handsome. You
know, he resembles my Robert when we were young. Oh, quite the
lady-killer, he was."

Vera rolls her eyes. She knew Robert, and he looked nothing
like Xander Lin, but that's Winifred for you. She just can't help
herself.

"He looks like he had a roaring life," Winifred says. "All these
fancy parties. Oh, look, a private jet! Did you know, back in Tai-
wan, this boy was so crazy about me, but I turned him down. Later
he became a millionaire, and he has his own private jet."

Vera sighs. "Yes, I'm sure that happened."

"Oh my, is that his yacht?" Winifred brings the phone closer to her face, until it is mere inches away from her eyes. "What did he do, this Xander? Was he in tech? I bet he was in tech."

"That's the thing. No one seems to know what he did for a living. In fact, no one seems to know much about him. Not even his girlfriend."

"How is that possible? You should see my daughter when she started dating. All day she was glued to her phone, texting every minute of every day. If she dated anyone new, she'd look them up online until she knew everything about them."

Vera frowns. "Yes, that was exactly what I thought." Actually, what she had really thought was *Huh*. And then she just didn't think much of it. Aiya. How could she have been so careless? She makes a mental note to add that to Aimes's list of suspicious behavior.

"What about his family?"

Vera shakes her head. "Haven't managed to find them yet."

"A boy as wealthy as him," Winifred muses, "doesn't die in silence. There must be many friends and family wondering where he's gone. They would've called the police by now to report him missing."

"Well, that's the other thing. The police can't seem to identify him."

Winifred stares at her. "What do you mean? It says right here, he is Xander Lin."

"Yes . . . except he's not. His friend calls him Thomas. The police call him John Doe."

"Why John Doe?" Winifred says. "What a strange name."

Vera gives a knowing smile. "It's a name they give to people whose identities they don't know."

"So, Xander Lin is a fake name. I knew it. It sounds very fake. My, my," Winifred says as she taps on more of Xander's posts. "An unknown person with a fake name. What was he hiding? Probably evading taxes, would be my guess." Then she gasps.

"What?" Vera says.

Winifred doesn't answer, merely brings the phone even closer to her face, her nose practically touching the screen.

"What is it?" Vera says again, louder this time.

"Look at this post! That is Qiang Wen from the dim sum place two blocks away," Winifred says excitedly, shoving the phone in Vera's face.

Vera grabs the phone and squints at it. Winifred has clicked on a post of Xander sitting at a table eating a zongji. In the background is an old Asian man carrying a bamboo steamer. The caption reads, "After a week of nonstop partying, there is nothing like the taste of home. Love you, Gramps. #family #grandfather #dimsum." She zooms in on the old man's face. The picture turns grainier as she zooms, but against all odds, Winifred is right, damn it. The old man does look familiar. But can it really be Qiang Wen?

"It's him, I'm telling you," Winifred insists. "So, this is his grandson? Oh my. Do you think he's heard? I'm guessing not, since the police haven't identified this young man. If they knew he's Qiang Wen's grandson, they wouldn't name him John Doe. Right? Vera? Hey, Ver-aah, what are you thinking?"

Vera is shaking her head slowly. "Qiang Wen's daughter couldn't have been married long. I know because he used to do tai chi with Jinlong. They often talked to each other about their families, and Qiang Wen always told him how worried he was about his daughter. So, how can he have a grandson in his twenties?"

Winifred's brow furrows, then suddenly clears as her eyes grow wide. "Oh my," she says with a delighted, horrified gasp. "An illicit affair? A child out of wedlock?"

"Tch," Vera says. "Nobody likes a gossip, Winifred."

"I'm not gossiping, I'm investigating."

Well, she's got Vera there.

"Are you going to confront Qiang Wen now?" Winifred says, her eyes bright with excitement.

"Of course not. This requires a gentle touch. If he doesn't know about Xander's death, I'm not about to break his heart without at least cooking him a good meal."

"Oh yes, very considerate of you."

Vera smiles. Already her mind is racing ahead. Because though she's just chastised Winifred about gossiping, she is in fact very curious about Qiang Wen's secret grandson. And she has a feeling that getting the truth out of him is going to require some finesse, some subtlety. Luckily for this case, Vera is nothing if not subtle.

EIGHT

QIANG WEN

Qiang Wen has just finished washing the last of his dirty cookware when the front door swings open with a tinkle. "We are closed," he calls out from the back without looking up. He shakes his head. Did he forget to flip the sign from OPEN to CLOSED? He swears, his memory is getting worse by the day.

"Lei hou, Qiang Wen," a familiar voice says.

Qiang Wen pops his head out of the kitchen and pauses in surprise when he sees Vera Wong standing in his little dumpling shop. "Ah, Vera," he says in Cantonese. "Long time no see. How are you doing?"

"Good, good." Vera smiles at him. "And you?"

"Same old." He wipes his hands on a towel and heads out into the shop area, where, for a painful moment, the two of them stare at each other awkwardly. He's always been friendly with Vera, but they could never be accused of being friends. He was much closer to her late husband, Jinlong, and she much closer to his late wife,

Yi Mei. "So, what can I do for you? If you're here to pick up some dinner, I do have some leftover dumplings. I usually have them for dinner myself. Let's see . . ."

"Oh, no. Actually, I came by to invite you over for dinner."

Qiang Wen stops moving. He peers at her. A dinner invitation from Vera? How curious. "What's the occasion?"

Vera licks her lips. She looks like she's struggling to find the right words to say what she's about to say, which is very strange, because for as long as he's known her, Qiang Wen has never seen Vera at a loss for words. She usually has the opposite problem, in fact. "Well," she says finally, "I thought maybe you'd want some company, given the tragedy."

"Tragedy?" Dread seeps through Qiang Wen's stomach. "What's happened? Is everything okay?"

Vera gives him a funny look. "Well, everything is okay with me, yes, but you're the one who has suffered a great loss."

"I—what?"

And now Vera looks vexed. "Your grandson, Xander? Thomas? What was his name?"

For a moment, the only thing going through Qiang Wen's mind is *Grandson?* Then it all sinks in with horrible coldness. "Xander. What about him? Has something happened?"

Vera's eyebrows have disappeared into her fluffy gray hair. "Are you telling me the police didn't even inform you about his death?"

It feels as though there is a slab of stone weighing several tons squashing Qiang Wen's shoulders. With some effort, he manages to stagger to a chair. He collapses onto it. "His death?"

"Oh. Oh no. You didn't know. Oh, Qiang Wen, I am so sorry. I wouldn't have—I would've—I'm sorry."

Qiang Wen squeezes his eyes shut, covering his face with one hand. He's vaguely aware of his hands shaking, and he only hopes Vera would assume they're shaking out of intense grief. Because the main thing blaring in his mind isn't *My god, Xander is dead.* It's *What have I done?*

He sits there for goodness knows how long, guilt searing an excruciating path round and round in his mind. After a while, he becomes aware of Vera patting him gently on the arm.

"Qiang Wen, you must be strong. The police haven't been able to identify Xander, so they haven't notified his family. You'll have to tell his parents."

"I . . ." Qiang Wen looks at Vera helplessly. "I can't."

Vera looks like she's trying very hard to hold herself back from saying something. Her mouth turns into a thin line and moves like she's literally biting back her words. Then she says, "Well, surely you can't leave his parents wondering what's happened to him. His mother is your daughter, right? You wouldn't want her to suf—"

"She's not my daughter!" Qiang Wen snaps.

Vera falls silent. She clears her throat. "Ah. Has there been a falling out?"

"No, you don't understand. I—" Qiang Wen struggles with what to tell her. "I don't know who Xander's parents are."

"But he's your grandson?"

Qiang Wen winces. "Not by blood."

"Oh." Vera leans back. "I see. An adopted grandson."

Qiang Wen doesn't answer. The less Vera knows, the better. Once more, his focus goes toward the heavy black lump sitting in his belly. Xander is dead. And Qiang Wen knows, no matter what anyone tells him, it is all his fault.

"You better come with me," Vera says after a while.

"Huh?"

"I came here to invite you to dinner, remember? The food will get cold. Come, grab your jacket. And if you don't mind, I'll just pack up those leftover dumplings and add them to the menu I've prepared for tonight."

Qiang Wen gapes wordlessly as Vera bustles to the kitchen, already whipping out a container and a pair of chopsticks seemingly out of thin air. She opens the massive steamer without asking for permission and begins collecting the dumplings in her container. "These look great, Qiang Wen! Still the same juicy dumplings after all these years." When the container is full, she closes it with a quick snap and comes back out. "Got your jacket? Ah, here it is." She grabs it from the hook and drapes it over his shoulders. "Let's go, mustn't keep the others waiting."

"The others?" Qiang Wen must be in a dream. Or a trance. Or some kind of fugue state. And he's somewhat grateful for Vera's unquestionable confidence; now that she has dropped a bomb in his life by telling him about Xander's death, she isn't merely leaving him to spiral in his thoughts like he surely would. She's leading him, as though he were a helpless child, to what sounds like a big dinner, and maybe that's just what he needs right now? He has no idea, but here he is, locking up his shop and hurrying after Vera.

"Oh yes, the others. They are quite a funny group of people. I think you will like them." She glances at him sideways. "Or maybe not. I don't know, but you will like the food, anyway." With that, she brisk-walks down the block with so much enthusiasm that Qiang Wen has to jog to keep up with her.

....

As Vera predicted, Qiang Wen does like the food. He likes it a lot. When Yi Mei was alive, their meals used to be more like this—varied, with at least five or six dishes to accompany the white rice they ate daily. After she died, Qiang Wen stuck only to leftover dumplings. To be clear, his dumplings are nothing to be scoffed at. They are juicy and flavorful and made from scratch every morning, and he makes six different fillings, so there's some variety, at least. But all he's had for the last twelve years are dumplings. Dumplings for breakfast, dumplings for lunch, and dumplings for dinner. His daughter asked him once if he wasn't tired of dumplings, and he'd wanted to tell her that he saw food only as sustenance, that he ate without really tasting, so what did it matter if he was eating the same thing every day?

But now he finds himself sitting at a table surrounded by strangers. "A funny group of people," Vera had said, and they truly are, just not in the ha-ha sort of way, but more in the why-is-everybody-here sort of way. He's still in a daze, and it's a struggle to remember who everyone is. The Latino man sitting on his left is named TJ, and next to TJ is his teenage daughter, Robin. On Qiang Wen's right is Vera, and on Vera's other side is a young Caucasian woman named Amy or something like that, and then on Amy's other side is a young Asian woman named Millie, who looks like she might jump out of her seat and run away at any moment. Though, Qiang Wen supposes, the same could be said for any of them, really. None of them look like they're delighted about being here.

And yet, for some strange reason, here they all are, and none of them is making a move to leave. It's got to be some sort of spell.

Maybe Vera is some sort of deity, or maybe some cunning fox spirit in the guise of an older woman. Her food is certainly bewitching. The past few years, food has turned to ash as soon as it enters Qiang Wen's mouth. He's been chewing for years without tasting. But now, as he sits there wordlessly, Vera heaps different steaming dishes onto his plate—spicy Mouthwatering Chicken, cold peanut noodles, braised beef shank, tea-flavored eggs—and for the first time in years, Qiang Wen is eating first with his eyes. He stares at each dish with newfound wonderment. They're all familiar, all of them things that Yi Mei had made before, and yet they're also different. Gingerly, he takes a small bite of the chicken, and true to its name, his mouth waters, his taste buds bursting to life. He chokes back a sudden urge to start sobbing and quickly takes a sip of tea.

"Now, Aimes," Vera is saying to the blond girl. "You stay away from the chicken, is too spicy for white people."

"That's—you can't say that," Robin says. "That's playing on stereotypes."

"What is that? Stereo what?"

"Stereotype. Like, making an assumption based on someone's race."

Vera looks confused. "So, what I should be making assumption based on? Age?"

"That would be ageist," TJ says helpfully.

"Okay," Vera says. "So, base on sex?"

Everyone except for Qiang Wen (who is in all honesty rather lost at this point) groans. "No, that would be sexist," Aimes says. "Anyway, it's fine, we can move on from this. I can take spice."

"So, sexist is not same as sexy?" Vera muses as she places some chicken on Aimes's plate. "I always thought that when people tell me I am sexist, they mean I am very sexy."

Qiang Wen wonders about the etiquette of leaping up and running away. Around him, faces are still, like everyone is wondering the same thing.

"Yeah," Robin says finally. "That's not what they meant when they said that."

"Aiya. And here I have been thinking: Oh, good job, Vera, over sixty years old and people still finding you sexy, like Michelle Yeoh."

TJ looks horrified at the combination of the words "Vera" and "sexy." Qiang Wen can hardly blame him; Qiang Wen's own cheeks are burning with embarrassment. But then he takes a bite of the tea-steeped eggs, and he wants to weep because he feels like a little boy again, running indoors after an afternoon spent climbing trees and biting into a tea egg. He can almost feel the comforting pat of his mother's hand on his head as he chews. He's forgotten what food made with love tastes like.

"Everyone have some dumplings," Vera says, plopping the dumplings on their plates. "Qiang Wen made them especially for tonight."

A bald-faced lie, but Qiang Wen doesn't trust his own voice to say anything, so he merely nods and watches as they all bite into his dumplings. There are murmurs of appreciation, and again that feeling of needing a good cry comes over him. These young people remind him of Xander. Qiang Wen sees in his mind's eye the look of delight on Xander's face when he first bit into a pork-and-chive dumpling. He had spoken so enthusiastically, with such sincerity. But that was the problem, wasn't it? He was such a charismatic kid. And Qiang Wen is a foolish and lonely old man. His daughter and grandkids are on the East Coast and unlikely to ever move back, and all that's left for Qiang Wen to do is tick along until, one day, he stops ticking.

"These are really good. Thank you, Uncle," Millie says to him.

"Yeah, these are delicious," Aimes says, popping a whole dumpling into her mouth.

Qiang Wen nods, still unable to speak for the lump in his throat.

"Not to be rude," Robin says in that monotone way that teens have perfected over centuries, "but why are we here again? I mean, food's great, thanks, but seriously, who are you? Who are all of you? My dad won't tell me shi—"

"Language," TJ jumps in. He gives everyone an apologetic grimace. "Uh, sorry about her."

"She speak her mind; I think that is good thing," Vera says. She nods at Robin. "I tell you who I am. I am Vera Wong, famous tea connoisseur and intermediate murder investigator."

They all stare at Vera. Qiang Wen's mind moves like sludge as he tries to work out what she's just said. Even after decades of living in America, Qiang Wen's grasp on the English language, though on the whole pretty solid, isn't good enough to capture the finer details. Did she really just say "intermediate murder investigator," or was that some subtle English joke that Qiang Wen can never seem to understand? Qiang Wen raises his hand slowly, like a hesitant schoolboy.

"Yes, Qiang Wen?"

"What do you mean, 'intermediate murder investigator'?"

"Good question!" Vera beams at him. "Well, I am not quite a

professional because no one has pay me to investigate murder yet. I'm sure they will start paying me soon, but now I will do the investigation to expose myself."

They all stare at her some more, the awkwardness growing in the room until it's almost a solid presence. Then TJ clears his throat and says, "Uh, Vera, did you mean you're doing it for exposure?"

"Yes, that is what I say. You young people need to listen better. Anyway, I am not amateur investigator, because I already solve a big murder case last year. Even the police cannot figure it out. They say, 'Vera, only you can solve this because you are a Chinese mother, you are very good at sniffing out wrongdoing.'"

"The police said that to you?" Robin says in a tone of voice that clearly sounds unconvinced.

"More or less," Vera says, completely unbothered by Robin. "Anyway, so now we are investigating new murder."

"We?" Aimes says.

"Well, mostly me. Because you all still beginner. Also, you all might be suspect, I don't know. Last year I make mistake and think this person is suspect, that person is suspect; now I learn from experience. I don't anyhow accuse you all of being suspect. Even though you might be." She gives them all a stern look.

The back of Qiang Wen's neck crawls as his skin breaks out in a cold sweat. He's somewhat dazed by what Vera has said, and he's only about seventy percent sure that Vera isn't actually able to read people's minds as easily as one would a glowing neon sign. His sign would read, I AM GUILTY. He shrinks lower onto his seat and wonders if Vera is in good enough shape to pounce on him if he were to make a break for it.

"Wha—" TJ sputters. "When you said to bring my daughter

and come by for a home-cooked meal, this wasn't what I was expecting."

"Well, is dinner and a show," Vera says. "You know, is good to underpromise and overdeliver. This is business advice for you, TJ."

"Cool," Robin says. "So, whose murder are we investigating?"

Vera's smile widens into a shark's grin. "I like you. You can be my apprentice. And now, let us begin."

NINE

MILLIE

What has she done? What has she gotten herself into? This is completely the opposite of what she'd been expecting when she told Vera about Thomas. Although, well, come to think of it, what had Millie expected when she told Vera?

Well, that was the thing. She'd been expecting much of the same that she'd gotten used to over the past few years, and that is a big load of nothing. Of course that was what Millie had expected when she spilled her guts out to a random old woman over tea. Any reasonable person would think the same. What could this nice old lady do, right? Right?

And yet, here she is in a house full of strangers and delicious food, and she wants to keep eating, but also her stomach is clenched so hard with anxiety that eating is out of the question, which is a shame because the food is so, so good, and—and—

Oh god, Millie is spiraling. She takes a deep breath and returns to her mantra: I am Millie. I am okay. I have done nothing wrong.

"You okay?" the pretty blond girl next to her says quietly.

Millie nods. She's about to ask the blond girl how she knew Thomas when Vera claps for attention. Which she gets, obviously. Millie has the feeling that Vera is used to getting attention whenever she wants to.

"Right!" Vera says. "We go around the table and say how we know this Thomas or Xander or John."

Silence befalls the table. To Millie's horror, Vera points at her. "You," Vera says. "You bring the case to me, so you start."

"Uh—" Millie looks around with the desperation of a trapped animal. "Um, okay. Yes. Right. Thomas was my friend."

"Who's Thomas?" Aimes says.

"Thomas is Xander," Vera says.

Aimes narrows her eyes. "I don't get it."

Vera sighs impatiently. "Thomas and Xander and John are all same person. Aiya, how come you don't know all this about your boyfriend? When I date boy, I know everything about them, even their blood type."

Millie's chest constricts. Boyfriend? This beautiful girl with hair like honey and eyes like storm clouds is . . . Thomas's girlfriend? Shame curdles Millie's gut. No wonder Thomas hadn't been interested in her.

Vera continues her lecture, oblivious to the storm raging inside Millie. "You listen to me, you young people, follow my advice when you date, you will not regret it. First thing you should find out when you dating someone is . . . ?"

"Is that a rhetorical question—oh, you actually want us to answer," Aimes says. "Hmm, their star sign?"

"No!" Vera snaps. "Although, well, yes, you should find out if they are born in the year of ox or ram, etcetera. But that is not first thing, that is maybe the third thing. Anyone else?"

"What they do for a living?" Robin pipes up.

"No! Aiya, what they teaching you kids in school? Although, well, yes, you should find out that also. Maybe that one should be second thing. Good job. Okay, but first thing you find out is: Who are their family?"

Qiang Wen nods in agreement, but everyone else looks dubious.

"If you know their family, you know a lot about them. Whether they are from good background or not. You trust me," Vera says, wagging a finger at them. "Aimes, next time you remember, must meet his parents first before you even date him."

"I . . . don't think that's possible, but thanks for the advice," Aimes mutters. Then she turns to Millie.

Millie finds herself at a loss for words at the sight of Aimes's gray eyes trained on hers. She envies girls like Aimes. Girls who are effortlessly beautiful, but more than that, girls who effortlessly belong. And everything about Aimes is so effortless. Even the way her silk scarf drapes over her shoulders so neatly and naturally. Millie has grappled with scarves a million times and still she can't get them to fall over her shoulders like that.

"So, how did you meet Xan?"

Xan. Just like that, so cool. Millie sounds the word out in her mind, turning the syllable over and feeling the shape of it. Xan. So unlike the Thomas she knew. But that was just it. She didn't know him, maybe. "Um." Her mind flails to come up with an answer. "I—well, we lived next to each other."

Aimes's eyes widen. "Wow, you fancy."

"Huh?" Now Millie really is at a loss.

"Xan lived in Haight-Ashbury, right? Houses there cost like, what, five mil at least?"

"What?" Millie can hardly keep the shock out of her voice. "He lived—" She stops herself just in time. Her thoughts race ahead of her. She's already made a huge mistake telling them that she and Thomas were neighbors. Too close to the truth. She needs to back away from that now.

But of course, it's too late. Vera, who is apparently an actual investigator instead of a lonely old woman with too much time on her hands, has noticed the suspicious air about Millie. "Thomas lie about where he live?" she says, her sharp eyes on Millie. "He does not live in Haight-Ashbury?"

Millie shakes her head dumbly. "I . . . I don't know. Maybe he has another place that I didn't know about. I mean, we weren't very close. I hardly knew anything about him."

"Oh, I think you a lot closer than you say," Vera says. Then, thank god, Vera turns to Aimes. "Have you not been to Thomas's house?"

Aimes shakes her head, looking guilty.

"Aiya!" Vera snaps. "What kind of relationship you two in? How can you not go to boyfriend's house?"

Aimes groans and puts her hands over her face. "Oh my god, it was a very casual relationship, okay? We weren't ever going to get married or anything like that. We were just dating."

Vera harrumphs. "I don't like this word 'dating.' Sounds so un-serious. Relationships are very serious; they are not just between two people, they are between two families."

Millie's heart aches because she understands it all too well. Back home in Yunnan, a relationship is exactly the way Vera describes; it doesn't just involve two people but two entire families. The rules are different here, and she's had to adjust her under-standing of so many things to get them. And as much as she hates to admit it, she's jealous of Aimes, and of Thomas, who seemed like they'd had a complete understanding of the rules here. She's had enough attention. She needs to divert some of it. Turning to TJ, Millie says, "And what about you? How did you know Thomas?"

TJ tugs at his shirt collar. "I knew him as Xander, actually. He was one of my clients. Not much else to say aside from that." He gives a weak laugh.

Next to him, Robin rolls her eyes.

"Oh," Aimes says. "You're his talent manager? Xan used to mention you. It's nice to finally meet you in person."

"Yeah," TJ says with less enthusiasm than Millie would've expected. "But I was never close to him or anything. I mean, not to say I don't work closely with my clients, I just—"

"Oh my god, Dad," Robin groans. "This is painful. He's going through a tough time because he's being canceled, and it's all my fault."

"It's not your fault," TJ says.

Robin rolls her eyes, but Millie spots the tiniest hint of a tremor in Robin's chin. The atmosphere is so thick Millie feels like she can't breathe. She's about to blurt out something when the doorbell rings. Vera gets up, tells them to remain where they are, and bustles to the front door. There is a male voice along with a child saying, "Hi, Grandma."

"My little Em-Em," Vera says, pure love palpable in her voice. She comes back to the dining room holding the hand of a little girl, a man who looks to be in his early thirties behind them. "Everyone, this my granddaughter Emma, and this her uncle Oliver."

"Oh," Oliver says, obviously surprised by their presence. "Sorry,

Vera, I didn't know you were having a dinner party. Didn't mean to crash it."

"Don't be silly. You take a seat here, next to Millie. She seems like good girl. Millie, Oliver is good husband material."

Millie's entire face feels as though it's burst into flames. Then again, it seems like Oliver is about to have an aneurysm, so at least she's not the only one dying of embarrassment.

"Vera," Oliver sighs. "Behave, or I'm taking Emma home."

"Don't be silly," Vera says. "We have dumplings."

As Oliver squeezes in between Millie and Aimes, he catches Millie's eye. Her face, which has already burst into flames moments ago, melts into bubbling lava. Because, oh my goodness, Oliver is very handsome. And Millie cannot be trusted around handsome men.

"Hi, I'm Oliver," he says.

"Millie," she says. Her voice comes out so tiny that Oliver has to lean in a little to catch it, and the nearness of him makes Millie even more flustered. "Millie," she says again, and this time it's a little too loud, and god, she wishes she wasn't so bad at this. She isn't usually bad at talking to men, but it's the whole Aimes-being-Thomas's-girlfriend thing, and the whole Vera-investigating-Thomas's-death thing, and there are just way too many things going on right now.

"Let me guess, Vera has rounded up a group of complete strangers and is spearheading some sort of inappropriate investigation that borders on illegal?" Oliver says to her.

Millie's head shoots up. Because, yes, exactly. She nods, and Oliver sighs and gives a wry smile. "Yep, that's Vera."

She watches as he introduces himself to the rest of the table. Everyone else seems unfazed or, at the very least, less fazed.

Emma is insisting on hand-feeding Robin a dumpling, and Robin is going, "Kid, get your paws out of my face." Vera is chatting to Qiang Wen in Cantonese, and Aimes and TJ are talking about social media. Millie seems to be the only one who's ill at ease, and she supposes it makes sense, because Millie is the only one with a dark secret—multiple dark secrets, actually.

"So, how do you know Vera?" Oliver says.

"She found me outside of the police station and decided to help me out. What about you? Are you her son?"

"Not biologically, but I think she's pretty much adopted me. And a few others." Oliver spoons some pork onto her plate before serving himself. A tiny spark of pleasure shoots through Millie at the gesture. "My brother was found dead in Vera's shop last year, and she decided to investigate his death. That was how I got to know her."

"Oh my god, that's horrible. I'm so sorry to hear that."

Oliver chews thoughtfully. "Thanks. It was a pretty dark time for all of us involved. Thank god Vera was there. She kind of gathered the four of us—we were pretty messed up, all of us—and took us under her wing, even though she also suspected each one of us of killing my brother."

Millie's head is spinning. "Okay, that sounds really . . ."

"Weird? Messed up? Like a mindfuck? Yeah, it was all of those things. But she worked it out in the end. And I'm grateful I have Vera and the others in my life."

Millie nods. Should she be grateful, too, that Vera is taking an interest in Thomas's case, or should she be terrified about what Vera might find out?

"What do you do for a living, Millie?"

The answer flops out automatically. She's had a lot of practice doing it. "I'm an air stewardess for private planes." "Stewardess," not "attendant," because it sounds sexier. And "private planes" instead of "commercial jets" so no one can go, *Nice, which flight? Which airline?* She even knows some of the basic training that flight attendants had to go through, just to make her lie extra convincing.

"That sounds like hard work," Oliver says.

Millie is somewhat taken aback by this. Most men, when they hear she's an air stewardess, say stuff like "That's hot" or "That's a cushy job" or something else that's equal parts creepy and demeaning. "Yeah," she says after a pause. "It is."

"I can imagine. Private planes would mean catering to the rich and famous, and they're not known for being easy to work for. Not to mention the jet lag."

Millie nods, her face reddening with guilt. He thinks she's a hard worker. She can't take any more of this. Time to deflect. "What about you?"

"I'm just a supe," Oliver says. "I do minor repairs for the tenants in the building."

"Oliver is writer," Vera says.

Millie almost jumps. How long has Vera been listening to them?

"I don't know if I would call myself a writer—" Oliver says.

"Silly boy, of course you are. He is freelance writer, has written for the *San Francisco Chronicle* and *Bay Area Times.* Very good articles too. I frame them up in my tea shop, you know."

Oliver grins at Vera, and there's so much affection in his expression that it makes him look like a little boy.

Millie looks away, her emotions warring inside her. She makes a big deal out of checking her watch, then says, "Oh no, look at the time. I have an early flight tomorrow, so I should go."

"Oliver, walk her out," Vera says with a sly smile.

"You don't have to," Millie says, but already Oliver is getting up.

"Make sure she don't get mugged before she get in Uber or bus or whatever," Vera says sternly.

"Okay, Vera," Oliver says.

Millie says goodbye to everyone, but before they can go down the staircase, Vera comes after them and pushes a heavy container into Millie's hands. "Some Chinese barbecue pork for you," Vera says. "You should eat more, you are too skinny."

Tears prick Millie's eyes. When was the last time someone had looked out for her like this? She manages a nod and turns away before Vera can see the tears that are threatening to fall.

Outside, Millie wraps her jacket tightly around herself, wishing she could disappear. Oliver stuffs his hands inside his pockets and gives her a quick smile. "Do you need me to call you an Uber?"

He's so nice. Why does he have to be so nice? She must get away from him. She mustn't let them see her with him. "No, it's fine. I'm taking the bus."

"Okay. I'll wait with you."

"You really don't have to."

"Oh, I really do. I don't want to get in trouble with Vera."

She can't help laughing at that. A young, confident man like Oliver being scared of Vera is somehow hilarious and yet utterly believable. They walk in amicable silence to the bus stop. Her phone dings with a text. She pretends not to hear it. It dings again. And again.

"You can get that; I don't mind," Oliver says.

"Sorry." She hurriedly takes it out and checks her messages. They're all from Mother.

Curfew's over.
Where are you?
Millie. Come home NOW.

Her mouth has turned into a desert. She tries to type quickly, but her fingers have gone numb. She manages to tap in OMW back before the phone slips out of her fingers and falls onto the sidewalk.

"Oh no," Oliver says, bending over to retrieve it.

Millie's instincts take over and before she knows it, she's practically assaulted Oliver in her haste to grab the phone from his hands. By the time she snatches the phone away from him, her breathing is shallow, and she's sure she must've scared him away.

Instead, Oliver says, "Sorry. I should've—I didn't mean to pry. I promise I didn't see anything."

"No!" she cries. It kills her to think that he's blaming himself for her weirdness. "It's just." Just what? It is true that she reacted so fast because she didn't want him to see what's on her phone. "Sorry, I just get weird about my phone. It's not you."

"Anyway, I hope it's not broken."

She checks it. There is a crack on one corner of the screen, but it seems to be working okay. "It's fine." She stuffs it back into her pocket.

They wait in silence for a few seconds, then Oliver says, "Not to be weird, and feel free to say no, but can I give you my number?"

She gapes at him.

"Uh. I didn't wanna ask for your number in case you didn't feel safe giving it to me," he says. "Is that weird? I don't really know how to do these things."

"No, that's not weird at all. It's incredibly thoughtful, actually." She doesn't deserve thoughtful. She shouldn't take his number. She shouldn't take his anything. She should disappear and hope Vera and everybody else forgets about her. But Millie finds herself taking her phone out once more and opening her address book. She taps on New Contact and says, "Yes, I would love your number." She didn't think she could possibly hate herself more than she already does, and yet here she is, reaching new lows. The smile of relief that Oliver gives her nearly tips her over the edge, and when the bus arrives a minute later, Millie jumps on quickly. She waves bye at Oliver, then spends the ride back staring at his number, trying to make herself delete it. Nothing good can come out of this.

But instead of deleting it, Millie does something else. Something completely ridiculous, something so unhinged that she doesn't dare to stop in case she thinks better of it. The bus is about to pass through a stop in front of a Target when she shouts, "Stop!" She clambers out, hurries into Target, and purchases the first prepaid phone she finds. It costs $19.99, plus tax, and Millie tears open the package as soon as she's finished paying. She saves Oliver's number in her new phone, then stuffs it deep into her handbag, covering it with her makeup bag and cardigan.

When she gets back and Mother grabs her arm and practically drags her to their place to interrogate her, Millie thinks about the secret phone. Just for a second. Then she banishes all thoughts of it and forces herself to focus.

"Why're you spending so much time at a tea shop in Chinatown?" Mother says.

Millie doesn't ask Mother how she knew about Vera's tea shop. Mother and Father are all-knowing. They are like gods. Sometimes, she feels like they know things before they happen.

Still, Millie tries lying anyway. "I just stopped by for some tea," she says meekly. Mother and Father like it when she's meek. Actually, most people like it when she's meek. From the corner of her eye, she spots Mina peeping out from her doorway, and Millie gives a shake of her head. Mina disappears, though no doubt her little sister is listening. Days like these, Millie misses her big sister Yara so much. Millie has never quite known how to be a big sister to anybody. She had hoped that she'd be the last, that Mother and Father would stop having kids, but of course they haven't. Mother and Father love being parents. She wonders, for the millionth time: What would Yara do? But Yara wouldn't be in this mess in the first place.

"You're wasting time. Time you should be spending on your job," Father growls.

"This old woman who owns the shop," Mother says, "she rich?"

Millie shakes her head quickly. Too quickly?

"What about the guy who walked you out?" Father says.

Millie knows better than to ask how Father knows about Oliver.

"He's nobody." His number burns a hole in her pocket.

"They all are," Mother says. "Until they aren't. He seems nice. Nice is good."

"Nice is easy," Father says.

"And we like easy, don't we, Millie?"

Millie looks down at the floor and gives a small nod. She should've known better than to go to Vera's tonight. She knows she's bad news. They don't deserve to be around someone like her. And she wishes that when her phone fell, it had smashed beyond repair so Oliver couldn't have given her his number. So many wishes. It's too bad none of them would do her any good now.

TEN

VERA

Vera can't remember the last time she's had so much fun. Then she feels guilty for thinking that, because she literally has weekly dinners with her newfound family and they are nothing but fun, but the thing is, there's just nothing quite like the heartwarming joy of gathering a bunch of new people who are obviously slightly terrified and brazenly accusing them of murder. And also, to her credit, Vera has refrained from outrightly accusing anyone of murder this time around. See? Old dogs can learn new tricks.

Though of course she is secretly assessing everyone in her house and measuring them up against the Vera Wong Formula for Murderers.

1. *Does the person reek of guilt?*
2. *Shifty eyes? Awkward silences? Constipated look?*
3. *Mysterious connection with the victim?*

She should patent her formula. Although, to be fair, so far all of the people here tonight, except for Emma and Oliver, are potential killers according to her formula, so maybe Vera's formula needs a little fine-tuning.

She tells Qiang Wen to help Emma with her chopsticks, then turns her attention to TJ and Aimes, who are busy talking about social media. Vera quite likes social media; it's a wonderful way to learn about the new generation. When Tilly was a teen, he hated having Vera or Jinlong knowing anything about his life. He was so protective over everything that had to do with his life. But now, young people can't seem to share enough about their lives with the world. It's very handy for nosy parents.

"I will make some tea," Vera says, gliding behind her counter. Once she's in her element, Vera's entire body goes through a metamorphosis; even the way she stands feels different. Making tea in front of an audience makes Vera feel like a butterfly emerging from a chrysalis, unfurling her glorious wings to luxuriate in the attention. She moves with liquid grace, patiently taking out dried rosebuds from a jar with a pair of chef tweezers and measuring them out on an old-school weighing scale. The scales are made from brass and have a little weight on the end that Vera has to slide with care until she is satisfied. Next, she sprinkles some dried osmanthus onto the small pile of rosebuds, the flakes so delicate that they fly weightlessly. The entire process, Vera feels, is laced with magic. A small smile plays on her mouth as she pours the hot water. When it is done, she glances up and says, "Tea is served."

That's when she realizes that Aimes has been recording her with her phone. There is a moment of silence as Aimes stares at her through the phone screen, mouth agape. Vera flaps an impatient hand at her. "Eh, Aimes, what you doing?"

Aimes snaps to attention. "Oh my god," she says, tapping at the phone. "Vera, that was . . . wow. I don't know what made me decide to record you making tea, but oh my god. We've got some amazing footage there."

"Aiya, what are you talking about?"

"No, seriously, that was so comforting to watch. Oh my god. I like to watch soothing videos before I go to sleep at night—I know, scrolling through my phone in bed is a terrible habit, I know, but to be fair, I'm not doomscrolling. I stick to these soothing village cooking videos."

"Village cooking videos?" Vera says.

"Yeah, there are lots of them from around the world. My favorites are the ones from China and Poland. Hang on, let me show you." Aimes goes through her phone and then shows Vera what she means.

Vera watches in wonderment. It's a video of a middle-aged woman in China butchering pork and cooking all sorts of delicious pork dishes from scratch. She even makes the dumpling skin from scratch. "People watch this?" she says.

"Oh yeah. Look, this one's got three million views."

"Is that a lot of views?"

"Yeah! You get paid per million views," Aimes says.

Vera is flabbergasted. "How much you get paid?"

"Well, it really depends on how you choose to monetize. You could have ads or sponsors and collabs with people in the biz, not to mention merch."

"Aimes, you speak English, okay? Don't use these silly words, like 'merch' and all that," Vera scolds.

"Oh, sorry. Okay, just to keep it simple, you should get paid around two thousand dollars per million views."

"Two thousand dollar?" Vera cries. She glances again at the video, where the woman is now kneading a ball of dough. "Just to cook this? This is such simple dish, I make almost every week!"

"Well . . . yeah. Because most of us don't do this, Vera," Aimes says. "Most people don't make—is she making noodles from scratch? Okay, yeah, most of us don't do that. We buy premade noodles from the supermarket."

"Aiya, you young people." Vera frowns at the video. An idea is starting to take shape. An idea that would kill two pigs with one stone. It would establish her as a social media star *and* find justice for Thomas/Xander. She nods to herself. Yes, it's the perfect plan. Straightening up, she clears her throat and makes her announcement. "I have decide that I will be new social media star."

Aimes and TJ look suspiciously like they're trying to hold back a smile.

"Now, how you post it?" Vera says.

"Whoa, hang on, you can't just post raw footage. You gotta edit it first."

Robin, looking over their shoulders, plucks the phone from Aimes's hand.

"Hey!" Aimes says.

"You're too slow," Robin grumbles. She settles down on the couch. Emma climbs up next to her, and Robin gives her a hesitant sideways glance. "What's up, kid?"

"What are you doing?" Emma says in her surprisingly somber voice.

"I'm about to show these folks how to edit a video in under five minutes. Otherwise we're gonna be here forever. You in?"

Emma thinks for a bit, then nods. She watches as Robin swipes away with expert ease.

Aimes, watching over Robin's shoulder, grunts. Once in a while, Aimes mutters, "Huh."

Vera smiles inwardly. Look at these three girls. She wishes Sana were here. She'd fit right in.

Within a few minutes, as promised, Robin holds up the phone triumphantly and says, "Done."

Vera snatches the phone from her hands and hits Play. The video is beautiful, a thousand times better than Vera expected, and she had very unrealistic expectations to begin with. She looks so gentle in it, so maternal, and she can see how it would be a soothing video to watch after a long, hard day. And the tea! The tea looks nothing short of magical. Those little rosebuds and the way they swirl when the hot water hits them. The only thing wrong with it is the music playing in the background.

"How you get rid of music?" Vera says.

Aimes frowns. "I wouldn't get rid of the music, that's part of the charm. Good choice of music, by the way," she adds, nodding at Robin.

"No music," Vera says with finality. "I have message to say in video. The music just get in the way."

"Oh," Aimes says. "You're gonna narrate it? Okay." She taps at the phone and the music disappears.

"Okay, now send me video to my phone," Vera says, "so I can post."

"Do you even have a social media account?" Aimes says.

"That isn't Facebook?" Robin says.

The two of them look at each other and grin.

Vera ignores this little show of impertinence. "I have you know, I am on both the TikTok and the Instagram."

"Wow, I would never have guessed," Aimes mutters.

"What do you use them for?" TJ says.

"To spy on my son, obviously," Vera says smartly.

Robin groans. "Dad, do not get any ideas."

TJ gives an affronted look, like how could she possibly accuse him of doing such a thing? But Vera catches a short glimpse of guilt, and she has to bite back her laugh. Obviously TJ is already doing the same thing she is. Parents, no matter where they are from, are the same all over the world.

Aimes is in the middle of sending the video over to Vera when there is a knock at the front door.

Vera calls down, "Come up! We all up here."

A few moments later, Officer Selena Gray shows up. The chatter in the room dies down. Selena stops at the last step and stares. "Sorry, Vera, I didn't mean to inter—wait. I've met you all before."

Vera looks around the room, noticing how intensely worried and/or guilty TJ, Aimes, and Qiang Wen look. In fact, Qiang Wen looks more than worried; he looks terrified. *Aha*, she thinks, making a mental note to jot that down later in her notebook.

Oliver climbs up the stairs behind Selena. "Oh, hey, Selena," he says.

"Hey." She smiles at him, then turns back to face Vera and the others, her eyes narrowing. "Vera, what is going on here?" Her voice comes out very, very tired.

"Oh, nothing, Selena. Just nice dinner party with friends."

Selena gives a pointed look at Vera. "Why are your friends people I have spoken to about a specific case that happened two weeks ago?"

Vera returns the look with an innocent one. "Oh? What case is it?"

Selena's jaw clenches and unclenches. Ignoring Vera, she turns to TJ and says, "Why are you here?"

TJ looks like he would very much like to be anywhere but here. He shoves his hands into his pockets and clears his throat. "I—well, Vera here invited me and my daughter for dinner."

"Yeah, I got that. How do you know Vera?"

Vera flaps at them. "Never you mind that."

"Never I mind that?" Selena echoes. "Vera, this is my job, and I really hope you're not snooping again."

"Me, snoopy? You know I am too busy to do anything like that. All day every day, I cooking for you and Tilly and Oliver and all the others, not to mention look after my tea shop. You think I have time to go snoopy everywhere? Hah!"

Selena doesn't look fazed by Vera's faux scolding. She raises an impassive eyebrow and says in a warning tone, "Vera . . ."

"Also, you should be thankful if I snoopy, because look what happen last time I snoop, eh?"

"What happened last time?" Robin pipes up.

Vera grins. "Ah! I solve murder case."

Selena pinches the bridge of her nose. "Vera, you put yourself and others in danger the last time you did that."

"Aiya, of course not, don't be so drama. There is no danger, the killer is harmless old man."

"How can a killer be harmless?" Aimes says.

"Exactly," Selena says. "The killer was most definitely not harmless, and Vera, whatever you think you know about this case, I can assure you, you don't."

"Ah, so there is case?" Vera says cunningly.

Selena's mouth shuts into a tight line. "There is no case. I do not know how you got in touch with all these people, and I don't want to know. You all should go home."

"Yes, officer, right away," TJ says, already grabbing his and Robin's coats. "Come on, Robin."

"Yeah, I'd better get going too," Aimes says.

Qiang Wen mumbles something under his breath and starts to shuffle out of the living room as well.

"Wait!" Vera calls after them. "You haven't taken leftover food. Later will spoil. I cannot eat all by myself." But with hasty murmurs of thanks, everyone leaves the room, and soon, the only ones remaining are Vera, Oliver, Emma, and Selena. Vera huffs at Selena. "You are lucky I like you so much and you are going to be my future daughter-in-law. That is very rude, ending my dinner party early. Look, I didn't even have time to give them their goodie bags."

"Ooh, goodie bags!" Emma says, reaching out for one.

Vera hands it to her and glowers at Selena. Then her face softens. "Aiya, I cannot stay angry with daughter-in-law. You come and take leftover food, give some to Tilly also."

"Vera," Selena sighs. "I'm serious, you can't involve yourself in this. It's dangerous."

"But it says is suicide, so how can be dangerous?"

Selena pauses, then peers at Vera with suspicion. "How do you know it's suspected suicide?"

Uh-oh. Vera chooses not to answer, her mind whizzing ahead to try to cover up her slipup.

"Vera," Selena says in a warning tone. "What exactly do you know about this case? This John Doe? And how exactly did you find these people who are connected to the case?"

"Uncle Ollie, is Grandma in trouble?" Emma says.

Oliver tugs the collar of his shirt. "Uh, I think she might be?"

"Auntie Selena, why are you being mean to Grandma?"

Selena breaks her intense eye contact with Vera for a second and looks guiltily at the little girl. "I'm not being mean to Grandma, I'm just trying to make sure she doesn't do anything silly, like place herself in the middle of a live case."

"Ooh, so it is a live case? There is live investigation going on?" Vera says eagerly. "But why, if it is suicide?"

Selena groans out loud. "Vera, just—" She takes a deep breath. "Just don't do anything that might put you at risk. Let me do my job, all right?"

The last thing Vera wants to do is get into a fight with her future daughter-in-law. She has resolved a long time ago that she wouldn't be the stereotypical mother-in-law. Her own mother-in-law had been a tyrant of a woman, always picking fights with Vera over nonissues, and when Tilly was born, Vera had made herself a promise that whoever Tilly marries, that person is going to be so incredibly grateful to have Vera as a mother-in-law.

"Yes, yes, of course, you don't worry about that," Vera says. "Now, you wait there and I pack you up some food, okay? You don't need to diet, Selena, you are very beautiful and healthy already, okay? You remember that now." Vera pats Selena on the arm and bustles away to pack up the food for her.

Selena takes the bag of food with a very quick, very strained smile. "Thanks. But please remember what I said? Don't go looking for trouble, Vera."

"Such nonsense you talking," Vera cries, waving her away. "I don't need to look for trouble at my age."

At her age, one does not have the time to look for trouble; rather, one goes on the hunt for it.

ELEVEN

AIMES

Aimes can't sleep that night. To be fair, it's been a while since she's been able to sleep naturally; these days, she has to take a melatonin pill if she wants to not lie awake in bed for at least an hour before drifting off to sleep, and twice a week, she makes sure she goes to sleep quickly by polishing off a cheeky glass of wine, or two. She likes to think of it as a "cheeky" glass, even though she's nowhere near British enough to pull off the word "cheeky." But it makes it sound cuter rather than the beginnings of a potential drinking problem.

Tonight, Aimes has opted for the melatonin pill instead of wine. She's eaten so much at dinner that two glasses won't do a thing now, and she really can't afford to go for a third glass. She's got enough problems as it is. Like the fact that Vera is connected to Officer Gray. What are the chances of that? Just her luck that the random old lady who had randomly found her at a café happens to be Officer Gray's mother-in-law. Or mother-in-law-to-be. Whatever, same thing.

Aimes turns around in her bed and buries her face in her pillow, willing the memories to stay away. Except, of course, they do the exact opposite of that. She recalls the day that Officer Gray paid her a visit. The horrible, sinking feeling when she saw Officer Gray standing there at her doorstep. They'd connected her with Xander. Of course they had, even though in her wildest dreams she'd hoped against hope that they might've missed that connection. How could they have? She and Xander had wanted the whole world to know that they were dating. It was their thing. The smart thing to do, she had said, and he had agreed. *Not so smart now, are you?* a small, awful voice says in her head.

More memories. Her and Xander propping her phone up on a stand and posing in front of it, laughing. Her surprise at how natural it all felt, how real. Even their banter with each other felt natural. Him donning a long blond wig and pretending to act like her, strutting everywhere and going, "OMG it's fall season! Give me a PSL, STAT!" until she laughed so hard that a drop of pee came out. They'd had fun, hadn't they? They weren't just lies, there had been something real underneath it all, no matter how flimsy.

With a groan, Aimes gives up trying to fall asleep and reaches out to turn the bedside lamp on. She knocks a couple of trinkets onto the floor before finding the light switch. Aimes's room, like the rest of her tiny apartment, is filled with useless knickknacks. Promotional material sent over by sponsors for her to peddle to her followers. There are so many of the damn things, it's overwhelming. Even the table lamp is a free gift from a clay potter who has fifty thousand followers online and wants her to help promote him. It's in the shape of a hand holding an umbrella. Aimes hates it, but her followers had gone crazy over it when she posted it to her Stories, so it's here to stay. Every time she gropes around in the dark to turn it on, though, she shudders when her fingers brush the lamp's fingers. *Blergh*. It's like having someone's severed hand on your nightstand. Why would anyone want that? Why does she still have it? Because. Because her followers love it. Because she is terrified that if she threw it away and she posts a photo from her bedroom and her followers see it is missing, they'd know. They'd know what a fake she is. And that is why Aimes's apartment is filled to the gills with things she hates. Including herself.

Dim light spills across the room. Aimes locates her phone, unplugs it, and settles back in bed with it. She opens Instagram. Fifty-seven DMs and over three hundred notifications from the last time she checked, which was less than an hour ago. Aimes's eyebrows knit together. That is way more messages than she typically gets in an hour. The notifications used to trigger endorphins, the likes nourishing her as tiny little pieces of vitamin C would. But now, the sight of the notifications and unread messages only makes Aimes feel overwhelmed. She taps on the DMs.

OMG Aimes, just heard abt Xan, are you ok??

AIMES I LOVE YOU NO MATTER WHAT!

OMG I'm literally in tears writing this.

Aimes's stomach sours. Oh no. It's happening. She opens DM after DM, only half reading them, the sense of dread seeping even deeper as she scrolls. Then one of them makes her stop. It has a link, and the message reads: **Is this true????**

The link leads Aimes off Instagram and onto TikTok. When it

opens, Aimes's heart stops for a second. It's a video of Vera. A video that Aimes had shot just earlier this evening but somehow already has over one hundred thousand views.

In the video, Vera makes tea calmly. The camera zooms in on her weathered hands mixing the ingredients, then pans out to take in the small, loving smile on her face. Aimes isn't surprised by how good the footage looks. She remembers getting sucked in herself while watching Vera, marveling at how comforting it is to watch her do something as simple as brewing tea. No, the footage isn't what bothers her. It's the audio. Vera has added a voice-over of herself narrating as she makes the tea.

"What happen to Xander Lin?" Vera's voice says, full of suspicion and maternal concern. "Xander Lin was a social media star, many of you probably follow him. But police find him dead, and what is more suspicious, he is called John Doe by police. Because it turn out Xander Lin is not his real name. So, what is? And why does it seem like nobody know who is the real Xander Lin? Join me, Vera Wong from Vera Wang's World-Famous Teahouse, as I investigate Xander's death. Is it murder? I don't know, but we will have good tea and good food as we look into murder. I mean death. But also possibly murder."

For a second, Aimes almost throws up. She feels bile rush up her esophagus and lightly thump her chest, then swallows it. Oh god. This is bad. She needs to put a stop to this. But although Aimes has only met Vera twice, she knows that putting a stop to anything Vera is doing is probably going to be an exercise in futility. Maybe if she came clean to Vera, the older woman might feel sympathy toward her and . . .

And what? Stop looking for answers? Unlikely. She's investigating an actual *death*, not just some Internet scandal. And what if

Vera's right about Xan's death being suspicious? Would Aimes really get in the way of a potential murder investigation just to hide her dirty little secret?

Aimes groans out loud. How did she get herself into this mess? She flings herself out of bed and paces around her room. Here and there, her feet catch on more unusable knickknacks and she wants to cry with frustration. There are exactly two corners in her entire apartment that aren't choked with clutter—her bed and one side of her couch, which is right next to the window. Those two spaces look pristine most of the time, because they are where she shoots most of her content for social media. If someone were to look through her Instagram profile, they would think Aimes had everything under control, that she lives in a beautifully curated space instead of the mess that dominates her life.

She needs to get on top of things. A choked laugh burbles out of her at the thought of it. She thinks this to herself at least seventeen times a day: *I'm going to get on top of things.* It feels as though life were a treadmill, and Aimes has to keep rushing just to keep up with everything that it keeps throwing at her. She stops moving and stands in the middle of her bedroom, ignoring the piles of clothes, random plates, books, and other crap around her. Get on top of things. Right. How should she begin to do that?

First things first: She needs to resolve the whole Xan thing. But how? She can't just keep hiding and posting content as though nothing has happened. That's not going to work. She needs to acknowledge his death. What would she say about it? Aimes goes to the living room and sits at her coffee desk / dining table / writing desk. She finds a notebook—one of many that she's been sent—a pretty one with a swirl of flowers on the cover and the words *She Will Move Mountains* in a beautiful cursive font. Aimes can barely move the lint out of her apartment, but whatever. She opens it and starts writing.

Get on top of shit.

1. *Xander—Make post about his death. How much detail to go into? Maybe the last time I saw him?*

Aimes winces. The memory of the last time she saw Xan stabs into her like a jagged piece of glass. She wishes she could excise it from her mind, slice it out like a rotting appendix. She'll have to make something up for her followers.

2. *Maybe start up a fund for his family?*
3. *How much do I post about his family? Find out more about them?*

With a sigh, Aimes crosses out numbers 2 and 3. If she starts up a fund for his family, people are bound to get curious about them. No, she needs to keep this contained, put all things Xan in a neat box so that she can shut it when the time comes and put it away where no one would ever think about him.

The small, hateful voice at the back of her mind says, *You could spin it into a huge story.* Aimes wants to hit herself at the very thought of it. She could not, would not, stoop so low as to profit from Xan's death. She's lost enough of herself online; she would not lose her soul as well. No, she wouldn't post about his death to gain sympathy and followers. She would only post enough to make it seem believable, then she would move on. Forget about this whole mess. She's not a ghoul.

Aimes catches sight of her framed diploma hanging on the wall and turns away sharply. She cannot stand the sight of the thing. A bachelor of arts in English Lit from Berkeley, like that was ever going to do anything in the real world. All it did was make her unemployable. They should tell you things like that in high school. That, actually, you can't be anything you want to be, and that studying something like English Lit would only prepare you for disappointment in life.

Because for as long as Aimes can remember, she's always preferred spending time with books rather than spending it in what her parents would call "real life." As a kid, and then later as a teen, she never went anywhere without a book in her hand. During family meals, while her cousins chattered and giggled with one another, Aimes sat quietly with her book, looking up once in a while to spear a roasted potato or give a polite smile to someone. Her parents were somewhat bemused by this, but they were mostly proud of it.

"My little bookworm," her dad would say, and her mom would roll her eyes with obvious affection. They were, in general, proud that unlike other kids, Aimes had her nose buried in a book rather than the phone screen. They failed to see that she was becoming someone ill-suited for the real world. That with her compositions, Aimes was spinning stories for herself to inhabit. And now she was still spending most of her time spinning fictitious stories, except she had, as it turned out, moved on from books to phones. What a disappointment she'd turned out to be. They'd expected her to be a writer; hell, Aimes herself thought she would become a writer too, but she's queried enough agents to know that she doesn't have what it takes to stand out, not in publishing, anyway. But coming up with catchy Instagram captions is a form of writing, isn't it? And so what if it turns out that Aimes's imagination is better suited to coming up with social media content instead of books? That's nothing to be ashamed of. She's good at it. Good at spinning stories for people to consume.

Except now maybe the stories have gone too far. Now that Xan is dead, Aimes has no idea what to do with their story. She can't tell the truth, that much she knows. She has to stick to fiction. She's always been so good at fiction. While her Berkeley friends went on to do impressive internships after college, Aimes had spun more and more stories to try to keep up with seeming like she was keeping up with them. And the whole time, she retreated deeper into her isolation. Because if any of them actually spent enough time with her, they'd know. They'd find out what a pathetic life she was really leading.

I can't go out Friday, I'm slammed with work. Yeah, my job at the San Francisco Chronicle *is ridiculous, but I hope I can see you guys soon!*

Oh, I got offered a better position at this literary agency, so I left the Chronicle. *I know, what an amazing opportunity, right? So anyway, I can't come to your housewarming. I'm so sorry, but I'm sending over a nice bottle of wine, okay?*

I can't join you guys for girls' night, I have a really bad cold. I wouldn't want to pass it to anyone. I'm making a gift basket for you girls though. I hope you have so much fun!

Aimes shakes her head. Snap out of it. She needs to focus. She needs to come up with a really good story now; otherwise, she risks losing everything she's worked so hard for. No one can know the truth about her and Xan. She doesn't want to profit off his death either. The best thing she can do is to shut this whole thing down.

After applying minimal makeup, Aimes sets up her phone on its ring light stand in front of her couch. She sits down, takes a deep breath, and hits Record.

"Hi, everyone. It's me, Aimes. I just—"

No. It's all wrong. She sounds so stilted. Everyone would know she's a fake. She shakes her head once more, rakes her fingers through her hair, and takes another deep breath.

"Hi, everyone. By now, many of you have heard the devastating news about Xan. I—"

No. Too melodramatic. She doesn't want to invite more attention. She needs to keep it as short as possible. But at the same time, she has to convey sadness—and she is sad, but she can't be over the top with it. God, how the hell did she land herself in this mess?

"Hi, everyone. By now, many of you have heard about Xan. I just wanted to say that I see all of your messages and I'm grateful for all of your support, but I will be taking a hiatus from social media while I grieve Xan. Thanks."

There. Succinct. Suitably sad, if there is such a thing. Definitely doesn't invite more questions. Aimes watches it over, scrutinizing every minute expression her face makes. Does she look sincere? Sad enough? Too sad?

The thing about living your life on camera is it makes you question every single observable thing about you, to the point where Aimes no longer knows what she is truly feeling at any given time. Like now, for example. She is torn up over Xan. But she feels the grief as though it is hidden underneath a thick pane of glass, as though she were watching someone else, someone who looks exactly like her, go through it, and she can only sense the faint stirrings of the grief through this other person who looks like her. Did that thought even make any sense? Or like when she plans Instagrammable activities, like the time she made soba from scratch by following a YouTube tutorial. She thinks she had fun, but when she looks back on it, she can't remember the actual sensation of fun. She remembers laughing and smiling, but she also remembers thinking, *I am laughing, this is good, the camera likes it when I laugh.* She remembers slurping up the noodles when they were done, but she doesn't remember what they tasted like. She only remembers going, "Mmm, delicious!" so they must have been delicious. Her entire life feels like this, a murky mess of memories she can only remember through the eye of her phone camera. Is that sad, or is that just the new normal for everybody?

Aimes realizes she's been staring at her phone for ages. The world feels like it's hushed, waiting for her to hit Post. There's that anticipation she's come to love and hate, the moments before posting new content, wondering if this is the one that will go viral. Enough of her posts have gone viral for Aimes to crave that endorphin rush. It's too bad that the rush lasts shorter and shorter each time. And right now, with this particular post, Aimes wants it to sink into obscurity, though for a large part of her, it's become second nature to hunger for the next viral post. God, she is such a mess. She squeezes her eyes shut and presses the Post button. When she next opens them, the post is live, and the likes and comments are already trickling in.

OMG Aimes you poor thing!!!

Babe call me, I'm here for you. xoxo

Holy shit, I just saw this, this is crazy! He was so young!

Aimes can't possibly feel more disgusted about herself. She tosses the phone onto the carpeted floor and trudges to her bedroom. She'll take a nap, sleep the day away, and when she wakes, this will all have blown over. Right?

TWELVE

TJ

The numbers are not looking good. Have they ever looked good? Well, yes, actually. TJ can remember a time when he'd looked at the numbers and they'd looked back and gone, "Yay! You did it!" They did that enough times until he gained the confidence to leave his old job and start up his new firm. But right now, the numbers are not saying, "Yay." They're saying, "Welp. You had a good run. Now run."

TJ buries his head in his hands and massages his temples. He's going to have to close up shop. There's no way around it. My god, but how did it get so bad in such a short time? He'd really thought—well, he hadn't actually given it any thought, but he'd hoped—that when push came to shove, he'd have enough saved up to at least keep things running for a while. But nope. One viral post was all it took to make this house of cards crumble.

He should have done the responsible thing and put an end to this farce of a business before it got him into debt so deep it jeopardized Robin's future. He'll have to let Kit, Lomax, and Elsie go.

The thought sickens him. Quite literally. He feels like he needs to curl up on a bed, clutching his head and moaning gently.

"—without an appointment," Elsie says right as the door swings open.

Vera stands there, looking like a triumphant warrior. Behind her, Elsie stands with an apologetic expression, holding a half-eaten bun.

"Vera." TJ sighs. "You can't just show up here unannounced."

"Sorry, boss," Elsie says. "She distracted me with a pork bun." Then to Vera, she says, "It's really good."

"I have more," Vera says, handing Elsie a big paper bag. "You share with those two outside, okay?"

"Ooh," Elsie says with a smile. "I'll just leave you two alone, shall I?"

That little traitor, TJ thinks as Elsie takes the bag and shuts the door. He can hear her out there going, "Hey, guys, pork buns!" And happy murmurs from Kit and Lomax. He should be grateful for small favors.

TJ regards Vera wearily. "If this is about Xander Lin again, I don't think—"

"No, not about Xander Lin."

"Oh." He hadn't been expecting that. "Okay. Well, what can I do for you?"

"I am looking for representation," Vera says with her chin up.

"Um . . . representation?"

"Well, that is what you do, yes? You represent influencers online?"

"Uh, yeah. But you're not an influencer." God, did that come out sounding as callous as he thinks it did? He really doesn't mean to be a jackass. "And I mean that in the best possible way," he adds.

In answer, Vera takes out her phone, taps on it, and shoves it in TJ's face triumphantly. TJ leans back, squinting at the phone screen. "What am I looking at here?" he mutters.

"Over one million views," Vera crows.

The screen shows Vera brewing tea. "Oh, sorry, I forget volume."

She taps on the phone and the volume turns on at maximum power, blaring in the small office. "WHAT HAPPEN TO XANDER LIN?"

"Oops, sorry," Vera calls out, tapping at her phone until the volume goes from deafening to somewhat manageable.

TJ watches in horror as Vera narrates the mystery around Xander Lin's death while brewing tea. The comforting footage accompanied by the chilling narration makes the whole thing feel so surreal that you can't help but stop and watch it, which is probably the reason why the damn thing has gone viral.

"Wh—" TJ opens and closes his mouth, but no words come out. His brain seems to have forgotten how to form coherent words.

Stop this! he wants to shout, to beg. *Stop digging, stop rousing people's curiosity, stop whatever it is you're trying to do, because I cannot afford another catastrophe.*

"Very good, eh?" Vera says. "Now, Aimes tell me if I get one million view, I get pay two thousand dollars. Just for ten-minute work! I can get use to this."

"That's not—it doesn't work like that. You haven't monetized this particular video," TJ hears himself saying. What is he blathering on about? Who cares about monetizing videos right now? Especially when said video is about Xander Lin?

"Okay, you are my manager, so you can manage the money part, simple."

"I'm not your manager," he croaks.

Vera looks at him quietly for a second, disappointment crossing her face. TJ feels like a little boy who has broken his mother's favorite bowl. "TJ," Vera says quietly, and TJ wants to wail like a toddler, "I am telling you I am a star. If you don't manage me, I go to someone else and then you will regret. But I am giving you chance because I like you."

"Hell, if he doesn't do it, we will," Lomax calls out from the doorway.

TJ cranes his neck to see Lomax and Kit peering at them from outside, both of them with half-eaten pork buns in their hands. "These are so good," Kit says.

"Yeah," Lomax says, "and that video you did is awesome. You're right, lady, you are a star."

Vera smirks and covers her mouth with one hand. "Oh, you young people really know how to make an old woman feel good about herself."

TJ gives her a flat look, like who is she trying to fool? He's only known Vera for a very short time, but already he knows that bashfulness is not an emotion Vera is familiar with.

"Did you make these from scratch?" Kit says through a full mouth.

"Yes."

"Even the dough?" Kit says.

"Oh yes, of course."

Kit and Lomax exchange a glance, and TJ has to keep himself from groaning out loud again. He knows that look. They're excited about Vera, and he can't blame them. There is nothing quite like footage of someone kneading dough to drive viewers insane. Especially when that someone is a grandmotherly figure like Vera. He can already see that Vera will, indeed, become a social media sensation. People would watch her gently kneading dough and chopping vegetables in the wee hours of the night for some comfort. Hell, TJ would've been one of those people if only he didn't know her personally and she weren't trying to ruin his entire life. He needs to do something. He can't just let Kit and Lomax run with this, not when his life is on the line.

"Okay, Vera," TJ says, "I'll take you on."

"Aw, man," Lomax says, "seriously?"

"A minute ago, you weren't interested," Kit says. "What happened?"

TJ shakes his head. "She makes the dough from scratch."

"Come on," Kit groans. "Let us do this, you know we'd do her justice."

Yeah, that's the problem, he wants to say. But to them, he says, "I have the time. I don't have that many clients anymore."

Kit's and Lomax's expressions soften, turning into ones of sympathy, and TJ hates himself for using his trump card with them. "Okay, boss," Lomax says. He turns to Vera. "You're in good hands, Vera. But if you ever need anything, any tips about social media . . ."

"Or an extra stomach if you cook too much food," Kit adds.

"Yeah, or that," Lomax says, "you know where to find us."

Vera laughs. "Don't worry, I feed you well."

As soon as Lomax and Kit leave, TJ releases a sigh of relief. He sags back in his seat, exhausted.

"Okay, so where I sign?" Vera says.

TJ bites his lip. But before he can answer, his cell phone rings. The screen says, **Roosevelt Middle School**. "Oh no," he mutters. In the split second that it takes him to pick up the phone, his heart rate has somehow managed to double. "Hello?"

"Hello! This is Anya Cobb, vice principal of Roosevelt Middle School. Please come pick your daughter up from school right away."

TJ swallows. His throat is a desert. "Is there—is she okay?"

"Yes, she is all right, but she is being suspended and needs to be picked up. Can we expect you soon?"

Suspended. TJ closes his eyes.

"Um. Hello?"

"Yes," he croaks. "I'll be there."

He hangs up and rises from the chair.

"Robin okay?" Vera says.

TJ blinks. Somehow, he's forgotten that Vera was sitting a mere three feet across from him. "No. I've gotta go."

"I come with you."

"Vera, no."

She follows him out of the office anyway. "I'm leaving for the day," he calls out to Elsie. "Can you lock up in here?"

"Sure thing." She smiles and waves. "See you around, Vera!"

"You drink that ginseng tea I make you, okay? Good for baby," Vera says as she hurries out after TJ. Just how many things has she made for TJ's employees?

TJ unlocks his car and slides in, his mind a scramble. He startles when Vera hops into the passenger seat. "Vera," he groans. "Seriously. This is a family matter."

"I have pork buns," she says simply, like that would make everything magically okay.

TJ starts to argue with Vera, but there isn't time. There never is enough time. His kid needs him, and it was all his fault, and he really shouldn't keep her waiting a minute longer. God, why do things have to be so complicated? He strangles the steering wheel as he drives, his mind going through all of the possibilities that could've landed Robin in a suspension, each one worse than the last. Cigarettes, drugs, stealing. When TJ thinks about how different Robin is, how quickly she's changed from his baby into this surly preteen, he wants to bury his face in his hands and wail. He can still remember her at age five, suddenly getting separation anxiety and clinging to his leg every morning, crying so hard at the gates of her kindergarten that she threw up. He'd been so frustrated at her then, and so torn up about leaving her, getting teary-eyed himself as he hurried away and blocked out her wails. But every evening when he picked her up, they'd have what he called a "luddle," which was basically a cuddle but extra long, and he had convinced himself that it was enough. But maybe it wasn't. Maybe she felt abandoned by him, over and over again, and that was why she was having such a hard time in middle school now. Maybe, maybe. That was parenting: a never-ending series of maybes.

TJ is so lost in thought that he barely notices Vera scurrying out of the car once he's parked outside of the school. He's only subconsciously aware of Vera's presence behind him as he rushes through the school doors and hurries down the hallway. And there she is, his not-so-little baby girl, sitting outside of the principal's office. *She looks so skinny*, he thinks. All elbows and knees. When did the baby fat melt away? TJ had loved that baby fat, the chubby thigh rolls, the round cheeks, the protruding belly. Robin looks almost like a stranger now. She looks up, and for a second, her face falls when she spots him. Then it hardens. TJ can practically hear the walls slamming into place around Robin, and he girds himself for yet another fight.

"What happened?" he says, and he immediately hates himself for saying it, because a good parent would've said, *Are you okay?* He adds belatedly, "Are you okay?"

Robin shrugs and looks down at her feet. The door opens and Mr. Burns, the principal, says, "Ah, you're here, good. Come on in."

TJ straightens up, pats Robin on the shoulder, and ushers her in. When he turns to close the door behind him, he bumps into Vera, who's slunk into the office with them. "What—"

"I'm her grandmother," Vera says to Mr. Burns.

Mr. Burns's eyebrows shoot up in surprise, and he looks back and forth from Vera to TJ to Robin, clearly wondering how in the hell the three of them could be related. Then he probably decides it's not worth pushing and says, "Ah, well it's nice to meet you, Mrs. . . ."

"Mrs. Wong." She takes Mr. Burns's hand and sits down primly across from his desk. She pats the chair next to her and says, "Come sit next to Grandma, Robin."

Robin, looking confused but also slightly amused, does so, leaving TJ standing awkwardly. Now it's impossible for TJ to tell Vera to get out. And what would he say to Mr. Burns? She's not really his mother? She's just some random old woman who's wormed herself into his life because of a death that's connected to him? He'd only be reinforcing Mr. Burns's opinion of them being a problematic family. So TJ gives a weak smile and sits down on the remaining chair, resigned to his fate.

"So," Mr. Burns says, sitting behind his desk. "I regret to inform you that Robin will be suspended for a week due to indecent behavior."

Robin rolls her eyes.

"What did she do?" TJ hears himself ask, and oh, could he hate himself even more than he already does? His voice sounds so thin, as though it didn't want to be heard. How can he expect anyone to take him seriously when he sounds like a lost, scared kid?

Mr. Burns clears his throat, looking uncomfortable, and TJ wants to hide behind his chair. "Well, Robin was asked last week to, ah, start wearing a bra."

And now TJ really would like to hide behind his chair, please. Somehow, he remains sitting, maintaining eye contact with Mr. Burns.

"But she continuously refuses to do so, and unfortunately, we cannot allow this to continue because it's disruptive to—"

"Robin, you are how old?" Vera says, interrupting the principal.

Robin, who has put her arms around her chest and curved in on herself, looks up. "Thirteen."

Vera cocks her head, regarding Robin for a bit. "Okay," she says to the principal. "I buy her bra. No need for suspend."

Mr. Burns blinks. "Mrs. Wong, I'm sorry to inform you that the suspension is still in effect. We did give Robin ample warning—"

"Oh, rubbish," Vera snaps.

"Excuse me?"

"Vera," TJ says, but Vera ignores him.

"I am being courteous to you," Vera says.

"You are?"

"You are bullying a thirteen-year-old child into wearing bra. That is very wrong, Mr. Bun, but okay, I look other way, I don't tell you how very creepy it is, not to mention you are infringe on her human right. So what if she don't want to wear bra? I don't wear bra. They dig into my skin and give me rash. You going to tell me off about that too?" Vera scolds, sitting up very, very straight so her chest sticks out. It is impossible not to glance at her (braless) chest as she talks.

TJ's mouth drops open. He would desperately like to forget all of this conversation right away.

"Well," Mr. Burns sputters, "obviously not, but you're not a student at my school."

"Oh? But I am at your school now. Am I being disruptive because my breasts not bound? They are very big breasts, they use to be B-cup, but after I have baby, they become C and they never shrink back."

"W-well—"

"But never mind that. Like I say, is okay. I look other way even though you are being so inappropriate and also my son is lawyer, he is going to be senior associate soon. His office is at the Embarcadero. He is very important and he is always saying, 'Ma, if you need help with anything, just come to me.' *And* he is soon to be engage to a detective. A police officer, very high ranking. She is very beautiful, and they will give me beautiful grandbabies. So, if I want to, I can push back against you and your bra fetish, but I am being nice, Mr. Bun."

"Burns," the principal mumbles, not quite meeting Vera's eye.

"What? You need to speak up," Vera says.

Robin looks suspiciously like she's biting back a laugh. TJ has no idea what his own face is doing, but his brain at least is going, *Whaaaa?*

"My name is Burns," Mr. Burns says.

"Yes, that is what I been calling you. Don't change subject. Focus. I say okay, I will take Robin to look for bra, and if we find one she like, then okay, maybe she want to wear it. But if she has sensitive skin like me, then you let her be, Mr. Bun, and stop looking at my granddaughter's chest."

"I wasn't—it was reported to me," Mr. Burns cries.

"And you tell whoever snitch to you to stop looking at her chest, yes?" Vera pauses expectantly.

There is a moment of silence.

"You don't find it worrying that someone keep staring so hard at a child's chest that they notice she not wearing bra?" Vera pushes.

"I'll . . . have a word with them," Mr. Burns says.

"Good. Otherwise my son, the important lawyer at big law firm, have word with you. And I am social media star, so I will splash this story all over the social media. You think I won't? I am Chinese mother, all I do is create conflict. You think CIA know anything about destabilizing? They know nothing compare to me!"

TJ almost feels sorry for Mr. Burns, who's gaping at Vera in open horror. Almost. But a bigger part of TJ wants to clap for Vera, except he doesn't because he's kind of really terrified of her right now.

"Now, I think we all agree education is number one important thing in child's life, so Robin will come back to school tomorrow. I always find this suspension thing very silly, don't you? Very anti-education. We don't do such thing in Asia, you know."

"I'm sure that's not true," Mr. Burns says. "Asian schools are known for much harsher punishments . . ."

Vera stares hard at him until his voice trails away. TJ can practically feel Mr. Burns's soul departing his body under Vera's unwavering stare. After an eternity, Mr. Burns mumbles, "Yes, well, thank you for stopping by, and we'll see Robin in school tomorrow."

"Good," Vera says. She takes out a plastic-wrapped bun and plops it in the middle of Mr. Burns's desk. "Pork bun for you. I make myself." With that, she stands up and says, "Come, TJ and Robin."

And, through TJ's mystified haze, they do.

THIRTEEN

VERA

So . . ." Robin says as soon as they're all back inside TJ's car.

TJ sits there with both hands on the steering wheel, not starting the car or anything. He looks slightly dazed.

Vera rolls her eyes. Why are men always so dramatic? She turns over her shoulder and studies Robin. "You okay, Robin? Want a pork bun?"

"Sure," she says cheerfully.

Vera gives her a grandmotherly smile as she hands Robin the last pork bun. "You eat more, you too skinny."

Robin takes a huge bite, her cheeks rounding like a chipmunk. She grins at Vera and says, "So that was pretty freaking badass, Vera."

Vera's finger shoots up and points straight at Robin, who stops chewing and freezes. "Robin, you are thirteen. You cannot call me by first name, very disrespectful."

"Oh," Robin mumbles. "Sorry."

"You call me Grandma," Vera says sternly.

Robin looks up at her. "Really?"

"Yes, what else you gonna call me? Auntie? I am too old to be your auntie. Don't be silly."

Robin smiles. "Okay. Well. That was pretty freaking badass, Grandma."

"Yes, my ass is quite bad."

At that, TJ snaps out of his stupor. He regards Vera with eyes so wide she can see all the whites around the iris. "I can't believe you just did that," he croaks. "You threatened the school principal."

"Oh, I don't know if I call it threaten. Why you have to be so dramatic, TJ? You young people always drama this, drama that. I just walk in there and I have discussion with principal, and he come to agree with my viewpoint, that is all."

"You literally threatened to use CIA tactics to destabilize him," Robin pipes up.

"Robin, don't talk with mouth full, very unladylike."

Robin shrugs.

"Now," Vera says, turning back to TJ, who shrinks away from her ever so slightly. "Take me to this address."

"But—" he begins, and Vera stares hard at him until, like Principal Burns, TJ sees the futility in arguing with her and starts the car.

She leans back, satisfied. Is there anything quite as invigorating as threatening people? When Vera was young, she used to read women's magazines, all of which swore up and down that there is nothing more invigorating than exercise and/or sexual activity. But they really missed out on storming into someone else's space and brandishing a good, solid threat in their faces. Vera makes a mental note to write a letter to the editors of women's magazines, telling them to suggest making threats as a good pastime for young women. Or maybe she should tell Oliver to write about it for the *Chronicle*. Oh yes, Oliver would appreciate that. He's always looking for new topics to write about.

On the way to Julia's, Vera receives a text message.

TILLY: Ma, what's this I hear about you
making a viral video about a dead guy?

Vera sniffs. Oh, Tilly. Always so dramatic.

VERA: New hobby. Doctor says you
have to keep busy in old age.

TILLY: Selena's worried.

Vera smiles a little at that. So! Her xifu is worried about her, eh? That's a sign of a good xifu, that is.

VERA: She worry too much. I will cook
some winter melon soup for her, will
stop her from worrying too much.
Okay, I am with friends, stop doing the
texting, very rude.

She watches as three dots appear, disappear, appear, and disappear next to Tilly's name. Then, finally, Tilly says, Okay, ma, just be careful please.

Vera is in a good mood when they arrive at Julia's. She expected Julia to be taken aback by TJ and Robin's presence, but when Julia opens the door, all she says is, "Vera, hi! And these must be your latest victims. Ollie told me all about it." Then, to TJ and Robin, she says, "It's best to just let Vera do what she wants. Hi, I'm Julia, Vera's last project, and this is Emma, my daughter."

Vera rolls her eyes. See what she means about young people being overly dramatic?

TJ shakes Julia's hand and introduces himself and Robin.

"I would invite you guys in, but I have to run to a photo shoot," Julia says. "I'm so sorry. Thank you for taking Emma." She hugs Emma before ushering her out of the house. "Listen to Grandma Vera, okay, sweetie?"

"Okay," Emma says.

"Dinner at six," Vera says. "If you are late, don't complain that barbecue pork all gone."

"I know," Julia says. She kisses Vera on the cheek. "Oh, Vera. Never change." Then she gives Emma one last hug and waves goodbye before climbing into her car.

Emma looks up at TJ and Robin. "It's you again," she says.

TJ gives her a weak smile. Vera needs to work on TJ's facial expressions. Half the time, he looks like he's about to burst into tears, and the rest of the time, he looks like he's constipated. "Hey, Emma."

"Hmm," Emma says, taking Vera's hand. "Grandma, are we spending the day with them?"

"Well," Vera announces. "We are going to look for bra for your big sister Robin."

TJ's mouth falls open. Robin's face turns red. Emma looks impassively at Robin. "What is a bra?"

"The question to ask is: *Why* is a bra?" Vera says.

Emma nods thoughtfully.

"Uh," Robin says, "do we have to? I don't really . . ." She looks down at her feet, her face still bright red.

Vera's heart twists. She has no idea what happened to Robin's mother, and she hasn't had a chance to corner TJ and bully him into telling her yet, but it's clear to her that Robin is badly in need of a motherly figure in her life. "You don't worry, Robin. Your baba will drop us off at fancy lingerie store and leave us privacy, so it'll just be us girls."

"Okay . . ." Robin mumbles.

"Uh, just how fancy are we talking here?" TJ says.

Vera shoots him a look. "What is price of daughter's confidence?" Before TJ has a chance to answer, she points to the garage. "Get Emma's car seat, is inside garage."

And less than ten minutes later, they are off once again. They get to Macy's, and Robin looks dubiously at it. "Macy's?" she says.

"You a bit young for Agent Provocateur," Vera says.

TJ makes a choking noise.

"Thank you, TJ, we see you back here in one hour."

As Vera walks into the air-conditioned building holding Emma's little hand and dragging Robin by the arm in the other, she feels a sudden swell of pure joy. Hasn't this been what she has dreamed about for years and years? To be able to go shopping with her grandkids. Oh, what happiness. Almost better than solving a murd—no. Nothing is better than the shot of serotonin that comes with solving a murder. Well, maybe this comes close.

She locates the girls' section and quickly identifies the most vulnerable salesperson and squawks at the poor woman until she comes hurrying back, her face hidden under a giant pile of training bras. Vera discards two-thirds of them with one quick glance and sends Robin into the changing room with four potential bras. Then she waits patiently with Emma outside the changing room.

"Robin, I not getting any younger out here."

"Oh my god, it's been, like, two seconds, Ver—Gran."

"Do you know how to put bra on?"

"Yes!" Silence. "No."

"You need help?"

"Yeah."

The door to the changing room unlocks, and Vera and Emma walk inside. Robin stands there, holding a bra to cover her chest.

"Okay, turn around," Vera says with surprising gentleness. She squints as she hooks the bra on, then adjusts the straps before patting Robin's shoulder and going, "There." They look in the mirror. "Is okay?"

Robin nods quietly, her mouth pursing. Her cheeks turn red once more. "How did you know I didn't . . ." Her voice trails away.

"How I know you don't want to buy bra with your dad?"

Robin nods.

"Who want to buy bra with their father? Nobody! But now you have me for this kind of thing."

Robin looks away abruptly, but not before Vera catches the glint of tears in her eyes. Vera pats her lightly on the arm. Robin sniffles and whispers, "Thanks. Grandma."

And now it's Vera's turn to get all misty-eyed. Clearing her throat, she says, "Okay, this one cut into skin or not? You like the color?"

"I like the color," Emma says. "Can I have one?" They both look down at Emma and burst out laughing. Emma frowns. "I want one too."

"Let's give it another ten years, kiddo," Robin says, ruffling Emma's hair.

Vera has to bite back a smile at the big sisterly gesture. She has seen this phrase so often online but never quite understood until now, but in this moment, Vera thinks, *The kids are okay.*

By the time they meet up with TJ again, Robin is in a good mood once more. TJ looks worried, but when he sees Robin's cheerful expression, Vera can see the tension melt away from his neck and shoulders. He glances at Vera and nods at her, and there is so much gratitude behind the simple gesture. Vera and TJ watch as Robin, one hand clasped around Emma's little one and the other carrying her bag of new bras proudly, skips down the street.

"Thank you," TJ says, his voice thick.

"I keep receipt in the bag, you don't forget to pay me back."

TJ laughs. "Of course, Vera." They walk for a bit in amicable silence. "She never met her mom, you know."

"What happen to her?"

TJ shrugs. "She was a one-night stand I had after a party. Didn't think I'd ever see her again. Nine months later, she came back to my place and boom, there was Robin."

"She don't want to keep baby?" Vera says.

"She had her reasons for not wanting to be a mother," TJ says. "She gave me a diaper bag, said, 'Do what you want with her. I can't.' And left. I don't remember much of those early days, they're kind of a haze in my head. I've never known panic quite like that before. But I do remember this: One night, Robin wouldn't stop crying. She was only about two weeks old, but those little lungs on her, oh man. I tried feeding her, I tried burping her, tried everything. I was so tired. I had no idea what time it was or when was the last time I had a proper night's sleep or when I last showered or had a hot meal. I still had her in my arms, and I just flopped to the floor on my back, and she was on my chest when I burst into tears. I wailed along with her." TJ snorts. "My sobs must've shocked her, because she stopped crying, and she looked at me and our eyes met and it was the first time she really saw me. I saw an understanding there. Oh, I know you'll say that's not possible because she was a newborn baby etcetera, but I swear, it was like things clicked for her, and she was like, 'Huh. Hey . . . Dad.'"

Vera smiles. "Oh, very possible. Yes, babies are very more aware than people think."

TJ nods. "I looked back at her, my nose still streaming from crying so hard, and I laughed. I said, 'Hey, kid.' And that was that. Up until that point, I'd been toying with the idea of putting her up for adoption or asking my parents to look after her, but after that moment, I knew she and I belonged together."

"You are good person, TJ. Not many young men can do like that."

TJ swipes an arm across his eyes. "Thanks. I try my best. I think we manage with most things, Robin and I. It's just things like this . . ."

"Like buying bra," Vera says.

TJ nods.

"I think if only problem so far is you don't know how to buy bra for your daughter, I will say you doing just fine."

TJ gives a watery laugh. "God, I sure as hell hope so." He takes in a deep breath and sighs. "Vera, what are you hoping for with us?"

Vera senses the undertones in the seemingly innocuous question and chooses to blithely ignore them. "Hmm? Well, today just buying a bra, that is all."

"No, I meant about this whole Xander Lin thing. Why are you

so"—TJ searches for the right word—"committed to the details of his death?"

It takes a moment for Vera to mull over the question. "When I see you, I know you are young person in need."

"Do I really appear that pathetic?"

"Yes."

"Oof. I can't say that didn't hurt."

"Call it mother instinct. I know immediately you need mother attention. And Robin, she desperately need grandmother attention."

TJ looks down at his feet. "My parents are on the East Coast. We see them once a year, twice at the most."

"Must be hard on you and them. But is okay, we do the best we can try. Now, I was saying, I see Millie, she come to me for advice on Xander death. And I see, oh, this is also young person needing my help."

TJ frowns. "Millie thinks his death wasn't suicide?"

Vera studies him from the corner of her eye. She likes TJ, and it would really be a shame if he turns out to be a killer. "Maybe?"

TJ grunts. "Vera, there's something you need to know about me—"

"Grandma, I'm hungry!" Emma calls back.

"Me too," Robin says.

Vera groans and shoots a hard look at TJ. "What is it? You tell me now."

TJ's mouth opens and closes. "I—uh, I'm hungry too?"

Vera grits her teeth, then she wags a finger in TJ's face. "TJ, you know I will get truth out of you even though you try to hide it. You are very bad liar."

TJ gives her a sheepish grin and scurries away, throwing an arm around Robin's shoulders as he goes.

Vera follows them with a thoughtful frown on her face, her mind tick-ticking along, patiently picking at all the odd angles of the case. If there is indeed even a case to be found. Still, when it comes to maybe-cases, there's no one more well suited to cracking them than Vera Wong.

Much later, Vera is back at her house, and Emma and TJ are finishing up their afternoon snack while Vera has wrangled Robin into helping her record her next viral video. Winifred had popped in bearing a tray of pastries, and the others were so delighted at getting free pastries that Vera hadn't had a chance to drive Winifred and her nosy self off.

"Come help me make the viral video, Robin," Vera had said, to which Robin had replied, "Bold of you to assume it'll go viral." To which Vera had replied, "Robin, why you insist on failing before you even try?" To which Robin had had no reply, and so here they are, with Robin shooting Vera from all angles as she prepares drunken chicken for tonight's dinner.

Behind them, Winifred hovers, clearly jealous of all the attention Vera is getting.

Robin's style is very different from Aimes's. Aimes had focused on Vera as a whole as she made the tea, but Robin chooses to focus on Vera's hands as she rubs the chicken with aromatics.

"You not getting my face," Vera complains after a while.

"Yeah, because what you're doing is really interesting."

"I think she is trying to avoid getting the wrinkles on your face," Winifred pipes up snidely.

Vera ignores her. "Nothing more interesting than my face. You stand farther back so you can catch my whole body. I work very hard to keep in shape, not to hide from camera."

Robin rolls her eyes but listens to Vera's request and takes two steps back. Vera watches her with a sharp eye, and when she's satisfied with the angle Robin is shooting at, she takes a deep breath and smiles, transforming from stern grandmother into a loving, jolly one. She pretends not to see Winifred rolling her eyes. Vera preps the drunken chicken and accompanying herbs and vegetables, places them into a large clay pot, and puts it on the stove, all the while wearing that comforting smile on her face.

When the chicken is finally simmering away, Vera looks up and says, "There. Like that, okay?"

"Yeah, that was pretty good," Robin says. "But the beauty in making content is the editing."

"Editing?"

"Watch and learn," Robin says. And Vera does. She watches and learns as Robin slices the video she recorded into short clips and plays around with them, zooming in one second and out the next, cutting the repetitive bits out and editing the colors. She adds some soothing background music, and before Vera knows it, she's watching an incredibly professional and utterly entertaining short video of herself making drunken chicken. "And now all we need is a clip of the chicken when it's done and you eating it."

Vera looks affronted at that. "Me eating it? Why you want to see me eating the chicken? Is this like some pervert video?"

"Or maybe like those kind of Korean videos where they watch people stuff themselves silly?" Winifred says. "Is called mukbang."

"No, god, you guys," Robin cries. "It's the thing you do with cooking videos. People need to see you eat it. Because, see, every story starts off with a promise."

"A premise," Vera corrects her magnanimously.

"No, a promise. Like, this video promises to create a delicious chicken dish. And then showing the final product and eating it is like fulfilling that promise: The chicken looks delicious *and* it tastes delicious. Get it?"

Vera glances over to the dining room, where TJ is half listening to their conversation. She wonders if TJ caught what Robin said. She wonders if he knows what a bright kid Robin is. She quirks an eyebrow at Robin. "Okay. Sound like the bullshit, but I go with what you say."

"Meanwhile, did you want to record narration for it?" Robin says.

"Oh yes!" Vera grabs the phone and clears her throat before hitting Record. "Hello, today I am making Drunken Chicken. You can find recipe in . . . Where can find recipe?"

"In the caption," Robin says.

"Okay. You can find recipe in caption. Now, we go back to talking about this Xander Lin. Very curious case. He is huge star on the Instagram and the TikTok, party with so many of you. I see many picture of him at big party with big people. If you are one of these big people in Xander photo, please slip and slide into my DM and tell me everything about Xander. This is very important, because I am concerned. I am concern about . . . a lot of things, really. And when I see Xander photo, something inside me connect with him. I think it is loneliness. I know all about loneliness, you see. My husband, he die many years ago, and I was all alone for very long time. No meaning in life, until last year, by good luck, man die in my teahouse. Police tell me is nothing, just accident only, but I know. Oho, I know. And I solve his murder, and when I do that, I gain new family. Now I do the same with Xander. I see people who are connected to him, they seem like they need help, so I help them. Please, help me do the same. Help me understand why such young man, so promising and so handsome, can die like this."

By the time Vera is done, the house is quiet. Robin, TJ, Winifred, and Emma are all staring at her. Vera starts feeling slightly self-conscious. "Is it not good?"

TJ clears his throat. "It's really good."

Winifred nods. "I think you will help this case a lot."

"Yeah, that was—and it pains me to use this word—but that felt really authentic," Robin says.

"What is authentic?" Emma says.

"It means 'real.' So much on social media is curated content," Robin says. "People are always looking for something real, something authentic. Something they can connect with on a basic human level."

"And that's Grandma Vera?"

"Yep." Robin looks at Vera, and Vera could swear there is wonderment in the teenager's eyes. "That's her all right."

And this time, it is Vera's turn to blush.

FOURTEEN

QIANG WEN

Is it wrong to lie? Qiang Wen knows it is, on the whole, not a great thing to lie. But what if it is a lie that never hurts anyone? A lie to make people feel good. And Qiang Wen has always been good at those, ever since he was a little kid. Like telling his mother that the new dress she bought was pretty and did not at all look cheap, or telling his father that the pepper beef he cooked wasn't too peppery, even though Qiang Wen couldn't stop coughing after every mouthful. But these are good lies, aren't they? Lies that help grease the wheels of life, because sometimes life can be so cruel, so jagged and harsh.

But maybe there is no such thing as a good lie. Because now, Qiang Wen's lies are catching up with him. And it's these lies that got him in this predicament in the first place. Lies that Xander came up with and Qiang Wen never refuted, lies that—

No. Qiang Wen needs to own up to his responsibility in this entire business. As much as he would like to blame everything on Xander, he can't. He was a willing participant. But, oh, he was so lonely. Excuses. Anyone can come up with an excuse for anything, even murder. Tears fill Qiang Wen's eyes as he looks at his phone. He hadn't even known what an Instagram was before Xander. Then Xander had downloaded it on Qiang Wen's phone and helped him create an account and followed a handful of people for Qiang Wen. One of them was Xander, of course, but the others were very interesting Chinese people who posted videos of themselves cooking Chinese food or doing tai chi or having family meals. Qiang Wen likes the last ones most; that's all he watches nowadays, just videos of strangers eating with their families. Sometimes he cries while watching these videos.

But now, Qiang Wen isn't looking at these strangers' content. He's scrolling through Xander's profile and letting the grief and guilt and confusion surge through him in overwhelming waves. There are so many pictures and videos of Xander, and Qiang Wen misses him so much he could practically hear Xander's voice, laughing with him, calling him "Ah Gong." His own grandchildren don't even call him that. They call him "Gramps," a horrible English word that sounds so grouchy, so harsh to Qiang Wen's ears. But when he tried to tell them to call him "Yeye" or "Gonggong," his own daughter had told him off and accused him of taking away their autonomy. Qiang Wen hadn't even known what an autonomy was; how could he take it away?

He smiles sadly at a video of Xander and him, both of them wearing matching aprons, making dumplings. His voice comes out tinny, barely recognizable. "The edges of the dumpling skin should be thinner than the center, so when you pinch it together, you don't get this horrible, thick layer of dough," Qiang Wen says in Mandarin.

"Never thought of that, Ah Gong," Xander says, obediently

rolling the edges of his dumpling skin thin. He looks at the camera and gives that heart-winning smile of his, switching to English. "Is there anything better than making dumplings with your grandfather? And these are seriously so good, you guys."

"So good," Qiang Wen repeats to the camera with so much earnestness that Xander laughs.

Had that moment been real for Xander? For Qiang Wen, it had been one of the sweetest memories he had, one of the happiest days in recent years that he could remember. But now he finds himself questioning what it had meant to Xander, and he hates that he's doing this. What does it matter if it didn't mean the same thing to Xander as it did to him? Surely all that matters is his own perception? But it does. It does, damn it. Knowing that it could all have been fabricated for social media hurts as much as if Xander had told him he hated him. It hurts so much that Qiang Wen could've very easily hurt Xander over this betrayal. He grips his phone tight before slamming it face down on the table with a sigh.

The best thing Qiang Wen can do right now is to forget about this whole thing. He takes a deep breath. He's going to let this go. Forget about everything that has to do with Xan—

The door swings open. "Ni hao, Qiang Wen!" a loud voice calls out.

All semblance of peace shatters and Qiang Wen's head snaps up, his heart immediately hammering hard against his rib cage.

In the doorway is Vera. But not just Vera. She is flanked by the man Qiang Wen recognizes as TJ and TJ's teenage daughter Robie? Or Rowan? Something like that. And the uncannily serious little girl Emma, who would be unnerving if she wasn't so dang cute. Qiang Wen stares at them as they pile into his little shop. Qiang Wen's dumpling place isn't really an eat-in restaurant.

There is only one small table with two chairs for people to sit at while waiting for their order, so the addition of four people, even if one of them is pint-sized, makes the space feel overcrowded.

"Uh," Qiang Wen burbles. It takes a moment for him to find the right words in English. "Can I help you?"

"Vera thought it would be nice to eat at your place for a change," the teenager mutters.

Qiang Wen is really not very good with teens. His own relationship with his daughter had deteriorated when she hit puberty, and he regards the teen years as a hideous time of strange hairs and even stranger odors. He gapes at this particular teen now, unsure of what to say to her.

She glances at him sullenly before shrugging. "Don't look at me, it wasn't my decision."

"Oh yes," Vera chirps. "Grab more chairs, Qiang Wen. You have some upstair? TJ help you."

"Uh." Qiang Wen's brain has stopped working somehow. This is an invasion.

"Ah, I find stool back here," Vera says, pointing to the kitchen area. "Look, there is stack of stools. Robin, you take one, TJ take two because he is very manly and strong."

"Um, I'm not sure . . ." TJ mumbles.

"You not strong and manly?"

"No, I mean like," TJ lowers his voice, "this feels like we're intruding on Qiang Wen's space?"

"Don't be silly," Vera cries. "Qiang Wen don't mind." She turns to Qiang Wen and gives him a sweet smile. "You don't mind, right?"

"Wh . . ." Qiang Wen's brain gives up trying to make sense of anything and he merely nods.

"See? He don't mind. Stools now!" Vera snaps, and Robin and

TJ stand to attention and rush to get the stools while Vera plops Emma onto one of the available stools and perches on the other one herself. "Qiang Wen, I want six pork and chive dumpling, six pork and shrimp dumpling, six pork and crab dumpling, and six vegetarian dumpling. Extra chili oil. Eat in."

"We don't do eat in," Qiang Wen says, but the words come out soft as a whisper, and already more stools have appeared around the small table, and four pairs of eyes are now staring expectantly, hungrily, at him. And so without quite understanding what is happening, Qiang Wen heads back into the kitchen, where he fills Vera's order, locating the right steamers and piling them on top of one another. He brings out the stack, staggering a little under its weight, and TJ jumps to his feet and helps him place them on the table. He could've sworn that there was no way that they could eat around this tiny table, but somehow, they make it work. Somehow, everybody has a pair of chopsticks—Emma has a pair of training chopsticks—and a little saucer of chili oil and vinegar, and somehow, everybody is eating his dumplings and arguing good-naturedly about which filling is the best one.

Is he allowed to enjoy this moment? It feels so wrong to Xander's memory to have a good time after his death, especially given that these people are only here because Xander died. If Xander were still alive, Qiang Wen's life would be the lonely, drab one he's always known, with the occasional visits from Xander as the only bright points in it. Qiang Wen watches in a daze as Robin patiently tears a pork and crab dumpling in half and helps Emma pick it up with her training chopsticks.

"Chew slowly," Robin instructs her. "I don't want you to choke." And this, coming from a surly teen, is somehow all the more touching because of its unexpectedness.

But just as Qiang Wen's heart fills with joy, Vera says, "Qiang Wen, you'll be happy to know that I am making very good progress on investigating your grandson's death."

Qiang Wen's throat tightens and he struggles to swallow.

"Well, I have post two viral videos already. Do you know what 'viral' mean? It is like virus, spreading very quick, from person to person. A Vera virus," she says proudly.

"That just doesn't sound like a good thing," TJ says.

Vera shoots him a dirty look. "It sound like the best thing. Why anyone would not want to catch Vera virus?" She takes her phone out of her bag and brandishes it at Qiang Wen. "Look! Second video, Robin help me make. She is very good. Has over five hundred thousand views already! That's half a million you know," she adds unnecessarily.

"Oh," Qiang Wen says weakly. "I don't understand what this has to do with Xander."

"My bad," Vera says. "I forget to turn on volume." She squints at the phone and fiddles with the controls. Loud noise suddenly spills from the phone. "WELCOME TO VERA WONG'S—"

"Sorry!" Vera calls out, lowering the volume. She shoves the phone back at Qiang Wen, who listens with mounting trepidation at Vera's narration.

Stop digging! he wants to shout. *Please, please stop.*

But the video continues playing, showing Vera cooking while the voice-over talks about Xander and how they desperately need to know what really happened to him.

"And I am getting a lot of the DMs," Vera says proudly. "You know what are the DMs? They stand for 'directly messaging.'"

"Just 'direct message,'" TJ mutters.

"People are doing the DM to me and giving me so much info."

"Most of them are irrelevant," TJ adds.

Vera's glare slices into TJ, and he shrinks back. "TJ, nobody like a no-sayer. No-sayers say nothing, that is why they called no-sayer."

TJ chews his dumpling sheepishly. "Sorry. I'm just . . . I don't know, it's kind of macabre to me to make content off a poor kid who died."

"Well, she's not just making content, Dad," Robin says. "She's trying to find out what really happened to him."

"Nothing happened to him!" Qiang Wen snaps.

They all look at him. Even little Emma. Qiang Wen wishes he could crawl into the kitchen and hide from all of them.

"Sorry," Qiang Wen says. "This is a tough subject for me."

Vera's face scrunches with sympathy. "Of course, Qiang Wen. He was grandson. I am sorry. I should be more sensitive to you. You don't worry about it, my friend, I will not stop until I am under the bottom of this."

What can he say to that? It's not like he can say, *No, I don't want to know what happened to my grandson because I don't want you to find out the truth.* He merely nods and says, "Thank you."

"Now, one of the DMs say, 'Vera, you are so fabulous, you have to come to this party on Friday. A lot of people that Xander party with going there, actually he been to this house before, I see on his photo.'"

Every pair of chopsticks, except Emma's, stops in midair. Everyone, except Emma, stares at Vera. After a moment, Emma, noticing the sudden silence, looks around at the table, then at Vera.

"Vera," TJ says in a wary voice, "are you saying you got an invitation to an influencer party?"

"What is influencer party? You mean influenza party? I hope not. At my age, if I get influenza it will be very bad. You know, I got a touch of pneumonia last year because—"

"Not influenza, influen*cer*," TJ says. "A party full of the who's who of social media."

"Oh!" Vera regards the question for a bit. "It sound like that kind of party, yes. Why?"

"Oh my god, can I go?" Robin says.

"No," TJ says immediately.

"What is big deal?" Vera says. "I get invite to party all the time."

They all continue staring at her until she adds, "You know, my weekly dinner with Tilly and all that. They are party."

"Yes, we play games," Emma adds.

"There you go," Vera says. "Very fun party. Everybody have fun."

"This is going to be a little bit different," TJ says. "Listen, Vera, I don't think you should go. I don't think it's safe."

"What nonsense," Vera says. "I am life of party, everybody say so. Back in the day, my friends and I go take a trip to Macau— oooh, the trouble we get up to. You know, we even get ban from nightclub in Macau!"

Robin's eyes widen. "Banned from a nightclub? Oh my god, Grandma, how did that happen? Tell me everything, and do not spare the details."

Vera opens her mouth to reply, but TJ rushes in with, "*Anyway,* I just don't think an invitation from a complete Internet stranger to a strange party is the safest thing to accept."

"You don't worry, TJ. I bring my police-grade pepper spray. Homemade! I make from Szechuan pepper, not only sting but make eyes go numb. Very effective. My soon-to-be daughter-in-law is in process of seeing if she can switch out the standard police issue pepper spray to mine." When they all look skeptical, she at least has the grace to look slightly sheepish. "Well, I am sure one of these days she will realize my Szechuan pepper spray is better than their old one."

Qiang Wen has been watching the exchange in a kind of stupefied horror so far, but now he finally snaps out of his daze and says, "Vera, I don't understand. What is it that you are hoping to get from this party?"

"Information," Vera says simply. "This is the kind of thing your grandson use to do all the time. I see on his profile he go to this party, that party, wah, very busy life. You don't want to get to know his friends? People he spend so much time with? Maybe one of them know what happen to him."

Qiang Wen's stomach knots painfully. Nerves? Fear? Guilt? All of the above? It is a struggle keeping his voice even. "This subject is too painful for me," he says finally. Next to him, TJ shifts on the stool, obviously uncomfortable. *Good*, Qiang Wen thinks. Grief should make others uncomfortable. It's designed to drive others away so he can mourn in peace. Except that doesn't seem to apply to Vera, who reaches out to pat his shoulder.

"I'm sure is very painful for you," Vera says. "I cannot even imagine. But don't you worry, Qiang Wen. We here to help. I promise you, I won't rest until I find out what happen to your grandson."

Nooo! Qiang Wen wants to wail. *I want you to do the exact opposite. Rest without finding out what happened to him.*

But that's not the sort of thing that a loving grandparent could say, is it? He's been backed into a corner now. He's tried to stay away, keep his distance from this whole thing, but clearly that tactic hasn't worked. He's like a fly obstinately buzzing into a glass pane over and over. Maybe what he needs to do is the exact opposite. Change his strategy. Instead of shying away, Qiang Wen needs to be like Vera and rush into this head-on. With a gulp, Qiang Wen meets Vera's eyes and says, "Then I'll do what I can to help you."

FIFTEEN

MILLIE

Millie is good at looking good; it's one of the few things she's good at, actually. A long time ago—feels like a lifetime ago, in fact—Mother had given her a crash course on hair and makeup and choosing the right outfits. The kind of thing any loving mom would do when their daughter comes of age, really. Except maybe Mother's lessons had been more . . . pointed.

A *straight brow,* she had said, while shaping Millie's eyebrows, *makes you look youthful and vulnerable. Men like that.*

Okay, so maybe not quite the kind of thing a loving mom would do for their daughters.

Millie pushes the traitorous thought from her head. She doesn't like having unkind thoughts about Mother and Father, especially after everything they've done for her. She owes them so much, and even if she worked three whole lifetimes, she would never be able to repay her debt to them. But she tries her best.

Today, for example, she takes care to pick her outfit. She goes for jeans and a dark green top, which makes her look even paler but brings out the peach undertones of her skin. Most American men prefer tanned skin, but there is a certain kind of man that is drawn to pale, vulnerable-looking women, and these are the men Mother and Father have advised Millie to look for. Men who want to protect her. It's good advice, Millie reminds herself as she swipes tinted sunscreen on her face. It's advice that caring parents would give to their daughters.

Her makeup is kept simple; Mother said that too much makeup would age you, and society as a whole much prefers young women to older ones. "Young and vulnerable," Mother had said, a mantra that has accompanied Millie for as long as she can remember. Just a layer of mascara, a light brown eyeliner, some blush, and a thin layer of lip tint. Millie steps back and studies her reflection. She looks so young, so much younger than her twenty-seven years. She looks like she could be a high school student. Exactly how Mother and Father said she should look.

She checks the time on her watch and grabs her purse. But when she opens the door, she startles, a gasp jumping out of her mouth. Father is standing right in front of her. How long has he been there? Was he listening to her getting ready this whole time? A hundred questions crowd through her head. Had she made any noises? Given herself away somehow? Does he know? What does he know? Is he angry? Is she about to be punished?

"Where are you off to?" Father says. Like Mother, Father is an immigrant, but you wouldn't know it from his English. It's completely unaccented, like a news anchor. Mother's English is like that too. They'd taught Millie much the same, making her watch hundreds of hours of news channels and scrubbing her original accent completely. In her dreams, the people talk in newspeak, without accents or emotions of any kind.

Now, Millie tries her best not to squirm under Father's gaze. "I'm meeting a—a date." The moment she says "date," she kicks herself inwardly. Oh god, why had she said that? She knows he would pry, of course he would, but she couldn't say "friend." He wouldn't believe her. She should've said she was . . . was what? Nothing she does goes unnoticed by Father and Mother. That is the price she has to pay for everything they have done for her.

"A date?" Father says, his eyebrows rising ever so slightly. "Tell me about him." Father's tone is kind, but Millie knows him well enough by now to know that it can switch very easily, going from Santa Claus to Old Testament god within a split second.

Tread carefully, she tells herself. Not that she needed the reminder. "He's nice. Very nice."

"Good. Nice is good. What does he do for a living?"

"He is a writer."

The faint edges of a frown appear on Father's face, and Millie's insides shrivel up. "A successful writer?" he says silkily.

Millie gives a vigorous nod.

"His name?"

She doesn't want to give his name. It is a betrayal to give his name to Father. She tries hard not to even think it, in case Father senses it somehow.

"Millie," Father says, and now the edge has reached his voice.

"Oliver," she says. "Oliver Chen." She didn't put up a fight after all. She never does. Millie has been raised to be a good kid, the kind who never talks back or has secrets from her parents.

"And how did you meet him?"

"The usual way." A lie. Millie trains her gaze to focus on Father's chin instead of his eyes. She wills her pores not to start sweating. Father stares at her for an interminably long time, and she swears he can look straight through her skull and read every guilty thought skittering through her brain. She can't stand it. She's going to burst. She's going to blurt out the truth to him. She—

"Okay. Well, have fun."

It takes all of Millie's willpower not to jump in surprise and squeak, "Really?" Instead, she nods and says, "See you, Father," then ducks her head and squeezes past him. He doesn't bother stepping back to let her past. Occupying a large space is something Father is very good at and something Millie is really bad at.

Millie brisk-walks out of the complex and doesn't stop until she's all the way down the block. The whole time, she thinks she can feel Father's eyes lasering her back. He would've told Mother by now. They work so well as a team, Father and Mother. Their friends probably envy their marriage.

By the time she gets to the bus stop, she is out of breath. She feels slightly lightheaded too, which is probably a sign that her breakfast hadn't been big enough. But Mother is very strict about food allowance, and Millie is on a 1,200-calorie meal plan to—of course—keep her looking young and vulnerable. Every week, Mother makes Millie do a weigh-in, and god help her should her weight fluctuate by more than three pounds in either direction. When the bus arrives, Millie is glad to find an empty seat. She rests her head against the window, watching the scenery change as the bus trundles into the city. San Francisco is probably the prettiest city she's ever been to. Not that she's been to that many cities, but Millie can't imagine a lovelier place than this one. It looks like something out of a storybook. Millie loves looking at the houses on the hills, making up stories about the people who live inside them.

She spots Oliver from a distance, and despite everything, her heart rate spikes. Something about Oliver feels different from the other guys she's gone out with. She smiles wide as she steps off the bus, and he gives her a friendly but nonsuggestive hug.

"Hey, how's it going?" he says.

"Good," Millie says, and she means it. It really is good seeing him.

"It was a nice surprise, getting your text," Oliver says.

Millie blushes. Mother would hate that Millie was the one who made the first move, but there's just something about Oliver that had captured her the first time they met. There is a note of poignancy in the way Oliver carries himself, and Millie recognizes it as the sign of a fellow dreamer. Though what Oliver could possibly dream about, she has no idea. Surely he has everything he could wish for.

"Yeah," she says, "I'm glad you agreed to come out and see me."

"Of course." Oliver grins. "I haven't been to this part of the city in a while."

They're at Alamo Square, right next to the Painted Ladies, an iconic row of Victorian houses that Millie loves but very rarely gets to see. They start strolling down the street.

"My god, it's so beautiful here. I wish I could take my little sister out here. She'd flip out."

"Aww, I didn't know you had a little sister. How old is she?"

That gives Millie pause. "Eleven." So young. She thinks back to what she was like at eleven and her chest tightens.

"Wow, quite an age gap between you two."

Millie elbows him. "Are you calling me old?"

"God, no. If you're old, I'm a pile of ash waiting to be blown into the wind." Oliver snorts. "What's your lil sis like?"

Millie sighs. "Honestly, I don't know much about her. We're

not that close. But I'd like to get closer to her. I feel protective over her."

"Pretty hard getting close to preteens. I was . . . well, let's just say I was not the most approachable kid when I was eleven."

It's hard for Millie to think of Oliver as anything but approachable. Maybe he's just trying to make her feel better. Time to change the subject. "This is truly my favorite part of the city," she says, gazing at the colorful homes wistfully.

"Yeah? Why's that?"

She shrugs. "Before I came to America, I don't know why, but I had it in my mind that all the houses in this country would look like this. I thought I would live in one of these houses." She laughs, and it comes out slightly more bitter than she expected. "That's probably really stupid, huh?"

Oliver nudges her with his elbow. "Well, if we're going to compare stupid childhood beliefs, I believed that a giant built the Golden Gate Bridge out of Lego bricks."

Millie laughs. "Aww, that's cute!"

"Not really, not when I believed it up until I was around twelve."

"What? How is that possible?"

"My dad told us the story, and I just didn't think to question it." Oliver gives her a look. "Do not tell me you're judging me right now, after what you just told me."

Millie raises her hands. "No judgment here."

"Whatever. I can sense the judgment oozing out of you."

"Are you saying I smell?"

"Only of judginess."

"Not a word from me."

"Oof, more judgment."

She laughs again and marvels at how easy it is to be with Oliver. Moments like these, Millie lets herself forget who she is and what she's done. She allows herself to leave Father and Mother behind and pretend she's just a normal person, a carefree young woman spending time with a cute guy she met who seems nice. Wholesome, the picture of the American Dream. Oh, Millie knows the American Dream is usually one filled with great wealth and power, but hers was never that. Her dream had always included a simple stroll down a pretty street much like this one with a guy who laughs at her jokes, and a golden retriever walking alongside them.

Then the truth catches up with her, and Millie feels almost winded at the reminder of it. She's the opposite of wholesome. Thomas is proof of that. And she doesn't know what the hell she's doing here with Oliver, especially given his ties to Vera. Millie has the sense to know that Vera is not someone you want to be messing with. Vera is not someone whose friends and family you want to be messing with, so what is Millie doing right now?

"You okay? You got real quiet all of a sudden," Oliver says.

"Yeah, I'm fine," she says quickly, trying to shake off the darkness. She deserves a slice of happiness, just for a while. For now, she can pretend everything is fine and they're a normal couple and she's not about to do what she always does. She looks up at Oliver and smiles, and she wonders if he can sense the sadness behind the smile. "Wanna get a boba?"

It's so easy, spending time with Oliver. Except he hasn't tried to hold her hand or anything, even after two dates. A week later, Millie is in her room, staring up at the ceiling, wondering what she's doing wrong with him. That first date of theirs, they'd ended up spending half the day together, laughing and chatting about nothing in particular, and then he'd given her a quick hug before she got on the bus to go back. Three days after that, they'd gone to Fisherman's Wharf and shared a lobster bisque in a bread bowl before walking aimlessly around the wharf and playing overpriced carnival games. They'd laughed so much that Millie noticed her cheeks hurting later that night. They were really good dates. A+, no notes. She can sense that he likes her. He can hardly keep his eyes off her. So why hasn't Oliver made a move on her?

She takes out her phone and considers sending him a text. But maybe that would seem desperate? *Girls should never make the first move!* Mother's voice booms in her head. Mother knows everything there is to know about dating. Millie opens up the text thread she has with Oliver and scrolls through their messages. Over text, Oliver is himself. Open, friendly, but showing very few signals of romantic interest.

"Ugh," Millie groans. She isn't used to being the one who's more into the other person. What a mindfuck it is, being in this position. It's even got her questioning her straight brows, for goodness' sake. She lets her arms flop back down onto the bed, but just as she does so, her phone buzzes with a text. She whips her arms back up like a striking snake.

It's a text from Vera. Millie swallows her disappointment, a split second before she perks up because, hey, it's a text from Vera! Maybe there's something about Thomas?

Millie, you come to my place now. Wear
something nice. Or not, is okay. Aimes will

bring something nice for you. Okay, see
you. Kind regards, Auntie Vera.

Millie frowns. Wear something nice? She taps out a reply. You mean something nice for dinner with everyone?

Then she waits with bated breath for Vera's reply. When it finally comes, it offers no clarity. Something nice that you young people wear. Kind regards, Auntie Vera.

Great. Very helpful. Thank you, Vera. Millie sighs, getting up from the bed and walking over to her wardrobe. Despite her drab living conditions, Millie has a surprisingly good choice of outfits to choose from, thanks to Mother. Mother is always giving her new clothes, and Millie likes to think that it's one of the ways that Mother shows Millie she cares. It's the kind of thing loving mothers do, right? Millie sifts through the selection, muttering to herself. What to wear? She reminds herself that she can't look too nice walking out of here, because it might pique Mother's and Father's attention, and what would she say if they were to ask who she's seeing? Maybe she can tell them she's on her way to see Oliver? But then what happens when that fizzles out to nothing? They'd be so disappointed, and Millie hates disappointing them.

In the end, she chooses a pair of figure-hugging black pants and a lavender-colored top. She definitely looks nice enough for a date. She puts on the usual light makeup and slips out of her room as quietly as a cat. For once, her luck holds. She doesn't see Father or Mother around, though that doesn't really mean anything. They're probably watching her through one of the many security cameras strewn about the place. They're very protective parents. She scurries out of the building, jumping at the slightest noise, and doesn't stop until she gets to the bus stop.

While waiting for the bus, Millie checks her phone, and dread bubbles up at the sight of a text from Mother.

Where are you going?

I have a date.

We need to talk about this guy
when you come home.

Millie nods to no one in particular and stuffs the phone back in her purse. She licks her dry lips. She can't keep lying to them about having dates, especially when the ones she's had with Oliver are going nowhere. What if they find out about Vera and how Millie got involved with her in the first place? Millie takes out her phone once more and opens up a matchmaking app. Unlike Tinder, it's an app geared toward people who are looking for serious relationships and not one-night stands. Millie swipes right without really looking at the profiles. By the time the bus arrives, she's swiped right on eight profiles and gotten two matches. She spends the bus ride to Vera's messaging back and forth with the matches. She feels so tired. By now, they all sound the same to her. *Hey, how are you, how's it going, what do you do for a living, for fun, where do you live, etcetera?* She answers by rote. Mother's voice tromps through her mind: *young and vulnerable.* She should turn that into a show tune or something; she certainly says the phrase enough.

She's in a foul mood when she alights in Chinatown. She trudges down the block, her steps heavy, and takes a deep breath before entering Vera Wang's World-Famous Teahouse.

The bell tinkles, and Vera calls out from behind the counter. "Ah, Millie, there you are! Just in time for tea. I make with jujubes and goji berries and white fungus, they are very refreshing and will give you energy."

"Hi, Ver—Auntie Vera," Millie says. She inhales the fragrance in the tea shop, her tense muscles unknotting slightly. There's just something about this place that takes Millie's guard down, for better or worse. She spots Aimes sitting at one of the tables and tenses back up. "Hi," she says.

Aimes lifts her chin at Millie. "How's it going? You look nice."

"Thanks, so do you." That's an understatement. Aimes looks gorgeous. More so than before, actually. She looks like the kind of girls Millie looks at on Instagram, the ones with thick, beautifully separated lashes, poreless skin, and full pouty lips. The ones with entire wardrobes that cost more than a luxury car. The ones whose lives look way too good to be true.

Aimes seems to notice Millie staring and says, sheepishly, "The clothes are secondhand. There's this really amazing vintage shop in Little Italy I can take you to one day. I'm pretty sure the stuff there are mostly knockoffs, but you really can't tell. Come here, I'll do your makeup."

"Oh, you don't have to," Millie says, blushing.

"Yes, she has to," Vera calls out. "You have to fit in, Millie."

"Fit in to what?"

"Ah," Vera says slyly.

"No, really, that wasn't a rhetorical question," Millie says. "I actually would like an answer."

"A party," Vera says. She pours out the tea with intense focus and totters out from behind the counter.

Millie wants to ask, *What party?* but she's sitting down in front of Aimes now, and Aimes is studying her face closely, and Millie doesn't want to say a word in case her breath smells bad. Aimes takes out a huge makeup bag, and when she opens it, Millie openly gapes. Aimes has an amazing range of makeup.

"These are mostly gifts from brands that want me to post about them," Aimes says. She picks out a bottle of foundation and holds it up against Millie's face, then rejects it for a different bottle. She pours out a dollop onto the back of her hand and uses a brush to swipe it all over Millie's face. "I know this is a little thicker than you're used to, but it's going to give your skin that porcelain effect everybody's into right now."

"Wah, Aimes, you are very good at this," Vera says, placing a tray on the table. She beams at Millie. "Aimes do my makeup too. I look fabulous, yes?"

Millie looks at Vera without moving her face and realizes that, yes, actually, Vera does look fabulous. Thanks to Aimes, Vera's skin is glowing and her lips have been painted a bright fuchsia, which should look garish but ends up making Vera look bold and devastatingly fashionable. "Yeah, you look amazing."

Twenty minutes later, Aimes sits back and surveys Millie. Vera peers at Millie's face. "This is not making me feel at all self-conscious," Millie says with a nervous laugh.

"What do you think, Vera?" Aimes says.

Vera nods. "Very good work, Aimes. She look not at all like herself. So glamorous."

"Gee, thanks," Millie says, but then Aimes holds up a mirror, and all of Millie's sarcastic remarks fly out of her head. The person in the mirror can't possibly be her, can it? She no longer looks young or vulnerable; she looks like the kind of woman who turns heads and breaks hearts with no remorse.

"Do you like it?" Aimes says.

Millie can only nod, not trusting herself to speak.

"Okay, enough staring," Vera says. "Now you get dress and we have to go."

Millie stands, still in a bit of a daze, and accepts the shimmery dress that Aimes hands her. Vera ushers Millie upstairs, and when Millie is done changing, she stares at the mirror in Vera's bedroom. *This is what a woman looks like,* she thinks. Not a girl. She is in her twenties, after all, and very much no longer a girl, but she hasn't felt like a woman in . . . ever, actually. Millie swallows, shuddering a little. Father and Mother would definitely not approve of this. She takes her phone out of her purse. No messages from them. What they don't know can't hurt them.

"Millie, ah, Uber is here!" Vera calls from downstairs.

Millie switches the phone to Silent mode and walks out of the room. Apparently she is off to a party.

Millie has been to several parties here in America. The guys she had gone out with had taken her to house parties, mostly housewarming or anniversary or birthday parties—celebrations that are confined to close friends and their plus-ones, where she spent the night trying to make small talk with the other plus-ones.

This party is nothing like those. First of all, it's in a mansion at Bernal Heights. Millie can't believe how lavish the house is when they first arrive, a five-story monstrosity that makes the Painted Ladies look like baby houses. She looks at Vera. The old woman must've made a mistake coming here. But Vera only pauses for a moment before saying, "I hope they have dumpling." Then she tightens her hold on her stack of metal food containers, squares her shoulders, and says, "Okay, come with me, ladies. And hold your containers properly. If you drop them, you will be in big trouble."

"I don't know about this," Aimes says. "I've never turned up at a party with so much food. Not even a Thanksgiving party."

"Aiya, why you got no manners?" Vera tuts. "Of course you turn up to party, you have to bring enough food to feed everyone, otherwise people go home hungry, then how?"

Millie purses her lips. She's got a feeling that Aimes is right about this being weird, but at the same time, nothing could make Millie go against Vera. And so Millie tightens her hold on the intense weight of the Tiffin tower and takes a deep breath before following Vera and Aimes up the steps and into what will no doubt be the wildest night of their lives.

SIXTEEN

VERA

If Vera were to be completely honest, she might say she is ever so slightly intimidated. Some might even say she is downright scared. But that would be ludicrous, because Vera does not do fear. Fear is for toddlers and tiny dogs, not for wise older ladies like herself. But then again, Vera would be hard pressed to explain the dryness of her mouth and the pitter-patter of her heart and the way her forehead has gone quite moist. *Hot flashes*, she thinks. Postmenopausal hot flashes. Yes, that would be it.

Also, for some reason, her legs are being rather difficult, refusing to climb the steps to the front door until Vera consciously wills them to. And then, when she's at the door, her arm refuses to move until she mentally directs all of her willpower into lifting her hand toward the doorbell. Her heart lurches as she pushes on the doorbell and hears it ring somewhere inside the house, above the loud music. She licks her lips. Goodness, but they really are dry for some reason. She must be dehydrated.

The door swings open just as Vera is considering running

away—not out of fear, mind you, but for health reasons, as doctors are always yammering away about how good jogging is for you—and the person who opens it is a young man who looks like he could be a freshman at college. "Yeah?" he says. He spots the Tiffin tower, over the top of which Vera is peeking. "Did we order Chinese takeout?"

"No," Vera says, but already he's turned his head to look over his shoulder, calling out, "Did someone order Chinese takeout?"

Another face pops out from behind the door. This time, it's a young blond woman. Her eyes widen when she spots Vera. "Oh my god. I can't believe you actually showed up! OMG!" She shoves the young man away unceremoniously and opens the door wide, stepping outside with a delighted squeal. "Vera Wong, I can't believe you're here. Okay, selfies now."

Before Vera can even react, the girl's phone appears in her hand and she puts an arm around Vera's shoulders. "Say, Veraaa!"

Vera conjures up an awkward smile and the phone flashes, once, twice, three times.

"Let me take that for you," the girl says, taking hold of the Tiffin tower. "Oof, it's heavy. What do you have in here?"

Food. Food, Vera can talk about. The answer flows right out, and for the first time since arriving, Vera does not feel tongue-tied. "Chinese barbecue pork. Salt and pepper squid. Black pepper—"

"Shut up!" the girl cries.

Vera blinks. "What?"

"I don't think she meant it in a bad way," Aimes mutters.

"That sounds crazy good," the girl says. "OMG, you are just so cute in real life, Vera. Can you adopt me please?"

"Oh," Vera says, slightly taken aback. "Yes."

The girl squeals and claps. "Yay! Okay, come on in. Rob," she barks at the guy, "don't just stand there. Help them with their containers. Sorry, Rob's my younger brother and he's totally a second child."

"Wait, what is your name?" Vera says, hurrying after the girl. The music is almost unbearably loud, and the house is full of young people.

"Natalie," the girl says. "Did I not tell you over DM? My bad."

Vera glances behind her to make sure Aimes and Millie are following her, and sure enough, they are. Millie is looking around with big, scared eyes, and Aimes is also looking around with big, scared eyes, although she is at least trying to not look too scared. Vera squashes the urge to look around with big, scared eyes as well. *Remember,* Vera reminds herself, *your ass is bad. Very bad. And that is a good thing.*

As they walk through the crowded living room, Natalie greets other guests smoothly, saying, "Look who I have here! Vera Wong, in the flesh! Isn't she the cutest?"

And the other guests turn, their eyes widening, their mouths opening into awed smiles, and Vera finds herself enveloped in a swarm of young people all clamoring for her to adopt them. It is somewhat nice, she supposes, in a bizarre way. "Okay, okay," she calls out, "I will adopt you. Yes, and you also. You, no, I don't like blue hair, you color back to normal, then I adopt you."

Next to her, Aimes and Millie share a look with each other. Do they think she didn't notice that? She'll have to have a chat with them about it. They shouldn't be jealous about her adopting these needy youngsters. Natalie shoos everyone away and leads Vera to the dining room, which has a massive hardwood table that can seat about twenty people comfortably. The table is laden with dishes, but Natalie waves at a server and asks him to remove all of it.

"All of it, miss?" the server asks.

"Yes, thank you." Natalie heaves the Tiffin tower onto the table and says, "Phew! That was heavy, Vera. Okay, how do I undo this?" She fiddles with the top latch until Vera flaps at her.

"Aiya, you don't anyhow play with it, later you break. Come, let me do." Vera unlocks the tower and starts taking the containers out. She directs Aimes and Millie to put down their towers as well, then goes around laying out the containers on the table. Altogether, there are five containers, all of them stuffed to the brim with food. She's only vaguely aware of movement around her, but somehow, when she glances up, a crowd has gathered around her, all of them staring with rapt attention.

"Tell us what each dish is," Natalie says, aiming her phone camera at Vera.

"Oh. Um. Okay."

Vera has always secretly thought that she would make a fine TV star. After all, she has it all—the looks, the grace, and the voice. But now, with all these phone cameras aimed at her, she feels strangely shy. When she speaks, her voice comes out meek and soft, very much unlike herself.

"Hang on," Natalie says, "let me just turn that down . . ." She taps on her phone, and the song that had been blaring through the house is muted to a low volume. "Okay."

"Um," Vera says. She swallows, then points a finger at the nearest Tiffin container. To her surprise, the finger is slightly shaky. "T-this is claypot rice. I cook the rice in a clay pot over charcoal fire and put Chinese sausage and chicken in it."

The audience oohs. "It smells so good," someone says.

This gives Vera a little bit of oomph, and she speaks louder, pointing to the next dish. "This one is San Bei Ji. Three cup chicken. The name of the dish is because you just use the same cup to measure everything, very simple but very delicious." She goes on to the next dish and the next, and before long, Vera realizes she is enjoying herself. She smiles at the cameras, flapping at them one minute and pointing sternly the next. She really was made for this. When she's done with the final dish, everyone cheers, and Vera blushes all the way from the roots of her hair to the tips of her toes. Applause from a roomful of people. My goodness. It feels so natural. She really is born for this kind of thing. She preens a little.

Natalie links her arm through Vera's and waves at everyone. "Okay, everyone, dig in!" As the crowd descends upon Vera's lovingly cooked feast, Vera leads Natalie away.

"I need to ask you question," Vera says.

"Sure thing," Natalie says. "We can go into my home office."

"What is it that you do, Natalie?" Vera asks as they walk down a beautiful hallway that reminds her of a five-star hotel. "You are in finance? Or maybe drug dealer? Only heroin money can buy this kind of house."

Behind her, Millie makes a choking noise, but when Vera turns around to glare at her, she averts her face and gazes up at the ceiling.

Natalie laughs. "No. Would you believe it, it's YouTube money."

"YouTube money?" Now Vera is truly and well confused.

"When I was, like, eight years old, my parents started a YouTube channel of me opening boxes and reviewing toys. It got really popular. I was basically earning millions every year. And now

I'm a bit too old to review toys, so I moved on to TikTok and IG, and I review other things, but really it was mostly the toy review thing that made all this possible."

"Review toy?" Vera echoes. Her head spins, trying to grasp the concept of a child reviewing toys and getting paid for doing it. When she recalls Tilly with his toys, all she can remember him doing was, well, playing with them. She never once thought of recording him and asking him to talk about the toys. Wow, did she ever miss out on a trick there! She'd been so busy making sure Tilly would become rich by going into engineering, medicine, or law, that she'd completely missed out on social media. Tch. Vera tucks this piece of information in her back pocket. She will bring this up with Julia later. Emma would be great at reviewing toys. Like Vera, she is devastatingly honest and articulate.

Natalie's office is as beautifully decorated as the rest of the house. A big picture window overlooks an aggressively pruned backyard. There is a small working desk, but the rest of the room is filled with easy couches and lined with floor-to-ceiling bookshelves.

"Take a seat anywhere," Natalie says, reaching into a cabinet and taking out glasses and a decanter. "Whisky? Vera, I can tell you're a woman who appreciates fine whisky."

Is she? Vera shrugs and nods. Well, she might as well launch straight in. "Natalie, how you know Xander Lin?"

Natalie hands Vera a glass of whisky, and Vera wrinkles her nose at the smell. Vera doesn't much care for Western liquors. On the odd occasion that she drinks, she prefers Baijiu—Chinese liquor that directly translates to "white liquor." It does smell like rubbing alcohol, but it gets the job done. One shot, bam, and you're good for the rest of the evening. Nothing like this whisky thing, a wishy-washy drink if she ever saw one. She tips the glass up and swallows the whole thing in one gulp.

"Vera!" Aimes cries.

"Yes?"

"You're not supposed to down it. Oh my god. I'm so sorry," Aimes says to Natalie, who laughs.

"Hey, I don't care how you decide to drink it. In fact, good idea, bottoms up!" Natalie empties her glass as well, then grimaces. "Holy shit, that burns. Wow. Okay, Vera, you're an even bigger badass than I thought. I like you."

"Thank you. And now, Xander Lin?"

Natalie takes a breath, setting her glass down on the table. "Yeah, so that's the thing, Vera. That's kind of why I asked you to come."

Vera leans forward and, to her surprise, nearly falls out of the chair. Goodness, the whisky might have been a tad stronger than she expected. She recovers smoothly. Barely anyone notices. She hopes. "What you mean?"

"I don't know Xander," Natalie says.

"What?" Vera, Millie, and Aimes yell at the same time. Vera flaps at them to be quiet. Who's the one doing the interrogating here? "What you mean you don't know him?"

Natalie shakes her head. "What can I say? I've never met the guy."

"But—" Vera's head swims, and she's pretty sure it's not just the whisky. Maybe whisky isn't as wishy-washy a drink as she'd thought. "There are picture, so many of them, of him partying here. I recognize your house from his photo. Aimes," Vera barks, "show Natalie."

"Oh, trust me, I know," Natalie says. "You don't have to show me, I've seen them. The thing is, in case you haven't guessed, I hold a lot of parties. Like, literally every weekend I have a party, and midweek I have a party, and sometimes on Mondays I have a party. You know, to get rid of the Monday blues. Lots of people come to these parties, they're really casual, and I let my friends invite whoever they want. I trust their taste. So maybe one of them invited Xander."

"Why you don't just ask your friend, 'Hey, who here invite Xander to my house?'" Vera says, mystified at Natalie's lifestyle. Party after party after party. Aiya, terrible habit. Once Vera is done with the interrogation, she will lecture Natalie on having too many parties.

"I did," Natalie says. "But no one would admit it. I don't know, I think people are feeling really bad about it or something. Makes sense, I guess, since he died."

"Then why invite us here?" Aimes says. "I mean, not that I'm complaining. I'm Aimes, by the way. Big fan of yours."

Natalie smiles, but it looks more like a grimace. "Um, well, I kind of . . . only invited Vera, and then she brought you two along. Which is totally fine! But I'm just saying, I didn't invite all of you. And I invited Vera because I was curious about this whole Xander thing and, oh my gosh, Vera, I love your videos and I wanted to meet you in person, and I figured I'd help you out with your investigation. I mean, this is totally like *Only Murders in the Building* and I'm Selena Gomez and, Vera, you're that Charles dude. Or maybe you're Oliver? Or both. You're like both of them squished into one fabulous character. Ooh, maybe we should do a podcast about it!"

Vera shakes her head. "Aiya, you not making sense. I don't want to do podcast, I want to find out what happen to Xander."

"And you can," Natalie says. "I'm sure that out there, among my guests, there must be someone who was close to Xander. This is your chance, Vera. Get out there and start talking to people. Get them to open up to you."

"What do you get out of this?"

They all turn to look at Millie in surprise. Vera hadn't been expecting that question to come from sweet, quiet Millie. Her hands twist in her lap, and she looks down and mutters, "Sorry. I didn't mean to be rude."

"No, don't worry about it," Natalie says. "Totally fair question. To be honest with you, everything I do, I do for content. So obviously, I'll be recording as much of Vera tonight as I can—she's blowing up everywhere. The Internet adores her."

Vera cocks her head to one side, studying this bright young woman in front of her. She can't decide if she approves of Natalie. On the one hand, Natalie is obviously ambitious, which Vera, as a Chinese mother, admires. But on the other hand, Vera feels somewhat exploited, because Natalie is using her. But on the other, other hand, Vera also admires Natalie's honesty and gumption. If she were in Natalie's shoes, she would've totally done the same thing, except she wouldn't have been so up front about it. Finally, she decides that she doesn't particularly like Natalie, but she also wishes that Tilly and Selena were more like her. If they were, Tilly would be a named partner at his firm by now, and Selena would be chief of the SFPD for sure. Also, it doesn't hurt that Natalie said the Internet "adores" her. As well they should.

"Okay," Vera says. "I go and ask everyone who know Xander." She stands and sways ever so slightly.

Aimes jumps to her feet and grabs Vera's arm. "Please be careful," she says under her breath.

"I am Chinese mother, I am incapable of being not careful. I know million and one ways that people can die in this very room alone."

Aimes gives her a look. "You know what I mean, Vera. You can't just ask random people if they knew Xander, that's not going to get anything out of them."

"I am—"

"Chinese mother, yes, I know," Aimes says.

"Then you know no one can keep anything secret from me." With that Vera marches out of the office with Aimes, Millie, and Natalie hot on her heels.

O ver an hour later, Vera is very drunk and has zero answers. Or rather, she has an answer—the same one from everyone. That nobody knows Xander.

"But you all see his photo, yes?" Vera says to a group of young people.

"Yeah, of course," one of them, a girl wearing a bright pink crop top, says. "I follow him, he's amazing."

"His life is amazing," the girl next to her adds.

"But no one has met him?" Vera says.

"We haven't. I actually tried reaching out to him, but he didn't respond, so . . . whatever," the girl in the pink crop top says. She notices Aimes for the first time, and her eyes widen. "Hey, you're Aimes! Weren't you his girlfriend?"

Aimes seems to shrink in size.

The girl turns to Vera and says, "Did you ask her about Xander? They were dating, you know. Tons of photos of them. You guys made a cute couple. I'm really sorry about what happened."

Aimes nods and mumbles something under her breath. It's clear, even through Vera's buzzed gaze, that Aimes looks very uncomfortable. She should press Aimes, she'll likely get some answers, but Vera finds that she doesn't have the heart to do so.

Instead, Vera lurches away from them and locates her next victim. The same conversation is repeated. Maybe she's too drunk to be doing this. Someone had offered her a test tube full of bright blue liquid, and Vera had said, "Chemistry is good for you" before downing the whole thing, and now she is beginning to question her life choices.

"I think we should take Vera home," Millie says to Aimes.

"But I have not find Xander friend," Vera says.

"I don't think anyone here has met him in person," Aimes says. "Or if they did, they're hiding it for whatever reason." She doesn't meet Vera's eyes as she says this.

"Why they would hide it?" Vera says. "He was famous superstar on Internet. I'm sure many people would love to meet him, and he has so many fans. Why are they hiding it? What are they hiding?"

"I don't know," Aimes says. "Come on, let's get out of here."

What are YOU hiding? Vera wants to say to Aimes. But she recognizes that Aimes is probably not in the best mood right now, and perhaps pushing her for answers isn't the thing to do. Vera is no longer a hot-blooded twentysomething-year-old. She is older and wiser, and she can afford to wait a bit before jumping down Aimes's throat and demanding the truth from her.

"Vera, how's it going?" Natalie calls out from the crowd.

Vera frowns at her. Is it just Vera, or is there something curious about Natalie? She claims not to have known Xander, but then why did she invite Vera here in the first place? Dimly, Vera remembers Natalie admitting that she invited Vera over for content. Right. Some part of her realizes that this probably means that Natalie has been filming her as she stumbles around and asks random people intrusive questions. She sighs. The night is a bust, and she has made a fool of herself.

"Thank you for having me," she says to Natalie. "I will go now."

"Aww, stay and have fun," Natalie says. "Everybody loves you."

"At this stage in my life, I know making early exit is better than making exit too late." Or something to that effect, at least. She hugs Natalie, gathers her empty food containers, and then leaves the strange and wonderful party with Aimes and Millie by her side. Her ears ring. Outside, the air is bitingly cold, reviving Vera's senses a little. She takes a deep inhale and sighs. "Well, that is strange peek into different life," she says.

"You shouldn't shout, Vera," Millie says.

"I am shouting?" Vera shouts.

"Yeah," Aimes says. "And you should stop. People who live here will think nothing of calling the cops on you."

"Sorry," Vera calls out to any neighbors who might have been watching. "Is very strange though," she whispers. "I really don't feel like I'm shouting."

"God, she is such a talkative drunk," Aimes groans to Millie, who cracks a sympathetic smile.

"Oh, I'm not drunk," Vera slurs.

"Yeah, okay, Vera," Aimes says. "Look, our car's here. Come on, let's get you home."

Vera wants to tell Aimes off because if Vera knows anything about life, it is that she is the caretaker of others, and not the other way around. But her head is spinning and her tongue is fuzzy and she can't quite remember what she was about to say, so she lets the two youngsters bundle her into the Uber. The driver greets them and begins to back out into the street. They zoom down a steep hill.

"Eh, slow down!" Vera snaps at the driver, her stomach lurching. "Later I vomit in your car."

"Lady, do not throw up in my car. I swear to god," the driver says.

"Then you better slow down," Vera scolds. Huffing, she turns to Millie. "So, how you find party? You like it?"

Millie sighs. "It's . . . different. I can't believe Thomas—sorry, Xander—used to go to those things all the time. It's like a whole different world."

"Yeah," Aimes says.

Millie cranes her neck to look at Aimes, who is sitting on the other side of Vera. "You must go to these things a lot too?"

Aimes shrugs. "Sometimes. Nothing as grand as that though. I don't know that crowd very well. I'm not big enough to be invited to anything like that."

"Don't say like that," Vera says.

"What?" Aimes says.

"Like you are embarrass or sorry. 'Oh, I am just small influencer girl, I don't deserve to go to fancy party.' No! Sun Tzu say something very wise in his time. You know Sun Tzu? Famous Chinese man, wrote *The Art of War.* Anyway, he say, 'Fake it until you make it,' so you fake it. Act like you deserve to go to that party all the time, their loss for not inviting you." Vera catches the driver's eye in the rearview mirror and adds, "You too, Uber driver."

He mutters something unintelligible. Aimes gives Vera a side-eye. "I don't think it was Sun Tzu who said, 'Fake it till you make it.'"

"Are you arguing about Chinese history with me?" Vera says, affronted.

Aimes blanches. "Well—I mean—but—"

"I know Chinese history like back of my hand." Vera holds up her right hand, then frowns at the number of age spots on it and puts it back down on her lap. Do her hands really have that many age spots? Maybe she doesn't know them as well as she thinks after all. "Anyway, is good advice. I always try to live by that advice; that is why my shop is called Vera Wang's World-Famous Teahouse."

Aimes gives her a wry smile. "Thanks for the advice. I'll try to remember that old Chinese saying."

"You do that." For a while, everyone is quiet, lost in their own thoughts. Then Vera peers at Aimes. "But Xander never invite you to these parties? Is quite strange, especially since he is your boyfriend."

Aimes shifts in her seat and turns to look out the window. "We didn't date that long."

"Yes, but surely he invite you to a party here and there," Vera presses.

"I think he knew it's not my kind of scene."

The driver whistles and shakes his head. Vera narrows her eyes at him, but he keeps his gaze resolutely on the road. Vera turns her attention to Millie.

"And Millie, you say you are good friends, but he never invite you to party either?"

Millie shakes her head. "Never even knew this side of him existed."

"You ladies been played by some guy," the driver blurts out. "I know, none of my business, but I'm just saying, from a guy's perspective, it's pretty obvious this Xander dude is a walking red flag."

"Thanks," Aimes mutters.

"Walking red flag," Vera muses. "I know what that means from the TikTok. You youngsters use it all the time. It means he is bad news."

"Yep," the driver says.

"He wasn't," Millie says, and the sharp anger in her voice slices through the thick alcohol haze. Vera raises her eyebrows but doesn't say anything. "He wasn't bad news," Millie says again. "He was kind, and we looked out for each other, and tonight made me feel like I lost him all over again."

"Oh, Millie." Vera puts her arm around the girl and hugs her close. "Is okay. It will be okay." She thought Millie might be crying, but when she glances at Millie, the girl's cheeks are dry. *Millie is such an enigma*, Vera thinks. She can't quite get a read on her. Millie strikes Vera as very weak in many ways, but then there are times when she shows strength of spirit that surprises Vera.

"We're here," the driver says, lurching to a stop. He sounds very relieved.

They all pile out, slightly dazed, taking in the cold air as the driver peels away.

"Well, that is very interesting night," Vera says. "Thank you for accompanying me to my first influencer party. I have a feeling I will be invite to more parties, and I will take you two as my plus-one."

"I think the fact that it's called a plus-one means you're only really supposed to take one person with you," Aimes says.

"Aimes, you are too young and pretty to be so irritating. Wait until you are my age, then you can nag people about this and that." Vera pats Aimes on the shoulder. "Okay, I will see you two soon, I hope."

They both say goodbye to Vera, and she turns to go inside her shop. Then she sees what's on the front door, and a shocked gasp cuts its way out of her.

"Vera? You okay?" Millie places a hand on Vera's back. "What's wrong?"

Vera can only stare at her beloved shop front. Millie and Aimes turn to look at what she's staring at, and they both gasp as well. *My goodness*, Vera thinks. *Just how much alcohol did I drink tonight?* "Did I do this?" she wonders out loud.

"What?" Aimes says. "No, Vera. What the hell? Your shop was totally fine when we left, and we were with you the whole night."

"Because, you see, in order to investigate murder last year, I had to smash up my own shop," Vera babbles. "And so I am a bit confused. Am I dreaming?"

"No," Millie says, pinching Vera's arm gently.

"Ouch."

"See? Not dreaming. Somebody really came and did this to your shop."

And for once, as Vera gapes at her store, which has dark red paint splashed all over its front, and the words *I SEE YOU* sprayed across the sign that says, VERA WANG'S WORLD-FAMOUS TEA-HOUSE, she doesn't know what to say.

SEVENTEEN

AIMES

Aimes has no freaking idea what the hell just happened. Actually, this is pretty much how Aimes feels most of the time, so nothing new there. But this time, as she takes in the horrific sight in front of her, the dark red paint that looks so much like blood, and those hateful words scrawled across Vera's beautiful sign, there is a lot more panic exploding all over her mind. Her thoughts are basically a mess of OMG *who did this, are they still here, are they watching us, do they know?* DO THEY KNOW I AM A TERRIBLE PERSON?

"Vera—" Aimes starts to say, not knowing what's actually about to come out of her mouth, when Millie squeaks.

"I have to go."

"What?" Aimes says.

"Sorry, I have to go." Millie is already running off. Aimes would've gone after her, except Aimes can't possibly think of leaving Vera alone right now. Damn, Millie is a lot more heartless than Aimes had expected. What the hell?

She shakes herself and shifts her focus back to Vera. Her rib cage feels like it's squeezing her lungs. Her breath comes out shallow and fast, and she has to remind herself to breathe. It's her fault. She doesn't know who did this, but she knows whoever it was did it because of her. "Vera, are you okay?" Her voice comes out with a significant quaver. God, she hopes she isn't about to cry.

Vera nods. She turns slowly to look at Aimes, and Aimes steps back without meaning to. Vera is probably the sharpest tool in the drawer, and she would totally see the awful truth lurking behind Aimes's eyes. "I think maybe I don't sleep here tonight," Vera says.

"Yeah, I think that's a smart choice. Um, do you have somewhere to stay?" For a horrifying second, Aimes wonders if Vera is about to ask to stay at her place. She gets a flash of her place, the endless mess that dominates all of her space except for her bed and couch. *Fake it till you make it,* Vera had said to her, and Aimes could sob with the accuracy of the saying.

"I do." Vera takes out her phone and dials a number. "Julia, something happen to my shop. No, it's okay. Just, someone vandalize it, and this time, that someone is not me. Yes, I'm okay. But I don't think I want to stay here tonight. Yes. Thank you. Sorry for bothering you." She hangs up and slides the phone back in her purse. "Julia will come and pick me up."

"Okay, good." Aimes looks up at the vandalized sign once more and then looks sharply away, her gut souring.

"Why you look so upset?" Vera says.

"What? Because your shop was vandalized, that's why," Aimes cries. "It's a really upsetting thing."

"Yes, quite. But is not your shop, is my shop. So why are you so upset, Aimes?"

Aimes gestures wildly. "I don't know, because you're my friend, and it's really upsetting when bad things happen to my friends? That's such a weird question to ask, Vera." But is it? Aimes knows she's being a lot more upset than called for, but it's not like she can tell Vera the truth, that she has a horrible suspicion that this was really aimed at her. And because of it, she's now gaslighting the old woman to throw her off the scent. Oh man, Aimes really is the worst person ever.

"Thank you for being so caring. You are like what they say, you know, the person who can feel what other people feel. The path— pathy—pathetic."

Aimes laughs, although it comes out more like a sob. "Empath. Not pathetic. Well, I am pathetic. I'm not an empath. I just—I think seeing this being done to your beautiful shop would upset anyone. I'm really sorry that happened to you, Vera."

"Oh, is okay, it means I am on right track," Vera says.

Aimes gapes at her. "Vera, you can't possibly keep looking into Xan's death."

"Why not?"

"Oh my god. I can't—"

Just then, a car turns the corner, heading toward them. "There's Julia now," Vera says with a smile, her voice thick with affection.

Julia parks the car, climbs out, and closes the door gently. "Emma's asleep in her car seat." She hugs Vera. "Vera, you okay? Oof, have you been drinking?"

"Only whisky," Vera says.

"Wow, okay, sounds like a good night. Hey, Aimes, right? You okay? Thanks for accompanying Vera tonight."

"Yeah," Aimes says weakly.

Then, finally, Julia glances up at the shop and stops smiling. Her jaw scrapes the pavement. "Oh my god, Vera, your teahouse!"

"I say to you, someone vandalize it."

Julia shakes her head. "I know, I know. I guess I wasn't—it didn't really sink in. Oh man, this is bad." She sighs, then takes both of Vera's hands in hers. "Vera, I say this with all the love in the world, but what the fuck did you get yourself tangled up in this time?"

Vera at least has the grace to look somewhat ashamed at that, which kind of surprises Aimes, to be honest. But then Vera squares her shoulders and says, "I am solving a mysterious case. A case that looks like it involve the foul play, if this is any indication."

"You need to tell Selena," Julia says.

Vera glowers at her. "You know what she's like, she will nag me to death and make me stop investigating."

"As she should!" Julia says.

"I will tell her tomorrow."

"Promise?"

Vera makes a noncommittal noise.

Julia groans out loud. "All right. I know better by now than to ask you to stop whatever it is you're doing. Wait, how do you know that whoever did this isn't still watching you right now? What if they follow us back to my house? I don't want to put Emma in danger."

My god, she's right, Aimes thinks. How could Aimes not even have thought of the possibility that whoever did this might still be here, watching this whole time?

"Oh!" Vera says, and now, finally, she sounds scared. They all look around frantically. Vera pushes Julia away. "You go home right now. I won't go back to your place, put you in danger. You lock all the door and window."

"But what about you?" Julia says.

"I'll stay with her." It's only when Vera and Julia look at Aimes that she realizes what she just said. Why had she said that? Argh! Take it back, quick! Except when Aimes thinks of Vera all alone in her little house, scared and confused and still drunk, she can't bear to take it back. "I'll stay with you here. I'll make sure the doors and windows are all secured."

"I don't like this," Julia says. "Maybe I should call Oliver or Riki to come stay with you."

"Don't be silly," Vera says. "Why you are so drama? Riki has Adi, he cannot come stay with me, and Oliver snore. So loudly too. No, Aimes will stay with me."

Julia looks like she's about to argue, but then she thinks better of it. With a sigh, she pulls Vera into another hug. "Okay, but be careful. And call me first thing in the morning." She pauses, then says, "Actually, don't. Because you wake up at four thirty. I'll call you first thing in the morning."

"Okay, okay, stop worrying. You go home now. Sorry I make you come out here for nothing."

"It's not for nothing. And you need to call Selena and tell her about this, otherwise I will."

Vera shakes her head as Julia drives off, then she says, "All right, we go in now." She stops. Aimes can practically hear the cogs clacking in her head. She rummages through her bag and takes out something. "Szechuan pepper spray. In case vandal waiting inside my shop."

"Oh my god," Aimes moans. Then stops abruptly when something hard is placed in her hand. She looks down to see a box cutter. "What the hell? Where did you get this? Was this inside your bag the whole time? Do you walk around with a box cutter?"

"I am helpless old lady, I need to protect myself."

"For the last time, you are not old." Still, Aimes can hardly complain about the box cutter now, can she? So she holds it tightly as they approach the teahouse. Vera unlocks the front door. *Still locked*, Aimes thinks. That's a good sign. Guilt overcomes Aimes, and she taps Vera's shoulder and indicates for her to get behind her. Aimes opens the door carefully and steps inside. Should she go, "Hello"? But if there is indeed someone lurking in here, then they'd know that she's here. Well, they would know she's here anyway because she just opened the front door. Oh my god, why is this so much harder than it looks in the movies? She should've kicked down the door and shouted, "Hands up!"

When was the last time Aimes had been this fearful? She's been scared plenty of times before, but she's pretty sure she hasn't felt fear like this ever. It's a different kind of feeling, something shaved down to the bone, something to do with pure survival. Her blood roars in her ears as she creeps into the teahouse, jumping at the slightest noise. She swings the box cutter left and right, just in case, then, finding the shop clear, starts climbing up the stairs. Her heart is not so much thumping as it is whirring, going at such a high speed that it's basically a constant whine. Aimes creeps into the living room, trying, and failing, to control her breathing. In every corner she thinks she sees a dark crouched figure. She stabs the air menacingly, then nearly jumps out of her skin when the lights come on.

Vera stands by the light switch, looking sheepish. "Sorry, I thought maybe turning on light will help. You want me to turn off again? You look like you having such fun."

"I'm not having fun," Aimes cries. This is too much. All of it.

The party, that glamorous crowd, the red paint. The adrenaline rushes out of her, leaving her shaky and empty. The box cutter slides out of her hand, and Aimes slumps to the floor. "It's all my fault."

"Oh, Aimes, what is it?" Vera rushes to her side.

"This, what happened to your shop, I think it's my fault."

"No, you were there with me the whole night, how can be your fault? You so silly."

"I didn't do it," Aimes wails. "But I think someone did because of what I did to Xan."

"Oh, my dear girl. What you do to Xander? You hurt him?"

Aimes opens her mouth to say no, to cover everything up with yet more lies, but what ends up coming out is the truth. "Yes, I did." Sobs wrack her body. "He came to me for help, and I turned him away."

"Why?" Vera's voice is gentle, and Aimes can't stand it because she doesn't deserve gentleness, she deserves cruel judgment.

"Because he wasn't even my real boyfriend!" Aimes cries. And there it is. The ugly truth. Aimes is nothing but a fake. How laughable that Vera had thought she needed to teach Aimes to fake it till she makes it, when literally nothing in Aimes's life is real.

"Oh, my dear, I think you need to start from beginning," Vera says. "You sit down. Come. Give me box cutter. I will make you tea."

Aimes lets Vera lead her to the sofa. She curls up on it, shaking and crying, while Vera bustles into the kitchen and gets a kettle going. Time passes, and a steaming mug of milky tea is placed in Aimes's hands. She takes a sip, and it is magical, rich and sweet and hot. Despite everything, Aimes calms down, just a little.

Vera sits down next to her and pats her on the arm. "Okay, now you better tell me from the start."

And so she does.

Aimes has always been good at most things. When she was little, she was a natural at everything she tried her hand at—piano, tennis, math. "She's a natural," her teachers would say, and she would beam with pride and chug along merrily. She only ever had to do the bare minimum to get good grades. Life was good. Life was easy.

Then she went to Berkeley, and she found that she was surrounded by other naturals. But worse than that, the other students hadn't gotten used to just coasting through life. Most of them weren't just talented, they were hard workers. For the first time in her life, Aimes wasn't above average. She was average. Then she was below average. And it was awful. She'd never realized how much she'd taken being above average for granted. Now, she felt like she was thrashing crazily in the water just to stay afloat.

The thing about Berkeley is that there is no humanly possible way to get through all of the reading that their professors handed them. Each professor happily assigned ten hours' worth of reading each week, seemingly forgetting that every student was taking at least four classes, which meant they ended up with forty hours of reading to do each week, in addition to essays and research papers that they had to turn in. Aimes pulled all-nighters. She managed to just about scrape through her classes, ending up with a B average at the end of the year. Meanwhile, it seemed like most of her friends were scoring As. Then, come senior year, they scored internships and jobs, while Aimes continued floundering.

By the time she graduated, Aimes was burned out to nothing but charred bones. She felt like she hadn't slept in four years, hadn't had a single break when she was able to fully let go of the stress of college. The thought of applying for competitive internships or grad school or whatever made her want to hide in a cave. She got a retail job instead, something that made her ache physically but provided some respite for her mind. And she started posting on social media. Just random photos at first. She had a good eye for making things look pretty. At first, she assumed that it was something most people were good at, but then she noticed that her accounts were growing at a rate that was much better than most of her friends'. An above-average rate.

That term, "above average," rekindled something in her. A small part of her that shivered back to life. And so Aimes dived into the world of social media. She embraced the role of content creator. Except, the truth was, Aimes didn't have much content to share. Her life was pathetic, there was nothing fun or interesting about it. While her fellow Cal alumni were working at places like JPL or getting law degrees at Georgetown, Aimes was . . . well, not doing much, really. And it was so incredibly, painfully embarrassing. She plodded along, learning how to do her hair and makeup so she looked enchanting on camera, learning how to capture the golden light by playing with her phone camera's features, learning this and that and growing her accounts at a consistent rate. Slow but steady, and meanwhile she was withering inside, watching her friends soar.

Then along came Xander. Aimes had liked a few of his photos on Instagram, and somewhere along the way, they'd started DMing each other. Casual messages at first, then somehow, their conversations deepened. Maybe they had sensed something in each other. Some kind of brokenness. Aimes had definitely felt it in Xander. Here was someone who might actually understand her. They often DMed till the wee hours of the night, until Aimes fell asleep with her phone in her hand. When she woke up, the first thing she did was DM Xander. Maybe she was a little bit in love with him. Or maybe she was just in love with the idea of him.

She asked him to meet up. Of course she did. How could she not? And, crushingly, he said no. He told her he wasn't looking for anything real, and he was sorry that he had led her on. Aimes felt heartbroken. Then she felt angry. Then she felt stupid. Why would someone like Xander, who had over five hundred thousand followers on Instagram, want to spend any time with her? She only had about ten thousand followers at the time. She should've just been grateful that he even deigned to DM her. She slunk away, licking her wounds.

The thing with Xander, though, is that he was a genuinely nice guy. He must've felt bad for her, because he reached out and apologized, and then he said, "I can't be your boyfriend IRL, but maybe I can be your online boyfriend?"

She didn't understand at first. She thought maybe he meant they could date virtually. Maybe he wanted to sext? She was at a low enough point in her life that she would not have turned it down.

But what Xander suggested was something completely different. Something far more valuable than companionship—a partnership. He pointed out to Aimes that cute couples posting fun, relatable, romantic content about their relationships got a ton of likes. And they could create so much content with minimal effort. Nothing fancy required, no expensive meals or flashy outfits or brand-name goods. Just the two of them having fun in front of the camera before going their separate ways.

Aimes was horrified. Then curious. Then, after some research, she was in. Xander was right, photogenic couples were a hot commodity. And the amount of content they could do was endless, and it could all be done in a small space. In her tiny apartment, even. And so they did end up meeting in person after all, but with very clear boundaries. Xander was somewhat less attractive in person, but so was Aimes, and so was every other influencer out there probably, so she didn't hold it against him. He was courteous but also kept his distance, and she understood that for Xander, this was purely a business agreement. In a way, it made Aimes feel good. She had a professional relationship, which surely meant she had . . . a profession, right? Anyway, she treated it as one.

They met every Monday at four in the afternoon, and each of them would prepare three different scenarios to act out. Six in total. They ranged from cute wake-up kisses to funny kitchen pranks to little inside jokes. Sometimes, in the spur of the moment, they'd eke out a couple more scenarios. They'd act them out in two hours, switching outfits between each scene, and then Xander would leave. They posted one video or photo each day. Aimes was also still taking tons of beautiful photos of her food, her coffee, and her makeup, and all of a sudden, she had a whole slew of content to share. Her follower count exploded. So did Xander's, and she was so happy for him when he hit one million followers. For the first time in years, Aimes felt good. She was doing something tangible, something that wasn't just treading water and hoping no one would notice her. In fact, she was being noticed. Brands were reaching out to her. A swimwear company, about a dozen makeup companies, even a travel company that wanted to offer her and Xander a couple's trip to somewhere "exotic." Xander said no to that, telling Aimes that going out of the country was out of the question for him. She tamped down the frustration, telling herself they didn't need to travel, they were doing just fine shooting in her tiny apartment.

Everything was going so well. She was on her way to a million followers. She had found her niche. She could face her college friends once more, and when they asked her what she did for a living, she could say she was a content creator without any guile.

Then Xander dropped a bomb on her.

"Oh dear," Vera says, "that sound like abuse."

"No, not like that. A figurative bomb. Like, bad news."

"Ah, I see. I like this phrase, dropping bomb on head. Okay, sorry. What did he say?"

Aimes takes another sip of her tea but finds the mug empty. She sets it down on the table and bites her lip before finally blurting out, "He wanted to come clean. He wanted to do a live video where we'd tell everyone the truth, that our relationship was fake, and that in fact, we knew next to nothing about each other. He said he had a huge secret that he'd been hiding, and he couldn't live with it anymore, and he wanted to expose it with my help."

"What is this secret?"

"I don't know," Aimes sobs. "I told him he was being ridiculous. I said no. He begged me. H-he cried." She squeezes her eyes shut, feeling hot tears stream down her cheeks. "He said what he had to say was so much more important than a follower count or anything. We got into a fight. He called me—we called each other horrible names. He told me I was a soulless fake, and I told him he was just as fake as I was, and I said—" She can't. She can't say it out loud.

"It's okay," Vera says, stroking Aimes's arm. "It's okay."

"It's not okay. I said if he ever dares expose our fake relationship, I would ruin his life. Oh god." She buries her face in her hands. "I didn't mean it. I don't think I did, anyway. I don't know. I was so furious and so scared. I was terrified. By then, I'd built this amazing community on Instagram—followers who felt like they knew me. Some of them had become friends. We chatted every day. I couldn't stand the thought of losing them. I knew that I'd gone overboard with Xander, so the next morning, I DMed him, apologizing. He didn't reply. I thought maybe he was ignoring me. Days later, I saw the news about him dying." Aimes chokes on her tears. "Maybe I could've prevented it if I'd just been brave enough to do what he wanted me to do."

Vera sits there quietly, taking a deep breath. Oh god, she must hate Aimes now. And although Aimes has known Vera for only a short time, she's terrified at the idea of losing her.

"Do you hate me?" Aimes says in a small voice.

Vera looks surprised. "Hate you? Why can I hate you?"

"Because . . ." Aimes flails. "Because of what I just told you. All of the lying I did, the 'fake it till you make it' bullshit. My whole life is fake."

"Ah." Vera grimaces. "I know one thing or two things about being fake."

"You? No way. You're, like, the most authentic person I've ever come across."

"Well, last year change a lot of things for me. Before I had good luck of man dying in my teahouse—"

"I really don't see how that's good luck," Aimes says, sniffling.

"I explain to you some other time. But trust me, is very good luck. May you find dead man in your shop one day."

"Nope, that just does not sound right."

"Okay, anyway, before that happen, I was very sad. I felt like you, like my life not going anywhere. I had nobody to talk to, nobody to cook for."

Aimes tries hard to imagine Vera as a lonely individual with no one to cook for, and the image is so heartbreaking she immediately pushes it out of her mind. How can that be possible? Vera is so outgoing, larger than life, how could she possibly have ever been isolated? Maybe she's just saying this to make Aimes feel better.

"But I don't tell anyone how sad I am. I pretend like everything is okay. I go for morning walk, I see same people, and I say hi to them. I never once ask, 'Hello, would you like to come to my place for tea because I am very lonely?' No. I just wave and smile like everything is fine. I send message to my son, do I tell him 'I am so lonely I cry sometimes, for no reason, just in the middle of day, suddenly a tear come out'? No, I don't do that. Instead, I text him and tell him to drink more water or exercise more to keep virile."

Aimes can't help but smile at the thought of Vera's poor son getting a text from her with the word "virile" in it. She reaches out and grasps Vera's hand. "I'm sorry you had to go through that."

"Is okay. It make me strong. Give me different understanding of life. I feel like I can understand you better because I go through it myself. So when you ask me, do I hate you? No, Aimes. I see you. I understand what you go through. We are exactly the same. Except my breasts are bigger than yours."

"What?" Aimes blinks, then bursts into laughter. "Vera!" How does she do that? How does she make Aimes cackle at a time like this?

"Don't worry, is because I breastfeed, so they get bigger. If you breastfeed, yours will get bigger too."

"Oh my god." Aimes wipes her eyes and smiles at Vera.

"You'll be okay, Aimes. So, maybe you struggle in college, so what? Doesn't mean you are bad person. My niece Sana, she drop out of CalArts, but does that mean she is not good artist? She is earning well over six figures a year doing art now, you know," she says with obvious pride.

"That's amazing." Aimes kind of hates Sana a little now. Who makes six figures doing art these days? And, if Aimes were to be perfectly honest, she also hates that Sana has an aunt like Vera. If Aimes had an aunt like Vera, life would probably be very different. She wouldn't be such a mess, for one. But it feels less bad being a mess, having told someone about it and not been judged for it. She takes in a shaky breath. "Thanks for listening."

"Of course. I'm very good at listening. Okay, so you don't kill Xander? Just making sure before I cross you off the list."

And somehow, Vera has whipped out a notebook and a pen and is watching Aimes expectantly.

"There's an actual list?"

Vera looks affronted. "Yes, of course. I take my job as private investigator seriously."

"Okay. Well, no, I didn't kill Xander. I might as well have, turning him away like that, but I didn't physically kill him, no."

"Okay, that's one suspect down." Vera crosses Aimes's name off with a flourish. "And now I think we should go to bed, get some beauty sleep, yes? You can sleep in Tilly's old bedroom."

For the next few minutes, Vera shuffles back and forth, handing a new toothbrush and extra blankets to Aimes. Aimes takes each item obediently. She's too exhausted to say or do anything else. Then, next thing she knows, she is being tucked into Tilly's old bed as though she were a kid again, and it isn't the worst thing in the world. Vera puts a blanket over Aimes and gives her a quick pat on the shoulder before padding softly to the door.

"Don't think too much, just go to sleep," Vera says, turning out the lights.

And for the first time in as long as Aimes can remember, her mind does not spend the next few hours ruminating on every little thing she's done wrong. Instead, she turns over, closes her eyes, and drifts off into a deep, dreamless sleep.

EIGHTEEN

VERA

Vera thinks it might be wise to let Aimes sleep past four thirty the following morning. Not wanting to leave Aimes alone in the house after last night's events, Vera skips her early morning walk. She's about to start cooking when someone knocks at the shop's door. It's Winifred, carrying a box of pastries.

"Aiya," she says in Mandarin as soon as Vera unlocks the door. "What happened to your shop front?"

"Don't make such a fuss, it's nothing." Vera's voice falters as she glances up at the door. In the daylight, the vandalism looks less scary, but the mess is far worse than she'd originally thought.

"Nothing?" Winifred cries. "This is obviously not nothing. What if they came back and burned down your shop? My shop is attached to yours; I don't want to be collateral damage in whatever shady thing you've got going on."

"There is nothing shady going on. What Chinese pastries did you bring today?"

Winifred gives her a look before opening the box. "This is

Korean sausage roll, Korean mochi bread, and my new invention, Korean-French cheese and kimchi croissant."

Vera shakes her head. "What tea should I pair it with?"

"How about"—Winifred smiles slyly—"boba?"

"Aiya!" Vera spits. "Boba! Boba is the bane of my existence. People think drinking tea is healthy, therefore drinking boba is healthy. What rubbish! Terrible invention, I tell you. It's full of sugar and additives and—"

"Okay, okay, I'm sorry I brought it up."

Vera trots behind the counter, where she studies the 188 cabinets in front of her. "Okay, I think I have the perfect tea." She opens up the drawer containing roasted barley and scoops some out into a bowl, then adds a few goji berries, followed by a sliver of licorice to reduce phlegm.

"So, who did you piss off this time?" Winifred says as Vera fills up the kettle.

"Well." Vera sighs. "It really could be anyone. I went viral on the TikTok, you know."

"Ha!" Winifred slaps the table triumphantly. "I always knew one day you would bring back some virus that would kill us all, I knew it."

Vera narrows her eyes. "First of all, that's not what 'going viral' means, and second of all, you thought I meant I have a deadly virus and you're not worried, you're happy? Really, Winifred, I expected more from you."

Winifred shrugs, not looking at all ashamed of herself.

"Going viral means my video was watched by everyone."

"What video?"

"Videos about . . ." Vera's voice trails off, then she abruptly stops and fishes her phone out of her pocket. She turns on the camera and hands the phone to Winifred. "Actually, help me shoot a video right now. This way, not horizontal. Aim the camera at my hands, yes, like that. But sometimes you also have to record my face, especially when I'm smiling or looking peaceful."

"Aiya, you don't need to lecture me on how to do this!" Winifred leaps up from the chair and holds the phone with the natural professionalism that every Chinese grandmother is somehow born with. She goes into an unnecessarily deep crouch, aiming the camera at Vera. "Okay, action. Lift your chin, Vera. Don't hunch your back. Don't move like that, it's jerky and looks strange on the camera."

Vera is starting to rethink the wisdom of making Winifred her cameraperson. But she keeps going valiantly, ignoring Winifred's constant stream of instructions.

"Elbows out! Out, out. Smile, Vera. Big smile! Bigger! Aiya, no good."

Turns out that all one needs to do to bring out the inner dictator in Winifred is hand her a camera. Thankfully, the tea Vera is making is relatively straightforward, and before long, she is done. She practically pounces on Winifred, snatching the phone out of her hands and shouting, "Done!" There. Hopefully Winifred gets off her power trip and returns to her normal, mildly irritating self once more.

Winifred snorts, muttering, "You need to work on your posture." Then she sits back down and begins to serve up the pastries. "So, these videos of you making tea are going viral? People really watch anything these days, don't they?"

"It's not just me making tea. I also narrate them. I'm investigating a death, you know." Vera is unable to keep the smugness out of her voice. "I am so busy these days. You're lucky you caught me this morning." She serves Winifred her tea, then leans back and takes a bite of the Korean-French abomination. Of course, as luck would have it, the croissant actually tastes amazing. Quite possibly the best pastry Vera has ever had. The richness of the cheese is perfectly cut through by the sour, spicy kimchi, and all of it wrapped up in buttery, flaky layers. Yes, please.

"It's good, isn't it?" Winifred says, watching her like a hawk.

"It's okay," Vera says.

Winifred sniffs. "You like it. Now, tell me, what does your investigation have to do with online videos?"

"I'll show you." Vera opens up the video editing app that Robin had downloaded for her and uploads the footage Winifred has just recorded. Then she clears her throat and holds her phone close to her mouth. "Now be quiet while I record the audio." She pauses, then hits record and speaks in English. "Last night, I go to very interesting party. This party is full of people Xander Lin hang out with, but what is interesting is that when I ask people about Xander, nobody seem to have met him. Why is that? There is something fishy here. As you youngsters like to call it, the math ain't messing. Who is Xander Lin, and why is it so hard to find people who actually know him? I know that social media is a bit of a tricky thing to use. You want to be authentic, but you also want to save face. Is easier to save face without social media. Your generation is dealing with so much. But I will promise you this: I don't stop looking into Xander Lin's death until I know the truth. Thank you for watching." She finishes recording and sets the phone down before smiling smugly at Winifred.

"Is that all? Not sure I get what the big deal is," Winifred says.

"Oh, you bitter old crone, you know I have the X factor and

you can't stand it. Now, drink your tea and help me clean up my storefront."

"There is no saving your storefront. You'd best get a new sign. You can order one online and have it be delivered by noon."

"And pay good money for shipping? I don't think so. Up you get. I have a homemade cleaning solution that will get any stains out."

As Vera scrubs her front door, her thoughts fly back to the events from the night before. Last night was probably one of the most chaotic nights that Vera has had in a while. Well, there was the night of Oliver's surprise birthday party and the fiasco with the ketchup and the blow-up unicorn, but that's best left forgotten. Last night, Vera learned that young people are very, very good at faking it. Maybe it has something to do with social media. This case is really shaping up to be very unexpected. She can't even begin to make heads or tails of it.

It is becoming painfully clear that Xander Lin was a scammer of sorts. And, given Vera's recent run-in with scammers, she isn't too chuffed to learn this about Xander. A guy who fooled others into thinking he was in a fun, cute, and loving relationship with Aimes. Sounds like an exploitative relationship. But then Aimes said he never once touched or said anything inappropriate to her, so what was his game? Was it really something as mundane as gaining followers? That doesn't seem right. And what was it that he'd wanted to come clean about? The fake relationship was part of it, but it sounded like there was something else. Maybe Xander wasn't straight, and he wanted to come out?

A deep sadness settles over Vera's heart at the possibility. She wishes she had known Xander sooner, so she could have plied him with fattening foods and nagged him off social media. Except maybe she wouldn't have done the latter, given she herself is a rising social media starlet.

She spots movement inside the shop and stops scrubbing at the door. "Aimes, you finally awake, you sleep in quite long," she calls into the shop.

Aimes peers out warily, blinking in the bright sunlight. "It's barely past seven in the morning."

"Like I say, you sleep in quite long. This is Winifred, she owns the Chinese bakery next door."

"Oh, hi! I thought the bakery next door was Korean."

Vera rolls her eyes.

"Yes, it is Korean. My grandfather was Korean," Winifred says.

"Hah!" Vera says. "I thought you say grandmother?"

Winifred pauses, her cheeks growing red. "You must have remember wrong, Vera. Early onset dementia is very common among the old—"

"Who are you calling old?" Vera snaps.

"Um, you've mentioned quite a few times that you're really old and are about to drop dead any day now?" Aimes says. Her voice falters when Vera shoots her a deadly glare.

"Haven't you heard?" Vera says. "Sixty is new forty. And my mind is as clear and sharp as a—a sniper rifle."

"Cool," Aimes says quickly. "Hey, you ladies shouldn't bother with that. I'll clean it up, okay? It's the least I can do."

It's clearly a harried attempt at changing the subject, but Vera appreciates the offer anyway. "Oh, you don't have to do that," Vera says, even as she dumps her scrubbing brush into the pail of soapy water. "Okay, thank you, Aimes. My back is killing me."

"So, how you know Vera? Are you one of her suspects?"

"She was, up until last night. But now she no longer a suspect."

Aimes smiles. "Yeah, thanks for crossing me off the suspects list."

"Okay, you clean that up and I prepare breakfast for you. Winifred, you got more of that kimchi cheese croissant?"

"I thought you say you prepare breakfast for her?" Winifred says.

"Yes, I make tea. You provide the croissant. And get one more for me also."

Aimes watches as Winifred ambles to her shop, muttering under her breath. "You didn't have to do that."

"Nonsense. I am doing Winifred a favor. That kimchi cheese croissant taste so bad, she won't be able to sell before they go off. Now, work fast. After breakfast, I take you somewhere."

Aimes looks like she's about to ask silly questions, like where are they going? Then she seems to think better of it and picks up the scrubbing brush. Vera smiles inwardly. Good girl, that Aimes.

It takes Aimes a surprisingly long time to scrub off the paint from the shop front. Really, she needs to get a better workout routine, she is so feeble, with noodle arms. Vera tells her this lovingly, and Aimes merely rolls her eyes.

She also takes a video of Aimes cleaning up the storefront, zooming in on the red paint and the threatening words. Then she narrates, "I think someone do something bad to Xander Lin and now they are scare because I am getting close to finding out truth. If you think you can scare me by vandalizing my teahouse, you are wrong."

Vera takes her time editing this video, combining it with the earlier one that Winifred had shot. Then she opens up TikTok and uploads it. She has so many notifications she can barely keep up with them. Her last video is now at over two million views. Funny how Sana and company are always complaining about how hard it is to get hits on social media. Vera will tell them that it is in fact one of the easiest things to do. She'll give them pointers. They'll appreciate that.

Within a minute, the notifications start piling up once more. Comments stream in.

OMG someone did that to your tea shop???!!

How dare anyone do that to you, don't they know you are a national treasure?!

Veraaa you're right, you must be getting close to the real killer!!

Vera smirks to herself. It's easy to see why people find social media so addictive. She can practically feel her endorphins rising as she goes through the comments.

"You know, reading the comments is a two-edged sword," Aimes says from behind Vera's shoulder.

"They are all very nice."

"For now. Don't be surprised, though, when the trolls show up."

"Why are you talking about fairy-tale creature?"

Aimes sits down with a huge groan. "Oh man, my arms are killing me. I think we're gonna have to get you a new sign."

"You need to eat more, your arms so skinny, like Hong Kong egg noodle."

"Okay, Vera," Aimes says with a roll of her eyes. "Have you checked your DMs yet?"

"Ah, I keep forgetting." Vera opens her DMs cheerfully and shows them to Aimes. "Look at that, so many fan mail."

Aimes smiles. "Well, you deserve them." They scroll through the messages for a while, most of them from people asking Vera to adopt them. Then Aimes starts. "Hey, did you miss this one?"

It's a DM from an obviously fake account, and it says, **Stay out of this, nosy bitch.**

Coldness prickles in the center of Vera's chest and spreads like melting ice across her torso.

"Vera, you okay?"

She blinks and forces a smile. "Don't be silly, of course I am okay. Why not okay? Just because of one silly message?"

But then she scrolls down and sees another message, sent from a different account. **Stop posting about Xander Lin, or I will make you stop, you old cu—**

Vera slams the phone down, making Aimes jump. "Silly people," she says.

"Vera, I really think you should take this seriously," Aimes says.

Vera tuts at her. "At my age, if I take everything too serious, I will get nothing done." Just then, a text comes in saying, **I'm outside**, and Vera smiles. "Let's go."

Julia and Sana are outside waiting next to Julia's car. As soon as they see Vera, Julia starts in on her. "Have you told Selena about the vandalism?"

"Oh, not this again," Vera groans. "You and Oliver are like naggy aunties."

"Vera," Sana says, "this is serious. Someone actually came here, like physically came here, and did this to your shop. You need to report this to the police."

"The police," Vera grumbles. "You know what they'll say.

They'll tell me, 'Stop looking into Xander Lin's death, blah blah blah.'"

"Maybe you should," Aimes says.

"You talking crazy talk," Vera says.

"Aimes is right. No case is worth your safety," Julia says.

"Okay, enough of lecturing. I am your elder, you have to respect me."

"Vera," Julia sighs. "I love and respect you like you're my own mom, and that is why I'm really concerned, okay? Will you promise me that you'll at least talk to Selena about this?"

Vera grunts. "I will think." *Not a chance in hell*, she thinks. Then she says, "Enough about me. Aimes, go do the hang out with Julia and Sana."

"Uh . . ." Aimes says. "What does that mean, exactly?"

"Well, you say you are unlike your name, all aimless. This is something Julia and Sana very familiar with."

"Gee, thanks," Sana says, but she's smiling even as she rolls her eyes. She turns to Aimes. "It's true though. I dropped out of college and was basically, uh, stalking a guy before Vera found me."

Aimes gapes at her. "What? But you're a super-successful artist."

"Aww, stop. Well, yes, I am," Sana says, flipping her hair over her shoulder and grinning. "But that only happened because of Vera here." She reaches over and wraps an arm around Vera's shoulders. "Before that, I was depressed and—um, like I said, kind of doing some light stalking. To be fair, though, it wasn't like I was stalking him because I was in love with him or something; it was because he'd stolen my art, and I wanted to find a way to get it back."

"Aiya, stop talking," Vera says. "You are not helping."

"And I was a stay-at-home mom stuck in an abusive marriage,"

Julia says. "So we definitely know what it's like to feel stuck." She gives Aimes a warm smile, and Vera spots tears glimmering in Aimes's eyes before she turns away.

After clearing her throat, Aimes says, "But—I don't—I don't actually know what I want to do. I did study English Lit at Cal, but I don't know if it is something I wanna do. Sorry."

"Why you are sorry?" Vera says. "Don't be sorry. You are young, there are million jobs out there, of course you don't know what you want to do. Is okay. That is why you have me to tell you what to do. And what you should do is the hang out with these two ladies."

Aimes's eyes dart from Vera to Sana to Julia and back to Vera. "I mean, I don't want to be a bother . . ."

"No, you're not," Sana says. "We hang out all the time, and we'd love for you to join us. Come on, we'll get ant cupcakes and chill at the wharf."

"Ant cupcakes?"

Julia rolls her eyes. "It's Sana's latest thing. She thinks we should be eating bugs."

"They're low carb, high protein, and friendly for the environment."

Vera smiles cunningly. "Get one extra, I give to Winifred. Now off you go! Bye-bye!"

She gives Aimes a little push and waves them off.

"Call Selena," Julia says over her shoulder.

"Stop nagging," Vera calls back. Then, with a happy sigh, she goes back inside her tea shop and gets to work. She's not about to let a good vandalism go to waste.

NINETEEN

TJ

This is pretty bad," Lomax says.

"Can't believe some asshole did this to Vera," Kit says, as she climbs the ladder with an electric drill in her hand.

"Oh, I always say when people get angry like this, it mean you are doing the right thing," Vera says.

TJ pinches the bridge of his nose. "Or it means you're pissing the wrong people off and you should stop for your own safety."

Vera shares a look with Robin. "Your father is very boring man, isn't he?"

Robin grins. "Yep, I've said that to him like a million times."

TJ watches as Kit unscrews Vera's old sign. Kit has mentioned in the past that one of the classes she took back at the juvenile facility is woodshop, but he never really appreciated it until now. He has a newfound admiration for Kit, and he's feeling extra useless, and he's really freaking stressed out about Vera's insistence on continuing her investigation. And he's just finished doing his books and there's no way around it, he's going to have to close up shop.

Everyone cheers as the old sign comes down. Putting on the new one requires more than a pair of hands, and TJ is surprised by how tiring the work is. He's never going to look at a store sign the same way again. Afterward, Vera invites them all inside for some Korean-French pastries and some Chinese tea.

"This kimchi cheese croissant is so good, Grandma," Robin says.

"Is it? Is okay, I guess." Vera frowns at TJ. "TJ, you okay? You not eating very much."

"Hmm? Oh, yeah, I'm fine." TJ takes another bite of the croissant just so Vera won't start prying. They really are very good, but he doesn't have an appetite.

"Have you reported this to the police?" Lomax says.

"Aiya, of course I have."

"And what did they say?" Robin says.

Vera pauses for such a long time that even TJ notices.

"Well," she says finally, "they say don't worry, it happen all the time."

"What happens all the time? People splashing your shop with red paint?" TJ says.

"Well, not my shop, but yes, they say this kind of thing happen to all shops."

TJ frowns. "I don't think it does. I'm surprised they're not taking it more seriously."

"Dad," Robin says, "I don't like the idea of Grandma being here all by herself, especially when someone's clearly out to get her."

"Yeah, I don't like it either," Lomax says. Next to him, Kit nods solemnly.

TJ gapes at them. What are they asking him to do here? "I

mean, yeah, I'm not a fan either. Can you stay with your son for a while?"

"Oh, no," Vera says. "Terrible idea. He just move in with girl-friend and I need them to make babies. They can't make babies if I'm there."

Oh lord. TJ massages his temple. "I think this is somewhat more urgent than your son and his girlfriend, uh, having . . . rela-tions."

"Nothing more urgent than me having grandbabies," Vera snaps.

"It's okay, Grandma," Robin says. "How about you stay with us?"

TJ shoots Robin a very meaningful look, which she blithely ignores.

"I cannot do that to you. There are obviously people coming after me, maybe dangerous people," Vera says with a dramatic flourish. "If I lead them to your house, how can I forgive myself?"

"Yeah, you're right," TJ says quickly. "Thanks for being so selfless."

"Then we'll stay here with you," Robin says.

"What?" TJ says.

"I'm going to have a sleepover at Grandma's."

"No," TJ says.

Robin crosses her arms and raises her chin at him. Then she seems to rethink her stance and lowers her chin, gazing up at him with Bambi eyes. Damn it. "Please, Dad?" she says. "I've never done this before, and all the other kids at school often mention how they stayed over at their grandparents' house and baked brownies and shi—I mean, and stuff."

"Yeah, you can't deny your kid that experience. That's messed up," Kit says.

She's not your grandmother! TJ wants to scream. But then he thinks of how Vera had stormed into Robin's school and laid down the law with Mr. Burns, and how she'd taken Robin out to buy bras, and he thinks of all the nutritious food Vera has cooked for Robin, and it hits him that . . . she is very much the grandmother Robin has always wanted. The grandmother he's always wanted, in fact. *I must be going mad*, he thinks, as he says, "Okay. But obviously I'm gonna have to stay over as well. Is that okay with you?"

Vera shrugs. "As long as you don't get in my way."

"Yes!" Robin whisper-shouts. She turns to Vera. "Can we bake chocolate chip cookies?"

"What is that European nonsense? No."

Robin deflates.

"We will make Chinese jiggly sponge cake. I am your grandmother, so this is now your heritage also, you better learn."

Robin grins again. "Okay, that sounds awesome."

TJ slumps in his seat. This is going to be a long day.

L ater that night, after Robin has been tucked into Tilly's old bed and TJ has helped clear away the thousand and one dirty dishes from the feast that Vera had insisted on making for dinner, TJ settles down on the couch. His stomach is still uncomfortably full from dinner, and despite himself, TJ has actually enjoyed spending the day at Vera's. He's felt, lately, that Robin is growing up way too quickly. Gone was the sweet, shy kid he adored, and in her place is a sarcastic, eye-rolling teen who kind of scares TJ shitless sometimes. But Vera has a way of somehow peeling back the years and bringing out Robin's inner child. Around Vera, Robin is sweet and sincere, and she smiles with abandon. It makes TJ's heart crack open to see how eager Robin is for some motherly affection, how hungry she's been. How could he have missed that?

Vera comes out of the kitchen carrying a tray with hot tea and a big slice of the jiggly sponge cake she and Robin made earlier.

"I couldn't possibly eat another bite," TJ says.

"Okay." She places the cake in front of him anyway, then sits down. "Tell me, TJ, what is it?"

"What's what?"

"You are worrying over something. I can see it the whole day, like you have something to hide."

"I don't—"

"And I know it involve Robin and Kit and Lomax."

"What? How do you know that?" TJ says, sitting straight up.

"Because you keep looking at Kit and Lomax like you kill their dog or something. So guilty face. And," she adds, as though she isn't done blowing things up, "I think has to do with Xander Lin."

"No, it doesn't. It doesn't!" TJ snaps, and he hears it then, the raw fear in his voice, turning it sharp-edged. He stares at Vera, his chest heaving, then he buries his face in his hands. "I'm sorry. I didn't mean to shout at you. I just—everything's falling apart, and I don't know what to do."

"How everything is falling apart?"

"We've lost too many clients, and I have to close down the office by the end of the week. Can't make rent. I fucked up."

"How you fuck up?"

"Robin." It feels wrong to say her name in this context, but he can't deny that the issues do involve her. "I had a difficult client. A lot of my clients are difficult, actually, but this one was particularly difficult. He was entitled, he'd harass me if he saw that his 'friends' booked a sponsorship and he didn't. He'd call me twenty times a day, leave me nasty messages, demand that I work harder, all that stuff. I should've fired him, but he was growing so fast, and I didn't want to lose him as a client even though he was a terrible human being. One night, I drank one too many beers and bitched about him to Robin. I just needed to spill, I guess, and for whatever stupid reason, I thought it would be okay to tell her this stuff. God, I'm an idiot."

"Robin is very mature kid," Vera says. "I can see why you tell her about it."

TJ gives a mirthless laugh. "Yeah, except then I went to bed, and what I didn't foresee happening was Robin taking my phone and sending an email to that client, firing him. And not just firing him. She said, 'You are a spoiled, entitled rich brat, and I no longer want to work with you.'"

"Ah," Vera says, somehow keeping her face straight.

"Yeah. Didn't go over well. He posted a screenshot of the email online, and obviously it went viral. A talent manager saying that to his client? Unheard of. Half of our clients dropped us within the next twenty-four hours. Kit and Lomax lost clients too, just because they work for me."

"Oh dear."

"Yeah. And Robin—I know she was just trying to protect me, I know, but . . ."

"Is hard not to feel a bit upset with her," Vera says.

"Yeah," TJ croaks. He hates to admit it. He hates to even think it to himself, to face the fact that, yeah, actually, part of him is angry at Robin. He blames himself for everything, mostly, but part of him blames her too, and knowing that makes him feel disgusted with himself, because what kind of parent would feel that way about their child?

"You talk to her about it?"

TJ shrugs. "I told her it's fine."

"Is not really fine if you have to close down business."

"No, it's not really fine."

"And what this has to do with Xander? Why you are so shady about him?"

"Xander," TJ groans. "Yet another incident that makes me feel like the worst human alive."

Vera doesn't say anything, merely studies him. Can he really tell her? He can't. Nope. He wrings his hands in his lap.

"I make a guess," Vera says finally. "Xander come to you and ask you to help him do some big news, and you say no."

TJ's mouth falls open. "How do you know?"

"Mother intuition." Then she adds, "Also, Aimes tell me Xander come to her wanting to do big exposé."

"I see." His voice comes out weak. He barely recognizes it. "Yes. That was what happened. The thing is, with Xander, it was . . . different. When I first signed him as a client, he made it clear that he wanted it to seem like we worked really closely with each other. He wanted to sell this image of having a talent manager who was basically at his beck and call. It didn't mean much to me at first. I was fine playing along. He'd write these captions about how we often had long phone calls into the middle of the night, strategizing his career growth, and how he could call me up for literally anything, like if he got a flat tire or something."

"Interesting," Vera says. "Why?"

"I guess for clout? Made him seem more legit, if his manager is willing to spend all this time on him. And he was actually a really low-key client in real life, so I didn't mind. Compared to my other clients, like I told you, Xander was low maintenance. I hardly ever heard from him. Until that day. The day before he died. He came to my office. I was so surprised. That was the first time I had ever met him in person, and he had come in unannounced. He told me he wanted to come clean online, tell everyone the truth, that we'd never even met and I only played a small role in his life, all that stuff. He said it had to do with some big bad secret he wanted to reveal."

"And you say no."

"Of course I said no!" TJ cries. "That was about a month after the fallout with my other client, the one that Robin emailed. I couldn't afford another scandal. That would've ended me. And I'd profited off Xander's lie. I'd gotten clients precisely because they said they saw Xander's posts about how attentive I was. I couldn't possibly do what Xander wanted me to do."

"How Xander react when you tell him?"

"Not well." TJ squeezes his eyes shut at the ugly memory. "He told me people like me are the reason why this country is morally bankrupt. I mean, I don't disagree with him," TJ says with a bitter laugh. "Then he said, 'I'm gonna do it anyway, with or without you.' And I freaked out. This is my livelihood. I got scared. I—I told him if he did, I would sue him for all he was worth. I told him if he even uttered my name publicly again, he would hear from my lawyer." TJ grimaces. It's almost physically painful reliving that day. He can still remember the blinding hot surge of rage that had overtaken his entire body. How his brain had felt like a heart thumping and thudding and burning. "I was despicable," he moans. "I was so hateful. And he looked so disappointed. He said I was one of the few people he thought he could count on, and then he left. And the next day, he was dead."

"Is that why all this time you acting so shady and not wanting me to look into his death?"

"Yeah. Because I'm a coward, Vera. And it's so painful thinking of Xander. I just want to push everything that has to do with him out of my mind. I know it's selfish. I know."

"Yes, it is selfish, but I also understand why you acting selfishly. You are parent. Not just to Robin but to Kit and Lomax. You feel responsible for them, so you cannot afford to risk this and that. I know. I am parent too."

Something inside TJ breaks, and he digs his knuckles into his eyes like a little kid. He wants to blot out the world. He wants to stop existing, just for a little while. "When the cops came to talk to me about Xander, I was so scared. And confused. They told me Xander wasn't who he said he was. I mean, what was that all about? I told them the truth, that I didn't know anything about Xander aside from him being an influencer, and they said from his posts, it sounded like I knew a lot more than what I was telling them. My god, I practically crapped my pants, Vera. I told them he may have embellished a little. I felt like complete shit. They looked like . . . like I was something sticky they'd accidentally stepped on."

"Ah, no, that is just cop being cop; they always look like they smell something bad."

Somehow, despite everything, TJ chuckles. "Yeah, they do, don't they?"

"I ask Selena once, you know, my future—"

"Daughter-in-law, yes, you've mentioned once or twice. Or three times."

"Well, I ask her once, why cop have that face? And she say, 'What face?' I show her and she laugh, then she say, 'I don't know, maybe because we deal with scumbags all the time?'"

"Scumbag, yep, that's me."

"Aiya, TJ, stop being so drama. Oh my goodness, you young people. Okay, so cops know that you not really have close relationship with Xander, so what? They don't care about that, they only care about whether or not you kill him. And you didn't, so what is problem?"

"I mean, when you put it that way . . ." TJ sighs. "I'm sorry I tried to talk you out of investigating his death. I would like to know what happened to him too. Even if it turns out he killed himself because everyone around him let him down. I should face it, take responsibility for what I did."

"Yes, don't worry about it, I was never going to listen to you, anyway."

"True."

"And Robin . . ."

"I know it's not her fault," TJ says.

"Well, sort of, but if you think about it, she get so angry when she hear that someone mistreats her father. Is quite touching, isn't it? Show you that you raise a fighter, someone who want to protect her family."

A warm, golden feeling spreads across TJ's body. He gazes at Vera in wonderment. "Yeah. You're right. All this time, I've been so carried away by the fallout, I never really spent any time thinking about the why."

"I think it show that you raise her so well."

TJ's cheeks burn, but it's not a bad feeling. "Do you really think so?" He's not even embarrassed by how needy his voice comes out sounding.

"Yes," Vera says simply. "Otherwise, I would not take her as granddaughter. I have very high standards, you know."

TJ snorts. "I'm glad to hear that she passed your test."

"And Kit and Lomax, they will be okay. They are good kids too, they will find place in the world."

"I don't know. I know they're great in person, and they've got good hearts and good heads on their shoulders, but on paper, they don't look so great."

"We will figure out. One step at one time, TJ. You don't have to take on the whole world at once. Just take one step."

TJ nods, feeling like the huge boulder that's been crushing him all this time has lifted, just a little. "I think I'm gonna have some of this cake after all."

"I know. No one can resist jiggly sponge cake."

Something about being around Vera makes TJ feel so safe, which is ironic given he's here tonight to make sure she is safe. Still, he can't complain. It feels nice, not being the one that everybody has to depend on for once. To have someone he can lean on. TJ bites into the airy soft cake and releases a long breath. Maybe Vera is right. Maybe, despite the shattered mess that his life has turned into, somehow, it's going to end up being okay.

TWENTY

MILLIE

Millie likes Oliver. Like, really likes him, in a genuine way that she hasn't felt in a long time. They've hung out two more times now, and she's pretty sure he likes her too. Usually she's so good at telling when guys are into her; she can sense it in the way their gazes touch her, quick and shy, darting away when she makes eye contact. But with Oliver, she can't be sure, and it's because she likes him, and the liking him is clouding her judgment. Father and Mother would—

It's best to not dwell on what Father and Mother would do.

Last night, Mother had knocked on her door before coming in—that's what they do, they knock, then without waiting for a reply, they go in. "What's going on with this guy you're seeing?" Mother had asked.

"We're taking it slow. Being careful," Millie said to her.

Mother had regarded Millie with such an intensity that Millie felt her skin shriveling, every inch of her wanting to hide from

Mother. *Somewhere out there*, she thought, *there are young women who aren't afraid of their mothers.*

"If it's not going anywhere, end it," Mother said finally. "You don't want to get hurt, Millie."

Millie nodded, the knots in her muscles loosening ever so slightly. *See*, she told herself, *Mother is just being caring. She cares about me.*

"One more date," Mother had said. "Then, if nothing happens, move on. I've taught you better than this."

More than anything, Millie hates disappointing Mother. She nodded again. "I know. I'm sorry."

"Young people nowadays," Mother had muttered as she left the room.

And now, as Millie sits on a picnic blanket at Golden Gate Park, she can't help stealing multiple glances at Oliver. He's rolled up his sleeves to his elbows and is taking out food he's prepared at home, and the sight is just so unbelievably sexy.

"—has been teaching me for weeks, and I think she'll be proud of me," he says. He stops and waves a hand in front of Millie's face. "Earth to Millie."

"Sorry," she says, snapping out of her daze.

"What were you thinking of?"

"Nothing," Millie says, squashing all thoughts of Mother deep, deep down. *Quick, change the subject.* She focuses on the containers of food. "Wow, Vera taught you how to make these?"

"Yup. I've been going to her place every week for cooking lessons. It's weird, I grew up in a pretty patriarchal household, and my mom was the one who cooked every meal. After she died, my dad took over, but he never got into it, you know? Like, I got the sense that he only cooked out of necessity. There was no love in the food. It was bland, and he rotated between three or four dishes. When I moved out, I didn't even think to learn how to cook or anything. I think that subconsciously, I'd internalized the whole gendered bullshit, and I was expecting my future wife to cook for me. God, I sound like an asshole." He scratches the back of his head, then adds, "And that's probably because I was. But I realized I need to work on myself. Unlearn all of the misogynistic crap I grew up with. Learn to cook actual good food. And Vera's a great teacher. I'm lucky to have her."

"Wow," Millie says. She hadn't thought it would be possible to like him even more than she already does, but here they are.

"Sorry, didn't mean to ramble. Okay, so here we have roast duck sandwiches, sweet and sour fish, and scallion oil noodles. And for dessert, black sticky rice with coconut cream."

"Wow," Millie says again. Can she not think of better things to say, for goodness' sake? When she is with other men, Millie is sweet and funny and cute, and when she is with Oliver, she is reduced to one-word answers only.

Mother's voice flashes through her mind. *Last chance; if nothing happens, end it.*

Millie knows Mother is right. She doesn't want to waste her time on someone who doesn't know what he wants. She deserves more than that. She needs to know if he likes her too.

"Here you go," Oliver says, handing her one of the roast duck sandwiches.

Millie takes a bite, and it is delicious. The duck skin is crispy, the flesh juicy, and there are julienned cucumbers and green onions in the sandwich that take it to a whole new level of freshness. "This is so good."

"Mmm. Oh yeah, good job, me," Oliver says, his mouth full.

Ugh, even when he talks with his mouth full, he's still so cute. Millie puts the sandwich down on her napkin.

"Uh-oh. What's wrong?"

She shakes her head. "Nothing." Can she say it? She can. Nope, she can't. "There's something I—" She chokes on the words and has to start over. "Oliver, I want to—" That came out sounding so wrong, and now Oliver looks worried, and can she blame him? Desperation catches hold of her, and she lifts her hand and places it woodenly on top of his. Oh god, this is painful.

Oliver looks down at his hand, then back up at her. Then realization dawns. Then, horrifyingly, horror appears on his face. Just for a split second, but still. Millie spots it and snatches her hand back.

"Millie—"

"Never mind," she says quickly.

"No, wait, I'm sorry. I didn't—"

"It's okay." She gathers her things. Her face is tingling, numb. She feels like she's been slapped.

"Wait, Millie. I'm so sorry. I thought we were just hanging out. As friends. I'm kind of clueless about these things, so, I'm sorry."

As friends? The words trigger something inside her, and suddenly, Millie is furious. Friends? She glares up at him. "How the hell can you possibly think we're just friends?"

Oliver's mouth drops open. "I don't know, I guess I assumed that anyone who wants to hang out with me wants to do so as a friend."

"What about Vera setting us up?"

Oliver winces. "Vera is always trying to set people up. It doesn't even matter who they are, as long as they're single, she will try to look for a partner for them. I—I'm sorry that you didn't know. I—she's tried to set me up with five people since I got to know her."

"I've been giving you all the signals!"

Oliver looks blankly at her, and Millie raises her hands before letting them drop limply by her sides. "So, you don't like me at all?" she says, not caring how desperate it makes her sound.

"I mean, I like you as a friend. I'm not looking for anything like that right now. I—and Millie, I'm like ten years older than you."

"So?" Since when is that an issue? None of the men she's dated ever complained about her being younger than them, and some of them are twenty years older than her.

"So . . . I don't know, it's kind of a big age gap. Look, I'm sorry. I didn't mean to take advantage of you like this, and I'm really sorry, Millie."

Tears sting the back of Millie's eyes. What's so wrong with her that he doesn't like her back? She hasn't been rejected in years. Mother's mantra has been tried and tested, and isn't that what every man wants—a young and vulnerable woman? She reaches out for Oliver's hand again. "It's okay if you didn't see me that way before. Maybe we can just have fun with each other. We're both single and lonely, right? What's wrong with taking pleasure in each other?" God, she sounds so desperate. She can't even tell right now if she actually wants to be with him because she really wants to or because it's what she thinks she should do. In the end, does the distinction between the two matter?

Oliver squeezes her hand before taking his away. "I'm alone, but I'm not lonely. And maybe you feel lonely, but you're not alone. You've got me, but more importantly than that, you've got Vera." He chuckles. "Vera will sort your life out, trust me. I was a mess when she found me, and I don't know how she did it, but whatever she did, it worked. Millie, you've got good people around you."

The kindness in his words only makes Millie feel even worse. Oliver isn't even interested in having a sexual relationship with her when she's practically offered it up to him on a silver platter. Has she lost it? Is she past her prime? Is she no longer young or vulnerable enough?

"Do you want me to take you home?" Oliver says.

Home. The thought of going back to Mother and Father right now makes Millie feel ill. They'll know. They'll see it on her face—she could never lie to them—and they won't be happy that she's wasted so much time with Oliver. A girl's worth, they always say, is in her youth. Once it's gone, the girl is worthless. Millie thinks about what they might do when they decide she's worthless, and her belly twists so hard that she almost pukes.

"Do you want to go to Vera's?"

She hears his voice from afar and feels herself nodding.

"Okay." Oliver begins packing everything up without complaint, and Millie feels another stab of guilt that he's gone to all this effort only for her to take one bite and then ruin everything. And he's done all this because he sees her as a . . . friend. Is this what friends do for each other? What a strange and alien concept.

They are silent on the car ride to Vera's. Millie keeps her gaze resolutely out of the window, and Oliver doesn't try to make conversation. When they get to Vera's, she jumps out of the car and rushes inside the shop without waiting for Oliver.

Vera is tending to customers inside the shop. "Oh, Millie. Just in time."

"In time for what?"

"Tea, of course. Silly girl. Sit." She peers out the window. "Is that Oliver with you?"

"Yeah," Millie says without looking. She hopes Oliver doesn't come inside.

"Oh, I guess he not coming in." Vera waves at the window, and Millie breathes a sigh of relief. Thank god for that.

She takes a seat at the remaining empty table and watches Vera pouring the tea for her customers. Something in the way Vera moves sets Millie's mind at ease. Her movements are slow and careful and gentle. The movements of a mom. Vera places a small teacup in front of Millie.

"Drink."

The tea is so bitter that Millie grimaces when it touches her tongue, but the next moment, it turns honey-sweet. She sighs, closing her eyes and sinking into the chair, letting the comforting taste of it cleanse her spirits. How does Vera know exactly what to give her? Millie stays like that for a long time, sipping tea and keeping her eyes closed. When she opens them, the customers have gone.

"What happen, Millie?" Vera says, sitting down across from her.

"What do you mean?"

"You look like sad person."

"That's kind of rude."

"Is it?" Vera takes a sip of her tea. "I know sad person because I use to be one. Also, Oliver text me and ask me to look after you."

Ugh. Somehow, knowing that Oliver did that makes it even worse. Now Millie feels nothing but animosity toward him. How could she ever think he was attractive? He's nothing but a wet, spineless mama's boy.

"I'm fine," Millie grumbles.

Vera looks like she's about to say something, but the doorbell tinkles and Aimes walks in. Vera's face brightens. "Aimes! Just in time for tea."

"Hey, Vera," Aimes says. "Sana and Julia mentioned how obsessed you are with protecting your skin from the sun. So look what I got you." She takes something out from her bag. It looks like a normal visor, but then she tugs at it and an entire face shield unfolds. "Tada! It's the latest visor design. It covers your entire face."

"Wah!" Vera cries, putting it on and admiring it.

Millie watches with a small prick of envy. She should've thought of getting something for Vera, especially since Vera has done so much for her. But, no, Millie is nothing but a selfish girl who only knows how to take and take and take. No wonder Oliver didn't want her.

"Hey, Millie, how's it going?" Aimes says, sliding into the seat next to her.

Millie blinks and gives herself a mental shake of the head. "Yeah, fine. You?"

"I'm . . ." Aimes takes a deep breath. "Not amazing, but I think I'll be okay." Biting her lip, Aimes gives Millie a small smile. "I have something to confess to you."

"To me?" Now Millie is thoroughly confused.

"Oh!" Vera says. "I just remember, need to take something from upstair. You girls talk, just ignore me." With that very fake-sounding announcement, Vera clomps up the stairs, leaving the two of them alone.

"Yeah, so . . ." Aimes licks her lips. "Um, Xander and I weren't really dating."

"What?"

"Our relationship was fake, all of it was made up for social media. He'd come over to my place once a week, and we'd work super efficiently and make a whole bunch of reels, and that was that. We didn't even hang out or anything. As soon as we were done, he was out the door."

Millie's head spins as she struggles to follow what Aimes is telling her. "But—I don't—what? So you're not his girlfriend?"

"No. Never was. I'm sorry I lied to you about it."

Millie shakes her head. "You don't owe me the truth. We barely know each other."

Aimes's expression is soft with sadness. "Yeah, I know. The truth is, I don't have that many friends, and you know what's funny, I never even realized it. I was living most of my life online, and online I've got a lot of followers and I considered them friends, but—ugh, I'm rambling. The other day, Vera got me to hang out with Sana and Julia—have you met Sana?"

Millie shakes her head.

"She's really great. So's Julia. I was spending time with them, and I realized that it's been forever since I did that. Just hung out with other women and do nothing but chat. It was so nice. And, um, this is going to sound like we're in kindergarten, but, um, I'd really like it if you and I could be friends too. We had fun at that influencer party, right?"

This is so far from what Millie has been expecting that for a moment, she can only sit there in stunned silence. Then Aimes's words sink in, and a lovely warm glow spreads from Millie's belly. A platonic friendship, pure and sweet. This, she realizes. This is exactly what she needs. A smile takes over her face and she nods. "Yes. I'd love that."

"Awesome."

Just at this moment, Vera bustles back down the stairs. Her timing is so impeccable that Millie has no doubt that Vera's been listening the entire time, waiting for the right moment to come back down.

"Ah," Vera calls out, "now we have kimchi cheese croissants."

Millie accepts a warm croissant and takes a small bite, watching Vera and Aimes dig in, chatting and laughing easily with each other. It's almost like watching a family sitcom, except somehow, Millie is in it. This is what a real family feels like. And she could be in it, as well. But only if she stops being Millie.

My name is Millie, her brain whispers. *My name is Millie.*

She grits her teeth so hard they clack. She's so tired of being Millie. The need to be part of Vera's family is so strong, so overwhelming. *It's impossible,* her mind whispers. *You can't. You don't belong. Go home. GO. HOME.*

The conversation stops abruptly, and Millie realizes she's just stood up so fast that her chair clatters to the floor. "I'm so sorry!" she says, bending over to pick up the chair. "Um. I have to go." Without waiting for a reply, Millie rushes out of the shop and runs all the way to the bus stop.

Her heart thunders at her and her blood roars in her ears. Why is life so unfair? Why couldn't she have a mother like Vera instead of the one she has now?

No. No use thinking like that. It won't change anything. She needs to go back and forget everything, leave Vera and that entire mess with Oliver behind. Yes. That is what she will do. That is the right choice. These are good people, and she needs to stay far, far away from them.

"My name is Millie," she whispers repeatedly, all the way

back, and each time she does, the name settles more firmly in her mind.

When she gets back, she creeps as quietly as she can into the building. The walls are thin here, and she does not want to alert Mother—

"You're home."

Millie jumps and turns around guiltily. Mother stands there next to Father. Oh god. She's told him. Of course she has. They're the perfect married couple. No secrets between them.

"Yes," she says meekly.

"How did it go?" Father says, his eyes glinting with eagerness.

It takes Millie a while to be able to swallow the knot in her throat so she can actually speak. "He's not right for me."

Displeasure tightens Mother's face. "How so?"

"Well. He's not interested in me." There. Simple as that. The truth.

"Impossible," Mother spits. "Why wouldn't he be interested in you? Look at you, you're beautiful."

Father nods, scratching his chin. "Did you do something wrong?"

"No! I did everything like you taught me." Only she doesn't know if she did; she had been so infatuated by Oliver that it had blinded her. She licks her dry lips. Please, please let them believe her.

"If you did everything I taught you, you would be in his bed by now," Mother says.

"We're disappointed in you, Millie," Father says.

Millie bows her head. "I'm sorry."

"We're disappointed in you because you lied to us."

Her head snaps up, horror dancing in her eyes. "I didn't—"

"You spent the day with that old woman," Mother says. "The tea shop owner."

"That wasn't—it was only an hour or two, and only because—"

"Shut up," Father says quietly. He never raises his voice, not even when he's angry, which somehow makes him all the more terrifying. "And listen to what you are going to do to make this up to us."

Millie shakes her head. "Please, don't. She's a poor old woman who lives on her own. I don't want to—"

"Want?" Mother says. "Since when does what you want matter, Daughter?"

Millie thinks of the sweet, warm laughter between Vera and everyone she knows. Normally, Millie would cower and say, yes, she'll do it, whatever they ask of her. But when she thinks of that moment back in Vera's teahouse and what Father and Mother want her to do to Vera, she can't bring herself to say yes. "I won't do it," she says.

Father and Mother exchange a glance. "Then maybe the time has come to teach you a lesson," Mother says. She reaches out for Millie.

There is only enough time for Millie to squeak, "No," before she is yanked forward, painfully, unforgivingly, and then she finds that she can't say anything at all.

TWENTY-ONE

VERA

What the fuck, Vera!" Selena snaps as she storms inside Vera's teahouse.

Vera gapes at her in shock and horror. "You talk to mother-in-law like that?"

"What?" Selena says. "You're not my—"

Tilly slides in front of Selena, standing between her and Vera. "Never mind that. Ma, Selena is just really worried about you. You didn't tell us about your shop getting vandalized. Oliver called and told Selena about it earlier."

"Yeah," Selena says, craning her neck to glare at Vera over Tilly's shoulder. "What the fuck? We've been over this, Vera. You're not a PI, and you can't let something like that go unreported. This is really dangerous. Someone out there wants to hurt you. How could you not tell us?"

Vera is still horrified by Selena's show of extreme disrespect—when Jinlong's parents were still alive, Vera had been the picture of perfect filiality. She practically bowed to them every time they spoke, and she never once called them by their names, never! It was always "Ma" and "Ba," and she spoke to them with the deference one kept for deities. And here is Selena shouting at her and saying "fuck" to her. Unheard of!

"Ma," Tilly pleads. "We're really concerned about your safety."

Vera gives herself a little shake, focusing on Tilly. "Don't be silly. Why you have to be concern? I am okay. I can take care of myself."

"You clearly can't," Selena says. "You need to come stay with us for a while, until we catch the perp who did this to your shop."

Ever since Tilly moved out, all Vera has ever wanted was to be invited to be a part of his life again. If anyone had told her last year that she would one day be invited to stay at his house by his girlfriend, she would've cried with joy. But now, all Vera can think of is *THE DISRESPECT!*

"No, thank you," Vera says icily.

Tilly closes his eyes for a moment. "Ma, I know you're angry right now, and we can absolutely talk about it, but for now, can we put that aside, and let's start packing your things, okay?"

Vera narrows her eyes at him. That's his lawyerly tone of voice that he uses when he speaks to a difficult client. He's trying to handle her. Hah, well, she'll show him that Vera Wong is unhandleable. "Thank you for kind offer, but no. I am able-body adult, I don't want to impose."

"You won't be imposing."

"You know what is imposing?" Selena says. "Imposing is you doing your own investigation into an ongoing case when you have no authority and no expertise, and then getting yourself tangled up in the mess."

"What you mean, no expertise? I solve Marshall Chen case,

didn't I? You all think his death is accident only, and if not for me, you would not have find out it is murder."

Selena takes a deep, frustrated breath. "Yes, and we thank you for your service, but that was just a one-time thing. You're not a trained detective, and I don't want to see you get hurt." The anger in Selena's voice gives way to sadness. "Vera, you mean so much to so many people. You take such good care of everyone around you. All I'm trying to do is convince you to take better care of your own safety."

The ice that has wrapped around Vera's heart thaws a little. She sniffs. "Hmph. Well, I appreciate that. But I don't want to stay with you."

"Ma, why not?" Tilly groans.

"Because, how you can have sexy time with me around?"

"Oh my god." Selena's hand flies to cover her eyes.

"Your new house is very nice, but is a bit small, and the walls are quite thin. I think you feel too self-conscious with me there to have sexy time—"

"Please stop saying 'sexy time,'" Tilly begs.

"And then how I get my grandbabies?"

Tilly and Selena gape at her in complete horror for a moment, then Tilly quickly turns to Selena and says, "Please ignore what my mom just said. I know you're not ready for kids, and I'm very happy to wait until—"

"What?" Vera squawks. "Not ready? Tilly, you how old? You think only women have ticking clock? Men also have ticking clock. Your sperm quality decrease as you age."

"Oh my god, please don't ever say the word 'sperm' to me again, Ma."

"Well, I am just telling you, I know many men think they can take it easy, unlike women, they don't have biology clock, but I am telling you, you do. And if sperm quality not good, then baby quality also won't be good. I want good quality grandbaby."

"Okay, maybe this conversation is no longer productive," Tilly says in his lawyer voice again.

"Don't worry about me, other people will come and take turn to stay with me. They sleep in your old room."

"Who?" Tilly says. "Oliver?"

"Well, Oliver's turn tonight, but last night was TJ and his daughter Robin, and night before was Aimes. See? I am in demand, I have revolving door."

"Nope," Selena says immediately, "that phrase does not mean what you think it means."

"Is mean I am popular."

"In a way," Selena says carefully.

"And Selena, you shouldn't be angry at me that I am investigating this case. I find out a lot of useful information about Xander Lin."

"Oh? Like what?"

Vera cocks her head to one side and gives Selena a sly look. Aha. She's about to start trading, and there is nothing Chinese mothers do better than trade information. "It depend on what you know about Xander Lin."

Selena's eyes bore into Vera's. Vera returns the hard look with her own piercing gaze.

"Well, we know that Xander Lin wasn't his real name," Selena says.

Vera throws her head back and cackles. "That old information? I know that from very beginning. His real name was Thomas."

Selena's eyes narrow. "And how do you know that?"

"I cannot say my sources."

"You know, this is getting real close to obstructing justice," Selena mutters.

"Is not," Vera says. "I know my rights." She doesn't. But she's hoping she looks like she does. Sometimes, looking like you know things is more important than actually knowing things.

"All right, Thomas what?"

"Ah, that I don't know. Okay, now you tell me what else you know."

"Honestly? Not much else. We've been slammed with other more pressing cases, and this one looks like a suicide, so I don't know why you're so intent on digging. There isn't much that's suspicious about it aside from not knowing his real identity and that shady bunch of people you found."

"Oh dear, and you still say you don't need my help? You clearly need all my help. And that 'shady' bunch of people are people who are connected to him."

Selena frowns. "No, they only appear connected to him."

"You mean Aimes pretending to be his girlfriend and TJ pretending to have close working relationship with him?"

"Yeah, and then that old dude—"

"Qiang Wen? He is Xander's grandfather."

Selena shakes her head. "Nope."

Now it is Vera's turn to stare. "What?"

"He's not his grandfather. I know it's what Xander posted online, but he isn't. They're not related. We've talked to Mr. Li Qiang Wen and confirmed it."

"WHAT?" Now Vera is angry. Apoplectic, actually. How many times has she spoken to Qiang Wen? How many chances has she given him to come out with the truth, and all this time, he's chosen to remain quiet? This is a betrayal of their deep, long-term friendship! Okay, maybe their friendship is neither deep nor long-term, but still!

"I think you might've just landed Mr. Li in deep shit," Tilly whispers to Selena.

Selena grimaces. "Sorry." Then she gives herself a little shake and goes, "Anyway, please just stop whatever you're doing, okay? The TikToks, the going to strangers' house parties . . . I was fine with you snooping until you pissed off the wrong people and endangered yourself."

"But is proof that I am on right path," Vera says. "Speaking of path, I am going to go for a walk now. You two leave and go have sexy time." She pushes them bodily out of the teahouse.

"Ma, don't do anything brash," Tilly says.

"And for the love of god, stop telling us to have 'sexy time,'" Selena adds. "And stop snooping."

"Yes, yes, my goodness you two are too young to turn into such nags." She locks up her shop. "Now stop worrying. Oliver will be here for dinner, he is big strong man."

They both raise their eyebrows. "We are talking about the same Oliver, yeah?" Selena says.

"Yes, Oliver Chen. Asian Thor."

"Oookay. Call us if anything happens. I mean it, Vera."

"When she is going to start calling me Ma?" Vera grumbles.

Tilly grabs Selena's shoulders and steers her away. "Okay, see you later, Ma!"

With an annoyed huff at their retreating backs, Vera starts marching down the street in the opposite direction with a strong sense of purpose. Elbows out, hands balled into fists, nostrils flaring. Fellow pedestrians who spot her in time scatter out of her path; the unfortunate ones who don't are barked at. As Vera marches, she thinks about all of the things she will say to Qiang Wen.

How could you betray our friendship?

Maybe that's a touch too dramatic, even for Vera.

You liar!

Hmm, has potential. But maybe the aggression is a bit high on that one.

Who are you, really? I don't even know you anymore.

She wishes she had more time to work on this, but already she finds herself just one block away from Qiang Wen's dumpling shop. Well, she'll just have to play it by ear.

She barges into the shop, startling two women who are lining up for their dumplings. "Qiang Wen! We need to—oh, sorry."

The two women gape at her. Behind the counter, Qiang Wen gapes at her. Vera gives the women a polite smile. "Sorry, I don't mean to cut queue. Which dumpling you getting? I recommend pork and chive one. Very juicy and flavorful."

"Um. That sounds good," one of the women says. "We'll get six of those, please. Thank you."

Vera watches, still wearing a polite smile, as Qiang Wen fills a plastic container with the dumplings. She notices with satisfaction how he darts little scared glances at her as he works. Good, he should be scared. The women pay for their order and leave, still throwing worried glances her way as they scuttle out the door. The moment the door swings shut, the smile falls from Vera's face, giving way to a truly impressive scowl.

"Qiang Wen!" she snaps, and Qiang Wen jumps. "You lie to me! You say Xander is your grandson, but he is not!"

She doesn't quite know what she was expecting from Qiang

Wen, but she definitely did not expect Qiang Wen to sag on his stool as though all of the energy has leaked out of his body. His head falls, and he mumbles, "In all the way that matters, he was my grandson."

He sounds so broken, so empty, that Vera can't help feeling strands of sympathy stirring within her. Argh! She is too soft-hearted, that's the problem. Jinlong used to say that to her. "You are too generous, too kind, too good. People will take advantage of you." Too good of a person, that is definitely Vera's problem. But, no, she must harden herself now.

"You best explain yourself to me. You owe me that much." Even as she says it, Vera thinks, *Does he?* He doesn't really owe her anything. But it sounded good coming out of her mouth, and Qiang Wen doesn't seem to have the wherewithal to refute her, so she decides she's glad that she's played that card.

"I will," Qiang Wen says. "Take a seat."

"This better be a good story."

Then Qiang Wen talks, and it is a good story. Because it is almost exactly like her own story.

TWENTY-TWO

QIANG WEN

Like Vera, Qiang Wen is an immigrant. And like Vera, his partner died over a decade ago—bone cancer. Unlike Vera, Qiang Wen's offspring has moved out of the Bay Area. "Too expensive, Ba. You should move too," she'd said. But he was too scared to leave Chinatown, and so he chose to stay put. He was fine, anyway. He had friends that he met up with twice a week to play mahjong, he did tai chi every morning, and he liked this part of the city.

The thing with being fine, though, is that when things change bit by bit, when life slides lemons to you in tiny little slices—like your mahjong buddies getting older and sicker one by one, so the mahjong sessions go from twice a week to once a week, then to every other week—it happens so slowly, so gently, that you don't realize it's happening until one day, there's no one left to play mahjong with. But because of the slowness of the deterioration, you don't realize that you're no longer fine. You continue thinking, *I'm fine*, and you keep chugging along even though the small speck of sadness in your heart has grown quietly into a boulder, without you even noticing. When your kids call, you tell them you're fine, and because they're busy and have a million things to do and you're just one of many things on their list they have to check off, they believe you.

Qiang Wen was fine. Everything was fine.

Then along came Xander. He wandered into the shop one morning, and they started chatting. Qiang Wen often chats with his customers; it's probably the best part of his job. But Xander was different. As they chatted, Qiang Wen recognized something in Xander. It was the way the corners of his mouth trembled ever so slightly when he smiled, like it took a lot of effort to keep the smile up. And that haunted, empty look in his eyes—Qiang Wen shivered. It was the same look he saw in the mirror every morning. The look of someone who had given up. And that was the moment Qiang Wen realized that he was far from fine.

Xander did not have enough money to pay for his dumplings, which was somewhat strange, given he was wearing nice clothes, but Qiang Wen didn't mind feeding him. They talked for nearly an hour that day, and Qiang Wen found himself telling Xander about his family and even showed Xander photos of them. Xander told him about his family back home in Indonesia. Then he glanced at the clock and jumped out of his seat, saying he had to go. After Xander left, Qiang Wen felt painfully empty. He shuffled about, doing mundane little tasks to keep his mind off the gaping hole in his heart. The thought pounded in his head: *I am not okay. Not okay. Not okay at all.* And he had no idea what to do about it. So there was nothing to do but keep puttering on as always.

A few days later, Xander came back. This time, he handed Qiang Wen a five-dollar bill. "For last time," he said.

Qiang Wen laughed and pushed the note back to him. "Keep it." Then he served up an assortment of his fattest dumplings.

They talked about everything. It had been a long time since Qiang Wen had held a conversation with someone who wasn't geriatric, and he found Xander's world really quite marvelous. Xander showed him the apps on his smartphone and helped Qiang Wen download a couple—a brain challenge game, which Xander said would be good for him, and TikTok, so he could entertain himself on slow days. He didn't tell Xander that every day was a slow day. The following weeks, Xander dropped by regularly, and Qiang Wen found himself looking forward to seeing him again. Whenever Xander's head popped into the shop, Qiang Wen got a joyous little glow, like the sun was shining directly on him.

And when Xander started to call him "Ah Gong," Chinese for "grandfather," Qiang Wen thought he might die of happiness. A grandson. A grandson who came to see him multiple times a week. A grandson whom he plied with food and fussed over and talked to.

Xander would take selfies with Qiang Wen and post them to his social media profiles with the caption "Hanging with my grandpa." And Qiang Wen could cry happy tears at how proud Xander was of their relationship. It was too good to be true.

Then, that horrible, earth-shattering day. The argument they'd had.

Qiang Wen did not tell anyone about this. What would he even say? He had a falling out with his only friend? What was he, twelve?

It wasn't until the police showed up at his shop that Qiang Wen found out the awful truth: Xander was dead. And Qiang Wen had to tell the cops that no, he wasn't Xander's grandfather. Yes, he knew that Xander was calling him that online, but no, there was no biological connection between them. And did he know that Xander wasn't his real name? No, he did not. Did he know Xander's real name? No.

It seemed that Qiang Wen knew very little about Xander after all, even though Xander knew practically everything there is to know about Qiang Wen.

"Did you give him any sensitive information, like your social security number or birth date or anything like that?" the police officer said.

Qiang Wen had told her no. It wasn't true, but what did it matter? Xander was dead. And one way or another, Qiang Wen would have to be fine, to keep going.

"Then you showed up," Qiang Wen says in Cantonese.

Vera has been listening with wide eyes, and when Qiang Wen says that, she lets out a heavy breath. "Oh, Qiang Wen. We crossed paths so many times. We stopped to say hi to each other once in a while, but why did we never talk, really talk?"

"Habit, I suppose."

"Yes, I think you're right. Stupid, stupid habit. We were both so lonely, we could've used a friend. But, no, we just remained in our little isolated circles, bumping everyone away." Vera gazes out the window, then turns back to him. "Well, never mind that. We're friends now, and friends tell each other the truth. Thank you for telling me the truth. But why didn't you tell me before?"

Qiang Wen looks down at his hands.

"Qiang Wen," Vera says. "What is it? What are you hiding?"

He can only shake his head, not able to trust himself to speak without bursting into sobs. "I'm sorry, Vera, I lied. I couldn't bear to face the truth."

After Vera's dramatic entrance earlier, he fully expects her to fly into a rage at this, but all she says is, "Ah, I thought so. Did he tell you he wanted to come clean about not actually being your grandson?"

Surprised, Qiang Wen nods. "How did you know?"

"He did the same thing with Aimes and TJ. And now I'm guessing he probably did the same thing with Millie too, but I haven't had a chance to speak to her. So. He wanted to tell everyone the truth. Why did that bother you?"

"It wasn't the fact that he was going to tell them we're not really related, it was . . . He was rambling, he was hardly making any sense. He kept saying he was leading a double life and he was tired of preying on people and—"

"Preying on people?" Vera says, sitting up. "Did he say how?"

"No. I asked him what he was talking about, and he said, 'It's safer for you if you don't know.' Seeing him like that, so scared, it made me scared too. I told him to please leave and take whatever dirty business he was involved in with him. He was as good as a grandson to me, but in his time of need, I turned him away." Qiang Wen moans. The truth is, the one who had betrayed the other was Qiang Wen and not Xander. "I tried contacting him after that. I regretted it almost immediately. But he never replied. I couldn't get ahold of him. And then the police came, and well, you know the rest."

"Preying on people," Vera muses. "He and Aimes were pretending to be a couple online. Could that be what he was talking about?"

"Pretending to be a couple online?" Qiang Wen tries to wrap his mind around that. "But why?"

"To get more likes. They could do cute little couple things for content."

Qiang Wen has no idea if that made any sense, but he nods and goes along with it. "I don't think it was that. He was really torn up about whatever it was. It sounded bad, like it was eating him up."

"I think you're right. The thing with Aimes is not wonderful, but it's not really the kind of thing that would bother someone like Xander too much, if he's okay with faking everything online."

"I didn't know he was faking everything online."

"Oh yes, everything. Many of the images were photoshopped, made it look like he was at some parties when he wasn't. I'm not sure if he did that with every party he pretended to have attended— no, he must have gone to a few of them, otherwise people would've noticed. Anyway, yes, he faked a lot of things online."

"What?" A deep sorrow stabs into Qiang Wen. Can it be true that he knew so very little about Xander? And why? Why would Xander have hidden so much from him? He should've known that Qiang Wen wouldn't mind, wouldn't have judged him. Again and again, Qiang Wen is realizing that he's failed Xander in so many different ways.

"You can't blame yourself," Vera says, reading his mind. "You were lost and so was he, from the sounds of it. And so was I, in fact. We were all just groping around in the dark, trying to find our way out of the tunnel. You did the best you could. You provided him with a safe place to go to and good food to eat."

Qiang Wen nods, sniffling. He takes some time to gather himself before asking, "What are you going to do now?"

"Well, I need to speak with Millie and ask her if Xander came to her about doing some sort of exposé."

"Millie is the only one of us who knew him as Thomas," Qiang Wen points out. "Maybe that means she knew him better than any of us."

"Good point. I think Millie definitely knows something. Ah, don't you worry, I'll get it out of her. There is no one as good as me when it comes to interrogation."

"I believe you." And he does. He's beginning to learn that life gets much easier when you hand over the reins to Vera.

TWENTY-THREE

VERA

Hi Millie, this is Vera Wong from Vera Wang's World-Famous Teahouse. How are you doing? Please call me back when you have chance. Kind Regards, Vera.—3:30 p.m.

Hi Millie, this is Vera Wong again. I'm not sure if you remember me, but I have a nice little teahouse in Chinatown and you been there a few times. Well you probably remember me. You must be busy, young people nowadays always so busy, but if you have chance, please call me. Kind Regards, Vera.—3:42 p.m.

Hi Millie, this is Vera again. I forgot that young people really don't like to make the phone call, so please ignore my last message. You can just send message back, no need to make the phone call. Kind Regards, Vera.—3:57 p.m.

Hi Millie, this is Vera. Seems like you have very busy day, but Tilly tells me if the ticks on the messages turn blue is mean the messages are read. I can see the ticks have turn from gray to blue, so I know you read my messages, which is good. I hope you having a nice day. I just have a question to ask you about

Thomas, so let me know when we can meet up. Kind Regards, Vera.—5:18 p.m.

Hi Vera, what was the question you wanted to ask about Thomas?—5:18 p.m.

Hi Millie, this is Vera. So good to see your reply! Your day is going well? Very busy? Kind Regards, Vera.—5:23 p.m.

Yeah, busy. So what was the question you wanted to ask?—5:24 p.m.

Hi Millie, Vera again. I think is better if we meet in person to talk about Thomas. I have learn quite a bit about him, is very hard to explain over WhatsApp. I am so old, my thumbs move very slowly on phone screen. I know Julia always say to me, 'Vera, you are not old. Sixty is the new forty.' But I think sixty is venerable old age, you agree right? Anyway, when you can come to tea shop? Kind Regards, Vera.—5:31 p.m.

I don't think I'll be able to for a while, so you need to tell me over text. If it's hard for you to type, then maybe you can send a voice note.—5:32 p.m.

What is voice note? Kind Regards, Vera.—5:35 p.m.

Oh, sorry I forget to say above, this is Vera. In case you don't know.—5:37 p.m.

What have you learned about Thomas?—5:38 p.m.

Sorry Millie, my arthritis acting up, I cannot play on phone too long. Will figure out this voice note thing and get back to you.—5:42 p.m.

Vera, please tell me what you found out about Thomas.—5:42 p.m.

Vera?—5:43 p.m.

TWENTY-FOUR

MILLIE

The door to her room bursts open. Mother and Father stand there, looking mutinous. Millie wishes she were the type of person who could act aloof, pretend that everything is okay, but she isn't. She's the type of person who cowers very visibly.

"What did you tell that old bitch?" Mother says.

It takes Millie a beat to realize she's referring to Vera, and something inside her turns sour at having Vera being referred to as a "bitch." Vera is the opposite of a bitch, and anyway, Millie hates that word so much. "I didn't tell Vera anything," she says in a small voice.

"Don't lie to us, you little bitch," Mother says.

Millie cringes. They always call her that when they're displeased with her. In the early days, they called her that all the time, and her older sister Yara had told her that it was because Mother and Father wanted to break her. Millie misses Yara so much. *Don't let them break you,* Yara's voice whispers in her head.

"Stop calling me that," she whispers.

"What did you say?" Father says.

A braver person would have screamed it at them. But Millie is so tired and hungry and so goddamn scared. She shakes her head. "Nothing."

"No, it wasn't nothing," Father says, walking toward her.

Millie hugs her knees to her chest, wishing for the millionth time that she could disappear. "I'm sorry," she blurts out before he gets to her. She always breaks before they can punish her even more. Yara was the fighter. She fought until she disappeared from Millie's life. Thomas was more like Millie, pliant and soft.

Father towers over her like a god. She sneaks one quick glance up before lowering her head. "I'm sorry," she says again. He grunts. Relief floods her. He's accepted her apology, for now.

Then Mother says, "We found your phone, Millie."

Oh no. Fear stabs into Millie's stomach, cold and sharp. The back of her neck prickles with sweat. Her phone. Her secret phone. How cunning she'd thought she was being when she bought it, but of course when Mother and Father confiscated her bag, they'd found it. *Stupid girl*, she scolds herself. Thomas would've never made that mistake. Her brother and sister were so much smarter than she was, and look what happened to them. Why did Millie ever think she could get away with this?

Father bends down so his face is level with Millie. She shrinks back. "Haven't we been clear about the rules of the house?"

Millie nods.

"Never mind that for now," Mother says brusquely. "We'll deal with your deception later. What does this Vera bitch know about Thomas?"

This time, Millie doesn't even try to fight them. She shakes her head vigorously. "Nothing. I promise. All she knows is that he jumped off the bridge. That's all."

"Then why is she saying that she's found out some information about him and needs to talk to you?"

There is a sliver of a second of confusion and hope—did Vera solve it after all? Then Father's hand shoots out, and before Millie knows it, he's grabbed her by the hair. Pain sears through her scalp, and she squeals. Vaguely, she spots someone's head popping through the doorway. Her little sister, Mina. Millie wants to tell Mina to go away. She shouldn't be seeing this. Then Father yanks and Millie forgets all about Mina. All she can do is squawk and flail in pain.

"We're going to have to clean up your mess, Millie," Mother says. "We're very disappointed in you. Do you understand?"

Gripping Millie's shoulder tight, Father gives her an unforgiving shake. Millie wonders if her neck is about to snap. She doesn't want to die. Despite everything, she wants to live. "I'm sorry!" she manages to gasp out. "Sorry, sorry!" He releases her so suddenly that she thumps onto the floor, out of breath, her face wet with tears and snot.

"We're gonna have to take care of this Vera, thanks to you," Mother says.

No, not Vera. Vera's warm laugh echoes in Millie's head, and she scrambles to Mother on her hands and knees. "Don't do anything to her. Please!" She grabs hold of Mother's feet. "I'm sorry, I'll do anything you want."

"You should've thought of that before involving her." Mother steps back.

"Mother, no!"

"Stop all this screaming," Mother snarls. "You'll wake your siblings up, you selfish little brat."

"Please, Mother!"

Father grabs her by the hair again and flings her backward as though she were a doll. Millie crashes into the wall and the breath is punched out of her. By the time she manages to peel herself off the floor, Father and Mother have stormed out, slamming the door shut. She runs toward the door, but it's locked. Of course it is. She pounds on it. "Leave her alone!" she shrieks.

Mother's voice comes through the door. "Millie, if you do not behave, we will have to fix you, do you understand?"

A promise. She knows Mother always follows through on her promises. Millie slides down to the floor sobbing. Yara had fought too. She remembers all the screaming, all the shouting. She remembers hearing Mother say those exact same words to Yara right before Yara left. One day, Yara was in the room next to hers, and the next day, there was Thomas. Thomas never met Yara, though Millie told him all about her.

Millie doesn't know how long she stays on the floor crying. It feels like forever. She runs out of tears at some point; she's so thirsty. Father and Mother have been sliding in just one glass of water every morning. "A kindness," Mother had said, and Millie was so stupidly grateful every time the glass of water appeared. Now she's cried and sweated and struggled so much that she feels like a desiccated corpse. She pulls herself up. She needs to warn Vera somehow. But how? Her phone is gone. The window in her room is much too small for her to climb through. She goes to it anyway and gazes out longingly. When she first arrived here, she spent many hours just looking out the window, searching for stars to wish on. Her reflection on the window catches her eye. Millie studies it.

For once, she doesn't have makeup on. Her face is red and blotchy and her hair is a mess, but she sees herself. "My name is Millie," she whispers. "My name is . . ."

Her face scrunches up and tears slide down her cheeks again. "Fuck you," she tells her reflection. "Fuck Millie. My name is Penxi!" She screams it. "My name is Penxi!"

There is a knock on the wall. Mina's voice, small and scared, comes through a hole. "My name is Channary."

Millie shuts her eyes, crying. "Hi, Channary."

"Hi, Penxi. It's Mina, by the way."

A laugh burbles out of Millie's mouth. "I know."

"But my name is actually Channary."

"It's a beautiful name."

"It's Cambodian. That's where I'm from. I don't think I ever told you that before."

Millie goes to the wall and places her hand there. "I'm from China."

"America isn't really like how I thought it would be."

"Well. This part of it isn't. But there are parts that are like a dream."

"Next week is my twelfth birthday. I was kind of hoping I would be able to celebrate it like American kids do, but I guess that's not something Mother and Father do, huh?"

So young. Too young. Millie rests her forehead against the wall. "You shouldn't be here. None of us should be here."

God, eleven. Despair threatens to swallow her whole. There is so much emotion surging through her. She needs to let something out before she bursts apart like an overripe fruit.

Millie goes to her desk and takes out a pen and paper. She sits down and takes a shuddery breath. Then she begins to write.

Dear Vera,

You know me as Millie, but my real name is Lin Penxi. I am from Yunnan, China. When I was twelve, I left my family farm and moved to Shanghai to live with my aunt, where I had hoped to become a star. Ridiculous dream, I know that now. But Shanghai has so many talent shows, and there are so many kids who do make it big, so I didn't think it was that ridiculous at the time. Anyway, I was auditioning for one of these shows when I met a man—he told me to call him Uncle Yang. I don't know his real name. Uncle Yang told me that American talent shows are where it's at, and I would be wasting my talent here in Shanghai. It all sounded too good to be true. And it was.

My parents aren't well educated. They were just as starstruck as I was when I called to tell them that Uncle Yang wanted me to go to America. He even paid them a fee. Isn't that amazing? I begged them to let me go, and they did. Papers were signed, Uncle Yang got me a passport, and before long, I was on my way to America. I should've known that things were wrong during the journey there. We went on an airplane at first, which was fine. There were seven other kids and teens with me. We were all very excited. But then we stopped off somewhere, I don't know where, and we were herded out of the airplane and led to a ship. Some of the teens asked why we were getting on a ship instead of flying to America, and Uncle Yang told them to shut up. That scared me, because up until then, Uncle Yang had been so nice to us.

The journey by sea took a very long time. Some of us got seasick. I was one of the ones who didn't, so I spent my time rushing back and forth, fetching water for the poor kids and cleaning up their vomit. The crew didn't seem to care very much at all about the sick kids.

Then at some point, we were taken from our rooms and marched into a shipping container. That was when the older kids started shouting. This teenaged boy named Ming struggled and fought, and one of the crew members hit Ming in the head so hard that he vomited. Most of us lost our fight then.

I don't know how long we spent inside the shipping container. It felt like it was never going to end. I was in some kind of daze when the ship docked; I could hear horns and other noises and I sat up. Then there was this monstrous noise and the container jerked to one side suddenly. We screamed and fell. I was sure we were going to die then and there. I clung to the floor as the container swung one way, then it clanged to the ground. I guessed then that they had moved us off the ship and onto the dock. Hours crawled by and nothing happened. We called out, shouting, though to be honest, none of us had much energy by then. The container smelled so, so bad. There were no toilets in there, you know. I can still smell it even now, more than ten years later.

I was half asleep when the doors were finally opened. Flashlights shone at us, blinding me. I sat up, confused, and a pair of strong hands grabbed me under my armpits and lifted me bodily into the air. I screamed and kicked, and something was placed over my mouth and nose. It smelled sharp, and it hit immediately, like a thick fog had suddenly settled over my brain. Then my head dropped forward and all went black.

When I woke up, I found myself in what is now my current bedroom. Two people—a man and a woman—were looking down at me.

"Hello, Millie," the man said. He had a kind voice. Reassuring.

I blinked up at them, my thoughts a blur. I knew some English then, enough to know that he was greeting me as Millie. The mistake actually gave me some comfort, because it proved that there had been some silly mistake, and once they knew I wasn't Millie, then everything would be put right. I was very stupid. "My name is Penxi," I said.

"That is very hard for Americans to pronounce," the woman said. She had yellow hair, like in the movies. I thought she looked very pretty.

"I'm sorry," I said, feeling bad about having a hard-to-pronounce name.

"That's all right, dear," the woman said. "But we've come up with a new name for you that we'd like you to remember."

"Millie," the man said. "It suits you, don't you think?"

"I don't understand," I said.

"It's okay," the man said. "We'll explain everything to you. We're very good at explaining things."

I just stared up at them, scared and confused and hungry and all sorts of other emotions swirling through me in a mess. "I want my mama," I said, and began to cry.

"Oh, my sweet child, I'm here," the woman said.

"No, I want my real mama."

"That's me, Millie. I'm your real mama. You must call me Mother from now on. And this right here is Father. We are your parents now."

I started crying harder, and Mother's face turned from gentle to something else. Something that scared me.

"Millie," she said, "I don't like the way you're behaving. Please stop making a fuss."

I tried to stop crying, I really did, but that only made me sob even more. And before I knew it, Mother had grabbed me by the arm and yanked me off the bed. Father caught my other arm, and together, they dragged me out of the room. We went down a long hallway—I dimly realized that we were in some kind of warehouse that had been converted into a living space of sorts. We passed by many rooms, all of them with the doors closed. Later, I would come to find out that these rooms were occupied by Father and Mother's other "children." People like me, who had been stolen from various countries and sold to Father and Mother. They became my brothers and sisters. They were from all over the world. I had an older sister Yara, who was from Russia, and an older brother Jeffrey from Nigeria, and there was Thomas, of course, who was from Indonesia, and now I have a younger sister from Cambodia. Mother and Father named her Mina, but I have just learned that her real name is Channary, which I think is really very beautiful. I wonder what Yara's, Jeffrey's, and Thomas's real names were.

Anyway, I am digressing because I don't want to revisit the memory of my first day here. But I will tell you, Vera, because you deserve to know the truth about how I became who I am now. You once said scammers are the lowest of bottom feeders, and I was so sad when you said that. I agree with you, Vera, I hate scammers too. But the truth is, I am a scam artist. So *were Thomas and Yara, and Channary is well on her way to becoming one as well. I hate that this is what we do, but we don't have a choice. Father and Mother made that very clear that first day when they held down my head in a bath full of water as I screamed and thrashed around. Water surged up my nose, down my mouth, choking me. I thought I was surely going to die. Then they pulled me up and said, "This is what happens to disobedient children. Do you understand?"*

I could only gasp for air like a fish out of water, and Mother snapped, "Do you understand, you little bitch?"

"Yes!" I cried. "My name is," I said slowly, "Millie."

A smile spread across Mother's face. She looked beautiful when she smiled like that. "Good girl." She patted my cheek. "Good, sweet Millie."

"Phew!" Father said cheerfully. "I could use some lunch after that. I bet you're hungry too, huh, Mills?"

"We've got a nice treat for you today. A welcome-to-America feast," Mother said. She raised her eyebrows. "McDonald's!"

I liked McDonald's. In my village back in Yunnan, there were no McDonald's, but there were a few in Shanghai, and I'd had the good fortune of having chicken nuggets from there once. They were delicious. And this was how Mother and Father broke me. Over the next few weeks, they punished me severely if I ever forgot to respond to the name Millie, until the name buried itself so deeply within my bones that I forgot my real name. Even in my dreams, people would call me Millie. Then, when they were sure that my old name and identity had been completely scrubbed from my mind, they began the lessons.

The first, and most important, lesson was learning English. I enjoyed this, actually, because a big part of it was watching American TV shows. I would be put in a room with a few other kids, and there, we would watch hours of random old shows like Friends and The Simpsons. It was the best part of my early days there. There were actual lessons too, of course, classes taught by Father where he went over the rules of grammar and tested us on our vocabulary and all sorts. He also glossed over a few other subjects like math and geography and history, because "You can't be a scam artist if you're an idiot." We didn't need to be scholars, but we had to know enough about American culture and history to be convincing.

The second lesson was with Mother, and this had to do with how to carry myself. "Young and vulnerable," she trilled. "This is how we like our girls here." She taught me how to stand, how to walk, even how to breathe.

The third lesson was about human interaction. "You're salespeople," Mother said. "You're trying to sell a product to them. You need to know how to hook their interest, keep it, and use it to your advantage. Sell the product."

"What is the product?" I can hear you asking, Vera. Well, the product depends on the kid. Thomas was your standard phone scammer. And here I can imagine you humphing with displeasure. I know, I know. You fell for a phone scam, and I hate the thought of it, Vera. I hope you know that. And I hope you know that Thomas did not have a choice. Father hated Thomas, I don't know why. He took every excuse he could get to beat the crap out of Thomas. We all have quotas to meet every month, and if we don't meet them, then we are starved or beaten or locked in our rooms for days. So that was

Thomas. He'd phone people and tell them the same thing you were told, that your credit card was used by someone else to make some extravagant online purchase. Or he'd phone people and tell them they're late on some government payment and now they've missed enough funds for them to lose their homes. Things like that. All of them despicable lies. Some of my brothers and sisters lost a bit of their humanity after a few years doing this. Some of them started to enjoy it, to see their victims as nothing but marks, but Thomas was never like that. He actively hated it, continued seeing his victims as people he was having to take advantage of, and he was angry at everything up until the day he died.

As for me, Mother got me to work on email scams until I was fourteen, then she said my voice sounded grown-up enough to start working the phones, so I was moved to that. Then, when I was sixteen, she said, "Would you like to start going out, Millie?"

I was so surprised. Up until that point, I wasn't allowed to leave the warehouse. Some of us were. My older sister Yara was one of them. She'd dress up all pretty—she was so beautiful, blond hair, big green eyes, and so tall and graceful—and she'd go out on what I imagine were very glamorous dates. I was so jealous of her. I was still a stupid kid then. What can I say? So when Mother asked me that, I immediately said, "Yes!" I had no idea what was in store for me.

So Mother taught me the new product: me. She'd prepared me, all this time, for this very moment. I just didn't know it yet. But I had been kept on a very strict diet and taught how to hold myself a certain way and to do my makeup in a very specific way, and Mother gave me all these

pretty clothes, and when she was done, I looked into the
mirror and was shocked at what I saw.

"You're beautiful, Millie," Mother said, and I hope it
doesn't make me sound arrogant to say that I agreed with her.

She uploaded my photos onto dating apps and filled out
my data for me. She registered me as a nineteen-year-old so
that I would be allowed to date any man. And she gave me a
script. We always had a script, whether it's for emails, phones,
or in-person scams. I was Millie, a student at Cal whose
major was undecided. I liked dating older men because boys
my age were hopeless. I was to be fun and must be a very
good listener, and then after a few dates, I would have some
kind of catastrophe: my dad got cancer, or the university
canceled my funding, or this and that. Basically, I would have
to be on the verge of losing my spot at Cal, and I really
needed some money quick.

The first guy I dated ghosted me as soon as I tried pulling
the scam, and that got me locked in my room for three days.
When Father and Mother let me out, they hugged me and
said, "Poor Millie." Then they gave me a treat—more
McDonald's. Break me, then soothe me, remember? It really
is a very good strategy on their part. I was scared of them and
grateful to them in equal measure. They then sat me down
and we had a debriefing session, where they went over
everything I did wrong.

The second guy I went out with, I managed to get seven
thousand dollars from. Mother and Father were so happy.
Father actually got a bit teary-eyed. They gave me more
McDonald's and told me they were proud of me. I was so
happy to have made them proud. And this became my

twenty-four-seven job. In order to meet my new monthly quota, I dated so many men, as many as five at a time, juggling them carefully so they would never guess that the sweet, attentive girl they were seeing was seeing multiple people at once. Not all of the scams were successful, of course, but enough were to make Mother and Father happy.

Here, I can feel you wondering how far did I go with these men to get money out of them? I don't think you'd want to know the answer to that, Vera. I'll say this much: I would have done anything to not be locked in my room for days with a bucket.

And now, I can sense you wondering, Why didn't I run away? I could get out, surely I could've gone to the police station and reported Mother and Father.

Aha. Well, here's where I tell you that Mother and Father are extremely clever people. They don't work alone. They're part of an international organization. Uncle Yang is just one of their many, many contacts. And with each child they bought, Mother and Father made sure that they always had something over the child. They told me that if I ever made the mistake of running away, that Uncle Yang would call up his friends and have my parents killed. That's the thing with all of us kids, we were all in this situation in the first place because we were all from impoverished families. None of our families had any connections. We were the children of farmers or sweatshop workers or street urchins. It would've been far too easy for Uncle Yang to have my parents killed. A pair of poor farmers in a tiny village in Yunnan? Nobody would give a shit.

Then, *after killing our parents, Father and Mother would hunt us down—and make no mistake about it, they would find us, no matter where we hid—and they would make an example out of us. My sister Yara, did I mention that she was a fighter? She ran away. I thought she'd made it out safely, but about a week later, Father and Mother came back to the warehouse and tossed something on the dining table. It was Yara's necklace. I was there, doing the dishes, and a couple other kids were there as well, cleaning up. Father and Mother made sure we'd all seen the necklace before they said, "Well, that was a shame. All that time and money we spent on her."*

I thought of my beautiful sister Yara, and I went on doing the dishes, but my hands were shaking too hard and I smashed one of the glasses. Earned myself twenty-four hours of being locked up in my room.

The other thing that Father and Mother often reminded us, as though all the threats weren't enough, is "You are all illegal aliens in America. There is nothing we hate more here than illegal immigrants. Not to mention the fact that you're not just illegal immigrants but criminals as well. If you go to the police, they will arrest you."

So. Now do you see why I didn't just escape? I had nowhere to escape to, and although I knew the cops would arrest Mother and Father if they knew about their operation, I was also convinced that I would be arrested as well. Especially since Mother and Father documented all of my scams. Not to mention my countless victims, who would only be too happy to testify against me. I would rot in prison as a scam artist, and rightfully so, I guess. But maybe all of this is just an excuse to avoid facing the truth, which is that I am a coward, Vera. I have forgotten the faces of my parents, and I'm sure that by now they have assumed that I died and moved on with their lives. I hope they have, anyway. Sometimes, in the very early mornings, when I wake up and I am in that state between sleeping and waking, I think, I'm home with Mother and Father. Sometimes I forget, you see, that they are not my real parents. Sometimes it's hard to remember what life was like before I came here.

Oh, Vera, I'm sorry this letter is so long. I didn't mean to ramble on and on the way I did here. Meeting you was the best thing that has happened to me in America. I remember that day so clearly. After Thomas disappeared, I thought that maybe there was a way that I could report it to the police without exposing myself and my other brothers and sisters. But every possible story I came up with felt so flimsy. I had no idea if Thomas was okay, maybe he'd made it out, maybe he managed to outsmart Mother and Father, or maybe not. That was why I was loitering outside of the police station that day. I was so scared and had no idea what was the right thing to do. I thought maybe I should just turn myself in, consequences be damned. If you hadn't found me, I would've probably given up and gone back to the warehouse. But you did find me, and you whisked me off to your magical little teahouse, and Vera, I need you to understand how much everything you've done meant to me.

I think I am going to die here. I have gone against Mother and Father in a way that is simply unforgivable, and I think they no longer trust me to behave myself, and when a child loses Father and Mother's trust, that child is no longer a useful product. They will discard me the same way they discarded Thomas and Yara and Jeffrey and probably others I don't know about. I've accepted it. But what I can't accept is what they might do to you, and all because of me. If I were less selfish, I would wish that I had never met you, but I am selfish, so I'm glad that I got to know you, but now you're in danger because of me, and I am locked up in this room.

I'm so sorry, Vera.

With love,
Penxi

TWENTY-FIVE

VERA

It's been quite a busy day for Vera, so busy in fact that she hasn't had time to think about Millie's strange texts. It was a good day, all in all. Her customers were a pleasant crowd, some of them regulars, the rest of them newcomers who heard about her from social media, and all of them were curious and respectful and wanted her to serve them tea based off her intuition, which is exactly how tea should be served—hot with a side of judgy but also motherly advice from Vera. Later tonight, Aimes will come over and spend the night here again, just so Vera isn't alone. Vera rather likes having people staying over at her house. Makes for a really nice change.

She's just drying the last of the teacups when there is a loud crash and the shop window seems to explode. A shard of glass whizzes across her forehead and she doesn't even feel it slice into her skin, but a moment later her vision is darkened by blood.

"Oh," she says. Stunned would be an understatement. Vera puts the dish drying rag to her forehead as the door flies open.

In walks the largest man she has ever seen in real life. He's so tall that he actually has to lower his head as he enters, and seeing his hulking figure in her tiny shop brings the phrase "a bull in a china shop" to mind.

"My window seems to have broken," Vera says. It is possible she might be somewhat shell-shocked.

"That would be because of the brick I flung through it," the man says.

"I see." She can't help but shrink back as the man advances toward her. His gray eyes regard her in a cold, detached way. The kind of look a predator would give to its prey. "What do you want?"

"You've been snooping around, sticking your nose where it doesn't belong," he growls. "You need to stop."

This is actually a scenario that Vera has fantasized about, strangely enough. In her fantasies, a generic bad guy would storm into her teahouse, maybe to rob her or something or other, and through her wit and charm and motherly kindness, she would help him see the error of his ways. She would then brew some tea for him, and they would talk about where he went wrong in his life and how he can fix it, and over the years, he would come to see her as his mom and attribute every good thing in his life to Vera.

But real life is nothing like fantasy, and Vera finds that there is no wit or charm or motherly advice in her right now. All there is, is sharp animal terror. Her entire body shakes with it. "Okay," she says. So simply, just like that, she's rolled over and given in.

"And nothing happened here, you understand? We know where you live. We know where that cute little kid and the single mom live. Don't fuck with us." And with that, he storms out.

Vera sags against the wall, her breath coming out in a ragged whoosh. Dear Goddess of Mercy, did that really just happen? It was much less exciting and much more terrifying than she had expected. And now that the immediate shock and adrenaline rush is dying down, she can feel the painful cut on her forehead, and my goodness, it hurts.

"Aiya, Vera, are you okay?" someone cries.

"Winifred," Vera says, still breathing hard.

"Ah! Your head! Come, sit down. Aiya." Winifred helps Vera onto a chair. "Let me take a look."

Vera winces as Winifred moves her hand aside.

"That will need stitches. I'll call Tilly. Or maybe you need an ambulance?"

"Too expensive," Vera says.

Winifred nods and calls Tilly, filling him in on what's happened. All Vera can think is *That man knows where Emma lives.*

"Tilly will be here right away," Winifred says. "What happened?"

"Someone threw a brick into my window. You didn't hear it?"

Winifred shakes her head, and Vera is glad that Winifred is hard of hearing. Hopefully it means that Winifred didn't see the man come into Vera's teahouse. He knows where Emma lives. Vera is going to have to step very, very carefully.

"Does this have to do with the death you're investigating?" Winifred says.

"Maybe," Vera mutters.

"Vera, you need to stop snooping. You're in danger! Oh, you poor thing."

Winifred heats up some water, pours it into a bowl, and dips a clean napkin into it. "Let me clean you up a little, you look like a scene from a horror movie."

Vera's thoughts are a mess as Winifred dabs at her face. And soaring above the messy swirl is the awful thought that keeps pulsing at her: *They know where Emma lives.* The thought overwhelms her and she grabs her phone. She dials Julia's number.

"Hey, Vera, what's up?"

"Julia, you listen to me. You take Emma with you and get out of home. Go stay with Oliver."

"Uh. What's going on?"

"Just listen to me."

In the background, Vera can hear Emma's voice going, "Is that Grandma?" Vera takes in a shuddery breath. Oh, Emma.

"Are you caught up in something bad?" Julia says in a low voice. "Have you told Selena? Does this have something to do with that dead guy you're looking into?"

"Julia," Vera snaps. "Just listen to me and go, okay?"

Julia sighs. "Okay. For how long though?"

"I don't know. But I will fix somehow."

Winifred is staring at her with wide eyes as she hangs up the phone. "What did she say to you?" she says in Mandarin.

"None of your business." She feels sorry for being so rude to Winifred, but she has no choice.

"Aiya! Look at you with blood pouring out of your head and me cleaning you up, literally cleaning up your mess, and you're telling me it's none of my business?"

Vera opens her mouth to argue, but just then, the door swings open and Tilly and Selena rush in.

"Oh my god, Ma!"

Selena takes one look at Vera and says, "We should get her to the hospital right now."

They help Vera to her feet and lead her out of the teahouse. As Vera settles into the back seat of Selena's car, she gazes out the window at her teahouse. Winifred stands at the door, wringing her hands.

"Don't worry, I will lock up the shop," Winifred calls out.

The shop, which has been Vera's refuge for so long, no longer feels safe. She feels exposed, her every step watched. She sinks deeper into the seat, wondering if she'll ever feel safe again.

The wound requires five stitches. Not too bad, all in all.

"It's not actually too deep," the doctor who stitches her up says. "Head wounds tend to show a lot of blood, so I know it looked alarming, but I think you're going to have minimal scarring."

Vera thanks him and sits there quietly for a bit, trying to gather her thoughts. Tilly is holding her hand and looking at her with such concern that she feels like a little kid. They drive home in silence.

Winifred has kindly swept away all of the broken glass on the floor, but still the shop feels cold and soulless, as though whatever friendly spirits had been there before have been scared away.

"I'll help you pack your things," Tilly says, helping her up the stairs. Vera doesn't bother arguing with him this time.

When they finally get back to Tilly and Selena's house, Vera feels like she's aged by a decade. She has always enjoyed telling people she is a helpless old woman, but it is only now that she realizes what being a helpless old woman really feels like. She sits at the dining table and stares at her hands while Tilly cooks dinner and Selena gets the guest bedroom ready. He puts a big bowl of beef noodle soup in front of her.

"Here you go, Ma." He sits next to her, and Selena on her other side, and they dig into the food.

Vera takes a small bite, then a bigger one. "This is very good."

Tilly smiles. "You taught me how to make it, remember?"

"He has pots of homemade broth in the freezer," Selena says.

Pride blooms in Vera's chest, then quickly deflates when she recalls the horrible thought: *That bad man knows where Emma lives.*

Seeing the change in Vera's expression, Selena puts her chopsticks down. "Okay, Vera, you've got to tell us what happened. Winifred said it was a hate crime. Did you see who did it?"

"I think we should give her some space," Tilly says.

Selena's mouth turns into a thin line. "Sorry. I just—this feels targeted. Especially taking into account the vandalism only a short while ago."

Vera shakes her head. "I don't know who did it. I didn't see."

Selena gives her a sharp look, and Vera's scalp tingles. Selena is way too good at sensing bullshit.

"Why do I feel like you're hiding something from me?" Selena leans forward. "Vera, if you know why this happened, you need to tell me right away. You were just assaulted, and—"

"Hey, come on," Tilly says, and now there's an edge in his voice. "Give her a break, okay?"

"I'm trying to help her."

"You're badgering her, so back off."

"Badgering?" Selena says. "Don't use your lawyer speak on me."

"Don't act like a cop with my mom."

Oh no. Things have gone very, very wrong. "Stop arguing," Vera says.

"We're not arguing," Tilly snaps.

"I'm gonna go for a jog," Selena says, standing up abruptly.

Tilly rests his forehead on his hand as Selena leaves the table. Vera wishes she could disappear. What just happened? The argument started so quickly that she needs to replay it in her mind to catch up. The front door slams shut, making Vera jump.

"I'm sorry I cause trouble with you and Selena."

"It's fine." Tilly sighs and picks up his chopsticks, gesturing at Vera to do the same. Then he lowers his chopsticks again. "Well, actually though, Ma, Selena had a point. I mean, she was being hard on you, but it's because she's been so worried about you. She's a cop, she can sense when things are really bad, and I know she's scared for your safety. I think that's why she was coming on so strong tonight. What is going on?"

Tears sting the back of Vera's eyes. The man had warned her about not telling anyone. But this is her son, surely she could tell him? But he's living with a cop, and she knows that once she tells Tilly, he will definitely want to tell Selena, and Selena would want to make an official report, and then it would be a whole thing. But maybe this is the best course of action to protect Julia and Emma? But what about Millie?

Cold fear seeps through Vera. Millie. Oh no. Vera has been so distracted by everything that she's forgotten about Millie. Where is Millie? What if, by coming clean about what's happened, she puts Millie in danger?

"Ma?" Tilly says.

"I am very tired, I think I go to bed."

Tilly sighs. "All right. I'll see you in the morning."

Vera goes into the guest bedroom and leans against the door. She takes out her phone and goes through the last few messages that she got from Millie.

A text message comes in.

JULIA: Vera, Tilly told me about the
incident. My god! Are u ok?? Does this
have something to do with you telling
me to go to Ollie's??

VERA: I'm ok. Everything ok at Oliver's?

JULIA: Yes everything's fine. Vera, WHAT
IS GOING ON??

VERA: I tell you later, too complicated.

Vera goes back to the message thread with Millie. Now that she finally has a chance to go through them carefully, she sees how strange Millie's messages are. They don't sound like Millie. Could they be from the man who had attacked her? She taps on the Reply button and then sits there for a while, her thumbs hovering over the screen.

What should she say? For the first time since Vera can remember, she feels completely out of her depth. And even though she has fulfilled her dream—staying over at Tilly's house—she feels so alone and so scared and so guilty. She has made a meal of this, hasn't she? And all because she started snooping. Now she has endangered the people she loves most.

Noises from outside make her head snap up. She goes to the door and cracks it open. It seems Selena is back from her run. *That was a short run*, she thinks. *I take longer walks, probably burn more calories.* Then she scolds herself for having such a silly thought.

"Hey," Tilly says.

"Hey," Selena says.

Vera braces herself for a heated argument from the two of them, but instead, Tilly says, "I'm sorry about earlier. I was being an ass."

Oh. That wasn't what she'd been expecting. She smiles to herself. *Good boy, Tilly.*

"No, you were right, I was being hard on your mom."

"It was coming from a good place."

"Yeah, I'm just so worried about her. All of my police instincts are going insane."

Tilly laughs a little. "Your Spidey senses are tingling?"

"Uh-uh, they're not just tingling, they are screaming. She's telling lie after lie, and it's so obvious that she's scared out of her mind, and oh my god, she is the most infuriating person I have ever come across, and I deal with hardened criminals every day. I think she's gotten herself involved in something really dangerous. I don't want her to get hurt. I mean"—Selena sighs—"she's already gotten hurt. I don't want her to get even more hurt."

"I know. Trust me, I get the frustration of having to deal with my mother."

Vera's smile turns into a frown. What did he just say?

"How about this," Tilly adds. "Give her a night to settle down, and then you can interrogate her in the morning?"

Another sigh. "Okay, I guess. She can't get into more trouble tonight."

"Will you forgive me for—"

"For being a lawyer?"

Tilly chuckles. "Yeah."

"Maybe I can overlook tonight's infraction."

"Thank you." There are smacking noises that Vera realizes are kissing sounds. She makes a face and closes the door gently. It's one thing telling those two to make grandbabies; it's quite another having to actually hear them.

In the quiet of her room, Vera studies the messages once more. She drafts a reply, then deletes it and drafts another. Everything feels wrong, every step feels precarious, like she is standing in the middle of a minefield. All alone.

Except she isn't alone, is she? She's just been so used to thinking that she is alone that sometimes, she fails to realize that she is far from alone now. Outside of this very room, in fact, there are two young people who care very much about her, and there's the little group that has become her family, and there's Aimes and TJ and Robin and Millie and Qiang Wen, who she can see are quickly becoming part of her circle, and if any of them were to have a problem, she would be annoyed—no, offended—if they didn't reach out to her for help. Would they not feel the same way about her? And Selena is right to have her Spidey senses go off, because yes, Vera is way out of her depth. And she is going to do something about it. She isn't going to revert to her old comfortable ways and isolate herself. Old dogs, it seems, can learn new tricks.

TWENTY-SIX

VERA

"Stop having sexy time, I have confession to make!"

Tilly and Selena gape up at her. Between them there is a very elaborate-looking board game.

"Oh, you are not having sexy time, never mind."

"My god, Ma, why would we have sexy—I mean, have sex out here in the dining room when you're staying with us?" Tilly says.

Selena, who can't stop being a cop for ten seconds, stands up and says, "You said you have a confession to make?"

Inside, Vera quails, but she makes herself meet Selena's piercing eyes. Goodness me, no wonder Selena makes a fine detective. Her gaze looks like it can see right into your soul. She would make a fine Chinese mother.

"Yes," she says. "I have been keeping secret from you about Xander Lin's case."

"Yeah, I know that, Vera. Come on, sit down and tell me what's going on."

And so Vera does. While Tilly looks on in open horror, Vera

tells Selena everything, from finding Millie outside the police station to going to see Aimes, TJ, and Qiang Wen to the attack this evening and what the man said to her. At certain points, Vera can see Tilly wanting to jump in, probably to tell her to stop talking until she hires a lawyer, but he holds himself back.

"Wait, and he said he knows where Julia and Emma live?" Selena says.

Vera nods. "I tell Julia to stay at Oliver's place."

"From what you've told me about this guy, that's not gonna be enough. Ideally I'd want a security detail parked outside their place . . ."

"We can ask them to come here," Tilly says.

Selena pinches the bridge of her nose, then says, "Okay. Just for tonight."

"A sleepover," Vera says. "I will go make snacks."

"Oh no you won't. Stay here," Selena says sternly. "I need more information from you."

While Tilly calls Oliver and explains the situation to him, Selena draws out more information from Vera. When Vera shows her the strange text messages from Millie, Selena mutters, "This feels really bad." She stands. "I'm going to the station to report this, and I'll have a car assigned outside in case the perp shows up here. And Vera?"

"Yes?"

"Thank you for telling me everything. Now, I'm going to need you to stay out of this, okay?"

"Okay," Vera says meekly, though of course she means exactly zero percent of that. But she knows by now it's useless to argue with Selena.

With a quick kiss (to Tilly, not Vera), Selena strides out of the house.

"Well," Tilly says, "that sounded about as bad as it could sound."

"Don't you start," Vera says, getting up and marching with renewed purpose into the kitchen.

"What are you doing?"

"Emma is coming here for sleepover. You think I let her go hungry?"

"It's nine p.m., so I think she's probably had dinner and will just go to sleep."

"Aiya, you don't know little children, they are always hungry. When you and Selena have children, I will cook nonstop for them."

Tilly gives a resigned smile. "Yeah, I know, Ma."

Vera has just finished making Chinese Rice Krispies (Rice Krispies Treats but with sesame seeds added to the mix) when Oliver, Julia, and Emma arrive. Emma is asleep in Julia's arms.

"Vera," Oliver says, "what happened to your head?"

"Oh, just a minor assault, no big deal." She turns to greet Julia, but to her surprise, Julia looks kind of . . . annoyed.

"Hey," Tilly says in a low voice to keep from waking Emma up. "You can put her in the guest bedroom."

With a nod, Julia walks into the guest bedroom. Oliver and Tilly give each other a bro hug. Before Vera can say a word, the doorbell rings again. Tilly goes to answer it, and Vera says, "Wait! What if it's bad man?"

"I don't think he'd be ringing the bell," Tilly says. Still, he looks through the peephole before opening the door.

Riki, Sana, and Adi file inside. "What's happened?" Sana says, then gasps. "Oh, Vera! Your forehead!"

"Hey, Gran," Adi says, giving Vera a hug. "What happened to your forehead?"

"Minor assault," Vera says, quite enjoying saying those words now. "I had five stitches."

"Assault?" Riki says.

Julia comes back to the living room, sans Emma, and glares at Vera. "I think you owe us an explanation."

Vera gives her a sheepish smile, then says, "I make Chinese Rice Krispies."

"Ooh, yes, please," Sana says.

Julia shoots her a glare. "Do not try to bribe us with food, Vera. You need to tell us what the hell is going on."

Vera deflates. "I know. I'm sorry."

"Come on," Tilly says. "Let's all take a seat. This is going to be a long story."

And so, over tea and Chinese Rice Krispies, Vera recounts the story for a second time that night. This audience is a far better one than the first, though, so this time, she really gets into the story, making dramatic pauses where needed and lowering her voice when she wants everyone to lean forward. They ooh and aah and gasp in shocked horror at the right moments, and none of them goes, "My god, Vera, what were you thinking?"

By the time she is done, Vera is pleased at their horrified expressions. Good storytelling, she thinks, is a lot harder than it looks, but she has obviously accomplished it.

"So, you were actually assaulted?" Julia says. "That wasn't just you embellishing as usual?"

Vera looks sharply at Julia. "Embellish? I don't even know what that is meaning, so how can I do it if I don't know what it is?"

Julia looks like she's about to argue, but then thinks better of it.

"So, some guy actually went into your shop and threatened you?" Riki says.

"That's supercool!" Adi says. Sana pulls his ear, and he says, "Ow! I'm just saying."

"Yes," Vera says. "It is exactly like in the movies. Like a James Bond villain, so big and strong. I thought surely he is going to kill me."

"Oh, Vera," Sana says, "you must've been terrified."

Vera takes a casual sip of her tea and hopes that her hand doesn't tremble. "Oh, you know, take a lot more than that to scare me."

"I would've been shitting my pants," Oliver says.

"Me too," Riki says. "You're really brave, Vera."

Vera has the grace to blush a little at this display of admiration. She deserves it, obviously, but also she recalls with perfect clarity just how terrified and helpless she had felt during the attack. "Yes, I am very heroic, I know that. We move on. What we are going to do?"

They all stare at her. "What do you mean, Ma?" Tilly says.

"Well, we can't just sit here when poor Millie might be in trouble!"

Oliver leans toward Tilly and asks in a soft voice, "She's told Selena about all this, yeah?"

"Yes," Tilly says flatly, "and Selena told you expressly, Ma, to let the police handle it."

"She did," Vera agrees.

"And?"

"And I disagree with her. And as her elder, she should defer to me."

Tilly smacks his forehead. "As an officer of the law, she definitely does not need to defer to you on this, and she's right, Ma. Look what happened to you today. You're sitting there with a busted head, for god's sakes."

"Aiya, you make big fuss out of nothing. This is just scratch, the doctor say it's nothing."

"You got literal stitches," Tilly says.

"Anyway, maybe Selena is officer of law, but she's not here, and you are not officer of law. You are my son, so you need to listen to me."

Everybody looks at Tilly with bated breath, wondering what he's going to say. And also probably feeling grateful that they are not him.

Tilly looks around the table. "Can one of you please talk some sense into her?"

They all shake their heads vigorously. "Sorry, bro, you're on your own here," Oliver says.

"Plus, I kind of want to get involved?" Sana says.

"Babe, it doesn't sound safe," Riki says.

"No shit," Julia says. "I had to leave my house because this guy knows where I live. It's not safe."

"Okay then, Sana, you can be my helper."

"I'll help too," Oliver says. When Julia glares at him, he shrugs. "Might give me ideas for my next book."

Riki sighs. "Fine, I'm in." Adi's eyes widen with glee, and Riki adds, "But not you, kid."

"Aw, man."

Julia groans. "Okay. The sooner we solve this case, the sooner the bad guy will be put behind bars, so I guess I'm in."

"You have got to be kidding me," Tilly says. "I let you all into my house and this is what happens?"

"Should've seen it coming," Sana says. "Come on, it'll be fun. Don't be such a lawyer, Tills, it's boring."

Tilly slumps in his chair. "Selena is going to be so pissed."

"She got him the whip," Vera whispers loudly to everyone.

"She means to say Selena's got me whipped, not that Selena gifted me a whip," Tilly says quickly, his face turning red.

"Whatever you say," Sana says.

They begin discussing all of the information that Vera has shared with them. Oliver raises his hand.

"Yes?" Vera says.

"I spent quite a bit of time with Millie," he says. "As friends. It was my bad, actually. I thought we were just hanging out as friends, but Millie had different ideas and we kind of had a falling out."

"Oof," Riki says. "That sounds tough."

"Yeah. Ah, at one point, I saw her get on the bus from Vera's."

Vera claps with excitement. "Which bus? Someone get a Google Map, now!"

Riki takes out his phone and opens the Maps app. He keys in the bus number and they all lean forward to look at the route.

"She went in that direction," Oliver says, pointing at an area of the map.

"Oakland?" Riki says.

There's silence for a moment. "Do you know where Millie lives?" Julia says.

Vera shakes her head.

"She could've gone anywhere. She could've just jumped on the first bus she saw to get away and then made a change later on," Sana says.

"Oliver, what else you know about Millie?" Vera says.

Oliver ponders the question. "We joked around quite a bit. She told me she likes to stargaze, and Thomas used to fold paper flowers for her to put in a vase on her windowsill. Oh, she calls her mom and dad 'Mother' and 'Father.'"

"That's . . . kind of creepy," Sana says.

"Yeah. I asked her about them once, and she clammed up. I got the sense that she was kind of scared." Oliver grimaces. "In hindsight, I should've questioned it more. It's becoming obvious to me now that she wasn't okay at all."

"No use looking at your behind," Vera says. "Look forward. So, we think this Millie's parents are hurting her maybe?"

"Well, hang on," Sana says, "didn't she tell you she came from China? Did her parents come with her?"

"You know what?" Oliver says. "She said something like, 'My parents grow all sorts of crops on their farm.' She said, 'grow,' present tense. So, maybe her parents are back in China?"

"Let's say they are," Julia says. "Where does that leave us?"

Vera sighs. "You kids are hopeless. Too much time is wasting. I better call for backup."

TWENTY-SEVEN

TJ

TJ is already in his pajamas when his phone rings. Vera's name flashes on the screen. "Hey, Vera, what's up?" he says warily. It's almost eleven p.m., and nobody ever calls with good news after eight p.m.

"TJ, is time to step up."

"What?"

"You come to me right now. I will send you the address. Bring Robin too."

"Vera, it's eleven p.m. on a school night."

"I will tell Mr. Bun that Robin will be absent for good reason. Tilly will write letter to him. He is a lawyer, you know."

"You've mentioned that. I don't think I should—"

"TJ, you know if it's not important, I wouldn't ask. I will send you picture. Hold on." There is a lot of rustling in the background, then Vera says, "Okay, check your phone."

TJ looks at his phone screen and utters a small gasp of surprise.

It's a selfie of Vera, and there is a bandage wrapped around her head. "Vera, what happened?"

"Major assault. Bad guy come and attack me, and I think it has to do with Xander Lin, and I think Millie is in trouble. You come here now." With that, she hangs up the phone.

TJ stares at the phone in his hand, then he looks up and sees Robin in the doorway.

"I'll go grab my jacket," she says, already walking toward her bedroom.

"Wait," TJ calls out. "I don't know about this."

Robin levels her gaze at him. "Really, Dad? Some guy attacked Vera and you're thinking of not going to her?"

When she puts it that way, it does sound ridiculous. "But you've got school tomorrow," he says weakly.

"Apparently I'll get a note from an attorney, so I think it'll be okay." She walks off and TJ sighs in defeat. Why did he even try arguing?

Less than fifteen minutes later, they arrive at what appears to be Vera's son's house. It is full of people who seem very excited to meet them. Robin is engulfed in hugs and Vera introduces her immediately to Adi, who is about her age and apparently a gifted child. Before TJ can take his jacket off, Aimes and Qiang Wen arrive, and there are yet more hugs and greetings all around. TJ is sleepy and confused—is there big trouble? But if there is, why is everyone so cheerful? He lets himself be led to the dining table, where there is a plethora of snacks. Someone places what looks like a cube of Rice Krispies treats in his hand, and he takes a bite. It's very good and has toasted sesame seeds added in, which gives it a nutty flavor. Maybe he's dreaming, he thinks.

"Okay, everybody," Vera calls out. "Thank you for coming to my mystery club."

"This is a mystery club now?" Julia says.

"I will think of better name later," Vera says. "Unless you have better idea now? Okay, I didn't think you would. Right. We are all here to solve mystery. As you can see, one of us is missing."

"Millie," Aimes says.

"Correct. We have a reason to think she is in danger." Vera fills them in on what has happened, and TJ listens with mounting horror.

"The guy literally said that to you?" Aimes says. "Stop digging? And you're not only continuing to dig, you're involving us in the digging?"

"Yes," Vera says. "I thought is very obvious. Why I have to spell it out for you?"

"Vera, I can't be involved in anything dangerous," TJ says. "I've got a kid to look after."

"I don't mind," Robin says.

"This is crazy," TJ says. "We're going."

"TJ," Vera says, "we need your help."

"I don't know what I'm supposed to do here."

"Xander come to you before he die, asking you to help him do exposé."

"Right, and?"

"And I think we should do the exposé."

"What are we exposing?" TJ says. "He didn't tell me what his big secret was."

"It doesn't matter," Vera says. "We do the exposé on what we know—that everything Xander do online is fake." She turns to

Aimes and Qiang Wen, both of whom look like deer in headlights. "Will you tell them?"

They look down at their laps for a second, then Aimes says, "We weren't really dating. We pretended to be a couple online, but it was purely business."

"I am not his real grandfather," Qiang Wen mumbles. "And when he come to me saying he wants to do exposé, I turn him away."

"He wanted to come clean about our fake relationship," Aimes says. "I told him no too."

TJ's insides squirm. He can't be here, around these people, spilling his secrets. He's told Vera, but that was under very different circumstances. But then he catches sight of Robin, who is watching him. His hands ball up into fists. He can't lie in front of her. "I turned him away too. He wanted to do a live video telling people how fake he'd been and how our working relationship wasn't actually as close as he'd made it sound, and I flipped out on him."

"Dad," Robin whispers. She walks over and wraps her arms around him, and TJ feels tears pricking his eyes. He hugs her back.

"I'm sorry," he says.

"It's all good." She smiles at him before going back to her seat.

TJ takes in a long, deep breath. "So, why do you want to do the exposé right now? How's that going to help us find Millie?"

"Because of theory," Vera says, looking around proudly. "I have one."

"Would you care to share?" Oliver says.

"Yes, yes, I'm getting there. I am doing the dramatic pause, don't rush me, Oliver."

"It's just, you know, you think Millie might be in danger . . ."

"Oh yes, good point. Okay, here is quick theory: I think Millie

and Thomas/Xander do some bad thing, maybe caught up in a
cult or something. Yes, probably a cult. My guess is maybe one of
those young people cult like a music festival—"

"You're getting off track," Sana says.

"Right, sorry. So. They are member of cult, and Xander maybe
use social media as a form of escape. He create this perfect life, a
life that he want for himself but can't have because of cult, and
then maybe after a while, he feeling a bit guilty, so he want to
come clean. The cult find out and they kill him, make it look like
suicide. Millie wants to report to police, but she is maybe too
scared, so she hang around outside the station until I find her and
save the day."

"You haven't saved the day yet," TJ mutters.

"Aiya! Stop interrupting, all of you."

There are murmurs of "Sorry, Vera."

Vera humphs, then continues. "Millie tell me about Thomas,
so I start looking into it, posting viral videos, becoming pop star
and all that, and the cult take notice and get scared. 'Oh no, this
Vera is a brilliant investigator and rising pop star. We must stop
her.' They try to scare me off by splashing red paint on my shop,
but I am not so easy to scare. So, they send bad guy after me, to
give me warning. And they lock Millie up because they are angry
because she get me involved." She gives everyone a triumphant look.

There is a pause. Then Qiang Wen says, cautiously, "Er, Vera,
you are done with theory?"

"Yes. Is good theory, right?"

They all nod slowly, digesting her words. TJ scans her theory
for holes, and finds about fifteen of them, but when he tries to
come up with a better explanation, all his mind spits up is a blank.
"So, you're going to say all that in your video?"

"Yes. And as my talent manager—"

"You're not technically a client."

"—your job is to make it go viral. Use all your contact to make it go viral, that's what a good talent manager does."

"Actually—"

Vera turns to Aimes and Qiang Wen. "I want you two in the video also. Tell everyone what you know about Xander."

They both look terrified at that. "I'll be crucified!" Aimes cries.

"I don't want any trouble," Qiang Wen mumbles.

"Trust me," Vera says. "Truth is always the right path to choose."

"Wow, Grandma," Robin says. "That almost sounded like it made sense."

"Tch, of course it does. Now, I cannot force any of you into doing anything you don't want to do, but we need to help Millie, and more hands helping is better than fewer hands."

TJ leans back in his chair, his mind racing. This is exactly the kind of thing he should be staying far, far away from. Especially after getting his bad rep. It's the kind of thing that could end his career.

Then again, his career is effectively over. He's given notice that he wouldn't be renewing the lease on his office space, and tomorrow he's going to tell Kit, Lomax, and Elise that the agency is going to shut down. So what is he so scared about? Isn't it better to go out with one final bang? And not just on any project, but one where the safety of a friend is involved.

"I'd just like to point out," Tilly says, "that Selena is going to be very unimpressed by all this."

"Just refresh my memory, Selena is . . ." TJ says.

"My girlfriend."

"Soon to be fiancée," Vera says.

"Ah." TJ swallows and goes back to panicking quietly. But again, he's doing this for a good cause. Yes, a very good cause. And it's not just him involved, it's this big group of people, and they seem like a good bunch. Except for Vera, who is definitely a bad influence. He looks at Robin. Is he putting her in danger? What would a responsible parent do?

It's the question he has so often asked himself, because even after thirteen years, he still feels like he's playing pretend. Pretending to know what it takes to be a dad. Pretending to know what the hell to do when things get tough. Pretending to have everything under control. And he's so tired of doing that.

Maybe the most responsible thing a parent can do is to be themselves. To show their kids who they really are. And when TJ looks back on the things he regrets most, it's the ones where he decided to play it safe. Like when Xander asked him for help and TJ turned him away. Deep down inside, TJ knows that if he says no to Vera right now, he is going to live to regret it for years to come. And if it turns out something bad does happen to Millie, he will probably regret it for the rest of his life.

He has to will every cell in his body to let his mouth speak. "I'm in."

TWENTY-EIGHT

AIMES

Aimes has never been so terrified in her life before. This has got to be a nightmare. This is her worst fears come true. She's literally had nightmares about this kind of thing happening. This, very specifically this. People finding out what a fraud she really is? Torture.

If Vera had asked her to do this just one month ago, Aimes would have said no. Hell no. She wouldn't have even thought twice about it. But here she is, actually considering it like it's a reasonable ask that won't at all ruin her entire life.

But someone's life might actually be at stake here, the little voice in her mind says. *Not her social life, but like, her actual life-life.*

And surely that is worth more than Aimes's reputation. Aimes grimaces. Gah, she hates her thoughts sometimes. Actually, she hates her thoughts all the time. But it's true. When she thinks of Millie, someone she really wants to be a friend, she feels a stab of concern. And, admittedly, those text messages that Vera showed Aimes really did look suspicious as hell.

And you owe it to Xan, the little voice whispers.

Damn it, it really had to go there. Her past with Xan flashes through her mind. They'd had fun sometimes, shooting those cute skits. He always kept his distance, but Aimes liked him. Not in a romantic sense but as a person. And then the way she had betrayed him—

"Hey," Sana says, placing a reassuring hand on Aimes's arm. "You okay?"

Aimes shakes her head, blinking hard to keep the tears from falling. "I don't know."

Julia appears next to her. "It's totally fine if you don't want to do it. You don't need to do anything you don't feel comfortable doing." And when Julia says it, it's clear that she means it, wholly. It's not just something she's said to make Aimes feel better in the moment only to judge her for it later on.

Aimes looks at Julia and Sana, and her mind goes back to that day when the three of them had hung out together and Sana and Julia had told her, over ice cream, how they'd met each other. What a mess they'd both been before Vera took them under her wings. Here are people who understand exactly what she's feeling, who know what it's like to be a complete fraud, to feel like a failure in every sense of the word, and now look at them. They've come through the other side. Maybe she can too.

Bitterness pierces Aimes's mouth. She betrayed Xander because she was a coward and a fake, and she doesn't want to be that person anymore. What is the point of becoming an influencer if she loses herself in the process? What is she going to influence people into doing when she doesn't even know what she is doing?

"Yeah, okay, I'm in too," Aimes says.

Julia and Sana wrap her in a tight hug. "You're gonna be great," Julia says.

"And even if you bomb, it'll be fine," Sana says. She looks at them both and says, "It sounded more reassuring in my head."

Across from Aimes, Qiang Wen nods. "All right. I'm not sure what is it you want us to do, Vera, but okay."

"Good," Vera says. She's already whipped out her phone. "Robin, come and shoot the video."

"I'm her cameraperson," Robin tells everyone proudly.

"She is very good," Vera says. "Robin, you shoot from that angle, okay? Remember, right side of my face is the good side. And don't make me have double chin."

"Grandma, you don't have to worry about double chins, you know you look like a bad bitch."

For a second, nobody in the room dares to breathe as everyone awaits Vera's response.

Vera nods slowly. "A bad bitch. Hmm. Yes, I like that sound."

The group breathes a collective sigh of relief.

"All right, everybody!" Vera calls out. "Places!"

"Wait, what?" Riki says. "Are we all in this video?"

"No. Just me, I am star, of course, and then Aimes, Qiang Wen, and TJ. The rest of you stand over there so you don't ruin shot."

"Geez, okay," Sana says. They all file obediently to one side of the room.

Vera primps her hair, then nods at Robin, who starts recording the live stream. Vera looks at the camera and says in an ominous tone, "Who is Xander Lin? I think I find out who he is. His name is Thomas, and he is a member of"—dramatic pause—"a cult."

Aimes can almost hear the *dun dun dun*. As Vera launches into her dramatic speech about Xander, Aimes swallows the growing lump in her throat. She feels like she's about to be sick. Can she really do this?

Someone places a hand on her arm. It's Qiang Wen. He gives her an encouraging nod. "You will be okay," he whispers.

Aimes nods, biting back her tears.

"—faking everything online, including his romantic relationship," Vera says. She looks over at Aimes and gestures for her to join in.

Here it goes. Aimes steps into the camera's line of sight. She looks straight into the eye of the lens. How many people are watching right now? "Um," she squeaks. She clears her throat and tries again. "Hey, everyone. It's Aimes here. I need to come clean about something. I've been faking everything on my profile. My place is a mess. It's not at all Instagrammable. But there are two small spots that I keep neat so I can make content with them. And, like my apartment, my relationship with Xan was fake. We weren't actually a couple. More like business partners. He would come to my place once a week, and we'd make content for an hour or two, then he'd leave."

Her voice trembles and she wavers. But then she sees the crowd of people in front of her, some of them complete strangers just an hour ago, and others more familiar faces, and all of them are looking at her with goodwill in their eyes. Sana's got her hands clasped in front of her and is wearing a *You go girl* expression, and Oliver is nodding at her to keep going. The sight of it bolsters her. Maybe her online life is about to implode, but if the trade-off is getting this group of people as her friends, it's worth it.

"The day before Xan died, he came to me and asked me to help him expose something. Some huge secret. And part of that secret was our fake relationship. He wanted to do a live stream to expose everything. I got scared. I had gone too deep with my lies, and I didn't want to be exposed for the fraud I am, so I told him no. And I have regretted it ever since. I am so sorry to everyone I have lied to."

"We forgive you, Aimes," Vera says, putting an arm around Aimes's trembling shoulders. "And it's not just Aimes who having fake relationship with Xander Lin. He also have same thing with his so-call grandfather and his talent manager."

This time, Qiang Wen takes the stage. Aimes steps backward and listens in growing sadness as Qiang Wen tells the world about how Xander filled a hole in his life that he didn't even know existed and how, like Aimes, he had turned his back on Xander in the end. TJ follows suit, and soon, a vivid picture is painted. One of a lost soul who, for whatever reason, wanted to create a perfect life online for himself.

"And now, Xander's friend Millie is missing," Vera says. "Millie is the one who bring this case to my attention. She is very sweet girl, here is a photo of her." Vera pauses, then says out of the corner of her mouth, "Robin, you are posting photo of Millie now, yes?"

"Oh!" Robin says. "Uh, okay, let me just . . . There you go. It's up."

"Okay, good. You all see Millie? She is very good girl, very sweet, and I am very worried about her. I am scare that something bad happen to her, same thing that happen to Xander. Because even though the police say his death looking like suicide, I don't think so. It's a bit too convenient for him to want to expose big secret and then next day is found dead. Don't you think so?"

"We're getting a *lot* of comments coming in," Robin says.

"We'll read through them," Riki says. He and Sana move to stand on either side of her, tapping on the phone screen and scrolling through the comments.

Aimes feels a tiny stab of jealousy at how well Riki and Sana work together, then she feels stupid for feeling jealous. She really needs to learn to stop comparing herself with everyone else.

"Thank you for your comments," Vera says to the camera. "We appreciate all your help. Any information you can give us about Millie will be very helpful."

"Um," Riki says. "Most of them aren't very helpful." He frowns. "I'm seeing a lot of guys calling Millie names, saying she scammed them and she probably scammed the wrong guy this time."

Aimes frowns, thinking of all of the interactions she's had with Millie. She sifts through their conversations and suddenly, little pieces of what she had thought were just awkward moments made sense. When Aimes mentioned Vera getting scammed, Millie had looked so uncomfortable. It had made Aimes wonder why, and now it's starting to make sense.

"Why you say such bad things about poor Millie?" Vera is scolding the phone.

"Maybe she was a scammer," Aimes says.

"Aiya, Aimes," Vera says in a harsh whisper, "we trying to get people to care about Millie, not trying to get them to hate her."

"I know, but there were things she said and did that made me wonder . . . and the thing is, I don't think she wants to do it. I don't think she wants to scam people. I think she's being made to do it."

Oliver's eyes widen and he raises his hand.

"Yes, Oliver?" Vera says.

"I think Aimes is right. I think maybe I was one of these guys that Millie was trying to scam, but I only ever saw her as a friend, so she ended it with me. That was right before those strange messages she sent your way, Vera."

Vera harrumphs. "Okay, so maybe Millie not so innocent after all, but I still think she is very good kid. I can tell her heart is good. Mothers can always tell these things. So, all you men out there that Millie scam, tell us everything you know about her."

"Um, the comments are getting really creepy," Sana says.

"Don't do the creepy!" Vera snaps at the camera. "What is wrong with you?"

Aimes mutters to Vera, "Welcome to the Internet."

"Oh! We got one that might be useful!" Riki says. "This guy says, 'I just knew she was up to something, cheating on me like the little sl—uh, let's gloss over that part—uh, okay, so I followed her home after our date." Riki's mouth twists in disgust. "Bro, what? That is creepy as fuck."

Sana jumps in and continues reading the comment out loud. "She got on the Greyhound for Oakland. I followed in my car. She got out in East Oakland. I was going to confront her, but then my other bitch called, and—" Now it's Sana's turn to look disgusted. "Ew, so you were cheating on her, but you're judging her for possibly doing the same exact thing? Men are trash. Except you, babe," she adds, kissing Riki's cheek.

"Okay, so now we know she lives in East Oakland," Julia says.

Aimes thinks again about what Millie has told her, snatches of conversation flitting through her mind. "She never said 'home,'" Aimes says, all of a sudden.

Everyone goes silent. "What?" Vera says.

"Millie. She never said, 'I need to go home' or 'I'm going home.' She always said, 'I have to go.'"

The mood in the room grows dark at Aimes's words. Aimes herself hadn't realized just how disturbing they were until they came out of her mouth. A deep sadness settles over her. Oh, Millie.

"I think," Aimes says slowly, "wherever Millie lives, she doesn't view it as her home. Maybe it's not a house? Maybe she's living in a dorm or something."

"I've updated Selena about Millie possibly living in East Oakland," Tilly calls out. He tugs on the collar of his shirt, even though he's wearing a T-shirt and therefore has no collar to tug at. "Uh, she's not very happy about what we're doing. Just FYI. She says to tell all of you to, and I quote, 'Go the fuck home and stop listening to Vera.'"

"She really need to learn to respect her elder," Vera says, "especially her future mother-in-law."

Adi, who's been tapping away at his phone this whole time, raises his hand. "Maybe it's a factory or warehouse or abandoned industrial park."

Aimes's heart sinks. No way.

He brandishes his phone at them. He has a map open with pins all over it. "There are a lot of abandoned industrial buildings in East Oakland. Thanks to gentrification, a lot of these places were shut down. There are spots that are basically mini ghost towns."

"You are very bright child," Qiang Wen says.

"Thank you, yes, I am. I go to a school for gifted kids, actually," Adi says.

"Okay, tone it down, little man," Riki says. "Good job though."

Aimes is so confused by what is going on right now. She's agitated with worry for Millie, but at the same time she's also feeling warm fuzzies because of this strange motley group, and she's also mourning the loss of her online identity—even though it's a fake one—and she's also feeling lightened by coming clean online, and it's just a lot of things to be feeling in one go.

But at the core of it, Aimes knows that what they are doing is the right thing, despite what Officer Selena Gray says. If it comes down to choosing a side between Vera and the law, Aimes knows where she stands.

TWENTY-NINE

QIANG WEN

What a strange time this is. How curious and how very, very strange. Is Qiang Wen supposed to be excited or sad or scared or maybe all of the above? One second he feels like crying, and the next he wants to hug someone while laughing. And most of all, he misses Xander so much he could wail with the emptiness it brings.

All of this stuff is beyond Qiang Wen. He's trying very hard to keep pace and pay attention to everything and solve the puzzle, but it's not so much a puzzle as it is a shattered mess they are trying to put back together. He's a simple dumpling maker; what does he know of scam artists and social media and "clout," a word that Vera has used four times in the last five minutes?

So Qiang Wen stands to one side quietly and observes the more energetic people as they debate and discuss with one another. He's good at observing. He's been doing that his whole life. His mind wanders gently back to the past, to more peaceful times when he had whiled away many a pleasant afternoon chatting to Xander.

Oh, he knows Xander is turning out to have been a scam artist of sorts, but that doesn't change anything about Qiang Wen's relationship with him. Xander will always be his grandson, no matter what.

He might have been involved in some really bad stuff, but he was also the guy who made paper flowers for his sister because she had nothing nice in her room to look at, and she once told him that her favorite flowers are daisies. He had smiled as he told Qiang Wen how his sister had the origami flowers in a plastic bottle that she had painted gold and placed on her windowsill.

He knows now that the girl is Millie, and his heart aches at the thought of poor Millie gazing at her window, past the paper flowers and up at the sky, wishing fervently upon any star she could find. Xander had said he wished she could have seen a prettier sight out of her window than the ugly old red building next to theirs. It was only a few meters away and blocked everything else out save for a sliver of sky.

Qiang Wen jumps. "A red building!" he cries.

The chatter around him pauses.

"Xander say there is nothing to look at out their window except for ugly red building. Big building, built really close to theirs, so close that you have to tilt your head to see the sky!"

Tilly picks up his phone and makes another call to relay the information. Adi types on his phone. Riki and Sana watch the comments section with eagle eyes.

"Comments are pouring in like crazy," Sana says.

"Yeah, we've got over a hundred thousand live viewers, by the way," Riki says, "just FYI."

"Sounds like an industrial park," Adi pipes up.

"That makes sense," Oliver says. "Warehouses and factories built in a cluster."

"There are over fifty in Oakland," Adi says, still typing madly into his phone. "I'm just looking at the Google satellite images now."

Qiang Wen watches the young boy in wonder. It's marvelous, the kind of information that is readily available these days. His heart could burst with joy at the thought of the world that awaits the younger generation. They will be so much better equipped to face the world than he ever was.

"Got it!" Adi says. "There's an abandoned industrial park in East Oakland that fits our description."

Vera gestures at Robin. "Okay, cut the live stream, we go now."

"What?" Tilly says. "No. Not a chance in hell. Selena will have a squad down there. She'll handle it."

"And let us miss fun?" Vera says. "After we do all the work? I don't think so! Oliver, get your car."

Oliver gives Tilly an apologetic grimace. "Sorry, but I do want to see how this one turns out."

Vera is already marching toward the door. "Why you all just staring like statues?" she barks as she snatches her jacket from the coat hook in the hallway.

That snaps Qiang Wen out of his puzzled daze, and he hurries toward Vera. He still isn't quite sure that he knows exactly what is happening, but he knows one thing for sure: He is not about to sit this one out.

I n the end, they all go to the location. Qiang Wen is in the back seat next to Tilly, with Oliver driving and Vera in the passenger seat up front. Sana drives the other car, with Aimes, Riki, TJ, and Robin in there. Julia has opted to stay behind with the minors.

This must be a dream, Qiang Wen thinks. And, funnily enough, he doesn't want to wake up.

"Ma," Tilly says, "when we get there, you are not to get out of the car. Do you understand me?"

"Why not get out of car? Then how I can see action?"

"You don't. That's the whole point. You let the police do their job. We're just going to be bystanders."

"I never been bystander in my life. That sound like very boring thing to be."

"It's a safe thing to be. Also, Selena says she will end our relationship if any of us gets in her way."

Vera gasps. "That is emotional blackmail!"

"She learned it from you."

Vera grunts. "Very good lesson from me," she says grudgingly.

"They might have guns," Oliver says.

"Yeah, that's a really good point," Tilly says. "These are actual hardened criminals we're dealing with."

"I know," Vera says.

From the rearview mirror, Qiang Wen can see that her face is alight with excitement. He sighs. "Vera, I don't think they are telling you these things to make you happy. They want to keep you safe. I think you better stay in the car."

"Of course," Vera says. "I won't get in way."

They all look at her dubiously, but none of them says anything more as the car zooms down the freeway toward their destination.

Surprisingly, Vera stays true to her word. When they get to the industrial park, she stays put inside the car even after Oliver parks. Maybe it has to do with Tilly clinging on to her like she's the last float in a shipwreck, but Qiang Wen likes to think it's because Vera has taken their warnings to heart.

Oliver has chosen to remain outside of the industrial park, well away from the action, but Qiang Wen can see that in the parking lot of the industrial park, there are already four police cars with their red and blue lights flashing.

"Oh my," Vera says, watching as the cops pile out of the car. "They look good, don't they? Oh, there's Selena! Ah, she looking very pretty, as usual." She looks around at the others, as if waiting for a reply from them.

"Yep, she is very pretty, Ma," Tilly says after a beat.

Qiang Wen and Oliver murmur their agreement.

"You know, she is so pretty, she probably get hit by men all the time."

"I think you mean 'gets hit on,'" Oliver says.

"That is exactly what I just say. And don't interrupt me, I am saying important lesson." Vera turns back to Tilly. "If you don't propose to her fast, she might get impatient and then leave you. Then how?"

"Are we really talking about this right now?" Tilly moans.

"When else to talk about it?"

"Maybe when we are not watching very exciting police raid," Qiang Wen offers. Although, he thinks, he would like to be present for this conversation as well.

"Yes, exactly," Tilly says. "Thank you, Uncle Qiang."

Qiang Wen flushes with pleasure at the honorific.

The next few moments, they watch in silence as the police, with guns drawn, break into one of the industrial buildings.

"Wah, they break down the door like is paper," Vera says. "Selena is very strong. We will have big and strong grandbabies."

Tilly takes in a breath, as though to say something, but then purses his lips instead. "Not worth it," he whispers under his breath.

Qiang Wen pats him on the shoulder.

"You should have park closer," Vera scolds Oliver. "I can't hear anything."

"Yeah, I kind of figured safety would be number one and all that," Oliver says.

"Haiyah." Vera opens the door, and they all shout and Tilly pounces on her before she can climb out. "Aiya! Let go of me! You are so heavy!"

"Stay. In. The. Car!" Tilly says.

Vera grumbles but closes the car door once more. Then she rolls down the window. Tilly still holds on to her. Cold night air fills the car. Qiang Wen catches faint shouts from the abandoned warehouse. He doesn't blame Vera for feeling curious; he himself is dying to know what is going on inside.

It sinks in then, that this is where Xander lived, and a great sorrow fills Qiang Wen. Oh, he understood all right, when they were discussing it, but seeing it in person now—this large, hulking building among other large, hulking buildings that were never meant to be anyone's living quarters—is something else. The whole area is abandoned, patches of wild grass growing out of the ground here and there, and the entire area is so dark and lifeless it's hard to believe there are people inside any of the buildings. Seeing it makes Qiang Wen angry at humanity as a whole. The whole place is without soul, a group of buildings built solely for capitalism's sake and then abandoned without a single thought, only to be taken over by Xander's captors. For the first time in a long while, Qiang Wen is filled with hatred.

"You okay?" Oliver says.

Qiang Wen blinks, looking over at the young man. "I can't believe this is where Xander live when he is alive."

"Yeah." Oliver gazes out the window. "You helped locate it though. You helped the rest of the people who are trapped in there. I think that was what Xander wanted."

Tears fill Qiang Wen's eyes and he nods, not trusting himself to speak. All this time, Qiang Wen has suppressed all of his memories of Xander because they had been too painful, but Oliver is right. He can sense, deep in his gut, that they have done the right thing, and he can only pray that the police have gotten here in time to save Xander's sister.

THIRTY

MILLIE

Millie often marvels at the way people—especially young people—say, so casually, that they're not afraid of death. Maybe people say that only because they've never actually stopped to consider it, but the thing with Millie is, she's been close to death so many times that she knows, beyond a shred of doubt, that she is very much frightened of dying. The numerous times that Father and Mother have punished her, Millie wailed and struggled, all of her sensibilities overwhelmed by a single overriding thought: *I don't want to die.*

But right now, Millie is too weak to do anything much about it. She can't remember the last time she was given any water or food. It must have been over two days ago. She should have known, really, that someone like her couldn't possibly live for long. Certainly not the lifespan of the average American. As she lies curled up in her bed, she considers that phrase: the average American. She wishes she could be an average American. What a privilege that would be. In her hands are the origami flowers Thomas had made for her, and under her bed is the letter she has written for Vera. Channary has promised that she will take the letter when she has the opportunity and keep it until the time comes when Father and Mother decide she is old enough to start scamming men in person, then she will find Vera and hand it to her.

What would Vera think then? Millie closes her eyes and tries to imagine all of the possible reactions that Vera might have. She might cry or rail at anyone who would listen. She would probably tell her daughter-in-law, the cop. Or maybe she won't tell her daughter-in-law right away because she might get scared. A small smile touches Millie's mouth. Yeah, right. Vera getting scared? Unlikely. One thing is for sure though—Vera would definitely demand that Channary be her niece and make sure that she is okay.

"Penxi?" Channary calls from behind the wall. "Are you okay?"

"Yes." A stupid lie, when it's obvious she isn't. Her voice comes out cracked and raw.

"I'm scared."

It takes so much energy to say, "Don't be."

There is a sniffle. "Are they going to kill you?"

Millie takes a long time to ponder the question, wondering if she should lie to Channary, but what is the point? Best for Channary to learn now just how dangerous Mother and Father can be. "Yes." How foolish Millie has been, to think that if she just behaved, if she just remained obedient, that she might one day be free. And now she'll end up just the same way as the others before her. Poor Thomas. She hopes he wasn't too scared when the time came.

Channary weeps quietly. Millie wishes she could wrap her arms around the kid. She tries to think of some piece of advice to give her, some wisdom that might help her, but her mind is blank. Finally, she says, "Don't forget your real name."

There is a loud boom, and shouts explode inside the warehouse. Millie jerks up, her heart pounding.

"Penxi? What's happening?"

"I don't know." Adrenaline pulses through her, giving her some strength. She pushes herself off the bed and tries to stand, but her legs are too weak and she falls, landing heavily on the floor. Pain lances up her arms and legs, and she gasps. There are more shouts from outside. She needs to know what is happening. She crawls to the door and presses her ear up against it.

People are shouting, "Get down! Hands behind your head! Down!"

Millie gasps. "It's the police," she whispers. "It's the cops." One last burst of energy shoots through her and she slams her fists against the door. "Help!" she screams. "Help us! We're in here!"

In the room next door, she can hear Channary doing the same, shrieking and kicking at her door. Down the hallway, every door is being pounded at by her siblings. Millie's heart is racing so fast she feels like she's going to explode. Footsteps pound down the hallway and someone shouts, "Get back from the door!"

She does so, moments before there is a thump so loud she feels it in her bones. Then another thump, and the door is flung open. Two police officers file in, guns drawn, and Millie raises her hands.

They lower their guns after making sure there's no one else in the room, then one of them says into his walkie-talkie, "We need a medic here." When he looks at Millie, his face is sad. "Jesus. What have they done to you?"

There are a million thoughts buzzing through Millie's mind, but when she opens her mouth, only one word comes out. "Channary."

"Is that your name?" the cop says.

Millie shakes her head. "My sister is in there." She points at the wall.

"They've got her."

And sure enough, Millie hears her wails clearly now that her door has been opened too. Millie tries to walk, but her legs give out, and the cop catches her before she falls again.

"Whoa, take it easy. Come on, let's get her out of here."

Outside of the room, the warehouse is in chaos, with what seems like a dozen police officers marching around.

"Penxi!" Channary cries. She runs toward Millie and throws her arms around her. Millie sobs, and hand in hand, they stumble down the hallway.

On the first floor, Millie finally sees the sight she's been dreaming of for over ten years. Father and Mother are being marched out with their hands cuffed behind their backs, their expressions mutinous.

Mother catches sight of her and snarls, "You little bitch. You did this. You're gonna be sorry."

"That's enough," the police officer holding Mother growls. It's Selena. She meets Millie's eye and gives her a little nod, and Millie returns it, then hangs back and watches as Father and Mother are led outside.

"What's going to happen to Father and Mother?" Channary says.

"Oh, they're gonna go away for a long time," the cop holding Millie says.

Millie's throat closes up with tears. If only Thomas could see this. And Yara. And Robert. Yara would say something snarky, like, "Who's the bitch now, bitch?" She smiles inwardly. *I didn't do this,* she thinks. *Thomas, you did it.*

Outside, Millie takes in great big gulps of the cold fresh air. Someone wraps a foil blanket around her and leads her to a waiting ambulance. Someone else says something about severe dehydration, and Millie nods, letting them lower her onto a stretcher. There is a sharp pain at the back of her hand, and when she looks down, she sees that someone has stuck a needle in it and is in the process of hooking her up to an IV drip. Channary is still holding her other hand, and Millie squeezes it to let her know it's okay.

There are more shouts, and Millie stiffens, but then Selena's voice says, "Let her through."

And moments later, Millie hears a familiar voice snapping, "Aiya! You hear my daughter-in-law! Let me through! My niece is in there, I am family."

"What's happening?" Channary says.

Millie smiles. Already, thanks to the IV drip, she's feeling a little less close to death's door. "Something good."

Penxi wakes up in the hospital room and isn't surprised to see Vera sitting next to her bed. She's been in here for three days now, and Vera hasn't left her side at all. It's been really nice having Vera there, though Penxi has been guilty of faking naps sometimes just to get Vera to stop talking.

"Penxi, ah, you know your eyes don't close all the way when you sleep?" Vera says by way of greeting.

Penxi yawns, rubbing her eyes. "Yeah?"

"You should close them all the way, otherwise you give future husband or wife big scare."

Penxi can't help but laugh. "Okay, Vera, I'll keep that in mind.

Gonna be a while before I find a partner though. I think I need to just not date for a while."

Vera nods. Then her face softens. "Selena give me your letter."

"Oh?" Penxi's cheeks warm as she thinks back to what she had written down. Argh, she'd written down literally everything, every dirty secret. When she wrote it, she didn't think she would ever see Vera again. And now here she is, having to face her after all that stuff she wrote about scamming people.

Vera reaches out and places her hand on top of Penxi's. "Penxi, ah, you are such brave girl. You been through so much."

Penxi swallows thickly. "I'm a scammer."

"You are human trafficking victim. No. You are human trafficking survivor."

It still seems surreal to think of herself with that label. Even after talking to Selena and hearing those words from her. "Human traffickers" was what Selena had called Mother and Father. Penxi knows it's true, but she never thought of herself as a victim of human trafficking.

Selena had assured her that the authorities would be reviewing her case with a sympathetic eye, given the circumstances, but still, Tilly had assigned one of his colleagues to represent Penxi anyway. He is unable to represent her himself due to a conflict of interest, but Vera says she will nag him into overseeing Penxi's case and making sure they have the best people on it. It has been a very strange, very wild few days, and through it all, Vera has refused to leave her side, flapping fiercely at anyone she thinks might cause Penxi any distress.

"How is Channary settling in?" Penxi says.

"So-so. Has many nightmares. Julia say Emma start sleeping with Channary so she won't be so scared."

Penxi smiles at the thought of little Emma soothing Channary back to sleep after a nightmare.

"They are trying to find her parents back in Cambodia."

"That's good."

"Adi and Robin have find your real parents, by the way."

Penxi sits up. "What? How?"

"These teenagers with their phones, how do I know? I have their phone number right here. You want to give them call?"

Penxi's mouth turns into a desert. It's been so long. What would she say? "Do they know what happened to me?"

"Yes, I think police already talk to them."

Penxi starts shaking. "I don't know what to say to them. It's been so long. What if they're angry or upset or—"

Vera squeezes her hand. "Penxi, look at me."

She does so, and lets the strength in Vera's eyes wash across her whole body.

"You don't have to say anything. They are your parents, they been so worried about you. They will only be happy to see you. I know this because I am a mother. Trust me."

Somehow, Penxi manages a nod. She watches wordlessly, her thoughts a complete scramble, as Vera makes the call, then passes the phone to her.

Though she hasn't heard their voices in over a decade, the moment they say, "Penxi? Is that you?" everything comes flooding back. Their smiling faces. The love in their eyes. The concern. She has forgotten what it was like to have real parents. Not Mother or Father.

Tears stream down Penxi's face as she says, "Mama, Baba."

THIRTY-ONE

XANDER
The Night Before His Last

Xander isn't his real name, but neither is Thomas, so Xander doesn't think it matters what people call him. And anyway, he likes the name Xander. Xander sounds like someone who's got his crap together. Xander sounds like someone who wears the latest Nike sneakers and drives a cool sports car. And, most importantly, Xander definitely does not sound like the kind of person who would spend all of his time scamming people out of their hard-earned money.

Xander is who he wants to be. But in the end, maybe he just can't help being a scam artist, because what started out as a little escapism has ended up being yet another huge lie.

He created this entire life because he needed an escape. Something to dream about, no matter how unrealistic. Xander knows it will never come true, but then he got carried away by the online world. By all of the beautiful people in it, and Aimes, so sweet and kind. When she asked him out, he had to turn her down. He couldn't date her, he didn't know how to keep up the ruse in person. He was so scared of losing her, so he turned around and offered her one thing he could: a fake relationship.

Those stolen hours at Aimes's place, making videos, are probably some of the best times Xander has experienced. He makes sure to keep them short, leaving her apartment as soon as they are done, but he wishes he could stay on. It was after one of these sessions, as Xander walked through Chinatown, that he found Qiang Wen's dumpling shop. He hadn't expected to make a connection with Qiang Wen, but Xander was lonely, and it was obvious that Qiang Wen was as well. And so, just for a few hours each week, Xander had someone to talk to. Someone who reminded him of his grandfather back home. And could he be blamed for wanting to add that to Xander's online life?

Then TJ had reached out to offer representation, and Xander was amazed. He now had not just a girlfriend and a grandfather, but also a career manager. The American Dream come true.

Except, as time went on, the dream turned into a nightmare. Mother and Father found out. Of course they did. He should've known they would. They were angry at first, then they saw an opportunity in it. They saw opportunities in everything; that was their problem, really. And they wanted Xander to use his online profile to scam more people.

Xander Lin was his own creation, his one escape from this hell he had somehow landed himself in, and he couldn't let Mother and Father dirty it. He'd had enough. He knew the risks. He'd seen what happened to siblings who stepped out of line. He'd experienced Father and Mother's violence himself. And Mother and Father were always so proud about having a contact within the police force, someone who would help them get out of trouble should anything come out. They'd convinced Thomas for so many years that if he ever went to the police, all that would happen is that he'd get charged as a scammer, but nothing would ever touch Mother and Father. But enough was enough. He was going to come clean online. Skip the police to circumvent the possibility of a dirty cop cleaning things up, and just reveal everything on social media. Burn this whole stinking operation to the ground. He'd end up in prison himself, but it was what he deserved.

He folded one last daisy for Millie. He hoped she would understand why he had to do it. Why he had to sell everyone out, even her. He hoped the police would be lenient on her. They wouldn't charge the younger kids, he was sure of it. But he needed courage. He didn't know if he could do it alone. It felt impossible, a larger-than-life undertaking that he had to shoulder alone, and he was so tired and so scared. All he wanted was one person, someone he'd connected with in the last few months, whether it be Aimes or Qiang Wen or TJ, to stand by him and tell him that, yes, he was doing the right thing. Someone who could help him show the fakeness of social media, prove that nothing was as it seemed. Someone who could hold his hand and tell him that he was doing the right thing. Because the one thing Xander was, was scared. He was piss-himself-in-his-pants-terrified, and he didn't know if he could go through with it, but he must. He had to. For the first time, Xander was going to do the right thing.

EPILOGUE

VERA

"Aiya, not to the left! You covering up the word 'teahouse'! Right a bit. Too much! Okay. Yes, there. Good."

"I still think this is a terrible idea," Selena says.

"Terrible," Tilly agrees.

"I think it's a great idea," Robin says.

"Yeah, and we'd be helping her on the tech side of things," Adi adds.

"That's what I was worried about," TJ mutters.

"I mean, she did uncover an entire human trafficking ring," Aimes says, "so you should give her some credit."

"Thank you, Aimes," Vera says.

"Suck-up," TJ says, without any real bite.

"I'm the suck-up?" Aimes says. "Who made her the sign?"

TJ stuffs his hands into his pockets and shrugs. "I didn't have a choice."

Riki and Oliver finish sticking on the sign and climb down their ladders. The group gaze up at the sign.

Vera clasps her hands to her chest. "Ah," she says, "isn't it beautiful?"

Above her shop, the sign now says:

VERA WANG'S WORLD-FAMOUS TEAHOUSE
AND PRIVATE INVESTIGATOR (CERTIFIED)

"Bit of a mouthful," Winifred the jealous grouch says.

"Jealousy not look good on you," Vera says tartly.

"Why would I be jealous? I have long line of customer every day coming in for my kimchi cheese croissant. I think if anyone is jealous, is you."

Vera shoots her a dirty look, but before she can come up with a sharp retort, Sana says, "Well, good job, everyone. Time for some tea?"

"And maybe some of those kimchi cheese croissants?" Penxi says.

Vera glares at her. "Traitor."

"Sorry. But they're so good." She turns to smile at her parents. "Right, Mama, Baba?"

"Yes," they say. Their arms are linked with hers, as though they can't bear to let go of her even for a second.

Winifred's face is seventy percent grin. "I'll go get them. Don't you worry."

Vera harrumphs. "All right, we best go inside then."

The group, consisting of Vera, Penxi, Penxi's parents, Sana, Riki, Julia, Emma, Oliver, Selena, Tilly, TJ, Qiang Wen, Robin, Adi, and Aimes, barely fits into the teahouse, but Oliver has brought extra tables and chairs, and they set them up outside. Winifred brings over tray after tray of pastries, and soon everyone is eating and chatting.

"You know," Oliver says, "this case has grown so big I saw it on the front page of the *New York Times* website."

"You do have to scroll down a bit," Sana says.

"Well, yes, but it still counts as the front page."

"What is headline?" Vera says. She can already see it in her mind's eye: "Vera Wong, Owner of Famous Teahouse, Solves Another Murder Case!"

Oliver's forehead scrunches as he tries to remember. "It was something like 'Married Couple Arrested in Bay Area Human Trafficking Ring.'"

"What?" Vera snaps. "Not even mention me?"

Oliver, who's only now seemed to realize that he's somehow landed himself in hot water, gazes back at her with wide eyes. "Um." He looks at the others, wordlessly pleading for their help.

"The article mentioned you a lot," Julia says. Oliver mouths *thanks* to her.

"Oh yes? What it says about me?"

"That you're a super sleuth," Aimes pipes up.

Vera isn't quite sure what a "sleuth" is, but from the way Aimes says it, she reckons it's a good thing, so she settles back in her chair with a smug smile.

"And they called you a 'TikTok personality,'" TJ mutters.

"Who is represented by you, Dad," Robin says. "He's gotten more business because of it."

"The TikTok personality?" Vera echoes. She likes the sound of that. She gives TJ a Cheshire grin. "I tell you I am a star, didn't I?"

"Okay, Vera, you were right. Thank you for saving my business."

"You are welcome," Vera says magnanimously. "And what will happen to these . . . human traffickers?" The two words are spat out with distaste.

At this, Selena says, "Well, we won't know until their trial, but my bet is they're going to be in a maximum security prison for the rest of their lives."

Penxi gives a grim smile. Vera reaches out and grasps her hand, giving it a tight squeeze before letting go. "I'm okay," Penxi says, but Vera knows that both the physical and mental scars that Penxi's captors have inflicted on her will be ones she carries with her forever. But she's got a strong support system now, and she's through the worst of it. Vera makes a mental note to ply Penxi with extra delicious food for the next two decades.

Clearly wanting to change the subject, Penxi turns to TJ. "So, your business is back up and running? That's amazing."

"Well, not quite. I don't have the funds to reopen the office just yet, so we're working out of my house right now, which is kind of chaotic, but also—"

"It's been awesome. I love having everyone over all the time," Robin says. "And I get to spoil Elsie's baby. She's such a cutie."

TJ gives Robin a tired smile. "It's . . . something all right."

"That sounds really great," Aimes says.

"Yeah," TJ says. "I've actually been meaning to reach out to you to see if you're looking for representation."

"Oh!" Aimes looks surprised, then she laughs. "I . . . you know what, I would've jumped at that before, but I'm actually taking a break from social media." She glances at Julia and Sana, and they give her an encouraging nod. "I think I need time to figure out what I want to do with my life."

"And that's okay," Julia says.

"Yeah," Aimes says.

Vera pats her on the arm. "You will be okay, Aimes, you a bright girl." Privately, Vera starts a list of careers she will suggest to

Aimes in the coming weeks. A psychologist. A lawyer. A wedding planner. She's going to have to brainstorm this. She looks around the tables and wonders who she should rope into a brainstorming session. There are so many choices. She settles on Qiang Wen. He's been less lonely ever since she's taken him under her wing, and Riki tells her that he and Sana often drop by Qiang Wen's place for dumplings, but he could do with a project. As though reading her thoughts, Qiang Wen meets her eye. They share a smile of understanding at each other.

"Ah, this is like a brasserie in Paris," Winifred says.

"What is it with you and France?" Vera says.

"What is it with you and pretending you are private investigator?" They narrow their eyes at each other.

"You know," Winifred says, "Paris is very beautiful this time of year."

"Oh, you've been?" Vera says.

"No. But it's something people say, isn't it?"

"I always want to go," Winifred says.

"It would be nice," Vera says. There is a moment of silence as the two of them consider it, then Vera says, "Aiya, cannot afford it. So expensive."

Selena and Tilly share a look with each other, then Tilly clears his throat. "Ma? If you want to go to Paris, I'll pay for it. You deserve a vacation."

Vera gapes at him. "I can't. Who run shop while I'm gone? I am pillar of community. Everyone fall apart if I leave." She pointedly ignores Winifred, who is rolling her eyes aggressively.

"I think we can manage for a bit," Oliver says.

"Just for a bit," Aimes says. "Then, you're right, we will start to fall apart."

For the first time, Vera is at a loss for words. "But I just start my PI business. I am expecting client anytime now."

"You know," Selena says, "murders do happen in Paris too."

"Oh yes," Winifred says happily, "big city everywhere will have plenty of murder. We will have such fun there, Vera."

Vera nods slowly.

"Grandma, you won't be a private investigator," Robin says, "you'll be a détective privé."

"See?" Winifred says. "Everything sound better in French."

Détective privé. Vera does like the sound of that. She looks around her with suspicion. "Are you all trying to get rid of me?"

There are immediate shouts of "Never!" but she catches what sounds suspiciously like "Only for a little while" being murmured from Selena's direction.

Vera harrumphs. She leans back in her chair and takes a sip of her tea. *Goodness me*, traveling at her age. Then again, if not now, when else? She looks up at her new sign once more, then says, "I hope you are not lying about murders in Paris. I will be quite disappoint if it turn out there is nothing to do there."

"Oh, I'm sure you'll manage to run into a dead body or two there," Selena says.

Winifred squeals. "A girls trip to Paris!"

"With murder," Robin says. "Can I go too?"

"No," TJ says immediately.

"When you graduate high school I take you," Vera says. "But, yes, for now, just me and Winifred." She finishes the last of her tea and smiles. "I think we are going to have all the fun." *Yes*, she thinks, and the French will most definitely find her a treat, she is sure of it.

ACKNOWLEDGMENTS

The first Vera book, *Vera Wong's Unsolicited Advice for Murderers*, took me on the most incredible journey. Most of you probably know by now how Vera popped into my head one night and how everything else got pushed back in favor of Vera. (This feels very appropriate. Vera would totally approve of pushing everything else back to make room for her.)

What I did not expect was the overwhelmingly positive response to Vera's story. The first book went on to sweep so many awards—it won an Edgar Award for Best Original Paperback, an Audie Award for Best Mystery, and a Libby Award for Best Mystery—and it became a *USA Today* bestseller almost a year after it came out. What an incredibly magical journey (well, Vera would argue that she saw it coming a mile away), and none of it would have been possible without the hard work of my tireless editor, Cindy Hwang; the team at Berkley Publishing; and my readers, who fell in love with Vera and spread the love through word of mouth.

It is only because of you, my dear reader, that a sequel could even exist. When I wrote the first book, I thought of it as a stand-alone novel. But thanks to you recommending it to friends and family, I was able to bring another Vera story to life. And what a story it is.

This sequel was inspired by actual events. My parents and I were in Singapore when my mom fell for a scam caller. I rushed her to the police station, where we told a kindly officer what had happened and filed a report. While filing the report, the officer shared with us stories about scammers and how they were often victims of human trafficking themselves, duped out of their home countries and forced to work as scammers by these traffickers. I felt such a whiplash of emotions. I'd come in filled with righteous rage that someone could be so cruel as to scam my mother, but within the space of thirty minutes, my heart was aching for them.

I could not stop thinking about it. I started to research the subject, and the more I did, the more horrific these stories became. Unfortunately, when it comes to the human trafficking aspect in this book, very little was made up.

I am very grateful to everyone who has kindly imparted their expertise with me while I did my research for this book, and everyone else who listened patiently while I whined to them about it. My family has had to put up with a lot, so thank you to them.

But this book is first and foremost for my readers. Because truly, without all of you, this one would not have been written, so thank you, to every single one of you who has read and loved Vera as much as I love her.

Photo by Donny Wu

Jesse Q. Sutanto is the award-winning, *USA Today* bestselling author of the Aunties series, *Vera Wong's Unsolicited Advice for Murderers*, *I'm Not Done with You Yet*, and *You Will Never Be Me*. Her young adult titles include *The Obsession* and *Well, That Was Unexpected*, and she has also written the Theo Tan children's fantasy series. She has a master's degree from Oxford University and a bachelor's from the University of California, Berkeley. She currently lives in Jakarta with her husband and two young daughters.

VISIT JESSE Q. SUTANTO ONLINE

JesseQSutantoAuthor.com

⊙ JesseQSutanto

♪ AuthorJesseQSutanto

Ready to find
your next great read?

Let us help.

Visit prh.com/nextread